T H E
PIONEERS

===

An American Family Portrait

BOOK FIVE

P·The Pioneers

Jack Cavanaugh

VICTOR BOOKS
A DIVISION OF SCRIPTURE PRESS PUBLICATIONS INC.
USA CANADA ENGLAND

Editor:
Greg Clouse

Design:
Andrea Boven

Cover Illustration:
Chris Cocozza

Maps:
Andrea Boven

Production:
Julianne Marotz

ISBN 1-56476-587-3

VICTOR BOOKS
1825 College Avenue,
Wheaton, Illinois
60187.

To my son Sam,
who, like Jesse Morgan,
is an intelligent and sensitive young man
standing on the doorstep of his destiny.

ACKNOWLEDGMENTS

To Jane Watson Wales and Erick—thank you for loaning me your books on frontier America. They were invaluable to me as you will readily see when you read the prairie chapters.

To John Mueller—your technical expertise constantly amazes me. I know of no one else who has your wide range of historical background on things like woodworking, plumbing, and factory furnaces, just to name a few. Thanks for all your comments.

To Mavis Sanders—for taking me to lunch at the historic Brown Palace Hotel in Denver, which provided a wonderful scene for this book; also, for your friendship, dedication, and diligent efforts that helped launch this series and my writing career.

To Greg Clouse and the Victor staff—three years ago you encouraged me as I made a transition to full-time writing. This year, the shoe is on the other foot, and I have watched as you have undergone some publishing changes. I pray that someday you will look back on all the changes that have taken place and see God's hand in it, if you can't do so already.

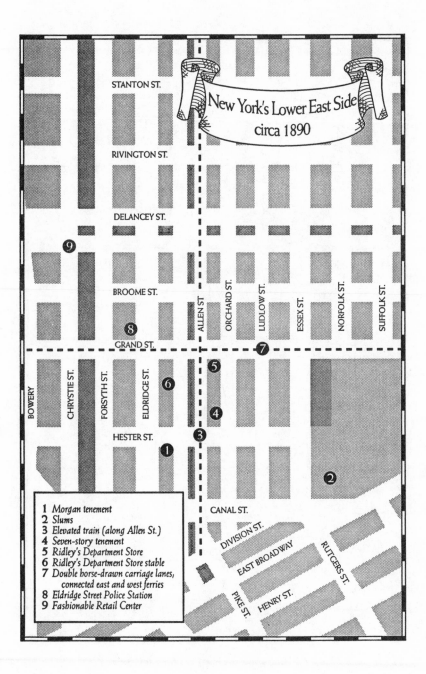

New York's Lower East Side
circa 1890

STANTON ST.

RIVINGTON ST.

DELANCEY ST.

BROOME ST.

GRAND ST.

HESTER ST.

CANAL ST.

DIVISION ST.

EAST BROADWAY

RUTGERS ST.

PIKE ST.

HENRY ST.

BOWERY

CHRYSTIE ST.

FORSYTH ST.

ELDRIDGE ST.

ALLEN ST.

ORCHARD ST.

LUDLOW ST.

ESSEX ST.

NORFOLK ST.

SUFFOLK ST.

1 Morgan tenement
2 Slums
3 Elevated train (along Allen St.)
4 Seven-story tenement
5 Ridley's Department Store
6 Ridley's Department Store stable
7 Double horse-drawn carriage lanes,
    connected east and west ferries
8 Eldridge Street Police Station
9 Fashionable Retail Center

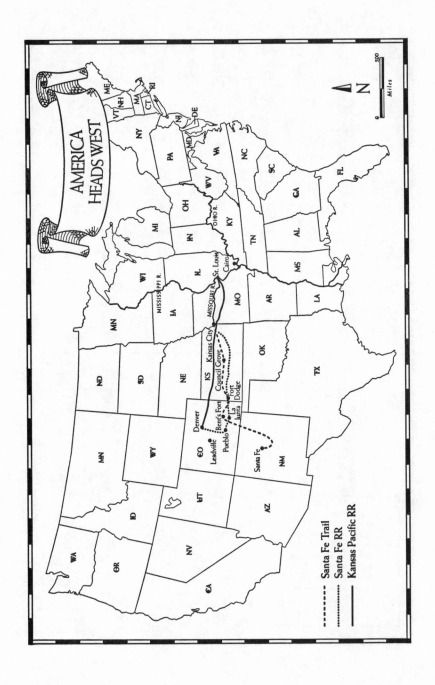

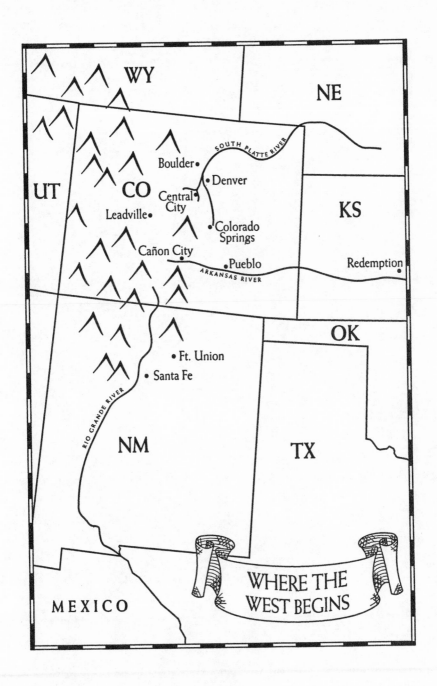

Chapter 1

JESSE Morgan didn't hear the cry for help. He was in another world.

Though his steps shuffled down the dark, odorous, trash-strewn brick streets of New York City's lower east side, his mind was in the Oklahoma Territory, crouched inside a Conestoga wagon, fending off the intense prairie sunlight with one hand and gripping a six-shooter with the other while Indian savages circled the wagon. In his mind he could see, huddled behind him and laying low against the wagon bed, golden-haired Charity Increase. She cast innocent eyes his direction. There was no fear in them. Why should there be? This wasn't the first time the two of them had faced death together. Her fair gaze only served to convey her love to him, and a calm confidence that he would once again rescue her from deadly peril.

With a rush of wind the Second Avenue elevated train screeched over Jesse's head. Cinders and ash from the locomotive plummeted to earth like outcast stars from heaven. They fell unnoticed. Jesse lifted his ever-present cap and brushed back brown hair that looked almost red in direct sunlight; at the moment, however, under the dim street lamps, it appeared mousy brown.

Normally carefree, Jesse's happy face was squinted and focused as he took aim at the mental images of red-skinned savages that played in his mind. He didn't hear the train's shrill whistle above; nor did he hear the thunderous rattle of its elevated tracks; nor did he hear the second cry for help, even though this time the scream was louder, more urgent.

Like weary horses heading for the barn, Jesse's feet carried his lanky body across Grand Street past the darkened windows of Ridley's department store with its ornate cast-iron facade that stretched around to Orchard Street. A fashionable emporium, Ridley's exuded an attitude of elegance and finery in a neighborhood that knew nothing of those things. Its stylish dresses with leg-o'-mutton sleeves and wasplike waists, its Queen kitchen cabinets, and its complete dining rooms with combination buffet and china closets, were all beyond the means of Ridley's immigrant neighbors.

The families that shared the city block with the emporium were stacked haphazardly on top of each other in rickety seven-story walk-up tenements. Men, women, and children worked in factories and sweatshops. Their meager wages were spent on potatoes, turnips, cabbages, carrots, peas, beets, and parsnips from wooden barrels at Hester Street's outdoor market. Ridley's department store only served to remind them what they couldn't afford. At least not yet.

But they could dream. And dream they did.

Not everyone dreamed of adventure and adoring young women like Jesse Morgan. Many dreamed of someday owning a piece of land, or running their own business. Some merely dreamed of escaping the three D's of the lower east side—dirt, discomfort, and disease.

With the twentieth century less than a decade away, an increasing number of them looked expectantly heavenward for escape from their daily drudgery. End-of-the-world predictions and prophecies, with a countless number of variations on a theme, were epidemic.

One ardent Broadway merchant boldly displayed a placard

on the front door of his business which identified the specific day the world would end. It read:

NOTICE!
This shop will be closed in honor of the King of kings, Who will appear about the twentieth of October. Get ready, friends, to crown Him Lord of All.

A smaller sign in the window advertised muslin on sale for ascension robes at twenty cents a yard. As the predicted date drew near, the merchant had closed his shop in anticipation of the Lord's imminent return. Six months later, the date having come and gone without visible incident, the shop was still dark. Rumor among the tenements was that the owner had starved to death waiting for God.

While some of the less religious neighbors clucked their tongues at the man's foolishness, another observed that God had indeed fulfilled the man's dream of heaven, in a natural sort of way. His interpretation of the merchant's passing received widespread acceptance. Such was the tenacity with which the tenement dwellers stubbornly clung to their belief that their dreams would come true.

For these tenement dreamers, pennies were the down payment on their dreams. Pennies scrimped and saved a few at a time. Pennies accumulated in a sock or jar hidden away in a secret place. The common belief was that—when enough of them were saved—these small copper disks could transform any dream, no matter how grand or intangible, into reality.

And there were no end of stories to sustain their convictions, stories that would convince the most hardened skeptic. One such story told of a Dutchman who had escaped the tenements and now owned his own shop in Brooklyn. Another story told of a young Jewish woman who once did sewing piecework, but who now owned her own millinery shop.

It was stories like these that sustained the tenement dwellers on muggy summer nights, when the days were long and hope was short, when the penny jar seemed more empty than full, and when the odors and noise and closeness of the stained tenement walls made life unbearable.

Gathering in the streets they would tell again the stories of those who had escaped the tenements as they gazed at the strip of stars that ran the length of the street between dilapidated buildings. For a moment they would forget the sixteen-hour workday, the pittance they were paid for piecework, and the roar of the factory machines that chewed up their lives and sometimes snatched an arm or a leg. And they would dream of the day they would escape the tenements, of the day they would be able to see more than just a strip of sky.

Like his neighbors, Jesse Morgan dreamed to survive. He was good at it; better than most because he practiced more. He dreamed at work, at home, and while in transit between the two locations. It was a way of life for him. He much preferred his clean, noble visions of glory over the grimy walls and dimly lit hallways of home.

His mother said he got his imagination from his father's side of the family. There was ample evidence to support her claim. Jesse's aunt was the well-known novelist, Sarah Morgan Cooper. A writer of dime novel adventures, her name was as familiar to readers of popular fiction as Mary J. Holmes, who injected a much-sought-after glow of romance into the drab lives of factory girls and kitchen maids; and Harlan P. Halsey, the author of *Old Sleuth,* a detective series with plenty of gore and breathless adventures illustrated with luridly colored paper covers; and Horatio Alger who, with his *Luck and Pluck* and *Ragged Dick* series, glorified the theme of worldly success.

Jesse's aunt contributed to this burgeoning repository of popular stories. The uniqueness of her contribution was that she added a spiritual element to her tales. The most popular of her works, the adventures of Truly Noble and Charity Increase, were based on moral premises taken from the Bible. In Mrs. Cooper's fictitious world, faithfulness and industry always won the day. Her hero, a sixteen-year-old orphan, never used violence except as a last resort; he always learned a moral lesson at the end of the novel; and he always, always won the heart and admiration of the lovely Charity Increase.

Though Jesse had never met his famous aunt, she had always sent him a copy of each novel soon after it was published. Within a day of its arrival he had devoured it; within a week he knew the story word for word; within a month he had generated several new story lines, variations on the book's theme.

When the first novel was delivered, Jesse was eight years old. He read it so many times the pages became limp and the cover crease wore so thin that one day the cover simply dropped off. From that day on, Jesse greeted the arrival of each new adventure with Christmas enthusiasm.

At first his mother was pleased with Jesse's newly developed passion for reading. She always assumed that as the years progressed his taste for reading material would likewise progress and mature. But as Jesse moved into and out of his adolescent years he showed no interest in anything other than dime novels. He turned up his nose at Victor Hugo's *Les Miserables* which his mother borrowed from their third-floor neighbor, Rabbi Moscowitz. Sharing his mother's growing concern over her boy's shallow reading fare, the Rabbi suggested Jesse might prefer something about the frontier, something more contemporary like *Huckleberry Finn,* written by an entertaining Western journalist.

Thinking the Rabbi had this time found the solution to her problem, Jesse's mother borrowed the book and presented it to him with a promotional pitch that would have made the author blush. Jesse never got past the first page.

Handing the Rabbi's much touted volume back to his mother, Jesse made it clear that he had no real interest in reading. He explained that the only reason he read was to enter the world of Truly Noble, where good and evil were easily distinguished, and where justice always triumphed.

Jesse never went anywhere without one of his aunt's dime novels. They were his portal to adventure. And once he stepped through that portal, nothing short of catastrophe could bring him back to reality, like almost getting run over by a streetcar, or walking headlong into a pillar—or a blood-curdling scream from an alley.

Jesse was passing the alley when the scream finally registered in his mind. Brick walls funneled the sound his direction. This time there was no thundering el to mask it. The cry was a naked, unobstructed plea for help.

"Gadzooks!" Jesse brought the word back with him from the other side of the portal. It was Truly Noble's favorite exclamation. The fictional character used it whenever he spied an injustice.

At the end of the alley stood a barrel containing a small inferno. One young tough, ragged, tattered, and soiled, stood with his hands on his hips as he supervised a mean-spirited form of tenement entertainment. Two other equally soiled boys his same size held a smaller lad by the arms and legs, bellyside up. They swung him back and forth over the fire.

At the apex of the swinging arc, the one furthest from the barrel, the lad's shaggy red hair brushed the brick pavement while his bottom pointed skyward; at the other end of the arc he reached a sitting position with his bottom hovering over the edge of the barrel and the fire. The flames leaped up from inside the barrel and nipped at the lad's bottom like playful orange and yellow puppies. Each time they did, the lad let out a scream.

"Finn! Tell them to stop!" he yelled. "Finn, this isn't funny!

Come on, Finn!"

From the look of terror on the lad's face, the prank had long since passed the playful stage. His cheeks were streaked with tear tracks. His pants smoldered. His scream was more than mere protest. It was the cry of a burn victim.

Jesse recognized the cry. He'd heard it before. He'd seen what happened when flame and flesh touch.

That's when the fire began beckoning to him. The boys and their prank softened to a blur. With horrifying clarity, the only thing Jesse saw was the flames. Flickering evil. Death's fingers. And he could sense that they saw him too. They recognized him from before. He was sure of it. It was as though the flames in the barrel had become bored with the boy. They turned their attention to him. Taunting him. Luring him.

The flames danced in the barrel as seductively as Salome danced before King Herod. Twirling. Leaping. Teasing. Mesmerizing him with their movements. They wanted him. As passionately as Salome wanted John the Baptist's head on a platter, so the flames in the barrel wanted him. And neither would they be satisfied until he was as dead as the desert preacher.

With invisible hands the fire spanned the distance between them, gripping his throat. Jesse's chest constricted. His heart pounded like it would burst. Though only a thin line of visible smoke could be seen snaking upward from the barrel, in Jesse's mind billows of invisible smoke filled his throat and lungs. Burning them. Depriving them of oxygen.

Jesse gasped for air. He coughed convulsively.

The sound of his struggle brought a pause in the action at the closed end of the alley. The swinging stopped, but the lad wasn't released. With his back laying on the ground and his arms and legs held up, he looked like a pig on a spit. His eyes joined the other three pair of eyes as they all turned to Jesse.

"Hey! Long John! Take a hike!" Finn, the overseer of the

prank, threatened Jesse with a fist.

The tough's description of Jesse was accurate. He was thin and lanky, making him appear taller than he actually was.

Jesse didn't move. He was aware someone was addressing him, but the voice was unclear, the way noises sound underwater. The only thing that *was* clear to him was the hypnotic allure of the fire and the death grip it had on his throat.

Finn stepped forward threateningly. By doing so, he blocked Jesse's view of the barrel.

Suddenly the spell was broken. The fire's seductive magic dissipated. Once again it had failed to claim him as a victim. Steadying himself with one hand against the brick wall, Jesse gulped down as much air as his crying lungs would hold.

Finn hitched his shoulders. "What? Are you some kind of crazy man? You think I'm talkin' to myself? Get outta here!"

"I heard a cry for help," Jesse gasped. His strength was returning. He pulled himself up to his full height, a full foot taller than Finn.

"Now that's where you was wrong," Finn said, jabbing a finger at Jesse. "You didn't hear nuttin'!" Without turning his head, he spoke to the other two boys. "He didn't hear nuttin', did he, boys?"

"Nope!"

"Nothin' to hear!"

The three older boys fastened their eyes hard on him. Jesse felt the force of their combined gaze. It unnerved him, but he held his ground. Someone had to stick up for the lad who was still dangling by his arms and legs.

Jesse shot the lad a reassuring glance. He wanted the boy to know that he wasn't about to be frightened away. But the look that Jesse got back puzzled him. Jesse had expected to see young pleading eyes, a silent cry for help. But the eyes that were situated below an unruly mop of curly red hair stared back at him with indifference, with a glint of hostility.

It didn't matter. Justice was threatened. What these bigger and older boys were doing to someone half their size was wrong. Jesse couldn't just walk away and let them continue torturing him. But then, what was he going to do about it?

What would Truly Noble do in this situation?

The question popped into his head, and not for the first time. On several other occasions the question had guided him. Each time Jesse had found a bit of wisdom from Truly Noble's adventures to advise him. This time was no different. The answer followed closely on the heels of the question.

It came in the form of dialogue from *The Demise of the Devious Detective,* the book he had just been reading, the very book that was even now tucked into his waistband wedged against the small of his back. In the narrative, Tru advised Docile Dan, a shy would-be detective's apprentice, how to approach a perilous situation:

"First, never rush into danger," Tru had said. "Always know what you're up against. Foolish action is worse than no action at all. Second, give peace a chance. Use violence only as a last resort. And third, do whatever is necessary to set things right. God smiles on the cause of a righteous man."

All right, Jesse mused, *so here's the situation. It's three against one. But who is it I'm up against? Three overgrown bullies picking on a kid half their size. What kind of person picks on someone smaller than him? A coward. All three of them—cowards. And a coward will always back down to someone his own size, or taller.*

Armed with the wisdom of his hero, Jesse Morgan boldly stepped forward and said, "Let the boy go."

Finn stared at Jesse in dumbfounded amazement.

Not used to having someone stand up to you, are you? Jesse thought.

With a dirt-smeared index finger, Finn rubbed the side of his nose and sniffed. He shook his head in wonder. A black-toothed grin spread wide between smudged cheeks. Behind him, the other two oafs let loose the lad and joined their leader, one on each side. The lad made no effort to get up from the ground.

Jesse found himself standing toe-to-toe with three adversaries. *The boy is their prize,* he reasoned. *Once he's out of their reach, once they have nothing to fight for, they'll back down.* He yelled past the line of grimy flesh that opposed him. "Now's your chance, boy! Get out of here!"

The lad looked stupidly at him.

"Through the gate!" Jesse pointed to the wooden fence that closed off the alley behind the boy.

The lad looked at the gate, then back at Jesse. He made no effort to move.

"If the gate's locked, climb over!" Jesse cried. "I'll take care of these three. Run, boy! Run!"

The boy stayed right where he was.

Finn laughed, showing even more black teeth. "He ain't goin' nowhere. Are you, Jake?" Finn turned to look at the lad. The boy shook his head. Finn chuckled as he turned his attention back again to Jesse. "You see, Jake there's my brother. He does what I say." Finn stepped forward, closing the distance between him and Jesse. "And nobody tells me what to do when it comes to me own brother."

Brothers. Jesse looked past Finn at the boy. His eyes were set close together, just like Finn's; and the two of them had a similarly thin jaw line. Why hadn't he seen the family resemblance before now? It didn't matter.

"Brother or not," Jesse said, "what you were doing was wrong. You could have hurt him."

"Then it's lucky you came along!" Finn cried with mock praise. "'Cause now we don't need to hurt him. We have *you.*"

Before Jesse could react, the two nameless oafs grabbed him by the arms. He was taller, but they were beefier. Instinctively Jesse struggled. Then he stopped. Not because he was overmatched, but because he remembered the words of Truly Noble: *Give peace a chance. God smiles upon the cause of a righteous man.*

"I don't want to fight you, Finn," Jesse said. "I was only concerned for the boy's safety. If you promise not to harm him, I'll take your word for it and be on my way."

"You don't want to fight me?" Finn asked, rubbing his knuckles.

Jesse shook his head. "No. It is my practice to use violence only as a last resor..."

A quick blow to the stomach ended Jesse's reply with a wordless *whoosh*. He doubled over, only to be hauled upright again by the bullies on either side of him. A second blow rolled Jesse's eyes back so far into his head, he feared they would never return to their normal position.

"You know," Finn said, rubbing his fists, "I've always used violence as a first resort. It works better that way; wouldn't you agree, boys?"

Jesse could hear the rumbling chortles of the two Neanderthals on either side of him. It took nearly every ounce of conscious effort for him to keep from blacking out. With what sliver of consciousness remained, he formulated a question: *What would Truly Noble do?*

But this time no answer was forthcoming. His brain— reduced by pain and lack of oxygen to the level of a mynah bird—could ask the question but not comprehend it. The question cycled endlessly in his head. *What would Truly Noble do? What would Truly Noble do? What would Truly Noble do?*

"I know!" Finn shouted triumphantly. "Let's have some fun!" Glancing at the barrel of fire behind him, he said, "Let's bob for embers! Bring him over here, boys."

Jesse felt himself being dragged deeper into the alley toward the blazing barrel.

"Since you're the guest of honor," Finn said to Jesse, "you

go first!"

More Neanderthal chortling as iron hands dragged him toward the fire. Jesse dug his toes into the bricks trying to stop them. They slipped and gave ground. As the group neared the barrel, Jesse closed his eyes to keep from looking directly at the fire. If he looked at the flames it would be all over for him.

Jesse felt his chances of emerging from his peril without serious injury beginning to melt like lard on a hot griddle. In full strength he couldn't out-muscle these two oafs, let alone now that Finn's two blows to his gut knocked the wind out of him like beans from a bag.

His captors' hands shifted to the back of his head, pushing it toward the flaming mouth of the barrel. Jesse could feel the fire's heat warming his face.

"Dunk his head, boys!" Finn squealed in giddy triumph.

One of the oafs spoke up. "Finn, I don't think this is such a good idea."

"Shut up! I do the thinking!" Finn screamed. "Stick his face in the barrel!"

Despite the order, there was a moment of hesitation. The skin on Jesse's face felt like it was glowing red. For reasons unknown, he opened his eyes. The flames in the barrel danced and leaped for joy beneath him. They crackled as if to say, "So you thought you could escape us...but we finally got you, didn't we? We finally got you."

His gaze transfixed on the flames, Jesse muttered in a trancelike whisper, "What would Truly Noble do?"

"What did he say?" an oaf asked.

"Shut up and stick his head in the barrel!" Finn shouted.

"But he said something!"

Finn screamed hysterically, "Shut up! Shut up! Shut up and do it!"

"O God, help me," Jesse cried as the flames grew hotter. He wondered what universe-threatening crisis had so distract-

ed the Almighty that He didn't have time to smile down upon
Jesse's righteous cause. Even so, if God managed to find time
to look down upon him, Jesse hoped the Almighty would do
more than smile. Right now a legion or two of angels would
be a welcome sight.

With every ounce of strength he had, Jesse pulled back.
Every part of him shook from the exertion. His arms and
neck became slippery with sweat. Drops of perspiration
dripped from his nose and chin; they hit the iron rim of the
barrel with a sizzle.

By some miracle, Jesse was managing to counter their
efforts. But for how long?

"Don't be shy, Long John," Finn laughed. "Here, let me
help."

Jesse felt another hand press against the back of his head. It
was too much. He had no chance against three of them. As
his face passed over the rim, the heat stung his cheeks and
nose and forehead.

O God, help me.... .

From the depths of the barrel yellow and orange flames
leaped joyfully. Like devils' tongues flicking upward, they
tried to lick him.

Jesse fought harder. It was no use. He couldn't halt the
downward direction of his head. *What would Truly Noble do?*

"Finn, stop it!" It was Jake, the one with smoldering pants.
His voice was quivering.

"Shut up!" Finn yelled at his brother. He pressed down on
Jesse's head even harder.

The heat was intense. The flames were near enough to
touch his cheeks. The fire's crackling taunted him: *Thought
you could escape us, didn't you? But there is no escape for you. Not
this time!*

Unexpectedly, the pressure against Jesse's head relaxed on
one side. "Did you hear that?" It was one of the oafish

helpers. He had let up. "A police whistle!"

The oaf on the other side let up too. "Yeah! A police whistle!"

"Both of you shut up and push!" Finn cried.

The whistle grew louder. Jesse heard it too.

"Finn, it's coming this way!"

The oaf was right. The whistle was definitely getting louder. It was coming from the far side of the wooden fence, but it was closing fast.

"Let's get outta here!" one of them cried. They both let go of Jesse simultaneously. The release was so sudden, Jesse bolted upright. He swung around and found himself facing Finn. Hurried footsteps echoed against the alley walls as the two oafs and Finn's younger brother rounded the corner where the alley emptied into the street.

The police whistle sounded furiously. It was immediately on the other side of the wooden fence. The gate shuddered as it took a blow.

With a sneer Finn pushed Jesse away, knocking him off balance. He headed for the open street. "I'm not finished with you, Long John!"

The whistle blew incessantly. The gate shuddered from another blow.

Catching his balance, Jesse leaped after the retreating Finn, hoping to hold onto him until the police crashed through the gate. But his arms and hands came up empty, catching nothing but air. With a thud he landed heavily on the bricks.

Jesse watched helplessly as Finn disappeared around the corner, heading toward Grand Street.

From the other side of the gate the police whistle blasted. The gate shook from the impact of another hit. It held fast.

For some reason the noise of the whistle, once a welcome sound, was now blasting with nerve-grating shrillness. Jesse rolled over onto his back and looked at the gate as it took another hit. He shook his head. It was a good thing Finn didn't know that Jesse's rescuer wasn't strong enough to break down a wooden gate. If he did, Jesse would be head-down in the barrel by now.

Jesse stared at the gate in amazement. It was incredible. How could a locked wooden gate, barely six feet tall, be such a formidable obstacle to a policeman? Another blow. The gate held. Why didn't the officer just scale it?

It was then that Jesse noticed it. The gate. There was no lock on it! Just a latch!

The whistle blew. The gate shuddered.

Disgustedly, Jesse picked himself up and ambled toward the gate. He lifted the latch with ease.

Had he not been so disgusted with the ineptness of the New York police department, he probably would have thought to step to one side after lifting the latch.

WHAM!

The gate flew open, slamming against Jesse's chest and chin. He stumbled backward and fell, his head smacking against the bricks. A black-clad form flew through the opening and landed full force on his stomach. Jesse's feet and head raised as the breath was punched out of his gut.

Through wincing eyes Jesse fought back the effects of the blow to see the face of the inept policeman who had nearly gotten him killed—first by failing to traverse a six-foot fence and now by nearly crushing him.

As his vision focused, fuzzy forms took on recognizable shapes. What he saw made no sense to him at all. Instead of a policeman, Jesse found himself staring into the face of an equally startled young lady. Her cheeks were red and puffed. A suddenly silent police whistle dangled from her lips.

Chapter 2

ARE her eyes always this incredibly round? Or is it because those magnificent brown orbs are mere inches away from me? And her skin—though flushed in the cheeks—is it always as pale and smooth as it appears this close?

These were Jesse's thoughts about the young lady who had burst through the gate and landed on top of him. Had it not been for the police whistle balancing on her full, soft pink lower lip, he would have mistaken her for an angel in answer to his prayer for help.

The whistle was a comical addition to an altogether attractive vision. It just perched on her lip, stuck there without support from the other lip which was otherwise engaged forming an expression of surprised embarrassment.

All of a sudden a flurry of hands pushed and pummeled and slid against Jesse's chest and stomach and arms as the young lady squirmed to get up. Her contortions caused the precariously perched whistle to lose its hold. With a noiseless thump it landed on Jesse's chest near the base of his neck.

"Get off of me!" she screamed.

Jesse's eyebrows raised at the absurdity of her command. "Get off of you? You're on top of me!"

His statement did little to slow her frenzied attempt to put distance between them. Jesse winced as her hand shoved against his shoulder, grinding it with her full weight into the bricks beneath him. He winced again as she jammed a knee into his belly. Then, just as she was making progress, the fabric between her hand and his shoulder slipped. With a whimper of surprise, she collapsed, her right breast smashing against his cheek and eye.

She bolted upright in feminine fury. "Mr. Morgan! I'm surprised at you!"

Jesse's face once again grew hot, but this time flames had nothing to do with it. His mouth hung open in silent protest. It was silent because he couldn't find words to defend himself against something he didn't do.

A fresh flurry of pokes and jabs pummeled him as the young lady renewed her attempt to disentangle herself from him. Just as she was shifting her weight from her hands to her feet, she teetered. Jesse raised a hand to her shoulder to steady her lest she fall again. Seeing his hand, she paused, then slapped it away. A mortified expression accompanied the slap.

Realizing anything he did to help her was going to be interpreted as an assault, Jesse went limp. He endured the gouging and jabs as best he could in gentlemanly fashion.

Once she attained secure footing, the young lady raised herself and jumped hastily away from him several steps. She busied herself brushing dirt from a full-length black linen dress.

Jesse waited a cautious moment, lest she find something offensive about his haste to get up. When he concluded it was safe for him to move, he lifted his head.

No sooner did he move when, out of the corner of his eye, he caught a flash of black linen. He froze. An arm swished past his nose as the young lady lunged at him, snatching the whistle from his chest. She jumped back as though he was a rabid animal, or a reptile, or worse—possibly the bogeyman.

"Well?" she said when he didn't move. "Are you going to get up or not? You look ridiculous lying down there on your back."

An exasperated sigh escaped Jesse's lips.

She ignored him. "Finn might not be as stupid as he looks," she said. "What if he gets wise to us and comes back?"

Jesse glanced toward the street. It was clear.

"Hurry!"

Jesse pushed himself up from the ground. As he did, bruises and scrapes—both those inflicted by Finn and those by the young lady—joined together in a chorus of complaint.

"Finn. You called him by name," Jesse said. "Do you know him?"

She wrinkled her nose in disgust, a commentary on the preposterous nature of his question. "I've never seen him or heard of him until tonight."

Neither had Jesse. But then, he hadn't seen this girl before tonight, either. At least he didn't think so. Yet something about her was familiar.

A thousand questions buzzed inside his aching head. *Who is this girl? And why did she do what she did?* Then it dawned on him. She had called him Mr. Morgan—how did she know his name?

"Well, I really must be going," the young lady said, giving her dress a final brush. You would have thought she was leaving a social gathering. With a brisk nod of her head, she tossed the police whistle in the air, snatched it triumphantly, and with a sweet smile headed for the street.

"Wait!" Jesse cried. "Who are you?"

She didn't respond.

"I haven't thanked you yet!" he cried.

Without stopping, cheerfully she called over her shoulder: "You're welcome."

Jesse ran to catch up with her. "Wait!"

By now she was in the street. From behind, Jesse reached for her shoulder, then thought better of it. The last time he did so it earned him a slap. Running past her, he stepped in front of her and blocked her path.

She pulled up abruptly, not looking at him directly. Her eyes darted to both sides, looking for a way of escape. She chose one side and moved that direction. Jesse stepped in front of her again.

"Mr. Morgan, I insist you let me pass." She still did not look at him directly, apparently preferring to speak to his chest. "It's not safe for a lady to be on the streets at night, especially with savages like Finn roaming around."

Jesse laughed. "Finn would be foolish to try anything with you," he said. "He'd be greatly overmatched."

"I'm glad I amuse you, Mr. Morgan," she said. Again, her words hit him in the chest. Jesse could see just enough of her eyes to see a glimmer in them. Her words might have been words of protest, but she seemed to delight in the exchange.

"That's the third time you called me by my name," Jesse said. "Do I know you?"

The amused glimmer vanished. Quickly. One instant it was there, then it was not. "There's no reason why you should," she said, her tone frosty. "Now, please step aside." Leading with her shoulder, she shoved past him.

"Wait!" Jesse cried.

But she didn't wait. She marched down the middle of the deserted thoroughfare in the direction of Grand Street.

He called after her. "You look familiar to me...I just can't remember where I've seen you!"

Jesse was not the type of boy that chased after girls. Ordinarily, he would have let her go her way without a second thought. Females had always been a disappointment to him. None of them were like Charity Increase. On occasion he'd thought that if ever he were to come across a girl that was like the heroine of his aunt's novels, he might change his mind. But the girls he knew bore no resemblance to Charity. No resemblance at all.

As a young boy Jesse used to regale the girls he knew with the adventures of Truly Noble. Passionately he would tell his aunt's stories, sometimes acting out the most exciting parts. He became so caught up in the tale at times the words seemed to flow from his heart, so closely did he associate with the hero of the story.

Without exception, every attempt he made to share the stories that meant so much to him met with disaster. The girls laughed at him before he ever had a chance to finish. Wide-open, howling mouths mocked him and his performance. Sometimes the girls mimicked his portrayal of Truly Noble, prompting a fresh outburst of laughter.

Usually, they interrupted him at the most dramatic part of the story, just as Jesse was getting caught up in it, at the very moment he and Truly Noble were merging into one and the same person. That's when they laughed. That's when Jesse was snapped back to reality, a reality that thought him silly. Immature. Foolish. Stupid.

Such was Jesse's experience with girls. It was this experience that made him realize a choice had to be made. He would have to choose between Truly Noble or girls. For Jesse Morgan it was no choice at all.

So when he chased after the nameless young lady who was heading toward Grand Street, he had no interest in her other than to find out why she had rescued him from Finn and his thugs.

"I want to ask you something!" From behind, Jesse caught the young lady by the arm. She swung around and faced him.

The gas lamp at the corner of Grand and Allen bathed them in an even, soft light. Round brown eyes, squinting just enough to convey a hint of mischief, gazed up at him expectantly. Jesse couldn't quite read them. Was the expectation he saw in her eyes one final chance for him to remember where he'd seen her before? Or was there something else?

She was shorter than him by a full head. The top of her hair was just below his chin, so that when she looked up at him the streetlight completely illuminated her face. Jesse was struck again by the smooth paleness of her face and hands. The alabaster quality of her skin was accentuated by black, full-length sleeves and a neckline that stretched up to her chin.

She lowered her head. Speaking to his chest, she said, "You said you had a question?"

Jesse figured the light from the streetlamp was in her eyes, so he stepped between the light and her so that his shadow fell across her face. It didn't seem to make any difference to her. She still didn't look up at him.

"I just wanted to know why you did what you did," Jesse said.

"Why I rescued you?"

Jesse grimaced. He wasn't comfortable with her choice of words. The thought that he had to be rescued was discomforting enough; the thought that he had been rescued by a girl was worse. He squirmed as though she'd just dropped a thorn in his pants.

He stammered, "Why you…felt the need…to scare Finn and his bullies away…with your whistle."

She lifted her head. Disbelief filled her eyes. She said, "Because they were sticking your head in a burning barrel, that's why!"

"Well, what I mean is, were you just walking by or do you go around looking for reasons to blow your whistle?" When the question first formed in his head, it didn't seem as dumb as it sounded when it came out.

With an air of forced patience, she said, "Mr. Morgan, I was walking home from work. As I passed the alley I heard scuffling and saw what was happening. Three against one. You didn't stand a chance. There wasn't much I could have done to help you directly, so I created an illusion. I ran around the block and approached the alley from the other side blowing my whistle. I hoped Finn and his ruffians would think I was the police."

"That's exactly what they thought," Jesse said.

"I'm glad it worked out," she said with a smile. "Now, I really have to be on my way."

"The Austin Factory offices!" Jesse shouted. "That's where I've seen you!"

A satisfied smile crossed her face.

"You work one of those typewriters!" Jesse said.

"And you deliver papers to my boss," she replied.

"So where did you get a police whistle?"

"My father gave it to me for protection. He doesn't like me walking alone on the streets at night. But I have no choice. I have to get back and forth to work."

"Where do you live?"

"Nearby."

Jesse nodded. For a few moments neither of them spoke, neither did they look at each other. In the distance an el locomotive sounded its whistle.

"Hmm!" Jesse shook his head.

"What?"

"I don't even know your name!"

The young lady smiled. "No, you don't, do you?" She looked past him as if she were looking for something and sighed softly.

"Well?"

"Well what?" she asked.

"Are you going to tell me your name?"

She wrinkled her nose playfully. "I suppose I could."

Another silence.

She giggled. "Emily. My name's Emily Barnes."

Jesse smiled. "Thank you, Emily. And thank your father for me. Tell him that police whistle was put to good use tonight."

"Good night, Mr. Morgan." Emily headed up Grand Street.

"Would you like me to walk you home?" Jesse asked.

Emily turned around. She continued walking, backward. "Thank you, but no." Turning again, she walked away from him.

Jesse watched her a moment, then retraced his steps down Allen Street toward home.

Emily walked as calmly as she could the length of the block. She wanted to look back to see if he was still there, but she resisted the urge though it kept building with every step. When she reached the end of the block she could resist no longer. Casually, she glanced over her shoulder.

He wasn't there. The lighted corner was vacant.

Turning up Eldridge Street, she ran parallel to Allen Street, her heels echoing up and down the street. When she reached Hester Street, she stopped. Struggling to control her labored breathing, she poked her head around the corner. The street was empty. Pulling back to the Eldridge side, she rested the back of her head against the corner building and waited. After several moments, she peeked around the corner again. Still nothing.

She let loose a perplexed sigh. There was no other outlet on Allen Street between Grand and Hester. He couldn't have already crossed Hester, could he? How else could she have missed him? She looked again. The street was empty.

Just as she was about to step into Hester Street, he appeared. She jumped back. Using the corner for cover, she watched Jesse Morgan stroll casually up the middle of the street. Emily's heart pounded as she watched him. About midway up the block, he entered the front door of a tenement building and disappeared.

Emily wrote down the number of the tenement and the

street name on a pad of paper. Taking one more look at the
building, she sighed and turned back toward Grand Street.

Chapter 3

WITH her thoughts on Jesse, Emily almost stumbled into Finn and his gang.

The street wanderers had found another source of amusement. This time it was a dead horse. Carcasses of animals lying unattended in the street were nothing uncommon for this neighborhood. Sometimes a fallen animal was left for two or three days before it was removed. The children of the tenements often played around them without so much as a second thought. However, the decaying stench of this particular black mare was enough to drive most people away. The putrid odor attracted Finn. He saw the stiff horse as another opportunity to torment his younger brother.

"Mount him up, boys!" he ordered.

Little Jake was lifted off his feet. He wriggled and squirmed in the grip of the two Neanderthals. Wrinkling their noses to ward off the rank odor and twitching their heads to shoo away armies of flies, they plopped the lad on the dead animal and jumped back.

"Ride 'em, cowboy!" Finn whooped.

Jake bounced off the cold flesh like it was a hot iron. The two oversized ruffians and Finn howled at the boy's terror.

"Get that cowboy back on his steed!" Finn shouted.

The two stooges corralled the screaming lad, grabbed him, and lifted him high for another ride.

Emily shivered in disgust as she witnessed this macabre entertainment. She fingered her whistle and wondered if the police ruse would work two times in one night. Then, just as she was about to blow the whistle, a burly head poked out of a tenement window three stories above the fallen horse.

"You! Down there! Get off our street! Go on, git!" the burly man shouted.

On the street below him the action froze. Jake dangled between the two oafs. Finn turned his attention to the source of interruption. He gestured angrily and shouted obscenities. "Mind your own business, old man!"

Another window opened and another head poked out, this time a woman: "Go home, Finn O'Shaughnessy! Go home before I tell your father what mischief you're up to this time!"

A third window opened. A man wearing a yarmulke and prayer shawl added his voice to those of his neighbors.

Finn's gaze bounced from window to window as a continuous barrage of orders were hurled at him. He took a step backward.

Emily put away her whistle. The growing chorus of neighbors had things well in hand. Retreating from her post she doubled back a few blocks and took an alternate route. She didn't want to run into Finn and his dunderheaded followers again.

Leaving the tenements behind her, Emily entered a high-class district of the city. The neighborhood through which she traveled was comprised of mostly brownstone houses, structures made of rough brown sandstone, a style that had been fashionable a couple of decades earlier. As a little girl Emily had thought the brown-colored houses were made of chocolate. The darkness of the night shadows reminded her of the mistaken childhood impression.

Cautiously she worked her way up Thirty-eighth Street toward Fifth Avenue. She avoided residents and passing carriages. At even the slightest sound she jumped for cover or scurried into a shadow.

The houses she passed, unlike the towering tenement structures, were only three or four stories high. There were other noticeable differences. These dwellings were more stately and better kept than the tenements; each structure housed only a single family; and there were no dead animals on the streets. These were the houses of New York's middle rich.

The middle rich were a new class of American citizen. They were not the wealthy older American families whose affluence was based on great landholdings and whose style and standards had prevailed up to the Civil War; nor were they the new rich who bought the homage and respect of the older families with gaudy displays of wealth. The middle rich families formed something of a bridge between the old and the new by wedding old traditions with new money. Counted among the middle rich were the Vanderbilts, the Livingstons, the Schuylers, and the Van Rensselaers.

Emily halted abruptly. What was that? She concentrated on listening. In the distance she could hear the rhythmic clop of horses' hooves and the crunching of carriage wheels echoing down the street. The sound grew increasingly louder.

She slid into the shadows of a large elm tree, positioning the broad trunk between her and the street. Breathlessly, she waited and listened. Several moments passed before a carriage sauntered by. From within the carriage she could hear the lilt of feminine cooing—light, giddy flirting words.

Emily leaned the back of her head against the tree trunk. She closed her eyes. There was nothing she could do but wait for the carriage to pass. Not until the street was silent again did she step from the shadows and continue on her way.

Upon reaching the end of the street, Emily squeezed through a gap in a low-cut hedge that lined the perimeter of the corner brownstone house. Crouching behind the hedge, she peered at an enormous white marble residence on the opposite corner.

The mansion resembled a Greek temple. Matching pairs of Corinthian columns supported the first and second floors on every side. Between the columns enormous multipaned windows stretched garishly skyward. A sculpted frieze rimmed the top of the house like an Olympic victor's wreath made of olive branches.

The white marble mansion stood out among the surrounding brownstone edifices like a diamond among rubies. Everything about it—from its creamy surface to its overstated stairway entrance to its prominent location on the most visible corner of the street—seemed to announce that no one within miles of it was wealthier than the owner of this house.

From her concealed position Emily studied the house. She took note of interior lights and movement. On the ground floor, the corner room closest to the street, draperies were pulled back from a window. Light spilled outside the room onto a grassy slope. Inside the room Emily could see rows of books on shelves. A figure paraded back and forth across the window. Male. Ample waistline. Dressed in a suit. He was talking to someone. Occasionally he would stop and gesture. His movements were emphatic. Forceful.

Emily sighed and shook her head. This would be easier if no one were home.

All the other windows in the house were dark, except for one dimly lit room on the back corner of the fourth floor. Emily studied the house for several minutes more. Nothing that she could observe changed. The man on the first floor continued to pace and talk. The fourth-floor room remained dimly lit. No other lights came on. Nor did she spy any other movement.

She checked the four arteries that converged at the corner intersection. They were clear of activity. She slipped back through the hedge and into the street, making her way noiselessly toward the marble mansion. A four-foot-high white wall served as a barrier between the house and the street. Its top railing rested on a seemingly endless series of identical posts that resembled stone flower pots. Hitching up her skirt, she scaled the wall near the back corner of the house. There was a soft thud as she landed on grass.

Staying low against the wall, she once again checked for signs of movement. From the front of the house she could hear the man's voice now. He was yelling, but she couldn't make out the words.

Emily moved into the shadow of the mansion. She ran her fingertips along the marble surface to guide her as she worked her way along its back side. She came upon a woodpile. It was stacked high against the house directly beneath a window. She looked to her left, then right. No one was in sight. Nothing moved.

Hitching her skirt again, she climbed the woodpile toward the window. Though no light shone through the glass, still she approached the window cautiously. When she reached the sill, she raised her head slowly until she could see inside.

The room into which she peered was the kitchen. It was dark. The only light came through a door from the front of the house at the end of a long hallway.

Just then Emily heard a loud snort. Then a whinny. Her heart jumped. Then it stood painfully still as if holding its breath.

To her left, at the corner of the house, a horse's head and neck emerged. The animal ambled down the middle of the street. As more of it appeared from behind the edge of the house, she also saw its rider.

A policeman.

As suddenly as it stopped, Emily's heart burst back to life. It pumped frantically as though making up for the beats it had missed. She slumped down and pressed up against the marble wall. She could feel her heart thumping through her chest against the cool marble wall.

The policeman rode casually, patrolling the street. When he first appeared, his head was turned away from her. He bent low in the saddle, peering into the hedge that was once her hiding place. Then, to Emily's horror, he straightened himself and swung his head her direction. Again he leaned forward as if by doing so his eyes could better penetrate the darkness.

Could he see her? She could see him. Clearly. The moon was bright enough she could make out his features. Broad, prominent nose. Thick, drooping mustache. Knobby chin. His eyes, though, were hidden to her. They lurked in the shadow beneath his hat. Just as she lurked in the shadow of the house.

Gripping the windowsill, Emily pressed even more tightly against the side of the mansion wishing there were a way she could melt into it. She considered closing her eyes, prompted by a childhood premise: *If you can't see them, they can't see you.* But the theory had proved itself false when she was a child; there was little chance that it would suddenly prove true now. So she kept her eyes open. She told herself to remain still and calm. He would be gone in a moment.

But he wasn't gone in a moment. The policeman pulled back on the horse's reins. The horse dutifully came to a halt. Leaning over even farther, the policeman stared into the darkness behind the marble mansion. Straight at her.

Emily's breathing quickened. Her chest rose and fell so forcefully, it seemed as if it would push her out of the shadows into the moonlight. Should she run? No. Let him make the first move.

For what seemed a lifetime, the policeman stared her direction. Then, without any sign of alarm, he clucked and spurred his horse forward. A moment later he was out of sight.

Now she closed her eyes. In relief. Her breathing soon returned to normal, but it took several extra moments before her heart was convinced it was safe to slow down.

Taking a deep breath, Emily raised herself above the sill again. Nothing inside had changed. She wedged her fingers in the vertical crack between the matching window frames. She smiled as the windows swung open like a pair of doors, freely and noiselessly.

Jumping onto the sill, she swung her legs inside. Beneath her was a massive table with a marble top. She stepped lightly onto the table, careful to avoid an eggbeater, a small hourglass egg-timer, a set of measuring cups, and various brushes that were methodically arranged on top. Pulling the windows closed behind her, she sat on the table and lowered herself to the floor.

Emily stood in a spacious kitchen with glassy white tile walls and a dark wooden floor. A massive coal-burning stove with an equally massive hood sat to her right on a hearth-stone. There was a shiny hot-water tank and porcelain iron sink on the wall opposite the stove. Water conduits traversing the ceiling gave testimony to an ample supply of bathrooms in the house.

Shifting her weight forward, Emily glided silently on her toes across the wooden floor. She stopped at the doorway and listened. All was quiet. Too quiet. What had happened to the shouting? Emily always preferred noise when she did this. Noise was a convenient indicator of people's location in the house. Silence meant they could be anywhere. They could appear without warning.

She paused, waiting for a noise, something that would indicate their location. She thought she heard a rustle of papers; but she wasn't sure, nor could she tell where the sound came from. Standing in the dark she shivered involuntarily. When she could wait no longer, she stepped from the wooden floor of the kitchen to hallway carpeting.

The far end of the hall emptied into a reception room at the front door. A framed archway marked the end of the hallway. Red velvet curtains adorned the archway, pulled to each side with gold tasseled cords. Palm fronds peeked out from behind the curtains.

When she reached the arch a mahogany stairway came into view on her right. Light from an open doorway illuminated the foot of the stairs. The room was the one in which she'd seen the man through the window.

She paused again to listen. She heard nothing. *This isn't good,* she said to herself. If the room was still occupied, there should be some sort of sound, even if it was just the turning of a page. But if the man and whomever he was talking to were no longer in the room, then where were they?

Emily stepped gingerly toward the stairs.

From inside the lighted room came the sound of a chair scraping against the floor. Then footsteps. Coming her direction!

Up the stairs? No, it would take too long. Back to the kitchen.

Emily whirled around. Her journey was a short one. She ran headlong into the chest of the man she'd seen in the window.

She screamed.

"What …?" the man cried. A sheaf of papers was knocked from his hands. They scattered across the floor.

The face that stared at Emily was as hard as the marble of which the mansion was built. Clean-shaved. Thin-lipped. A mole prominent below his right cheek.

At first, the man was as startled as Emily. Then, taking a step back, he took a good look at her. Gray eyes clouded with fury.

"Emily!" he thundered. He looked at her clothes. "You've been out on the streets again, haven't you?"

Before she could answer, two men appeared behind her from the lighted room. One had thinning, soft brown hair and matching eyes. His beard and mustache were so thick, they completely concealed his mouth. The other man had oily black hair. Plump cheeks rested on each side of a stylish mustache. A rectangular patch of beard rested on his chin. The vertical strip looked like it was pasted on.

The man with the oily hair poised himself to grab Emily should she attempt to get away. "Mr. Austin, are you all right?" he asked. "Is anything wrong?"

Austin shook his head. He made no attempt to conceal the fact that he was annoyed. "It's only my daughter. Go back into the study. I'll join you momentarily."

Without hesitation and without another word, both men obeyed; but not before the oily-haired man squinted a suspicious eye at Emily.

As soon as the two men were in the study Austin muttered a curse. "Of all nights, Emily, why tonight? First them, now you!"

Emily didn't respond. She bent down and gathered up the papers.

"You know how important this night is to me and your mother! Of all the selfish, stupid things to do!"

Emily reached for a sheet of paper next to her father's foot. As she did, she saw her reflection in the shine of the shoe. Of course. Why hadn't she noticed it earlier? Her father was dressed in his finest attire—black suit and tie, white turned-up collar. A top hat was waiting somewhere to complete the fashionable ensemble. This was the night of the annual ball for the Four Hundred.

It was the social event of the year. Every year Mrs. Astor hosted the party of parties for New York's four hundred wealthiest couples. And for the last ten years Emily had heard her parents grouse every time they read the invitation list printed in the newspaper. This year, however, was different. This year they had received an invitation. This year their name was printed in the newspaper. This year it was someone else's turn to grouse. For this year Franklin and Eleanor

Austin would be among the guests attending Mrs. Astor's exclusive soirée.

Gathering the last of the papers from the floor, Emily stood and handed them to her father. He didn't reach for them. He stood as still and as cool as stone. His granite gray eyes drilled into her.

"You'll be late," Emily said softly.

Her father snatched the papers from her hands. "I'll settle this matter with you later! Go to your room and stay there!" Austin thundered into his study where the two men were waiting for him.

Emily sighed. A confrontation with her father was exactly what she had hoped to avoid. She trudged wearily up the stairs.

Angry voices started up again in her father's study.

Now they talk business! Now they make noise! Why couldn't they have been doing this when I was... . Emily paused at the top of the stairs. A curious thought struck her. What had her father said?

Of all nights, Emily, why tonight? First them, now you!

What kind of business would keep him from Mrs. Astor's party? It would have to be something of unprecedented importance.

Stepping softly, Emily descended the stairs. She maneuvered as close to the doorway as she dared, close enough to hear the voices clearly.

Austin: That fire was over fifteen years ago!

Oily man: That's what I told him! Fifteen years. What does it matter now? Fifteen years is ancient history!

Had Emily not heard the oily man's voice earlier, she still would have identified it as belonging to him. It was as oily as his hair. The other man's voice fit his appearance too—soft and gentle, even though he was unmistakably agitated.

Soft man: What does fifteen years have to do with anything? Lives were lost in that fire!

Oily man: Only two lives!

Soft man: Only two? Only two! How many deaths are needed to make it a tragedy? Besides, for me it's personal. One of those lives lost belonged to a friend. A good man. A very good man. He helped me through a difficult time in my life. Not only me, he helped a lot of people.

Oily man: He was a labor agitator.

Soft man (angrily): Ben was a preacher! Yes, he was vocal about labor reforms, but only because he wanted a safe workplace! He cared for people. There was nothing in it for him; what he did, he did for others.

Austin (impatiently): Fine. You've convinced me. He was a good man. It's a shame he died. But what does that have to do with anything? I've shown you the report. The fire at the factory was an accident. Now, good-night, gentlemen.

Soft man: I heard the fire was deliberately set.

Austin: Nonsense!

Soft man: That means that the people who died in it were murdered.

Austin: Ridiculous! Read the report!

Oily man: That's what I keep tellin' him, Mr. Austin, but he won't listen to me. What was I to do? He talked of goin' to the papers. What was I to do? The only thing I could think of was to bring him to you, us bein' in your employ and all. I figured we owed you that much.

The front door latch clicked. Emily jumped. The Austins' coachman stepped through the door, his hat in his hand. Spying Emily on the stairs, he nodded. Emily nodded in return and indicated with her hand that her father was in the study. It was an unnecessary courtesy. Her father's bellowing announced his location.

The coachman nodded again, this time with a grin and a sly look in his eyes. He had caught her eavesdropping. He knew it. She knew it.

Emily swung about and hurried up the stairs to her room. She wanted to hear more of the conversation. She had her reasons. But the coachman's presence preempted any further eavesdropping. It was just as well. The anxieties of the evening had exacted their toll. She was exhausted.

With a sigh Emily closed her bedroom door behind her. She crossed the spacious room and placed the police whistle and the pad of paper she carried on her vanity. Bending over, she looked at herself in the mirror. A wrinkled nose summed up her assessment. She pulled the tie from her hair. Thick brown tresses fell to her shoulders. Using her fingers for a comb, she ran a hasty hand through her hair. She picked up a hairbrush, then set it down again. She'd brush her hair later.

A single bed was shoved against one wall opposite a brick fireplace. Emily fell onto the bed. Rolling over onto her back she closed her eyes. She sighed again. As she lay there, slumber crept toward her like an incoming fog.

Then she remembered something. Her eyes shot open. She jumped up and went to a correspondence desk that was adjacent to the fireplace. From beneath a stack of papers she uncovered a diary and opened it. Retrieving the pad of paper upon which she had recorded Jesse Morgan's address, she placed it beside the diary. With the utmost care she penned his address in her diary. When she was finished, she stared at what she had written and smiled.

Then she sifted through the stack of papers. Finding what she was looking for, she pulled the sheet of paper out from among the rest and set it before her. The top half of the page was filled with writing from edge to edge with but a single word:

Jesse Jesse

Jesse Jesse Jesse Jesse Jesse Jesse Jesse Jesse Jesse Jesse Jesse Jesse
Jesse Jesse Jesse Jesse Jesse Jesse Jesse Jesse Jesse Jesse Jesse Jesse
Jesse Jesse Jesse Jesse Jesse Jesse Jesse Jesse Jesse Jesse Jesse Jesse

Loading her pen with ink, Emily added:

Jesse Morgan Jesse Morgan Jesse Morgan Jesse Morgan
Jesse Morgan Jesse Morgan Jesse Morgan Jesse Morgan
Jesse Morgan Jesse Morgan Jesse Morgan Jesse Morgan
Emily Morgan Emily Morgan Emily Morgan Emily Morgan
Emily Morgan Emily Morgan Emily Morgan Emily Morgan
Emily Morgan Emily Morgan Emily Morgan Emily Morgan
Mrs. Jesse Morgan Mrs. Jesse Morgan Mrs. Jesse Morgan
Mrs. Jesse Morgan Mrs. Jesse Morgan Mrs. Jesse Morgan
Mrs. Jesse Morgan Mrs. Jesse Morgan Mrs. Jesse Morgan

Chapter 4

I hope you'll excuse me, but I don't have time to stop and chat," Clara said.

The woman sitting daintily across from her smiled sweetly. Maybe a little too sweetly. She had friendly hazel eyes. Matching hair was neatly pulled up and coiffured in modern style supporting a fragile pink hat with feathers. Delicate hands were folded serenely atop a book which she held in her lap.

In contrast, Clara Morgan's eyes had a natural sad or worried slant to them. Her hair was pulled up too, but not for style. She hooked stray strands over her ears whenever they fell between her and her sewing. Dried-out fingers continued stitching even as she glanced up to talk.

"I'd offer to help," the woman said apologetically, "but I've never been any good with a needle."

"We each have our gifts." Clara spoke the words flatly. She turned back to her stitching. For a moment her eyes refused to refocus on her work. They burned horribly. She could only imagine how red they looked. After a few blinks her sight cleared, but the effort did nothing to soothe the burning.

"Maybe I could make us some tea," the woman offered.

"Kettle's on the stove. Tea's on the shelf above it," Clara said curtly. She pursed her lips. She was behaving rudely and she didn't like it. What was it about this woman that was causing her to act this way?

Her guest rose from the chair. She placed the book on the end of the bed which was but an arm's length away. Then she busied herself at the stove—stoking the wood, placing the kettle over the fire, and taking the tea from the shelf.

To Clara, the woman looked every inch a Southern belle. Her arrival in a polished black carriage had drawn the attention of the entire neighborhood. A multitude of children and curious grown-ups had accompanied her up the stairs, trailing behind her as her pink dress swished and rustled down the hallway.

A small tenement girl wearing little more than rags was propped up against a soiled wall. Her older brothers stopped pitching pennies long enough for the woman in pink to pass. "Mama! Mama!" the girl shouted. "There's a angel in our building!"

Clara glanced up to check the progress of the little girl's angel. The woman in pink may have been a stranger to needles, but she was no stranger to cooking. Her hands moved deftly as she prepared two cups of tea. "How strong do you like your tea?" she asked.

"Tea's gotta last until I get paid again," Clara replied.

The woman nodded and fixed two cups of weak tea. She set one cup on a scarred wooden table next to Clara, who received it with a nod. Then the woman resumed her seat, holding her cup of tea in her lap like a perfect lady.

The room fell silent. From beyond the door the squeak of a pump handle from the tenement's only source of water could be heard. It squeaked continuously, pausing only long enough for an exchange of hands.

"When do you have to have them done?" the woman asked, referring to the pile of knee pants stacked on the bed.

"Tomorrow morning, 6 A.M. sharp."

"Tomorrow morning?" her guest cried. "The entire pile?"

Clara nodded without lifting her eyes from her work. For

each pair of pants, she turned them up and hemmed the legs; she then sewed on four flap buttons before laying them in the completed pile and grabbing another pair. "If I don't have them done by that time," she said, "the sweater will give the next batch of work to someone else."

"The sweater?"

"He contracts with the garment factory for piecework like this. Lowest bidder gets the contract."

"And how much—if you don't mind me asking—do you make per piece?"

Clara looked up at the woman. "A cent and a quarter—not that it's any of your business."

The woman reflected on the price quote. "That's not much," she said. "And how much do you pay for rent?"

Clara stared at the woman a long time.

"I apologize," the woman said sheepishly. "I'm being too bold. It's none of my business."

Clara forced herself to be polite. But it was quite evident the woman didn't belong here. She had too much color about her—the brightness of her dress, the sparkle of her eyes, even the color in her cheeks. These stood in sharp contrast to the brownish-gray, drab hues to which tenement dwellers were accustomed.

Clara wondered if the woman felt as conspicuous as she looked. She wondered how a woman of such obvious wealth felt sitting in a dilapidated tenement room.

The room's only door bore heavy scars. One panel had been replaced with a piece of wood several shades lighter than the original wood. The room's monotonous wallpaper was a faded green print. A row of six shallow shelves built into the wall served as the pantry. The shelves were covered by a long piece of cloth so thin you could read the can labels through it. Next to the pantry was an old wood-burning stove. A single bed took up the length of the wall opposite it. Clara sat with her back to a window that overlooked Hester Street, while her visitor's back was to the door.

"Six dollars a month," Clara conceded. "That's what we pay for rent. It could be worse. Not everyone in the building is as well off."

The woman's eyebrows raised in surprise.

"We have a window," Clara explained. "We get sunlight every day. One of the rooms further down the hall gets sunlight once a year. They have no windows. The family that lives there knows the exact day and hour of the year the sunlight comes between the buildings, through the courtyard door, and through their door into the room."

"How awful!" the woman said.

Clara nodded. "Plus, there's only Jesse and me sharing this room. On the sixth floor there's a German family that has a room this same size. Except there are nine people in their family. Husband, wife, and his mother, along with six children. There's only eight of them left. A couple of months ago the mother threw herself out the window."

"Lord, have mercy!"

Clara smiled wryly. For some odd reason, shocking the woman of substance with the reality of tenement life gave her a strange sense of pleasure.

"And Jesse," the woman said, "how is he doing in these surroundings?"

"He's surviving," Clara said. "Just like the rest of us. Hopefully, it won't be long before we'll be out of here."

"When do you expect that might be?"

Clara shook her head. "Hard to say. Been saving every penny I can. Maybe a year, maybe two. Then I can send him to school."

The woman looked pleased. "What school does Jesse want to attend?"

Clara frowned. "Jesse doesn't rightly want to go to school.

But he has to if he's going to make something of himself. When the time comes, he'll go."

"What are his interests?"

Clara's hands plopped into her lap. The work stopped. She looked at the woman and spoke sharply. "At the moment his only interest is daydreaming. He wastes most of the day pretending he's Truly Noble."

"Oh my," the woman replied. She stared in silence into her teacup.

Clara rubbed tired eyes. *Why did I go and say that?* she berated herself. Picking up her piecework, she began stitching again. In a more conciliatory tone she said, "When Jesse was little he wanted to be a fireman."

"Until his father died," the woman said.

Clara nodded.

"That must have been an awful time for him."

"He still hasn't gotten over it."

"Of course he hasn't."

"He blames himself for his father's death."

"Why? Jesse was only five years old when that happened!"

"He feels he should have done something to save his father."

"Jesse was there? He saw the fire? I didn't know that."

Clara nodded. "He'd gone with Ben to the factory. When the fire broke out, Ben had Gerald—one of the workers at the mission—hold Jesse while he went into the building to help people get out."

"How awful for Jesse!"

"And when Ben didn't come out, Jesse wanted to go into the building and get him. By then it was completely engulfed in flames. It was all Gerald could do to hold Jesse back."

"He sounds so much like his father."

"He's a Morgan," Clara said. "Thinks he can save the world." Her terse comment prompted another downward glance by the woman and more awkward silence. Clara chastised herself again. *What is making me say things like that?*

Without looking up, the woman spoke softly. "Ben was a Morgan for such a short time. His zealousness following the war was his way of trying to make up for his past." She smiled and raised her head. "Father was so proud of him when he and J.D. attended seminary together. I remember him beaming, 'Two sons following their father in the ministry! Who could ask for any greater blessing?'"

The woman mused a moment at the recollection.

She continued: "Then, when Ben graduated and turned down offers of big-city pastorates to work among the poor and destitute, Father wept. He said Ben's mother would have been so proud of him."

Clara said, "It was Ben's way of proving he was worthy of being the recipient of the Morgan Bible. Everything he did, he did to prove he was worthy to be a Morgan."

"He didn't have to prove anything to us."

"He felt he did." Clara's breathing grew shallow. Her anger rose inside of her as she spoke. "Every day he tried to prove it. That's what drove him so. I have to admit, it was that fire inside that first attracted me to him. He was so zealous, so passionate. He was unlike anyone I'd ever met. While everyone else was planning their careers, their futures, he found fulfillment in thinking of others first. There wasn't anything he wouldn't do to help someone. He helped them find work. He gave them money. He read them Bible verses. He weaned them off alcohol."

The woman in pink smiled warmly. "Ben needn't have concerned himself about being accepted by the family. His actions merely proved what we already knew. He was a Morgan."

"Was he?" Clara asked coldly. She tried to hold back the mounting anger, but it had been building for too many years.

"Is it a Morgan trait that made him turn down the financial security of a church pastorate? Is it a Morgan trait that prompted him to bring his bride to this den of filth? Is it a Morgan trait that would make him leave his wife and new-born son in the middle of the night to help some nameless drunk? Is it a Morgan trait that made him completely disregard his family and run into a burning building to rescue people he didn't even know?"

Clara's cheeks were flushed. Her chest was heaving with anger. But she didn't care.

The woman in the chair was subdued. She said nothing.

Setting aside her sewing, Clara stood abruptly. "I'm glad you're here," she said, managing to regain control over her emotions. She pushed back her chair and got down on her hands and knees. Reaching under the bed, she pulled out a large book and handed it to the woman.

The woman had to set aside her cup of tea to receive it. She did so with a look of concern.

"I would like to return your family's Bible to you," Clara said.

The woman took the Bible reluctantly. "This should be passed on to Jesse," she said.

Clara shook her head. "Ben told me all about the family tradition behind the Bible. Considering the fact that he is no longer around to fulfill his obligation of choosing the next recipient of the Bible, it should be returned to the person whose name is printed above Ben's name."

Almost reverently the woman lifted the cover of the Morgan family Bible. Printed on the inside was a list of names dating back to 1630. Benjamin McKenna Morgan was the last name on the list; above his name was printed his father's, Jeremiah Morgan.

"Are you sure you want to do this?" the woman asked.

"It's only fitting."

The woman looked up at her. "Father died last year. I'm not sure what he would have wanted…"

"Then give the book to J.D. If I'm not mistaken, he was your father's initial choice."

The woman stared at the Bible with sad eyes. She closed the book. Her gaze went from the Bible to Clara. Her face was a picture of tenderness and love. "Clara, let us help you. Let me talk to J.D. and Marshall and Willy. We can help Jesse…"

Clara cut her off. "Jesse and I will not become a Morgan family charity. We have done well for ourselves considering the circumstances. Thank you, but no."

The woman placed a comforting hand on Clara's arm. "But Clara, dear, think of…"

The door behind her opened and banged against the chair upon which the woman had been sitting. A capped head accompanied by a ready grin poked through the partially open door.

"Jesse!" Clara said. "I'm glad you're home. There's someone here who wants to meet you."

"Gadzooks! I can't believe it!" Jesse couldn't sit still. The carriage bounced with his excitement. "I can't believe it!" he repeated. "I'm sitting in a carriage with Sarah Morgan Cooper! Sarah Morgan Cooper, the author!"

A sea of faces filled the windows on each side of the carriage as it sat in the middle of Hester Street's bustling outdoor market. Pushcarts came to a halt. Sellers and buyers alike craned their necks to see who was in the fancy carriage.

"I hope you like my new novel," Sarah said. She sat on the edge of her seat with her hands in her lap. She was pleased at Jesse's reaction, but seemed distracted by the people surrounding the carriage. It wasn't so much their staring that bothered her, but the emptiness she saw in their eyes. She'd heard of the mental attrition that accompanied poverty and a poor diet. But she'd never seen it before. Had the tenements taken their toll on Jesse's mind too?

"Like it? I love it!" Jesse cried. He held it up to look at it again. *Danger at Deadwood: Another Exciting Truly Noble Adventure.* One panel on the cover showed Truly Noble wearing a sheriff's badge holding off four cattle rustlers with a six-shooter; another panel showed Chastity tied to a barn post while a sinister black figure put a match to a pile of hay. On the lower right corner the author had written: *To Jesse. May you find the strength that comes from goodness. Your aunt, Sarah Morgan Cooper.*

"It's the least I can do for my favorite reader," Sarah said.

"This is great! This is really great!" Jesse beamed.

"Are you ready to go?" Sarah asked. "I promised your mother we'd be gone thirty minutes at the most."

Jesse looked out the window at the mob of people who, at least for the moment, wished they were him. He nodded enthusiastically.

Sarah leaned forward. Her pink dress rustled as she reached up and knocked on the top of the carriage. She sat back. The carriage lurched and they were on their way.

Jesse bounced back in his seat, but not to relax. He wanted to get a better feel of what it was like to ride in the carriage. He ran his hand along the leather interior, more interested in the carriage itself than he was of the passing scenery.

"Have you traveled much?" Sarah asked him.

Jesse shook his head. "Mother tells me that she and Father took me to Ohio soon after I was born. Took me to see Grandpa Jeremiah. Of course, I was too small to remember any of it."

"I remember it," Sarah said with a smile. "It was a family reunion of sorts. Your father was so proud to have a son. You should have seen the way he held you—I've never seen a man handle a baby with such care."

Jesse smiled at the image that came to his mind. "Other than that trip," he said, "I've never been out of the city. But I'd like to someday."

Sarah said, "I remember my father taking me to Cincinnati when I was a young girl. The way he tells it, I threw a tantrum one time when he was leaving to lecture at the seminary. He let me ride to the main road, but when we got there I refused to get out. So he took me with him!"

She laughed at her own story.

"It became an annual event after that," she continued. "The thing that made me remember the trips was that one year—just before the war broke out—I happened to meet Harriet Beecher Stowe at the school. She and I had a lovely talk, just the two of us. We sat on a bench outside. It was a wonderful thrill for me to meet her."

"I know exactly how you must have felt when you met her," Jesse said, grinning.

Sarah blushed. "Well, I'm certainly not as famous as Mrs. Stowe. But I was thinking how different it is now that *I* am the one who is the author."

"I'll bet being an author you travel a lot," Jesse said.

"Mr. Cooper and I have been to England and Europe. We have been invited to the White House twice, once by President Grant and then again by President Arthur shortly after President Garfield's assassination."

Jesse sat forward in his seat. He seemed to have forgotten all about the fact that he was riding in a carriage.

"Oh!" Sarah cried, "You'd be interested in this. Mr. Cooper and I were fortunate to attend the Centennial Exhibition at Philadelphia's Fairmount Park."

Widened eyes indicated that Jesse was indeed interested.

Sarah smiled in response. "Have you heard of the Corliss steam engine?"

"Two thousand five hundred horse power!" Jesse said.

"We were there on opening day when President Grant and Dom Pedro, the Emperor of Brazil, started it. The funniest thing happened," she giggled. "When the emperor learned the number of revolutions per minute of the great Corliss engine, he replied, 'That's more than most of our South American republics!'"

Jesse laughed.

"You have a quick mind, Mr. Morgan," Sarah said, pleased that he caught the humor.

The carriage took them toward the better side of town as tenement buildings gave way to businesses, then brownstone houses. Sarah felt herself relax. No longer were they in an ocean of humanity. No longer was the carriage an object of great curiosity. It glided down the street virtually unnoticed by pedestrians and travelers alike.

For the remainder of the ride Sarah Morgan Cooper delighted in telling Jesse stories, which included descriptions of the other sites she saw at the centennial exhibition: Pullman palace cars, totem poles, Swedish stoves, Benjamin Franklin's press, George Washington's coat, vest, and breeches, and a variety of architecture that was as fascinating as the exhibits themselves.

Clara Morgan stood in front of the clouded mirror that hung behind the door. Peering into it she saw a drab, colorless woman. Her cheeks were sunken and chalky. Her eyes were tired and drooping. Dull brown hair, gathered at the crown of her head, showed little life.

She was not one to stare at herself in the mirror for any length of time. In fact, though she used the mirror daily to fix her hair, rarely did she even look at herself. But today, prompted by the colorful presence of her husband's half sister, she took the time.

Had Sarah not visited, Clara probably would not have noticed the toll the tenements had taken upon her. What was to notice? She looked like every other woman in the building. Sarah Morgan Cooper brought color to the tenement. She stood out like a rainbow against a flat gray sky.

Jesse saw it too. How could he fail to notice the difference between his aunt and all the other women of the tenements? The thought concerned Clara. In the absence of color, Jesse had been content to supplement the hues of his dreary world with his imagination. But how would he respond to real color? More precisely, how could an overworked seamstress mother compete with a famous novelist?

Clara spoke to the mirror. "You're all I have left, Jesse. I'm not going to let you chase after some elusive rainbow."

From the commotion on the street, Clara surmised that the carriage had returned. She stepped to the window and looked down at the throng as Jesse stepped out of the carriage, waving to them like some well-known statesman. He gripped his treasured new novel securely under his arm.

Clara considered hiding the new book once he was asleep, but then thought better of the idea. Jesse would destroy the place looking for it. It was best to let him keep the book. But at least she had the satisfaction of knowing she'd dispensed the Morgan Bible. In her mind the Bible was a greater threat than the novel.

She recalled the way Ben used to tell the stories of the men whose names appeared inside the front cover. His face would shine with the excitement of a little boy as he told the tales of Drew Morgan and the others. He used to regale little Jesse with the stories long before the boy had the capacity to understand them.

Clara decided it was best that Jesse not hear the stories again. They were dangerous stories, especially for a boy like Jesse. He was easily influenced by fictional stories. How would he respond to true accounts of the Morgans' exploits? The boy would probably get himself killed within a week trying to act like a Morgan.

"It's for your own good," Clara said as she watched her son wave enthusiastically to the departing carriage. A solitary tear streaked her colorless cheek. Clara made no attempt to stop it.

Chapter 5

SAGEAN'S last words to him that day were threats. "I can't keep makin' excuses for you, Jesse! Mr. Ruger thinks I'm daft for keepin' you on. Maybe I am.... You've gotta get your head outta the clouds and make somethin' o' yourself! You're not a lad anymore! And if you don't start pullin' your weight...well, ...I truly hate to say this, Jesse, I do... but I'll have no choice but to let you go... father or no father."

It was Sagean's loyalty to Jesse's father that got Jesse the job at the Ruger Glassworks Factory. Albert Sagean, the foreman of the factory, was one of Ben Morgan's success stories. Ben had literally pulled the drunken Sagean out of the gutter. Taking him to the Heritage Mission, Ben cleaned him up, fed him, and got him sober.

Never once, though, did Sagean feel he was someone's reformation project. Ben befriended him. Gave him odd jobs to do around the mission. Talked to him. And listened. No one had ever listened to Sagean like Ben.

"The man believed in me when I'd given up on myself," Sagean would later testify of Ben Morgan. "It was October 12, 1872—I remember it like it was yesterday—Ben was leadin' the Sunday service. I was praying jus' like he tol' me to, when all of a sudden a double miracle took place! First, God saved me and gave me a new life for my old worn-out one. But that wasn't all! That very night, God took away my desire for drink."

Those who were closest to Sagean were not convinced at his professed conversion. "It won't last," they agreed among themselves. And they weren't without precedent. History was on their side.

This wasn't the first time Sagean had straightened his life out; nor was it the twelfth time. If his pattern held true, Sagean would dry out for a week or two, get a job, and begin to put his life in order. Then, after a couple of weeks of success, he'd feel so good about himself, he'd take a drink. And then another, and another. He wouldn't stop until he lost his job and ended up facedown in the gutter again. So when Sagean insisted that this time was different, those who knew him didn't believe him. Like vultures they circled, waiting to hear that someone had seen him facedown in the gutter again.

They circled in vain. Albert Sagean was a new man.

When Ben Morgan learned that Sagean had been a glass-blower in Grafton, West Virginia, the preacher went to Will Ruger and convinced the majority owner of Ruger Glassworks to give Sagean a job. Eighteen years later Sagean was still there, having worked himself up to the position of foreman. He never forgot that it was Ben Morgan who had started him down the path that he had been walking for eighteen years.

So when Ben's only son needed a job, Sagean jumped at the opportunity to repay a kindness. Under union rules, glass-blowers were required to employ their own help. So he convinced his best blower to hire Jesse.

On his first day, Jesse was introduced to the glory hole—a sarcastic nickname for the glassworks furnace. Those who worked the glory hole had to endure intense heat. Many youngsters who had worked it sustained disabling injuries that factory officials attributed to personal carelessness or inattentiveness. However, the boys who could put up with the heat and danger of the glory hole were afforded a special measure of respect from the other workers.

Jesse got one look at the glory hole and wouldn't go near it. And no amount of persuasion could change his mind.

The blower that had hired him wanted to fire Jesse right then for his unwillingness to make an attempt at the job, but Sagean intervened. He suggested that Jesse was probably better suited to be a mold boy anyway.

So Jesse was given a second chance. The duties of a mold boy consisted of squatting in a cramped position for hours at a time at the end of the blower's tube attending the molten glass while it took shape. The job entailed lengthy spans of inactivity interrupted by quick hands and precise timing.

It was the periods of inactivity that were Jesse's undoing. Though his hands were poised, his mind remained active. And when he should have been capturing the blown glass, his mind was partnered with Truly Noble—confronting a corrupt banker, or spoiling a presidential assassination, or descending into a mine to rescue the innocent Charity Increase. The blower's curse would bring him back to the factory. But by then the piece had to be scrapped.

On the day that Jesse ruined three vessels in succession he was fired.

Though Sagean was disappointed with Jesse, he didn't give up on him. The foreman remembered how Ben Morgan refused to give up on him when everyone told the preacher he was wasting his time. Unable to get another blower to hire Jesse, Sagean hired the boy himself to be an office boy and runner.

The new position suited Jesse fine. It gave him time alone —travel time during which his mind could wander, or if the errand required travel by horse-drawn trolley, time to steal a glimpse at a few pages of Truly Noble's adventures. That's when he began carrying a book in his waistband to work every day.

While performing his duties Jesse didn't waste time. He had too much respect for Mr. Sagean to do that. But then, neither did he strive to be the fastest courier in New York. It seemed the perfect job for him. Mr. Sagean liked him. The work was easy. And he and his mother were making a living. While Mr. Sagean pushed him to apply for other jobs that paid better and had opportunities for advancement, Jesse had no desire to do anything else.

So when Sagean threatened to fire him, Jesse was concerned. But an even greater concern made him stick to his request.

"I'd only be going home thirty minutes early," Jesse reasoned. "I'm going to be on that side of town anyway. What good would it do to come back here? I'd get back just in time to leave again."

Sagean shook his head. "Thirty minutes isn't the issue, Jesse. It's your attitude. Your unwillingness to make something of yourself. A boy six or seven years younger than you could do this job!"

In the end, the foreman agreed to let Jesse go home after making his delivery to the Austin Factory office. But he made Jesse promise to use the extra time to think about his future.

It was exactly Jesse's future that prompted his request to go home early in the first place. His immediate future. Ever since his run-in with Finn and his thugs in the alley, the street tough had made it his mission to waylay Jesse on his way home. Up until now it had been a battle of wits instead of a battle of fists, and Jesse wanted to keep it that way.

Each night Jesse took a different route home, sometimes traveling all the way down to Henry Street before working his way back to Hester Street. Finn countered by posting his two oversized followers and his younger brother Jake on various street corners as lookouts. It helped that Finn didn't know exactly where Jesse lived.

Jesse's next move was to alter his time schedule. He waited long enough for the lookouts to think he had already slipped past them. Once they abandoned their posts, he would use the very routes they had just vacated. Today, by going home a half-hour early, he hoped to slip by Finn's lookouts before Finn even positioned them.

Hopping off the trolley at Grand and Forsyth Streets, Jesse carried the sealed envelope he was delivering through the pedestrian traffic toward Delancey Street and the Austin Factory office. It troubled him that he made Mr. Sagean angry. But the early hour was an opportunity Jesse couldn't pass up if he was to keep Truly Noble's favorite axiom: *Fight only as a last resort; and then, only to defend yourself or others.* Jesse decided he would work an extra hour the next day. By doing so, he not only would make Mr. Sagean happy, it would fit perfectly into his strategy to avoid Finn by altering his time schedule again.

Bounding up three flights of stairs, Jesse arrived at his delivery destination.

The clatter of typewriters slowed as the young ladies who were manipulating the keys looked up at him. There were three rows of desks, each with a pair of feminine eyes peering over a large black typing machine. Behind the second machine a familiar pair of eyes gazed up at him with a look of delightful surprise. A warm smile accompanied the gaze. Jesse recognized her. Emily Barnes. The girl with the police whistle.

"Get back to work, girls!" a thin, bespectacled man wearing a white shirt and red suspenders groused at them. The increased clatter of machines indicated their compliance.

"What took you so long?" the man yelled at Jesse.

Jesse held out the envelope without comment. The office manager snatched it from his hand. Jesse had learned that there was no pleasing this particular office manager. "What took you so long?" was the only greeting he had ever heard from the man. There were a couple of times Jesse knew for a fact that a delivery was not even expected. Yet still the office manager greeted him with, "What took you so long?"

"What are you standing around here for?" the office manager bellowed. "My girls will never get any work done if all they do is ogle you. Get outta here!"

Jesse couldn't help himself. He glanced at the girls on his way out the door. Sure enough, one of them was ogling him. Emily.

"Barnes! Get back to work!" the office manager screamed. He slammed the door shut, banging a slow-moving Jesse in the head.

If the multistoried brick tenement buildings were sheer cliffs, then the movement of humanity at their base was a river and Jesse would have to swim upstream to get home. Strands of pushcarts lined the edges of the street for as far as he could see. Sellers and buyers swirled in little eddies around the carts, haggling over the price of fish and vegetables and fruit and breads. Horse-drawn wagons navigated slowly down the middle of the street like great riverboats. The chatter of transactions and conversation and gossip roared against the vertical walls like the sound of rapids.

Jesse waded into the stream. Normally, Hester Street had cleared by the time he came home. Given the circumstances of his early arrival, he liked it better this way. He could just blend into the ripples of humanity. This would make it more difficult for Finn to spot him, although the troublemaker probably wasn't looking for him yet anyway. The ease with which he would make it home today made Mr. Sagean's disappointment in him easier to digest.

Still, he was cautious. He kept to the middle of the street where it was less crowded. Here, he could move abruptly in any direction if necessary. On the sides, he could easily get boxed in and trapped by a row of carts or a cluster of buyers and sellers. As he worked his way down the street, his eyes never stopped moving. He always kept at least one escape route in sight.

To his left a woman in a soiled white apron lifted a herring high above her head, extolling its freshness with a voice that cut sharply through the general din. She caught the eye of a woman shopper and reeled her in with a challenge to test the freshness of the fish. "Look at the way the sun glistens off those scales," the fish woman said. "And smell!" She shoved the herring under the buyer's nose. "Have you ever in your life smelled fish this fresh before? You haven't, have you?"

Behind the fish woman's cart a cluster of men in suits and hats sat in a circle of chairs. The smallest of them, a man with a wide mustache and a grating, high-pitched voice, was arguing that President Benjamin Harrison owed New York for his election. "If Harrison knows what's good for him, he'll revise the pension policy! That's what I say! This country owes a debt to our old soldiers!"

All around him heads bobbed in agreement.

"Apples! Apples for pies!" A husky man's voice pulled Jesse's attention toward the middle of the street again. "Apples! Eat them fresh! Bake them! No better value for your money! Apples!"

Finn!

When Jesse saw him, he stopped so abruptly a man behind him plowed right into him. The man muttered a sharp complaint; his breath was warm on Jesse's neck. The man pushed Jesse aside, disgusted by his sudden closeness to another man. Jesse, however, was barely aware that someone had run into him. He didn't hear what the man said. Didn't see his angry face when he passed. All Jesse could see was Finn walking straight at him!

The street ruffian wore a felt derby. The dark shadow cast

by the rim concealed his eyes and half his nose. Had it not been for the red-headed Jake at his side, Jesse might not have noticed Finn in time. The two boys were just a few hundred feet in front of him, passing the steps that led to Jesse's tenement. Finn walked jauntily, as if he owned the market on Hester Street.

Jesse was in luck. They hadn't spotted him yet. A young woman leaning out a second-story window caught Finn's eye. He glanced her direction, smiled, and tipped his hat. Jake was preoccupied with something on the ground. He was kicking a stone.

Jesse's instincts told him to turn and run; this was no time to think. Common sense butted in and argued that any sudden movement might catch Finn's attention. Jesse's racing pulse urged him to work out a compromise between his instincts and his common sense, and to do it quickly. Finn was almost upon him.

Jesse looked to his left. If he could get to the circle of men behind the fish woman, he could possibly blend in with them before Finn caught sight of him. Then, after Finn passed, he could slip behind him and up the steps into the tenement.

But what if Finn spied him? Worse yet, what if for some reason Finn glanced back and saw him go inside the tenement? He would be plainly visible on the steps. No. He couldn't risk Finn finding out where he lived.

Do something! Jesse chastised himself. *If not left, then right! Away from the house!*

Jesse took two quick steps to his right, then froze. His heart seized.

A large wagon blocked his way, filled with furniture and chairs. The legs of the chairs stuck up in the air like dead birds. But it wasn't the wagon itself that stopped him. Seated on the back of the wagon, pitching pebbles, were Finn's two oafish cohorts.

One of the oafs had just lofted a pebble high into the air. It hit a ragged boy on top of the head. The boy rubbed his head. He looked up at the sky. "Hey! It's raining rocks!" he cried. All the other youngsters around him joined him in scanning the sky for falling pebbles.

The two oafs roared. They tossed another pebble.

Jesse backed away from them slowly, careful not to draw their attention. There was only one direction left to him, the one his instincts told him to take in the first place. He turned his back on Finn with but a single thought: Put as many people between him and Finn as quickly as possible.

Just as Jesse was turning, Jake looked up from the stone he was kicking. Their eyes locked. The boy's mouth fell open in startled recognition.

"Finn, look!" Jake cried. "It's him!"

If Paul Revere had been as successful in rousing the colonials to action as Jake was in rallying Finn's forces, the English would have been thrown off the continent in a matter of weeks. Finn had Jesse in sight before he had time to take a single step. Moreover, the two oafs also heard Jake's alarm. They spotted Jesse too.

Four hungry pair of eyes locked on Jesse. Like an animal rendered motionless by the bright light of a fire, so Jesse stood transfixed, staring at his predators and they at him. For the briefest moment, everything and everyone around them faded to the background. Crowded Hester Street was reduced to five people. Four against one.

Jesse's heart had stopped in fear. Nor did he breathe. In fact, the only physical sensation that Jesse could feel was his own sweat as it pushed through his forehead and upper lip in beads.

"Git 'em!" Finn shouted.

Grabbing his derby to keep it from flying off, Finn sprang forward. The two oafs on the wagon were closer, but slower. Jumping down from the wagon, they lunged at Jesse.

The sudden movement toward him broke the paralyzing spell. Jesse dove under the fish woman's cart just as the first of the oafs was reaching him. He hit the ground and rolled under the cart.

One of the oafs dove after him. His reflexes a bit slow, the oaf didn't dive quickly enough. The entire cart shuddered as the top of the boy's head rammed into one side just as Jesse was emerging from the other. A seeming waterfall of herring poured down upon Jesse. The herring woman screamed in surprise at seeing Jesse roll by her feet, then in horror as she saw her fresh fish littering the ground.

Jesse scrambled to his feet. Behind him, the second of the two oafs chose to go over the cart rather than under it. He leaped onto the herring cart and grabbed the back of Jesse's shirt.

Furious, the fish woman removed her apron and began swatting the oaf who was sprawled atop her fish with a series of blows, wailing all the while that the oaf was crushing all her beautiful herring. The oaf cringed with each blow, but he wouldn't let go of Jesse's shirt.

His partner managed to shake off the effects of hitting his head on the cart and was coming at Jesse under the cart, grabbing for his legs.

Keeping his feet at a distance, Jesse turned and swatted at the arms of the oaf holding his shirt. The fish woman continued to whale upon his head. Still, the oaf's grip held. From beneath the cart, the other oaf inched closer to his legs.

Without letting up on his struggle to free himself from the oaf, Jesse glanced up to check on Finn. A devilish grin beneath a derby greeted him from the far side of the cart.

In near panic, Jesse pulled harder to break the grip on his shirt. Finn looked for a way to get around to him.

"Gotcha!"

The oaf beneath the cart grabbed hold of Jesse's ankle.

Just then, the tie of the fish woman's apron snapped like a

whip. With a howl, the oaf atop the cart let loose of Jesse. His hand flew to a triangular welt forming on his cheek.

"No!" Finn cried.

Jesse pulled back, managing to drag the oaf on the ground with him from under the cart. Finn lunged over the cart in an attempt to grab Jesse before he could get away.

The weight of two young men proved to be too much for the cart. With a crack, the axle snapped. The cart tilted precariously to one side, dumping herring, an oaf, and Finn on top of the other oaf on the ground in one grand, odorous pile.

The fish woman's wailing took on an added note of anguish as she beat Finn and the others repeatedly on the head. They, in turn, struggled to get up, slipping and sliding on the once-fresh herring.

Jesse took advantage of the development. Fighting his way through the crowd that rushed to see the excitement, he headed toward Allen Street and the elevated train tracks.

Chapter 6

A train whistle pulled Jesse toward the elevated tracks on Allen Street like metal shavings to a magnet. On a previous encounter with Finn, Jesse had used the el to make good his escape, managing to jump aboard the train just as it was departing the station. Finn and the others were left behind at the platform. They could do nothing but curse and stomp and watch helplessly as the train pulled away.

Of course, during that escape the timing worked out perfectly. Jesse shuddered at the thought of what might have happened had the train's departure been delayed by just a few seconds. Finn and company would have boarded the train and Jesse would have found himself trapped in a fast-moving box high above the city streets.

As he ran toward the el tracks again, he wondered if his luck would hold for a second escape. He paused long enough at the foot of the steps leading to the elevated platform to see if Finn was indeed coming. Allen Street, though busy, was wider and not nearly as crowded as Hester Street. It was sparsely populated by pedestrians and an assortment of wagons and carts. Jesse had a clear view of the corner at Hester Street.

Above him, the train whistle sounded. Three blasts. The train was about to leave.

Timing, Jesse thought, nervously tapping the railing. *Everything depends on timing.*

Three figures bolted from Hester Street. Finn led the way, his derby in hand so that he could run faster. Behind him, but keeping pace, were two heavier figures. Jesse stifled a grin. Even at a distance he could see bits of herring stuck to their clothing.

Three more blasts from the train above. It would be pulling out now.

Jesse glanced up at the departing train. Like all steam locomotives, it set into motion with a lurch and then slow progress. Too slow? Finn and the oafs were coming on fast.

Just as Jesse was about to race up the steps, he caught the amused grin of a man attending a newsstand. The stand was situated under the wedge of the stairs leading to the el. Magazines of every description were mounted on a board to best display the front covers. A table beneath the display had stacks of magazines and books and newspapers. The attendant at the stand had been watching Jesse, had followed his glance to the train and to the three running figures. He'd evidently surmised what was happening. Jesse's predicament seemed to provide him a measure of amusement in his business day.

Jesse bounded up the steps to the departing el. There were two flights of steps leading to the platform. A level platform separated them. Safety panels along the railing closed in the stairway.

At the top of the first flight of stairs Jesse paused on the platform. The cars on the train were still inching down the track. Finn was charging full speed, shouting.

"He's goin' to catch you!" The voice came from below. The man at the newsstand was looking up at him with a grin.

Jesse leaped up the second flight of stairs. At the top step, he fell to the ground.

The train was picking up speed.

His chest against the wooden platform, Jesse struggled to get up.

Running with all his might, Finn fixed his eyes on his lanky prey as Jesse ascended the stairs to the el. The leader of the hooligan band checked the progress of the train as it pulled out of the station. Years of street instincts came into play as he determined his chances. His mouth split wide with a brown-toothed grin. "You won't get away this time," he muttered.

Turning his head slightly, he yelled, "We got 'im! Hurry! We got 'im!"

Finn flew past the newsstand and an amused attendant. Running full speed, he grabbed the pole at the bottom of the stairs and used it to swing himself around without losing momentum. Feet pounding on the planks, Finn sailed up the first flight of stairs, across the platform, and up the second flight of stairs. He reached the station platform just as the last car was passing by.

With a well-timed leap, he landed on the steps of the moving car. A thunder of footsteps told him his boys were close behind. Stepping up, he turned just in time to pull first one, then the other oaf on board just as the car left the end of the platform.

Their chests heaving, the three made their way up the aisle of the last car, looking from seat to seat for Jesse Morgan. Finn retorted unkindly to the wrinkled noses and remarks of the other passengers at their pungent presence. He took his time, savoring his victory. He had finally caught the illusive Morgan. There was no escape for him now.

Jesse crouched in the darkness. Waiting. Listening.

Finn was a vocal person. Every other time Jesse encountered him, the street ruffian was shouting threats or orders at someone. If Finn was nearby, Jesse would hear him. At least, that's what Jesse was counting on.

Still, it was best not to be in a hurry. So Jesse waited.

When he was sure it was safe, he came out from behind the

newsstand. The surprised look on the face of the attendant was as satisfying as applause for a well-played game.

The stunned attendant looked up at the train platform, then back at Jesse. Suddenly, he put it together. "You sneaked back down the stairs and jumped from the landing behind the newsstand!"

Jesse smiled and nodded, enjoying his appreciative audience.

"I would have bet they had you!" the attendant said. "Very clever!"

"Thank you." Jesse took a modest bow.

With Finn and his cohorts rumbling harmlessly down the track, a pleased Jesse turned toward home.

An unruly patch of red hair caught his eye. Jake was descending the el train stairs. With shorter legs, he was unable to keep up with his brother. He had missed the train. Jumping off the last step, he came face-to-face with Jesse. His face registered shock, just like that of the newsstand attendant; but unlike the attendant, his surprised expression also harbored fear.

Jesse didn't know why, but for some reason he snatched the boy by the arm and then didn't know exactly what to do with him. The boy swung his fists and screamed and kicked. Jesse managed to hold him far enough away that none of the blows landed.

"Let me go!" Jake cried.

"I'm not going to hurt you!" Jesse said.

"Let me go!"

"Quit struggling!"

"Let me go!"

With a firm grip, Jesse dragged the boy back to the stairs and forced him to sit down on the first step. It proved to be a good place to control the boy. Jesse's body blocked his escape to the street, the panels blocked any side exit, and every time the boy tried to scramble up the stairs, Jesse's long arms easily pulled him back down.

"Sit still! I said I wouldn't hurt you!" Jesse yelled.

But the boy punched and kicked and tried to bite Jesse. When every effort was exhausted, Jake finally calmed down. Just looking at him, Jesse knew it was a temporary calm at best. He had the look of a trapped animal. Give him a chance, any chance at all, and he would bolt.

"What are you going to do with me?" Jake asked.

"I'm not going to do anything to you."

"Then why did you grab me?"

Jesse didn't have an answer to that question. It was just instinct. And now that he had him, Jesse didn't know what to do with him.

"I just want to talk with you," Jesse said.

The boy's eyes narrowed with suspicion. "About what?"

Something inside of Jesse stirred as he looked down at this boy. Red curly hair seemed to leap chaotically from Jake's head. His face was a canvas of freckles and dirt smudges. His eyes were green and clear. The clothing he wore had rips in both shoulder seams, exposing fair skin. For some reason, Jesse wanted to help this boy. The way his father used to help people. Lift them out of a pit of despair and give them hope.

"Why do you let Finn treat you the way he does?" Jesse asked.

The boy stared at Jesse like he was crazy. "He's my brother."

"That's no excuse for him to treat you like he does."

The boy stared at him, trying to figure out what Jesse was really after. "It's not so bad," the boy said. "Especially, lately."

"Finn has stopped doing mean things to you?"

Jake shrugged. "Not completely. He just doesn't have as much time now that we're chasin' you."

"I see," Jesse said with a wry grin. He tried a different approach. "Let me ask you this: What do you want to be when you grow up?"

Without hesitation, the boy replied, "I want to be just like Finn!"

"Why on earth would you want to be like Finn?"

"'Cause people do what he says and everyone's afraid of him!"

"You want people to be afraid of you?"

Jake nodded his head eagerly. "And to do what I say."

Jesse leaned closer to the boy. "You're better than that, Jake!"

Freckles rode the ridges on the boy's forehead. He didn't understand.

"Let me put it this way," Jesse said. "You can be whatever you want to be. When I was a little younger than you, I wanted to be a fireman. I loved the sound of the bells, the way the horses charged full-gallop down the street, and the way the smoke rose from the steam engine. I loved watching men climb ladders into the flames and rescue women and children who were trapped inside the burning buildings."

Jake's eyebrows raised. He was listening intently. "You're a fireman?"

"No," Jesse pulled back. "I said I wanted to be a fireman when I was younger."

"So, why didn't you become one?"

"That's not important," Jesse said. "What I'm trying to tell you is that you don't have to be like Finn. There are more important things you can be!"

"But I want to be like Finn!"

A stream of exasperated air escaped Jesse's lips. Then an idea came to him. "Do you know how to read?" he asked.

The boy shook his head.

Jesse pulled a Truly Noble book from his waistband—*Danger at Deadwood*, the book his aunt delivered to him personally. "Have you ever heard of Truly Noble?" he asked the boy.

Jake shook his head again, but his eyes stared eagerly at the adventurous scenes depicted on the cover.

"This is Truly Noble." Jesse pointed to the representation of his hero on the cover. "And this is Charity Increase."

The boy wasn't as interested in the girl.

Jesse opened the book. "Listen. I'll read you part of the story."

Jake didn't object immediately, so Jesse launched right into the tale. For more than half an hour Jesse read to the boy. After the first few minutes, Jesse took a seat on the step next to Jake. The boy showed no hint of wanting to run away; he was caught up in the story, which pleased Jesse greatly.

What surprised Jesse more than the eagerness with which Jake listened was the exhilaration he felt sharing the adventure with someone else. And not just the adventure, the moral lessons as well. He took immense satisfaction in feeling he was molding and shaping a young life.

As Jesse closed the book, little Jake looked up to him. "I know what you want to be when you grow up," he said.

"You do?"

Jake nodded. "You want to be a hero, just like Truly Noble."

Jesse smiled at the boy. "I suppose I do."

Chapter 7

SEVERAL days passed and Jesse never once saw Finn or Jake or the oafs on the streets of the lower east side of the city. On the first day, Jesse just considered himself lucky. But by the fourth day, he began to wonder if his encounter with Jake might be paying unexpected dividends. He imagined Jake telling Finn about the reading session on the el train steps. Maybe his kindness to Finn's little brother had earned him a pardon from the street desperado.

Could it have been that easy? Jesse wondered.

On the fifth incident-free day, Jesse took a direct route home for the first time in over a month. He was feeling good about himself and life in general. Not only did it appear that Finn was backing off, but Jesse's efforts to appease Mr. Sagean at the glassworks factory had not gone unnoticed. His boss' mood was pleasant again.

Strolling casually home, Jesse turned onto Hester Street. The first stars of the evening dotted the overhead strip of sky. There was just enough chill in the spring air to make breathing an invigorating experience.

With the steps of his tenement in sight, and still no sign of Finn, Jesse's thoughts turned homeward. Ever since his Aunt Sarah's visit, his mother had been unusually quiet. Plus, she was working harder than ever. Each night she sewed later and later. She would be sewing when Jesse fell asleep, and when he awoke the next morning he would find her still sewing. She insisted she'd slept, but the weary redness of her eyes gave testimony that it hadn't been much.

When Jesse commented that her sweater was asking too much of her, his mother informed him that she had requested the extra work. She said she was tired of living in the tenements, that Jesse needed to be in college, and that with a little extra effort they could possibly enroll him in a college by fall.

Given his mother's extra effort, Jesse couldn't bring himself to tell her that he didn't want to attend college. He knew he would have to tell her someday. But with fall a good half-year away, he figured he had plenty of time. Somehow he'd find the words.

A thought struck him. If he wasn't going to college, the money she'd been saving for his tuition could be used for other things. They could move out of the tenements sooner. Maybe right away! That would certainly please his mother. With a sharp inhale, Jesse determined to find a way to tell his mother about college tonight.

Then the anxiety set in. He felt more comfortable about the evening when he thought he had six months to come up with a way to tell her. He wanted to tell her. He just didn't want to do it tonight. He hated the look she got on her face whenever he disappointed her.

Well, he reasoned, *she's going to be disappointed sometime. Tonight or six months from now. Might as well get it over with. Then we can get on with plans to move out of the tenement.* He attempted to reassure himself. *She'll agree that this is for the best. It may take a while, but she'll see that I'm right.*

With a step of resolve Jesse placed his foot on the stairs of the tenement building. All of a sudden, a movement to his right caught his attention. He glanced that direction.

Gadzooks!

Jesse's heart burst into a gallop. His feet did a little dance, preparing themselves to run.

One of Finn's oafish disciples was running toward him!

Jesse glanced to his left, expecting to see the other oaf coming at him from the other side. But the street was empty. Jesse turned that direction to run.

"Wait!" the oaf cried. "Morgan! Wait! I need your help!"

On a scale of believability, the oaf might just as well have been declaring that Finn had been awarded sainthood. Jesse started to run.

"Morgan! Morgan!"

Jesse's thoughts switched to a familiar mind-set—escape. First, he scanned the street for signs of Finn and the other oaf. The street was clear. Good. Now, which route? Horse-drawn cars? Too slow. The el again? Too risky and too obvious.

"Morgan! It's Jake!"

Like a stick thrown at Jesse's feet, the oaf's words tripped him up enough to interrupt his stride. It was a trick. But the sound of the boy's name was enough to get him to wondering.

"Morgan! This is no trick!"

Keep running, Jesse told himself.

"The boy's gonna jump! He's tryin' to kill himself!"

Jesse whirled around, yet continued to back away from the oaf. He held out both hands, motioning the oaf to stop the pursuit. The oaf stopped. So did Jesse, but he was ready to run again at the first sign of trickery.

The oaf bent over. His hands were on his knees. He tried to speak and catch his breath at the same time.

"Seven stories high...says he's gonna jump...won't listen...says he wants to talk to you..."

"I don't believe you!" Jesse's head swiveled from right to left, then back again, his eyes never once leaving the oaf.

"Finn's been real mean to him," the oaf panted. "Was slappin' Jake around on the roof of a tenement...all of a sudden, Jake jumps up on the ledge to get away from Finn...when

Finn came near, he threatened to jump...I'm not foolin', Morgan!"

"Why does he want to talk to me?"

Still bent over, the oaf shook his head. "I don't know...all I know is that he says that he'll jump unless he gets to talk to you."

Jesse knew why the boy wanted to talk to him. It was because of their time on the el train steps together. Jesse had befriended him. He had shown the boy that not everyone was like Finn. Something he'd said or read to the boy had gotten through to him.

"Well?" the oaf said, straightening himself up. "Are you gonna come, or not?"

He made it sound as if Jesse had a choice. Since when was Finn giving him choices?

"And if I don't?"

The oaf squinted his eyes and shook his head sadly. "I wouldn't want to be you if the boy kills himself. Finn would blame you for not comin'."

So much for choices. But knowing something of Finn's demented mind, Jesse knew that the oaf was right.

What would Truly Noble do in this situation?

The question came to Jesse's mind effortlessly. And when it did, Jesse wished it hadn't, because he knew exactly what the fearless hero would do.

"All right," Jesse said, finding it difficult to believe that the words came out of his mouth. "Take me to Jake."

Trailing a good eight feet behind the oaf, Jesse followed him back up Hester Street to Forsyth Street where there was a seven-block row of tenements. Several times the oaf glanced over his shoulder to see if Jesse was still following.

Leaving Forsyth Street, the oaf led him between two tenement buildings. Trash and soiled papers and rags littered the way. Overhead, the day's wash was stretched between the buildings on row after row of lines looking like the ragged banners of a destitute nation. Children played on fire escapes, pausing to watch the parade of two pass beneath them.

The oaf stopped at a splintered, swollen wood door. He opened it and motioned Jesse inside. Jesse stopped well short of the door. With a sardonic grin, he shook his head and indicated that the oaf should go first. With the slightest of shrugs, the oaf swung wide the door and stepped inside.

Jesse grabbed the door before it closed. He glanced behind him in the alley. The wash waved in the breeze, the trash rustled restlessly, the children had returned to their playing. There was nothing to indicate that it was a trap. Jesse didn't know if he should feel relieved or not. He looked into the doorway. The oaf's backside waddled purposefully up an enclosed stairway.

A sick feeling rose inside Jesse's mouth. He wanted to slam the door and run. But if he did, and Jake jumped to his death, Finn would be after him like never before. Besides, what if he had managed to touch some spark of humanity in little Jake? Wasn't he obligated to follow through with his missionary effort?

What would Truly Noble do?

Jesse followed the oaf up the stairs.

The stairway switched back and forth seven times before a door led to the roof. The oaf opened it, stepped onto the roof, and held the door open for Jesse.

Stopping several steps shy of the landing, Jesse craned his neck to take in as much of the roof as possible. Finn and the other oaf were standing on the far side, glaring toward the stairs. Jake was not in sight.

"He's over there." The oaf pointed to a portion of the roof Jesse couldn't see.

Shooing the oaf away with his hand, Jesse said, "Stand back from the door."

The oaf followed Jesse's directions. The door swung shut and Jesse found himself standing in total darkness with no idea what was happening on the other side of the door. *That was not smart,* he muttered. *Now what? Forward or back?*

He hesitated, realizing that the longer he took to decide, the more time he was giving Finn and the others a chance to move into position to pounce on him.

Four quick steps. He threw the door open and braced himself for an attack.

The oaf beside the door gaped at him with lazy eyes. Finn and the other oaf had not moved. Jesse felt like a fool. But a fool who was still not going to let down his guard.

Stepping through the doorway, the entire roof came into view. Smoking vents popped up like mushrooms scattered across a gray, gritty surface that crunched with each step. A cool breeze blew in from the river. The city spread out in each direction with the exhilarating perspective of a bird. A panorama of stars stretched from horizon to horizon—not just a strip, but a whole sky full of them. Had the situation allowed it, Jesse could have spent hours staring at the stars.

Jake's position on the ledge of the building dispelled all pleasurable thoughts with a heart-pounding thud.

"You're responsible for this, Morgan!" Finn yelled. He took two threatening steps toward Jesse. The oaf beside Finn grabbed his arm and held him back.

The oaf closest to Jesse whispered, "I've never seen Finn this crazy. Just get Jake down off that ledge!"

Jesse turned his attention to the boy. He was sideways on the ledge, one shoulder hung over the street, the other was on the building side. His head was lowered as though it took all his concentration on the ledge to keep his balance. With nervous eyes he glanced at Jesse, then right back at the ledge. The boy's rags, normally stained and dirty, were heavy with dust and grime. His arms and face were covered as well. It was difficult to make out what was dirt and what were bruises. There was a dark half-moon under one eye. Pieces of twigs and straw stuck out of his red hair.

"I don't want to be like Finn no more," he said, half crying.

Finn lunged at Jesse. The oaf had to fight to keep him back. "You've turned my own brother against me!" he screamed.

The oaf that had ushered Jesse to the roof went over to help restrain Finn.

Jesse inched his way toward the boy on the ledge. He kept a cautious eye on Finn. "You don't have to be like Finn," Jesse said, doing his best to speak evenly, reassuringly.

"He hurt me, Jesse." The boy started to cry. "Hurt me bad."

"He won't hurt you anymore. We'll see to that."

Jesse checked the oafs. It was an uneasy alliance he shared with them. But so far, they were doing their job. Finn was restrained.

"You're safe now," Jesse said to the boy. "Come off the ledge."

Jake kept his eyes fixed firmly on the ledge. He shook his head. "They can't hold Finn forever."

"Do something!" Finn screamed at Jesse. "Get him down from there!"

"He's up there because of you!" Jesse yelled back. "It would help if you'd calm down! It would also help if you promised not to hurt him anymore."

"Sure. I promise. There. All right?"

"He doesn't mean it," Jake said.

Jesse wasn't convinced of Finn's sincerity either.

What would Truly Noble do? If talking didn't work, Truly Noble would grab the boy. Even at the risk of his own life.

Jesse maneuvered himself around a metal vent. He inched closer to Jake. The boy was about eight feet beyond his reach. Jake was shivering.

"What if I get…" he stopped because he didn't know the names of the oafs that he'd been running from for weeks. He turned to them and asked their names.

"Philemon," said the one.

"Elihu," said the other.

"Really?" Jesse asked.

The two oafs nodded their heads.

Jesse turned to Jake again. "What if I get Philemon and Elihu to promise to protect you from Finn? Would that help?"

Jake raised his head to look at the oafs.

"We won't let Finn hurt you no more," Elihu said.

"No more," Philemon agreed.

That seemed to assure Jake somewhat. He smiled at the thought of having a couple of allies. But the thought proved to be a distraction to his concentration. With a puppy-like yelp, he lost his balance. Arms twirling like windmills managed to keep the boy from falling over the edge.

Jesse had taken a step closer as the boy first lost his balance. He was poised to leap and grab Jake, but he drew back as the boy regained his balance, careful not to make any movement that could send the boy over the edge. Jesse's heart fluttered like a wild bird trying to break out of its cage. He gasped for air to calm himself, without ever once taking his eye off the boy.

"Jake, are you all right?" he asked.

"I'm scared," the boy replied.

"Jake, boy, come down from there," Finn pleaded. "I won't hurt you no more. I promise. Really. I promise!"

For the first time Finn sounded sincere. The boy seemed to listen.

"Jake," Jesse said. "Turn toward me. Slowly, turn toward me."

Jake teetered on the edge. "I can't!" he cried.

"Yes, you can!" Jesse said. "Hold out your arms. Turn toward me, and I'll grab you."

Jake laughed nervously. "This would make a good Truly

Noble adventure, wouldn't it?"

Jesse laughed, from nervousness as well as from the fact that the boy remembered Truly Noble. So he had made an impact after all! "It would make a great Truly Noble adventure!" Jesse said. "Now, slowly, very slowly, turn toward me."

With concentrated effort, Jake worked his feet on the ledge, scooting them ever so slightly; first one, then the other. For an instant, he lost his balance, but then managed to regain it.

"You're almost there, Jake," Jesse said. He eased closer to the boy. Only four feet separated them. "Now reach out your hand."

With extreme care, Jake stretched his right hand toward Jesse.

"Now look at me, Jake."

The boy froze.

"Jake! You're almost there. Look at me!"

The boy lifted his gaze until he was looking straight at Jesse. A slight smile creased his lips.

"That's right, Jake! You're going to make it!" Jesse said.

Two feet. That was all the distance that separated their hands.

Holding Jake's gaze with his, Jesse smiled. His mind raced: One step. Grab his hand. Plant your foot. And hold on. One more step. Just one more.

Something caught the toe of Jesse's shoe. He stumbled forward.

No! No! Dear God, no!

Jesse tried to catch himself. He couldn't. His momentum was forward. His knee crunched into the gravel on the rooftop. As he fell forward, he reached for Jake. Jesse's head turned skyward, looking for something to grab hold of. The boy's arms flailed helplessly. A face distorted with terror looked down at him. Jesse's hands groped for Jake's arms but came up empty.

There was nothing he could do. The force of his fall landed

squarely on the boy's legs sending little Jake over the ledge. In horror, Jesse watched as one moment he saw the body of a boy and the next moment all he saw was an empty sky.

Jesse's head slammed against the side of the ledge. Instinctively, his eyes shut to fight back the flash of light that accompanied the blow and the inevitable pain. In the darkness of his mind, he heard the scream of little Jake as he fell. Then, for an agonizing second, all was quiet.

"Jake! Jake!"

It was Finn's voice, on the edge between sanity and blind rage.

Jesse managed to open his eyes. He was surrounded by a forest of legs as Finn and the two oafs leaned over the edge of the building looking down toward the street.

"He killed my brother! He killed my brother!" Finn screamed.

The next thing Jesse knew, Finn was on top of him, landing blow after blow after blow. Jesse's resistance was purely instinct. He was too numb to defend himself. His numbness was such that he didn't even feel Finn's blows, though he knew that they were crashing upon him with unbridled hysteria.

Then there was nothing. The blows stopped. Finn's weight was lifted off him. The next thing Jesse knew, he was being hauled to his feet. After several forced blinks, his eyes came into focus.

"Get outta here! Go on, get outta here!"

One of the oafs was yelling at him—he was too disoriented to know which one. The other oaf had Finn pinned to the ground.

"I'll kill 'im! I'll kill 'im!" Finn ranted.

The oaf pushed Jesse toward the stairs.

"What about Jake?" Jesse asked.

"What do you think? He's dead!" There was thunder in his voice.

Finn broke free from the restraining oaf. The one closest to Jesse caught him, just before he reached Jesse.

"It was an accident!" the oaf yelled at Finn.

Dazed, Jesse took an apologetic step toward Finn. "I'm sorry...I was trying to..."

Finn lashed out and grabbed Jesse's shirt. And what Jesse saw in Finn's eyes cut through the dense clouds in his head. Never before had Jesse seen a murderous intent in a man's eyes. But the piercing cold glint in Finn's convinced Jesse that no amount of words would take it away.

The other oaf recovered and wrestled Finn's hand from Jesse's shirt.

"Go! Get out of here!" he shouted.

Jesse turned and stumbled. It was still difficult for him to believe what had happened. It took him two attempts to find the door latch and swing it open. He descended into the darkness of the stairwell.

The two oafs watched Jesse leave. When he was out of sight, Finn calmed down and they relaxed their grip. Finn collapsed onto the rooftop, rolled over, than sat with his arms around his legs. He looked up at the two oafs. And chuckled.

His chuckle turned into a laugh. Then a roar.

From the far side of the ledge, a small head with unruly red hair popped up. One of the oafs went over and helped Jake back over the ledge from the padded fire escape on which he'd landed.

"Did I do good, Finn?" the boy cried.

"You did good, kid! Real good!" Finn said.

Chapter 8

J ESSE Morgan was swallowed up by darkness. The only
sensation of which he was vaguely aware was that of
descent. Rubbery legs somehow managed to keep him upright
as he stumbled down the stairs, slamming from one side of
the enclosed stairwell to the other. He plummeted deeper and
deeper and deeper into the reeking bowels of the building. He
couldn't stop himself. His momentum carried him. He was
pulled down by forces he could not see, let alone counter.

But the dimly lit stairwell was like dawn's early light compared to the inky blackness he felt in his soul. Never before
had he experienced such hopelessness and despair. Such
emptiness.

The pounding of his feet on the wooden steps echoed cru-
elly in the cavernous stairwell:

*You killed him...you killed him...you killed him...you killed
him...*

He covered his ears to block the cursed accusation. The
voice only grew louder. Pounding now, against his ears. There
was nothing he could do to stop it. He couldn't run from it.
Like the banging of a judge's gavel, it hammered over and
over in his head.

Halfway down the last flight of stairs, he lost all sense of
balance and crashed through the door at the bottom of the
steps. The alley's brick walls and iron-rod fire escapes and

flapping laundry tumbled around him as he collapsed with a bone-jarring thud.

He lay there, waiting for the spinning to stop. Loose papers and trash swirled around his head. Then, with a moan, he rolled onto his back. He stared dizzily at the gathering of tenement children high above on the fire escapes whose play was halted by his abrupt appearance.

Jesse's tears blurred their startled expressions.

Jake's playmates. How will they react when they learn of his death? Any moment now, the news of his tragic fall will reach them. They'll hear about the man who was trying to save him, but who instead pushed him over the ledge. They'll race to the far side of the building. They'll see his lifeless body. They'll stare at his twisted limbs, his spilled blood. It will give them nightmares tonight. The memory will haunt their dreams for years to come.

Jesse scrambled to get up.

Must get away. Can't stay here. Can't be here when the announcement comes. Couldn't bear to look at their faces. Couldn't bear to see their expressions when Finn points to me as the man who pushed Jake over the ledge.

With his right hand waving in front of him like a blind man's cane, Jesse felt his way out of the alley. He staggered over boxes, plowed into barrels, stumbled into the middle of Forsyth Street where he pulled himself to a stop. He stood there. Hurting. Dazed. Confused.

Which way to run? Home? No. Must get away. Must think. Think of some way to explain. To tell Mother. What to say to... The thought brought a fresh infusion of tears. *...to Jake's parents? What can I say to a mother whose son I've just killed? I'm sorry? I was trying to save him, but I killed him instead? Would it help if I told you I wish I had died in his place?*

Words. Nothing more than words. Sounds riding the air. What comfort are mere sounds to a mother who has just lost a child?

His tears flowing unchecked, Jesse staggered toward the East River. He was oblivious to the way people stared at him as he passed by. He never heard Finn and Jake and the two oafs laughing at him from the rooftop. Nor did he take note of the female who hid behind a corner, then followed after him.

Jesse was thirteen years old when the Brooklyn Bridge was completed. Along with the rest of New York, he and his mother attended the dedication. Never before had the cities of New York and Brooklyn witnessed such an event. President Chester Arthur was on hand to inaugurate the festivities. Dubbed the eighth wonder of the world, the bridge had taken fourteen years to construct at a cost of $15 million and at least twenty lives.

On a splendidly sunny day, the dedication of the bridge opened to unprecedented fanfare. Buildings were draped with red, white, and blue bunting; the river beneath the bridge was a solid mass of flagged vessels; both shores teemed with celebrants. There was music everywhere, cannon salutes, and the ringing of bells as President Arthur and New York Governor Grover Cleveland led a procession across the bridge.

When night fell, a mile-long ribbon of lights sparkled across the expanse of the bridge. Fourteen tons of fireworks lit the black sky, culminating with a breathtaking display of five hundred rockets that burst into showers of silver and gold. Accompanying the visual spectacular was a chorus of bells, brass bands, choral voices, and horns blasting from every ship and boat on the East River.

From the day of its dedication, the bridge had been one of Jesse's favorite places. He would go there at every opportunity to watch the ships glide among the silver sparkles on the water's surface, or to enjoy the openness and fresh air that the river-front buildings blocked before it could reach the tenements.

It was to the bridge that Jesse ran when he thought he'd killed little Jake. This time there were no bursting rockets. No bells. No chorus of voices. Just the haunting whistle of the wind as it played the bridge's steel wires like strings of a harp. Other than the pockets of light surrounding the passageway lamps, the bridge was fittingly shrouded in darkness. Jesse stepped onto the pedestrian promenade and made his way to the middle of the span. He leaned trembling hands and arms on the rail and gazed upriver. A regular, but not steady, stream of pedestrians passed behind him. He wondered if they could tell how shaken and frightened he felt.

To calm himself, Jesse inhaled deeply the moist, heavy East River air. He told himself to calm down, not to make any hasty decisions. First, he had to sort things out. But that in itself was a nearly insurmountable task. Emotions and thoughts swirled endlessly in his head powered by a heart rate that rivaled the revolutions per minute of the Corliss engine. His stomach responded by raising the level of bile in his gullet. Jesse fought it back by taking another long draw of air. He tried to clear his mind, to think of nothing.

On the river below him, a schooner approached directly, then disappeared beneath the bridge as it headed out to sea. The light of the moon sparkled on the water, mixing languidly with the lights of the city at river's edge. The lights were interrupted by a dark strip of land nearly two miles in length and barely seven hundred and fifty feet wide that lay just offshore. Blackwell's Island. Light from a single residence illuminated but a small portion of the land mass.

That's where you're going to end up unless you get control of yourself, Jesse told himself.

Blackwell's Island. Known by every mother and child in the vicinity. Children jokingly accused each other of residing there. Mothers threatened to send their children there if they didn't obey. Originally a pasturage for hogs, Blackwell's Island was now a lunatic asylum.

"Got an extra bed?" Jesse asked the lighted building.

A sliver of sarcastic levity. The futile gasp of a desperate man.

The longer Jesse stared at the island, the more he felt he belonged there. All levity aside, he thought he could hear voices coming from Blackwell's Island. Depressed souls chanting his name.

Jesse...Jesse...Jesse...Jesse...Jesse...Jesse...Jesse...Jesse...

The dark river below joined the chorus, undulating in hypnotic rhythm. Beckoning him.

Let yourself go. Why endure the misery? There is no hope. No one will understand. So why try? Just let go. One step. Let the inky blackness engulf you, numb you, free you. The torturous thoughts will stop. Your pain will cease.

The voices from the island joined in refrain:

Jesse...Jesse...Jesse...join us...join us...join us...join us...

"Come here often?"

The voice, though soft and pleasant, startled him. The face that accompanied the voice was equally as pleasant. A young woman. Innocent, wide brown eyes. He'd seen her before.

Jesse tried to disguise his fright by remembering her name. "Emily...Emily..."

"Barnes," Emily Austin said. She repeated it for him. "My name's Emily Barnes."

"The young lady with the police whistle," Jesse remembered.

She pulled the whistle from her waistband. Holding it between two fingers she smiled impishly. "A woman can't be too careful," she said.

The woman and the whistle reminded Jesse of Finn. He glanced behind Emily. "You're alone?"

"No," she replied. "I'm here with you." Then, she added with a grin, "And my whistle, in case you get any indecent ideas."

Jesse protested, "I would never!"

Emily shook her head with mock sadness. "Too bad," she said, replacing the whistle in her waistband.

Jesse didn't know what to make of the woman who stood with him on the bridge. But he knew it was the second time that she had rescued him. The first time was when Finn tried to stick his head in a burning barrel. The second time was tonight. Her presence rescued him from the dark voices from beyond the bridge railing that called to him.

Maybe it was her sudden appearance on the heels of such a dark, desperate moment, but for some reason Emily seemed more real, more human, more alluring than anyone he'd seen before. The soft yellow glow of the bridge lights made her smooth skin and brown hair appear luminous.

"You never answered my question," Emily said.

"Question?"

"Do you come to the bridge often?"

Jesse smiled and tried to act nonchalant. Turning his back on Blackwell's Island, he walked casually to the sea side of the bridge. Emily followed him, which gave him more pleasure than he wanted to admit to himself. Leaning on the railing, he gazed at the Statue of Liberty which stood against a black night. "The bridge is one of my favorite places," he said. "I come here as often as I can."

Emily joined him against the rail. "Me too," she said.

The two of them nearly had the promenade to themselves. Side-by-side, Jesse and Emily gazed at the statue in the harbor. The lapping of the water was the only sound to be heard for a full minute. Emily turned around and leaned her back against the railing. She squinted her eyes upriver.

"Are you familiar with Blackwell's Island?" she asked.

Jesse didn't turn around. "I've heard of it."

"I come here to look at it. It inspires me."

With furrowed brow and disbelieving eyes, Jesse turned to

her. "An asylum inspires you?"

Bright eyes met his. "I know it sounds strange," she replied, "but that's because you don't know who I really am."

"You're not Emily Barnes, a typist at the Austin Factory offices?"

Emily shook her head. "That's only my disguise."

"Your disguise?" Jesse was intrigued. The woman standing next to him—between her attractiveness and mystery—had succeeded in making him forget all about his problems. At least for the moment.

"Have you ever heard of Nellie Bly?" she asked.

"You're Nellie Bly?"

Emily laughed. "Of course not! Though I want to be like her."

Jesse shook his head indicating he hadn't heard of this Bly woman.

"Don't you ever read the newspapers?" Emily asked. "Last year Nellie Bly beat Phileas Fogg's around-the-world record!"

"Phileas Fogg?"

Emily looked at him incredulously. "You need to read more, Mr. Morgan!"

"My mother thinks I read too much."

"Phileas Fogg is the hero of Jules Verne's book, *Around the World in Eighty Days*."

"I've heard of the book," Jesse said lamely.

"Well, Nellie Bly, a writer for the New York *World* newspaper, beat the eighty-day record!"

"Impossible!"

Emily smiled in triumph for the woman she idolized. "Seventy-two days, six hours, eleven minutes, and fourteen seconds. She rode on ships, trains, in jinrikishas and sampans, and on horses and burros."

The amazement on Jesse's face clearly delighted Emily. Then his expression turned to puzzlement. "What does that have to do with Blackwell's Island and you being in disguise?"

Emily laughed. Her laughter had a girlish lilt to it. "You should see the expression on your face, Jesse Morgan!" she said.

Jesse straightened his face into serious lines.

This too amused Emily. She overcame her amusement long enough to explain: "Nellie Bly became famous when she wrote a series of newspaper articles on Blackwell's Island. She feigned insanity to get into the asylum. Then, observing the inhuman conditions firsthand, she recorded the horrors with her pen. The resulting news articles prompted an investigation which brought about needed reforms at the asylum."

Head-nodding indicated Jesse was beginning to understand. "And you want to be like Nellie Bly," he said.

"I *am* like Nellie Bly," Emily cried with a fair amount of indignity.

"You've written newspaper stories?"

Emily crinkled her nose. "Written, yes. Published, no. At least not yet. But I'm still gathering research."

"At the Austin Factory?"

Emily nodded with all seriousness. "Being a typist is my cover. It puts me in a position to see important papers and files. I suspect there is widespread corruption, graft, and possible criminal activity in Mr. Austin's enterprises."

Jesse was clearly impressed. Here was a woman who lived the danger and excitement he only dreamed about. Now the rescue in the alley made sense. Being an undercover reporter, this woman was accustomed to danger. And when she didn't want to talk with him afterward—she was protecting her cover.

"But why are you telling me this?" Jesse asked. "You're exposing your cover."

Emily didn't have a ready answer to his question. She looked down. The way her eyes darted from side to side indicated she hadn't anticipated the question. Then, her eye movement slowed and ultimately fixed on a pine plank near her foot. She sighed and shrugged. "A person can get lonely during an undercover assignment. You look like a person I could trust. I took a chance."

"Your secret is safe with me," Jesse said quickly.

Emily's eyes filled with reassurance. "I knew it would be."

Chapter 9

HAD a person been listening for footsteps on the promenade of the Brooklyn Bridge, he would have thought a single person was coming toward him, so perfectly did Jesse's and Emily's footfalls match each other. It was an observation that did not go unnoticed by Jesse.

Their matching stride, her arm close enough to him that he could feel her warmth, the scent of her perfume, the way their eyes met and held each other—all these things distracted Jesse temporarily from his grief over little Jake.

He welcomed the distraction. It was as though her presence reminded him that there was still life for him to experience. Never before had he experienced the level of sensation he was currently feeling for Emily. It was as though the two of them were creating some sort of invisible field between them, one that heightened all his senses. Every word she spoke, every glance was charged with life. Even the wind off the river was crisper. The air they breathed was saltier. Lights were brighter; sounds sharper.

"Tell me about yourself," Emily said, giving him one of those electric glances. "What do you do when you aren't delivering envelopes or rescuing little boys from their big brothers?"

The unexpected reference to Jake was a blow. It hit Jesse hard, temporarily evaporating the sensation field between them. Jesse looked away, trying to shield from Emily the painful effects of her question.

"Did I say something wrong?" Emily said.

Jesse shook his head. Images flashed in his mind. Jake on the ledge. His arms flailing. The empty sky. The scream.

Emily stopped. "Something's bothering you." She reached out and touched Jesse's arm. The warmth of her fingertips sent a charge through him. It brought Jesse to a stop. "Tell me what it is that's bothering you," Emily said, her hand now resting fully on his arm.

For an instant, Jesse was pulled between tragedy and ecstasy; images of Jake and sensations with Emily battled inside his head—*Jake, scared, on the ledge...Emily's wide, brown eyes, friendly, concerned...flailing arms, Jesse reaching, reaching for Jake, but grasping nothing... the warmth of Emily's hand on his arm...an empty sky, an echoing scream...Jesse, please tell me, maybe I can help...*

Jesse fought to remain in the present, with Emily. He considered telling her about the incident. He wanted to tell her. He was sure she would understand. She'd witnessed Finn's cruel treatment of his little brother. But another thought stopped him. How would Emily react when she learned that it was he, not Finn, who had pushed Jake over the ledge? Would she pull away from him when she learned it was he who killed Jake? He didn't know for sure. He couldn't take that chance; or more correctly, he didn't want to take that chance. He decided a general response would be sufficient.

"I just had another encounter with Finn, that's all," he said. He waited eagerly for her response.

Emily gazed at him with sympathetic eyes. Her silence encouraged him to say something more.

Jesse looked away. "I'd rather not talk about it," he said.

"Did Finn hurt you?"

"No, he didn't hurt me." It was a true statement. The pain

he felt was self-inflicted. He'd only hurt himself by being so clumsy, by being such an oaf.

Emily removed her hand from his arm. Her eyes saddened. She was disappointed that he refused to confide in her. Jesse's heart ached as the wind cooled the place her hand had warmed. He changed the subject, hoping to find a topic that would invite her hand to return to his arm.

"My aunt was in town recently," he said. "You and she have something in common."

Emily looked at him with an expression of mild interest.

"She's a writer…like you. Only, she doesn't write for newspapers. She writes adventure novels."

"Novels? What's her name?"

"Sarah Morgan Cooper."

"I've heard of her," Emily said, clearly impressed. "Are her books good?"

"None finer, even if she is my aunt," Jesse said proudly. Reaching behind him he pulled out his copy of *Danger at Deadwood* from the back of his waistband. He held it out to Emily.

She read the first few paragraphs while he watched.

"Impressive!"

Jesse beamed.

"It's not everyone who has an author for an aunt."

The excitement level in Jesse's voice rose. "I rode in her carriage through the city. Apparently, my whole family on my father's side has led exciting lives. You should have heard the true stories my Aunt Sarah told me. Their names are all listed in a…"

He stopped abruptly, both speaking and walking.

"What?" Emily stopped too.

When Jesse began to speak again, he spoke slowly. His eyes glazed over, focusing on the events of the past. "The family names are listed in a Bible… which she was holding. What was she doing with the Bible?"

"What Bible?"

"My family's Bible," Jesse explained. "It's been in the family since the early seventeenth century. When I was young I remember sitting in my father's lap. He pointed to the names that are recorded in the front of the Bible and told the story associated with each name. Strange, I hadn't remembered that for years..."

"Maybe your father gave the Bible to your aunt," Emily suggested.

"My father's dead. Killed in a factory fire when I was five."

"I'm sorry," Emily apologized. "I didn't know."

"So what was she doing with the Bible?" Jesse wondered aloud. He pondered his own question for a moment. Unable to come up with a suitable explanation, he continued:

"Anyway, as I was saying, there's a list of my ancestors in the front of that Bible. The first name is that of Drew Morgan. He was a Puritan who endured the persecution of Bishop Laud in England. Drew Morgan led an entire village of people—the village of Edenford—to escape to America. That's how the Morgan family first got here.

"Then there was Jared Morgan. When he was young, he was a pirate. And then during the Revolutionary War, he assisted Benjamin Franklin in France. Jared had two sons who fought on opposite sides of the Revolutionary War. One of them was hanged by the British to protect his brother, who was caught as a spy. And then there's my father. He was given the Bible by his father following the last great civil conflict."

Jesse stopped to catch his breath. He chuckled.

"What?" Emily asked.

"One of the stories Aunt Sarah told me about her brother is rather interesting. She had three brothers. One is a minister near Cincinnati. He only has one leg. His other leg was shot off at the Battle of Fredericksburg. Another of her brothers is an artist. Willy. He's had sketches printed in almost every major national magazine. And then there's Marshall," Jesse chuckled, which prompted a grin and closer attention from Emily. "From what Aunt Sarah told me, her brother Marshall hated Southerners before the war something fierce!"

"So?" Emily said. "A lot of Northerners hated Southerners."

Jesse nodded. "Apparently not with the same passion as Marshall! So guess who he married?"

Emily shrugged.

"A Southern belle!"

"Really?"

Jesse nodded with a grin. "But only after she captured him raiding her farm!"

Emily shared his laughter. "A Southern belle captured your uncle?"

"The way Aunt Sarah described it, my uncle's wife dressed up like a soldier to protect herself from raiding parties, both Union and Southern. And when my Uncle Marshall wandered onto her farm, she captured him and chained him in the barn. For a long time, my uncle believed she was a Rebel private!"

"How did he find out that she was a female?"

"It was during the shelling of Vicksburg. They were running to some caves for shelter and her cap fell off."

Emily laughed. "She sounds like the kind of woman I could admire."

By this time Jesse and Emily had walked under the bridge's cathedral-style arches and had reached Chatham Street where the New York side of the bridge began. They slowed to a stop now that their direction was no longer dictated by a single pathway. Though it was obvious that the time had come for them to part, neither of them seemed in any hurry to do so.

"Thank you for sharing my walk with me," Emily said. "I'm glad we happened to be on the bridge at the same time."

"I'm glad too," Jesse replied. "I enjoyed walking with you."

Emily smiled. She gazed at the ground. Jesse cleared his throat and stretched his arms slightly.

"Well, I'd better be on my way," Emily said.

Jesse nodded. After a few moments when she made no attempt to leave, he said, "Would you like me to walk you home?" Before she could answer, he added, "Seems I asked you that once before and you declined."

Emily laughed. "Yes, you did. And the answer is still, thank you, but no. After all, I have my…" she touched her waistband.

Jesse nodded. He completed her sentence. "…police whistle." After another pause, he said, "Then, maybe you could escort me home."

Emily laughed. Jesse was taken by the sound of her laughter and the way her eyes sparkled when she laughed. She caught him looking at her eyes. Neither she nor he looked away. Jesse felt like he was being drawn into two glistening brown pools. He knew he could drown in those eyes and die a happy man.

She glanced away. Jesse caught his mouth hanging open. He closed it and cleared his throat again.

"Well, good-night," he said.

"Good-night."

"And don't worry. Your secret's safe with me."

"Secret?"

"Being undercover as a typist."

"Oh! Yes, yes…" Emily sputtered. "Sometimes I get so caught up in my own cover that I forget it's a cover. Thank you for keeping my secret."

"Well, good-night."

"Good-night, again," Emily said. Her fingers fluttered a little wave and she turned and left Jesse standing alone on Chatham Street.

Leaving the lights of the bridge behind him, Jesse reentered the dark streets that led home. The night shadows of the towering tenements loomed across his path like giant specters.

With each succeeding step a measure of the evening's romance and laughter and good times faded until the events of just a half hour previous seemed a distant memory. In their place rose the unwanted feelings he thought he'd shucked off—guilt, depression, hopelessness—now stronger than before.

He tried desperately to hold on to at least one swatch of pleasant memory, the image of Emily's brown eyes in the soft lamplight. But he could not. Row after row of tenement buildings haunted him with an alternative, more gruesome image. Empty ledges. All of them set against a black sky.

Jesse fought the unwanted mind pictures by keeping his eyes lowered. He stared at the bricks. Uniformly placed. Orderly. Some cracked or misaligned. Some sunken where the earth had given way beneath them. When he reached Hester Street, he was careful to make sure nobody saw him. He stayed in the shadows as he worked his way halfway up the block, eventually reaching the tenement steps that were opposite his home.

Clearing trash from the corner where the steps and the building joined, he huddled in the shadows. With his knees hugged tightly against his chest he stared up at the window of his room. His mother's back was to the window. Her head was lowered; it was bobbing slightly. She was sewing. She was always sewing.

Then, as though by intuition she sensed someone was looking at her and turned her head toward the window. She squinted into the darkness. Instinctively, Jesse pulled himself tightly into the corner. He watched as his mother's eyes glanced up the street, then down it. Apparently seeing nothing unusual, she began to pull back. She stopped and looked again. Something had caught her eye. She stared intently straight across the street. At the steps. Straight at Jesse.

For a long moment she stared. Jesse held his breath. He didn't move. He could feel her eyes on him, her gaze working its way through the darkness, searching for something but not quite able to focus on it. After a moment, she pulled back again, sat down, and resumed her sewing.

She hadn't seen him. But from the look on her face, he knew she was looking for him. He was later than usual coming home. Her face against the window had shown lines of worry.

Jesse sighed as he stared at the back of his mother's bobbing head. A shiver shook him when he realized the pain he would cause her. All of his life she had been patient with him. She had been content to let him develop at his own pace. Even in his transition from childhood to adulthood, she was patient. She told him that someday he would find his calling, but she never pushed him. She was content to let him find it on his own. Her insistence that he go to college was simply her way of providing him a fresh field in which he might discover his pearl of great price.

As for Jesse, deep inside, he always knew that someday his mother's patience would pay off. That someday she would be proud of him.

But that was unlikely now—now that he had killed a boy.

Jesse buried his head against his knees. He saw flailing arms. Little Jake's frightened expression. An empty sky.

In one afternoon, everything had changed for him. His entire life had been knocked off-balance.

Jesse sniffed back tears. He scolded himself. *It's time to grow up. Be a man. Think! Use that brain of yours. What are your options?*

In his mind he became Truly Noble. He went back to the tenement building to investigate the incident. In this scenario, he questioned Philemon, one of the oafs. Wracked by guilt, Philemon confessed that the whole thing wasn't Jesse's fault! According to the oaf, Jesse hadn't stumbled—he'd been tripped! Moreover, little Jake wasn't really dead! He was in the hospital, recovering from a broken bone or two. He was expected to recover fully. At the hospital bedside, little Jake, his red hair tousled, would greet him with a smile. He would thank Jesse for saving his life. Then, he would look up at Jesse and say, "Someday, I want to be just like..."

Stop it! STOP IT!

In anguish, Jesse squeezed his eyes shut and banged his head against his knees. Then he lifted his head and looked around him. The initial blurring of his vision gave way to familiar shapes. Dark shapes. Hester Street.

This is real life! Face it! Jake is dead! You pushed him over the ledge! Face it! FACE IT!

A feeling of determined resolution filled him, as though he'd been injected with a dose of adulthood. With a sharp inhalation, Jesse set aside his fantasies and stared at reality's cold, hard face.

Fact number one: He couldn't bring Jake back to life.

Fact number two: Nothing he could do could make up for what he had done.

Fact number three: He had to own up to what he had done, to take responsibility for it.

It was over fact number three that Jesse stumbled. He thought again of the anguish he had brought to two mothers—little Jake's and his own. How could he face them? And then there was Finn. There was no chance Finn would ever forgive him. Jesse would be running from Finn for the rest of his life as long as he stayed in the city.

As long as he stayed in the city!

The phrase flashed before him like a golden key, the key that would unlock the door to his mystery. He needed to prove himself—to prove that what happened on the roof was an accident, to prove his true character. But as long as he stayed in the city, he would be nothing more than an office boy running away from Finn every night on the way home from work. But somewhere else, where he could get a fresh start, things would be different. But where would that somewhere else be?

West.

In the West. That's where boys become men.

Jesse sat up straight. It all made sense now. And his Morgan family history confirmed it. Drew Morgan became a man when he left England for the New World. Jared Morgan became a man away from home as a pirate. Esau and Jacob grew up when they went to war. And it took another war for his own father to straighten out his life. Going West. Being on his own. Proving himself as a man. Then he could come home with his head held high. Then everyone would be able to see that one rooftop incident was an accident in an otherwise noble life.

Jesse stood and stepped from the shadows. He glanced up at his mother. Her head bobbed dutifully as she sewed. He thought about leaving her a note, then dismissed it. It would be better for him to get established first. It hurt him to think of the grief she would feel not knowing where her son was, not knowing what had happened to him. But it was better this way. Someday she would understand.

He stepped into the street, under the stars. Looking at the back of his mother's head, he said, "Good-bye, Mama. I'll make you proud of me. You'll see. As God is my witness, I'll make you proud."

Jesse Morgan turned and walked down Hester Street. He headed west.

Emily watched him from the corner of Hester Street, confused as to why Jesse chose to sit in a dark corner for so long. She watched as he emerged from the shadows and spoke something to one of the tenement windows. Then, when he left, she followed him. As she passed the tenement, she looked up at the window, the one Jesse had spoken to. She saw the back of a woman's head. It was bobbing up and down.

For well over a mile Emily followed Jesse. She broke off her surveillance only because it was getting late. She grimaced at the thought of trying to explain her whereabouts to her father should he catch her again.

Shaking her head, she watched as Jesse faded into the darkness. Where was he going at this time of night? With a shrug, she turned toward home, losing herself in thought as she relived the moments she'd spent with Jesse on the bridge.

At midnight, Clara Morgan could wait no longer. She threw a shawl around her shoulders and stepped into the dark night looking for Jesse. She retraced the most direct route between their house and the Ruger Glassworks Factory. The factory was shut up tight. Dark as a tomb.

She went to Albert Sagean's tenement building, waking three families before she found one that knew which room the Sageans occupied. The groggy foreman informed Clara that Jesse left work at the normal time. He then donned his clothes and joined her search.

After an hour, Sagean sent Clara home to see if Jesse had returned during her absence. Her hopes rose as she climbed the tenement steps and opened the door, then fell just as quickly. The room was as empty as she had left it.

As calmly as she could, she made herself some tea and sat in her chair. But she didn't sew. Her sweater would be angry with her come morning, but she didn't care. Clara Morgan had more important things to do. She rocked back and forth in her chair and prayed. She prayed until morning.

By mid-morning Albert Sagean appeared at her door. He had seen no sign of Jesse. Neither had Jesse shown up for work. Clara thanked him and accepted his offer to help, but there was nothing more she could think for him to do. With repeated assurances that Jesse would show up unharmed,

Sagean returned to work.

Clara Morgan went to the third floor. She knocked on the door of Rabbi Moscowitz, the man who had lent her the books for Jesse and the only spiritual man she knew of in the building. Tenderly he welcomed her inside and listened to her.

It was in the Rabbi's tenement room that Clara Morgan first wept for her missing son.

Chapter 10

IT had been three days since she and Jesse had strolled the promenade. Yet the memory was still fresh even though Emily had played it over and over in her mind a hundred times.

At work, every time the Austin Factory office door opened, Emily glanced up expectantly, hoping it was Jesse making a delivery. She had given considerable thought to how she would handle their next encounter. When he came through the door, she would pretend to be hard at work. Then, she would casually glance up and notice it was him. By then, of course, he would already be looking at her. She would smile at him discreetly—not a full smile lest she appear too eager, but enough of a smile for him to know she remembered fondly the night on the bridge. Her eyes would convey a sense of mystery, so that anyone looking at them would get the impression that they shared a secret. That ought to drive the other girls in the office crazy! In her bolder thoughts, Emily considered adding a seductive wink.

But for all her preparation, Emily had yet to be given the opportunity to carry out her planned nonverbal exchange. Three days came and went without a delivery from Ruger Glassworks. On the fourth day she was so busy concentrating on typing a table of inventory figures, she didn't hear the door open.

In the background she heard a mumbling sound followed by, "...from Mr. Sagean at Ruger Glassworks."

When the words "Ruger Glassworks" managed to penetrate the intensity of her concentration, Emily's head bolted up from the row of columns. In that instant, all her planning and practice were forgotten, so eager was she to catch a glimpse of Jesse. She flashed a smile filled with anticipation.

Her smile was met by a dirty-faced boy who couldn't have been more than ten or eleven years old. His ears stuck out wide, and he wore his cap on the back of his head in a jaunty manner. His clothes and arms and hands were soiled with soot.

The boy's eyes widened wolfishly when he saw the way Emily smiled at him. He tipped his hat and winked awkwardly. "Name's Jeb," he said. "What's your name, good-lookin'?"

Emily scowled and returned to her columns of figures. Her face flushed hot. The two girls she worked with tittered at her embarrassment.

"Get back to work, girls!" the bespectacled office manager ordered. "And you," he snatched the envelope from the boy's hand, "what took you so long? Go on, get out of here! Out! Out! Out!"

The office manager shoved the boy out the door and slammed it behind him.

The tittering, though stifled, continued.

Emily kept her head lowered. She stared at the rows of numbers before her, but she didn't see them. At first her humiliation blinded her; but then, as embarrassment turned to concern, her mind's eye assumed full temporary control of her vision, interpreting the row of numbers before her as nothing more than long blocks of gray. In her mind, Emily saw Jesse huddled in the late-night shadows; then she saw him talking to the tenement window; then she saw him walking, walking, walking into night. The darkness enveloped him. Then there was nothing. Only black.

She pushed back her chair.

"Miss Barnes, where do you think you're going?" The office

manager stood with his bony fingers firmly planted on his hips.

"I'll be right back," Emily said.

He blocked her way to the door. "Sit down and get back to work!" A long, skeletal finger pointed to her typewriter as though she might have forgotten where she worked. The other typewriters were still, their operators preoccupied with the office drama.

"I'll just be a minute," Emily insisted.

"Sit down!" the office manager shouted. His mean, squinting eyes challenged her.

"Mr. Stewart, I must talk with that boy."

The typists tittered.

Stewart shot them a hateful glance which promptly set the typewriters to clattering again.

"Mr. Stewart..."

"Miss Barnes, either you return to your place right now, or..."

Emily had had enough. She reached out and shoved the scrawny office manager aside with ease; he couldn't have weighed more than a scarecrow. The office door swung closed behind her to the sounds of Stewart's bellowing.

She caught up with the sooty boy halfway down the block. Since he had offered his name, she used it to get his attention. Turning, the boy saw her coming. He stopped, faced her, and grinned a goofy grin.

"Why didn't Jesse Morgan deliver the envelope from Ruger Glassworks today?" Emily asked him.

The boy's face screwed up in a puzzled expression.

"You know him, don't you? Jesse Morgan?"

"Sure I knows him."

"He normally delivers messages for Ruger Glassworks. Why didn't he do it today?"

Clearly disappointed that Emily was interested in Jesse and not him, the boy sneered, "Do I look like his mother?" The boy turned and walked away.

Emily grabbed his arm.

The boy shook free, as though Emily's touch had somehow soiled his already filthy shirt. "Don't touch the goods, lady!" he cried.

"Just tell me about Jesse!"

"He don't work there no more. All right? Now leave me alone."

"What do you mean he doesn't work there?"

"Jus' like I said. He don't work there. Ain't worked there for three days now."

"Did he quit? Was he fired?" Emily asked.

"What? Now I'm the foreman? What do I know?"

"Just tell me!"

A wolfish smile appeared as the boy's eyes wandered up and down Emily. The boy looked so silly, she would have laughed out loud except for the fact that she thought that by doing so she might not get any more answers.

"What'll you do for me if I tell you?" the boy asked suggestively.

Emily let loose a calculated chuckle. "Do for you? How old are you? Eight? Nine?" She deliberately guessed young.

The boy was duly insulted. "I'm eleven...twelve in six months!"

Emily grabbed the boy's arm, this time with a much firmer grip, the kind that a mother would use on a child throwing a tantrum. "I'll tell you what I won't do for you!" she said through clinched teeth. "I won't tell my three older brothers that you have been following me around for days making crude and suggestive remarks!"

The boy studied her face, apparently trying to ascertain if she did indeed have three older brothers. Emily squeezed his arm tighter.

"You really got it bad for him, don't you?" the boy said.

Emily squeezed his arm tighter.

"All right! He just didn't come in one day," the boy said. Sarcastically, he added, "Now please, don't tell your big brothers on me, please! I promise I'll leave you alone. I'll never do it again!"

Emily let go of the boy's arm.

He adjusted his shirt and backed away from her. "What a waste," he said. "You and that beanpole Morgan fella. What a waste. Listen, good-lookin', when you get tired of him, come look me up!" He winked.

Emily sneered at him, turned, and walked away.

When she entered the office, she found Mr. Stewart sitting in her chair behind the typewriter. His arms were folded, his head was cocked to one side in a superior manner. A grin graced his scarecrow face.

"Miss Barnes," he said in an oily, condescending tone, "gather your things and get out. You're terminated!"

Emily was not devastated by her dismissal as an office typist, but then neither was she pleased by it. Her untimely termination brought an abrupt halt to an investigation just when she was uncovering some interesting facts. The conversation she overheard in her father's study about the Austin Factory fire had piqued her interest. If indeed the fire had been set deliberately, it was a more dramatic story than the one she was working on.

Just yesterday she had read the initial report. It listed the names of the two people who had died in the fire: Molly (last name unknown), a little girl who was employed at the factory. Her body was never recovered. And Benjamin Morgan, identified as a labor agitator.

Jesse's father?

The men in her father's study had said the fire occurred fifteen years ago. Jesse said he was five years old when his father was killed in a factory fire. The arithmetic was right. And suddenly, an element of personal intrigue was injected into her factory fire investigation, intrigue now roadblocked by her dismissal.

Prior to her investigation of the fire, she had concentrated on cataloging miscellaneous improprieties in the Austin financial empire—payoffs, overpricing, and dangerous working conditions. Though none of these things in themselves was sufficient to earn her a story in a newspaper or magazine, she was hoping that the sum total of the transgressions might gain an editor's attention. That and the fact that she was investigating her own father's company.

The father-daughter angle had an ironic twist to it, one that Emily planned to work to her advantage. Naturally, she had considered what her father's reaction would be when the story broke. He would be outraged. But once his initial anger passed, she expected that he would understand. It was business. The same kind of aggressive tactic he had used to earn his money: You set your sights on what you want and you go after it. There was nothing personal about it.

Emily truly believed this because this was how she had been raised. There was nothing personal about life in the Austin household. The marble mansion housed three individual lives who happened to share a common street address. Father had his varied business enterprises; Mother had her world of art in which she was a wealthy patron; and Emily had her life—separate and distinct from her parents. It wasn't that Emily's parents didn't care for her; they did. And once Emily understood the nature of their compassion, she came to accept it as an equitable arrangement.

When she was younger, Emily shed a multitude of tears over her parents' seeming lack of interest in her. The way she saw it, she craved their attention and they doled it out in meager spoonfuls. However, when she was older, her attitude toward her parents changed. The transition occurred about the time she began reading the investigative articles of Nellie Bly. The reporter's graphic depiction of the filth of tenement life and the misery of sweatshops and factories made Emily realize how well her parents cared for her. True, they cared for her the same way they cared for the carpet in the entryway and the horses in the stable, but they did indeed care.

As she thought about it more, she came to realize that her expectations of her parents had been too great. They shared with her what they had—a home, food, clothes, and an education. In return, they asked nothing of her, other than that she not demand too much of their time. But the capstone to understanding her parents came when she realized that it was *she* who had been unreasonable. When it came to love, tenderness, compassion, and any degree of emotional warmth, her parents were bankrupt. All these years she had wanted something from her parents that they did not have!

She later called it the Day of Understanding. She saw it as the day she grew up. From that day she stopped coveting her parents' attention. She no longer dreamed the silly dreams that had so obsessed her childhood. She no longer stared at her bedroom door at night, hoping that her mother would pop in and sit on the edge of her bed and, for no reason at all, talk girl talk. She no longer dreamed of walking into her father's library unintentionally interrupting a meeting, only to be swallowed up in her father's arms while he boasted to his guest about his daughter's beauty.

Life became so much easier for Emily following her Day of Understanding. She was no longer disappointed with her parents, because she no longer expected anything from them. In fact, this newly discovered philosophy had such an impact on her, she applied it to all of life: Don't expect anything from anyone. If they let you down, you won't be disappointed since you didn't expect anything from them anyway; and, if they do something that pleases you, it will be a pleasant surprise.

So Emily wasn't devastated when the bespectacled scare-crow at the Austin Factory office terminated her from her typist job. She didn't expect the mean-spirited man to be reasonable. The investigation into the factory fire would just have to wait until she found another avenue to the company files. Meanwhile, there was a new mystery at hand for her to solve. Where was Jesse Morgan?

The thrill of a new challenge welled up inside her. Jesse's location was a mystery, a mystery she was eager to pursue since it had a romantic element to it. The very thought of tracking down the elusive Mr. Morgan gave Emily a pleasurable chill.

Chapter 11

"CAN you tell me where I might find the supervisor?" Emily stood at the entrance to the Ruger Glassworks factory, if there really was such a thing as an entrance. The entire side of the building was opened up, displaying a hive of activity inside. Men with puffed cheeks stood atop boxes blowing into long pipes. At the opposite end of the pipes glass bubbles formed, each one attended by a squatting boy. In the center of the facility was a huge brick furnace capped with a hood that funneled the smoke through the roof. Boys—mostly small and nearly all of them dressed in tattered knickers with suspenders—stood at makeshift tables performing a variety of chores. Some cleaned tools and molds while others performed finishing work on recently blown glass bottles.

She had spoken to a slight boy carrying a bucket of water. He stopped and stared at her when she asked the question. His eyes were wide and sad. And he had an oversized upper lip that looked too large for his face.

"Supervisor?" Emily repeated. "Foreman. Do you have a foreman?"

The boy's grin spread so wide it nearly cut his face in half. He pointed to a corner in the rear of the building.

"Thank you," Emily said. She entered the work area.

Heads popped up throughout the factory. Work stopped. Young eyes followed her progress from the front of the building to the rear. Some of the blowers shouted for their boy to pay attention; others earned a slap on the back of the head. But Emily noticed that even the blowers, who were older men and who had to keep their heads down, followed her out of the tops of their eyes.

"Hey, good-lookin'! Couldn't stay away from me?"

Emily rolled her eyes in disgust when she saw Jeb, the big-eared boy who had delivered the message to the Austin office in Jesse's place. She ignored him.

"That's the woman I was tellin' yous about," Jeb said, loud enough for her to hear. "You wouldn't believe the way she was comin' on to me!"

Emily resisted temptation and swallowed a retort intended to humiliate the boy. He was obviously trying to get a reaction out of her. She wouldn't give him the satisfaction. Ignoring him, she walked to the back of the factory.

The factory office was little more than a raised platform with a desk. Seated behind the desk was a large man with a heavy whisker shadow.

"Are you the foreman?" Emily asked.

Red eyes peered over the desk at her. Emily could feel her own eyes beginning to burn from the heat and smoke. "Would you like to place an order, Miss?"

Emily shook her head. "I'm looking for someone who used to work here. Maybe he still does."

The red eyes squinted at her.

"Jesse Morgan," she said. "Does he still work here?"

The man stood up. From atop the platform he towered over her like Goliath over David. A hand motioned Emily to the steps that led up to his level. He produced a chair and Emily sat opposite him.

"My name is Albert Sagean," the man said. "I'm a friend of the Morgan family as well as being Jesse's boss. How is it that you know Jesse?"

"I'm glad to meet you, Mr. Sagean. My name is Emily..."

"Austin," Sagean said. "I recognize you. I delivered a report to Mr. Austin at your house last year, and I saw you coming down the stairs."

Emily was relieved he interrupted her. She was about to introduce herself using her undercover name of Barnes.

"As I was about to say," Emily continued, "I know Jesse from the Austin Factory offices when he would deliver paperwork to us. And, well, when he didn't show up today, we became concerned."

The corners of Sagean's mouth turned up, not in humor, but in wincing skepticism. "This personal concern on the part of the Austin Factory for an office boy is admirable," he said, "but a little out of character."

"Well, we at the office have grown quite fond of Jesse," Emily said with a nonchalant wave of her hand. "And when Jeb told us that Jesse had not shown up for work for the last three days, naturally we were concerned."

Sagean sat back in his chair. He folded one arm across his belly and rested the elbow of his other arm upon it. With his thumb and forefinger he pinched his upper lip as he considered her words. Then, a sudden twinkle sparked in his eye. His hand stilled as it attempted to cover a smirk.

"I can appreciate your *corporate fondness* for Jesse..." he leaned forward slightly as he said the words.

Emily felt the color rise in her cheeks. She ignored it in the hopes it would fade quickly.

"...and we share your concern for him." The smirk faded quickly. Sagean's eyes took on a troubled appearance. "Fact is, he's missing. Three nights ago, his mother came looking for him. He hasn't been home since." Sagean leaned forward again; this time he was deadly serious. "Do you have any idea where he might be?"

The man's concern was genuine. Emily felt it. The distress

they shared over Jesse's disappearance created an immediate bond between them. "The last time I saw him was three nights ago. At the Brooklyn Bridge. We strolled along the promenade together."

When Emily walked into the glassworks factory she had no intention of revealing anything of a personal nature. She came to gather information, not disseminate it. But once she saw the concern in Sagean's eyes, they became partners in this crisis. And the things she said were said for Jesse's sake.

"What time was it when you last saw him?" Sagean asked. He sat forward in his chair, eager for clues.

"It was about ten o'clock when we left each other at Chatham Street."

"Ten o'clock," Sagean repeated as he worked his upper lip. Thinking and speaking at the same time, he mumbled, "His mother woke me up three hours later..."

Emily waited for the results of his ruminations. She got another question instead.

"And you haven't seen him since?"

There was a moment's hesitation as she thought. "No, that was the last time."

Sagean nodded and returned to his pondering.

Emily felt badly about lying to her partner in crisis, but the question came up suddenly. How could she explain that she saw Jesse again while she was spying on him?

"Have you spoken to Jesse's mother about this?" Sagean asked.

Emily shook her head. "I've never met Mrs. Morgan."

Sighing heavily, Sagean turned to his desk and wrote something on a scrap of paper. "Miss Austin, would you do me a favor?"

"What would you have me do?"

"This is Jesse's home address. He and his mother live on Hester Street. Do you know where that is?"

Emily nodded.

"Would you be kind enough to go there and tell Clara Morgan what you just told me? I know it doesn't seem like much, but any information would be welcomed. I'm sure of it." He held out the paper to her.

Though she didn't need the address, Emily took the piece of paper. "I'll go there right now," she said.

They rose together.

"And one more thing," he said. "If you see Jesse, or hear from him, will you let me know? I feel responsible for him. An old debt to his father."

Emily nodded.

As she walked out of the factory, not nearly as many heads followed her due to the fact that Sagean stood high on the platform and watched her go himself. With an elbow resting on a forearm, he worked his upper lip with his free hand.

"Imagine that," he chuckled. "Jesse and Franklin Austin's daughter!"

A deep breath didn't calm her. Nor could she seem to do anything to remove the silly grin that was plastered on her face. She couldn't help herself. She felt like skipping. It excited her to talk and act openly about Jesse. It was a new experience for her.

Privately, she had dreamed of Jesse. Secretly, she had followed him. And while both of these dalliances had provided pleasurable sensations, they couldn't begin to compare to the emotional intoxication she felt when she walked by his side on the bridge. Without doubt, that was the best feeling. The thrill of this new experience, however, took her by surprise. There was no other way to describe it. Talking openly with other people about her Jesse sent her heart soaring.

Being the private person she was, Emily had never discussed her feelings with anyone. Most of her education came at the hands of adult tutors. What little interaction she had with other girls her age disgusted her. She thought them immature, brainless creatures who were being raised as breeding stock for wealthy families. As a result, Emily's life had been compartmentalized: public things you discuss with others, private things you keep to yourself. This was the first time the division between the two compartments began to blur as her professional investigation and private love life commingled.

The fact that Jesse was missing didn't take the shine off her excitement. There was no reason for her to expect the worst. She was confident he would reappear and that there would be a satisfactory reason for his disappearance. Who knows? Maybe it was God's way. Emily wasn't sure she believed in God, but if He existed she was certain this was the kind of thing He would do—bringing her and Jesse together.

Passing Ridley's department store, Emily turned down Allen Street. Her heart skipped a beat with the thought that she was one block away from meeting Jesse's mother.

Sometimes the depth of her feelings for Jesse frightened her. From the first time she saw him walk into the Austin Factory offices, something about him struck her. She'd spent hours trying to figure it out. It wasn't his bearing, though his boyish gait had an innocence that attracted her. It wasn't his eyes, though the spark of quickness in them revealed an intelligent mind. It wasn't his smile, though the very thought of it sent goosebumps down her back. It wasn't his position in life, since he had none to speak of. There was no single thing about him that explained her attraction to him.

Finally, Emily summed it up with one word. An intangible word, but for her it captured that invisible quality about Jesse that so attracted her to him.

Passion.

Jesse was passionate about life. He oozed passion. In the office his passion stood out like a beacon in a sea of sterile numbers and columns. And just the thought of his passion warmed her bedroom at night in the white marble mansion. Jesse Morgan didn't have what her parents had, but he had everything they didn't have. In him, Emily knew she would find the love that she never found at home. And she would willingly exchange a white marble mansion with all of its comforts for one long embrace in Jesse Morgan's arms.

Her thoughts were snapped from introspection back to her immediate surroundings when she recognized red-headed Jake, Finn's little brother. The boy was on the opposite side of the street running her direction. He wasn't running from anything or anybody—this time—it was just a typical boy's hurried stride. He disappeared into an alley, the same alley in which Jesse had his scuffle with Finn.

Emily slowed her step until the boy disappeared. She stayed on the far side of the street away from the alley. Though it was daylight and she had nothing to fear from Finn, still she thought it best to keep as much distance as possible between her and anyone associated with him. However, she couldn't resist taking a quick look down the alley as she passed.

"Where you been?" Finn's voice carried out of the alley clearly.

He was sitting on a wooden barrel. At his feet were the ashes and charred metal hoops of the barrel that had been used to torture Jesse. Finn's two oafs stood oafishly around. One leaned against the brick wall and picked his teeth, while the other stood looking bored with his shoulders slumped and his hands thrust in his pockets. Finn took a swing at Jake as he approached. Jake ducked expertly.

Emily looked forward and quickened her stride.

An oafish voice echoed from the alley. "Not the same without that Morgan fella around...where do you think he went?"

Emily stopped. She was far enough past the alley that she couldn't see Finn and he couldn't see her. She cocked her head and tuned an ear toward the alley.

"Probably threw hisself into the river!" Finn's voice said. "I'll never get over the look on his face when…"

Clop, clop, clop, clop, clop…

A horse and carriage came down the street between Emily and the alley. She moaned in frustration. Picking up her skirt, she dashed behind the carriage to the other side of the street. She approached the corner of the alley on her toes even though the sound of the passing carriage was still loud enough to cover her footsteps.

Laughter came from the alley.

"I did good, Finn, didn't I?" Jake cried.

"Naw, you nearly messed up the whole thing!" Finn cried.

"But you said I did good!" Jake protested. "He thought I was dead!"

"Anybody coulda done what you done," Finn said.

"I know," one of the oafs said, "if he ever comes back, we can dress little Jake here up like a ghost and haunt him!"

Finn liked that idea. He laughed loud and the others followed his lead.

"Yeah," Finn sighed. "Jus' not the same without the beanpole around."

A couple walking down the street approached Emily. A small mustached man, with his arm crooked, escorted a taller woman. They stared suspiciously at Emily when they saw that she was listening to what was being said in the alley. It piqued their attention. They looked at her, then stared down the alley to see to whom she was listening.

Emily rolled her eyes in frustration. Why didn't they just announce her presence to Finn? She turned and walked briskly down the street ahead of the annoyingly inquisitive couple. But she wasn't finished with Finn.

She circled the block the way she did the night she rescued Jesse. Once again she used the wooden fence to hide her approach. For some reason, she reached into her waistband and pulled out her police whistle. Maybe the memories of that previous night prompted her. She just felt better with it in her hand.

Finn's voice could be heard again. She reached the fence, crouched down, and listened.

"...the el, maybe ol' Thad can give us a few laughs."

"I'll meet ya there," one of the oafs said.

"Where you goin'? You didn't tell me about this." Finn reminded Emily of the scarecrow office manager, always having to know what everybody was doing.

"Poppa needs me to run him an errand," the oaf said.

Finn mimicked the oaf's voice in a singsong manner, "Poppa needs me to run him an errand!" Everyone laughed, including the mimicked oaf.

"Yeah, it's somethin' I gotta do."

"Then do it!" Finn shouted. He was clearly annoyed that the oaf was leaving him. "Come on, boys," he said to the others.

There was a shuffling of feet as the gang left the alley.

Emily remained still. She wanted to make sure they were clear of the alley before she made a move.

The gate latch sounded.

Emily stifled a gasp.

The wooden gate swung open. One of the oafs stepped through. When he saw Emily crouched against the fence, his face twisted in a puzzled expression. He looked at her with an expression an explorer might use upon discovering some never-before-seen insect species.

Emily launched herself into him and the oaf reacted the same way the explorer would react if the unknown insect attacked. Startled by her movement, he jumped back. With him off-balance, the force of Emily's leap threw them both against the wall. The oaf's head banged against bricks. Dazed, he looked down at the woman who was pressed against his chest. His hands fumbled mindlessly in the air.

"Listen to me!" Emily cried. "You tell me what I want to know or I'm going to blow this whistle." She deliberately raised the whistle to her lips. "Police will come running and when they get here, I'll tell them that you tried to ravish me!"

"Who...who are you?" the oaf sputtered.

Emily placed the whistle to her lips.

"Wait! Wait!" the oaf cried.

She lowered the whistle, but pressed herself harder against his chest to keep him against the wall. But for how long? She had to act quickly. Already the element of surprise was beginning to wear off. The oaf's eyes were focusing; what little mind he had was kicking into gear.

"Tell me what you did to Jesse Morgan," she said.

If such a thing were possible, the oaf's eyes grew wise. They narrowed to slits and stared at her. "Who are you?" he asked.

"I'm the one who is going to send you to Blackwell's Island!" she shouted, placing the whistle against her lip again. "You know Blackwell's Island, don't you? Where all the crazies live? That's where you're going to end up unless you tell me what you did to Jesse Morgan!"

Her reference to the island achieved the effect she'd hoped it would. The oaf's eyes glazed over again in confusion and fear. But only for a moment. Beefy hands grabbed her shoulders. Effortlessly, he lifted her away from him. He regained his balance.

The whistle was in place. Emily took a deep breath.

"No! Don't blow the whistle!" the oaf cried.

"Then tell me!" Her words were mumbled because the whistle was still pressed between her lips.

"It was a prank." The oaf described the incident that led Jesse to believe he had killed Finn's little brother.

"When did this happen?"

The oaf looked at the sky. "Two...three nights ago."

"And where is Jesse now?"

"I don't know."

Emily threatened to blow the whistle again.

"Blowin' that whistle won't make me know something I don't know!"

She looked into his empty eyes. They seemed incapable of deceit. "Then let go of me," she said.

The oaf released her. "Sheesh!" he said, shaking his head. "Can I go now?"

Emily stepped cautiously away, giving him plenty of room to leave. She nodded, the whistle still at her lips.

The oaf ambled past her, took one look back, and shook his head. "All she had to do was ask," he mumbled.

Emily waited until she was sure he was gone before slumping against the brick wall. A practical joke. On the promenade Jesse had said Finn had done something to him. No wonder he looked so troubled. How awful! He thought he'd just killed Jake! Armed with this new information, she headed for Hester Street. At least now she had something concrete to tell Jesse's mother.

Chapter 12

THE tenement stairs that led up to the Morgans' room were dark. There was a gritty, sticky feeling to them as Emily wound her way up. The smell of stale urine was heavy in the air. She had read Nellie Bly's explicit description of life in the tenements, and she had passed by tenements all her life. But reading and imagining did not do justice to the feeling of filth she was experiencing. It encompassed her—it was under her shoes, on the walls, over her head; even the air that touched her skin was tainted with filth. She made a mental note: Once Jesse was found she was going to write a story about this particular tenement building. The world needed another graphic tenement story to convince them of the hopelessness of the people who lived behind these walls.

The absence of light in the hallway made it difficult for her to locate the Morgans' door. Once she did, Emily straightened herself and brushed the front of her dress with a flat hand before knocking. This was Jesse's mother she was meeting. She wanted to make a good first impression.

Her knock resulted in a hollow sound that echoed up and down the hallway. Three rooms down from her a door swung open. An old woman's head poked out, her hair streaked with gray, her face covered with wrinkles. The woman glanced down the hallway, looked Emily up and down, pulled her head back in, and slammed the door.

The way the sound of the knock carried in the hallway, Emily could understand how the woman might have thought it was someone knocking at her door. That, or the woman was a busybody. Either way, Emily hesitated knocking again when no one answered. But after several moments without a response she felt she had to give it at least one more try. She knocked again and waited. No response, not even from the woman three doors down.

A disappointed Emily stepped carefully as she made her way back down the stairs. Fresh air and the bustle of Hester Street vendors greeted her as she exited the building. She turned and looked up at the Morgans' window, the one Jesse had spoken to the last night she saw him. There were no draperies. Unlike that night, this time she could see no one in the window, nor was there any movement evident in the room.

Checking the step before she sat down, Emily positioned herself on the tenement steps and waited for a woman who, she supposed, bore some resemblance to Jesse. Her mind drifted back to the last time she was on this street. It was from that street corner she watched as Jesse cleared away the rubbish from the shadows over there.

Emily stood and looked across the street, over carts of apples and carrots and onions. The corner that Jesse cleared was filled again with trash; as though the rubbish union of Hester Street, unable to abide a clean corner, had ordered it filled again. The sun was such that there were no shadows. The corner gave Emily a thought.

While still keeping an eye open for a woman who looked like Jesse, Emily crossed the street to Jesse's corner. Kicking the trash out with her shoe, she stood in the corner and looked again at the Morgans' window. She wasn't expecting to see anything different, she just wanted to view the window from the angle Jesse had viewed it three nights previous.

What was Jesse thinking as he sat here and stared at that window?

Next, Emily positioned herself in the middle of the street, just like Jesse had done that night. Standing in the street, she ignored the stares of passing pedestrians as she stared at the window. A wagon loaded with squash working its way down the middle of the street pulled to a halt.

"Move it, Miss!" shouted the driver of the wagon, a barrel-chested man whose shirtsleeves were rolled halfway up his arms. He sported a large black mustache that reached beyond his cheeks and curled upward at the ends.

Emily frowned at the interruption. It was as though the answer she was looking for was just beyond the horizon. If she was patient, if she would just give it time, it would come to her.

"Come on, Miss, outta me way! I got a load here to deliver. Dream about your beau on the side o' the street!" The horses snorted impatiently, as though they too were annoyed at the delay.

Emily held up a hand, signaling to the driver for a moment more. The driver snorted like his horses. *Give it a moment more. It will come. It will come.*

"Come on, Miss! You're standin' in the middle of the street!"

"All right!" An angry Emily scowled at the man, but she stepped back and let the wagon pass.

As the wagon passed, without looking at her and speaking to no one in particular, the driver said, "She's a loon, that one is!"

Emily stepped again into the middle of the street. She stared at the window and opened her mind. The answer was there. All she had to do was coax it and it would come. She imagined the way it was three nights ago. Dark. A hint of chill in the air. She imagined she was Jesse Morgan. *I've just been tricked by Finn into thinking I've killed Jake. How would I feel?* An overwhelming sense of loss swept through her. And guilt. And pain.

She cursed Finn for his callousness. He was nothing more

than a brute animal. A man like Finn could not begin to comprehend how Jake's faked death could crush a sensitive soul like Jesse. Emily pursed her lips in disgust. Then she chided herself. *Hate Finn later. Right now, concentrate on how Jesse was feeling. Concentrate. The answer will come. It will come. What was Jesse thinking as he stood here?*

Emily thought back to the events of that night. Following the practical joke, Jesse went to the bridge where she found him. She smiled at the remembrance. Feeling the closeness of his presence as they walked along the promenade, that boyish grin of his...

Emily Austin! You can be your own worst distraction at times! Squeezing her eyes shut, she forced herself to maintain Jesse's point of view.

After leaving her at the bridge he came here, sat there in the corner, and stared up at the room at his mother. Then he got up and stood here. In this spot. He said something to his mother—to the back of her head—and then he walked away...he walked away into the darkness.

What did he say to her? What would a young man who thought he had just killed a boy tell his mother that he couldn't say to her face? The answer is right here; it's right here!

"Hey, lady! You're blockin' the road!" another wagon driver cried. This one was younger, cruder in appearance, with a scar on his chin. His wagon was empty. "Get outta the way!" he shouted.

Emily squeezed her eyes tighter still. She almost had it! Just a moment more...

"Move or I'll run ya over!"

Think! Jesse was devastated. What would a devastated young man say to his mother that he couldn't tell her to her face?

"I'm gonna count ta three!"

If you can count that high, Emily thought. *No, no! Think! Refuse to be distracted! What was it that Jesse couldn't tell his*

mother to her face? Think! He was devastated...in agony...what
would...of course! What if she didn't understand? By telling her,
he would risk disappointing her, possibly even losing her love.

"Lady, I'm starting to count! One! Two..."

Jesse couldn't risk losing her! Two losses in one night would be
too much for him. So what would he say to her?

"Three! Time's up, lady!"

What would he say to his mother?

"You asked for it, lady!"

"That's it!" Emily shouted.

Her outburst startled the horses. The driver struggled to
control them.

"That's it! He told her good-bye!" Emily cried happily. To
the wagon driver, she shouted, "If you thought you'd disappointed your mother and you couldn't tell her, what choice
would you have but to leave?"

"What's my mother got to do wid this?" the driver yelled.

"And if leaving is going to disappoint her," Emily shouted,
"you couldn't tell her that either! At least not to her face. So
you tell her from right here!"

"Tell who what? You're crazy, lady!" the driver shouted.

"It all makes sense!" Emily danced in the street for joy, then
made a path for the wagon to pass.

"Someone needs to lock you up, lady," the driver shouted
at her as he urged his horses forward. He hadn't gone far
when he twisted himself back toward Emily. "Hey, lady!
What's my mother got to do wid this? Has she been talkin' to
you about me?"

Emily didn't hear him. In her excitement she bounded up
the steps of Jesse's tenement. She ached to tell Jesse's mother
what she had figured out. She didn't know *where* Jesse went,
only that he was headed toward the Hudson River, but she
knew *why* he left. That was half the puzzle! He left on his own
and he left for a reason. At least he wasn't kidnapped or killed

or the victim of some other terrible fate.

Back up the tenement steps. Emily thought that maybe in her excitement Jesse's mother had slipped past her, or maybe she was visiting a neighbor in the building and now was home. She hadn't considered that before.

Nearing Jesse's floor, Emily was greeted by sounds of children playing in the hallway. When she reached the floor she saw four boys and a little girl. All of them were under ten years of age. Emily guessed the little girl was not yet five. The boys were standing hunched over. One at a time they tossed something toward the wall. The oldest looking boy grinned as the other boys grimaced and moaned; he walked over to the baseboard on the wall and picked up the tossed items. Pennies.

"Excuse me," Emily said, weaving her way between them.

Without exception, they stared at her as she went by. Their scrawny bodies were draped in torn shirts and frayed britches. The little girl smelled like she needed a change of pants. They all stood facing Emily and watched her knock on the Morgans' door.

Emily waited. She glanced at the children. They were still staring at her.

"She ain't home," the oldest boy said.

"You know the woman who lives here?" Emily asked.

The boy shook his head from side to side. "I only know she ain't home."

"Do you know where she went or when she'll be back?"

Another shake of the head. "I tol' you, lady! Only know she ain't home."

"So you did." Emily produced the small tablet of paper she carried with her and a pencil. She wrote:

Mrs. Morgan,
You don't know me. I'm a friend of Jesse. When I learned
he was missing I became concerned and investigated the mat-

ter. And although there is not enough room on this paper to explain all that has happened, I want you to know that I believe your son is fine. He is not in any danger. I am going after him and when I find him, I'll send you word.

Emily paused. How should she sign the note? Sincerely? A friend of the family? And what name should she use? Austin, or her professional pen name Barnes? She chuckled. She had written *Emily Morgan* so many times she was tempted to write that. Oh well, someday. In the end she decided on leaving off the last name altogether. She signed:

A friend,
Emily

As she looked the note over, she imagined Jesse's mother reading it. Naturally, she would be filled with questions. But at least it would give her a measure of comfort. Emily smiled as she thought of the day she would finally meet Jesse's mother. *Oh, so you're the one who left me that note!*

A chorus of giggles brought Emily back to the tenement hallway. Her nostalgic smile faded as the children laughed at her expression. With businesslike briskness, she folded the note and looked for a place to put it. Not between the door and the jamb; it might fall out. The best place was under the door. Slipping the note into the room, Emily nodded to the children and left the building.

"I can reach it!"
"No you can't! Let Sonia try!"
"Just...a little...farther..."
"Come on! Sonia can do it easy!"
With his face pressed against the floor, one of the boys who had lost his pennies in the hallway contest reached for Emily's

note. The others stood over him.

"You can't do it! Your fingers are too fat!" the oldest boy said.

The boy on the floor pulled his hand out. Red lines and bunched skin marked his hand where he'd forced it under the door. With his cheek still pressed against the wooden floorboards, he closed one eye. "I can see it!"

"You're just gonna push it further away! Let Sonia do it!"

The boy pushed his fingers under the door again. "I'll get it this time," he said.

The others watched as he wedged his hand under the door. "Do you got it?" the oldest asked.

"Almost."

"You're not gonna get it."

"It's right at the end of my fingertips." He pulled his hand out and rubbed it. "I can't get it," he said.

"I told you!" said the oldest boy. Turning to the little girl, he said, "Sonia, reach under there and get the piece of paper."

Little Sonia folded her arms and scowled. "No!"

"Why not?"

"Don't want to!"

"Come on, Sonia, please?"

"No!"

"Pleeeaaassse?" The other children gathered around her and begged her.

"I said no!" Her lower lip protruded.

The oldest boy had an idea. "We'll let you pitch pennies with us!"

This got the toddler's attention. One of the other boys punched the oldest in the arm. He whispered, "Mom will kill us if she finds out we let Sonia pitch pennies!"

"Shut up!" the eldest whispered back. "I'm not really gonna let her do it!" He took a penny from his pocket. "See this penny, Sonia? It's yours if you get that piece of paper for us."

Sonia's eyes grew big as she stared at the penny.

"Under the door," the eldest boy got down on his knees and pointed. He put his head on the floorboards and looked under the door. "See? Right there."

Little Sonia joined him, pressing her chubby cheek against the floor.

"Do you see it, Sonia?"

"Uh-huh!"

"Get it and you can have this penny!"

Sonia reached her hand under the door. Head to head with her, the eldest of her brothers watched as little fingers touched the edge of the paper, then got hold of it and pulled it under the door. As soon as the note cleared the threshold, the older boy snatched it from her hand. He jumped to his feet. The other boys gathered around him, craning their necks to look at the note.

"James, you're the best reader, what does it say?"

The group shuffled itself so that James could see the note without anyone losing his position in the process. The eldest among them lowered the note so James could see it. The reader read silently for a moment.

"It's not a love letter!" James cried. "There isn't a mushy word in it!"

The boys groaned.

"Where's my penny? I want my penny!" Sonia screamed.

The eldest boy pushed the paper close to James. "You're lyin'! This is a love letter! That lady's face was all mushy!"

"I want my penny!"

The more the oldest boy insisted the note was a love letter, the more the others began to deride him for being wrong. At first he defended himself, then he retaliated by wading up the note and pelting James in the forehead with it.

"Hey!" James retrieved the wad and threw it at the eldest boy. He missed.

"I'm gonna tell Momma! I want my penny!" little Sonia screamed in the melee.

Another boy grabbed the wad and threw it. The wadded note sailed up and down the hallway as one boy after another was pelted. James ducked as the wad whizzed by his head. It flew down the stairway. Back and forth it went down several flights of stairs until a man on the third floor threatened the boys for making noise. The boys scurried out of the stairwell and into an alley, followed by Sonia crying for her penny.

Emily's note to Jesse's mother burrowed in with all the trash at the foot of the stairs on the tenement's third floor.

Chapter 13

WHAT'S this?"
Like a booming double cannon blast, the two words broadsided Jesse's slumbering ears. He winced, but his senses were slow to rally.

Wooden prongs poked his side. Once. Twice.

The twin pricks of pain did what words failed to do. Suddenly Jesse was awake. More than awake. All of his senses, which had moments before been comfortably nestled in the warm sands of slumber, were now charged with electricity. It was this sudden intensity that undoubtedly made the tines that were inches from his face look so sharp, and the man holding the pitchfork loom so large.

Jesse rolled over and attempted to back away from the pointed threat. His retreat was blocked by a large oak tree. The night before he'd used the exposed roots as a resting place for his head. Even if he could get around the tree, his way would be blocked by a wooden wall, the side of a building which had no visible doors or windows.

"What are you doing on my property?"

"No harm, sir," Jesse cried, his voice cracking.

The man standing over him was indeed large; his midsection was as wide as the oak tree he was guarding. Heavy jowls hung on both sides of a hairless head, with the exception of two uncharacteristically bushy gray eyebrows which looked like they were pasted on. The man wore a large discolored white apron that bore a collection of stains with a rainbow of colors, that is, if there were such a thing as brown rainbows. Some of the stains looked as fresh as this morning, others looked older than Jesse. Thick forearms covered with blond hair extended down to sausage-like fingers curled around the handle of the pitchfork which kept Jesse at bay.

"If you intend no harm, then what?" the armed man challenged.

"I'm a traveler, nothing more, sir," Jesse stammered. "Just passing through."

Thick eyelids lowered suspiciously. "A traveler, huh? With no bag of clothes? No food? Only a fool would set off without provisions. You must be a thief!" The man cocked his head slightly. A look of recognition narrowed his eyes even more. "You're that Akins boy, aren't you? The one that's been stealin' chickens?"

"I'm not a thief!" Jesse cried. "And I don't know anyone named Akins. Jesse Morgan, that's my name."

"Can you prove it?"

Jesse's brow furrowed. He'd never been asked to prove his identity before. It seemed a perplexing dilemma. *How do I prove I'm me?* All his life his identity had been established by association, by the people and places that surrounded him. He was Jesse—Ben and Clara Morgan's son; the Jesse Morgan who lived on Hester Street; the Jesse Morgan who worked at Ruger's Glassworks Factory. How was he to prove his identity to a man who knew none of these people or places? And the only things he was carrying were the clothes on his back and a Truly Noble…

"Yes, I can prove it!" Jesse cried happily. He pulled *Danger at Deadwood* from his waistband. Cautiously extending it to the man standing over him, he pointed to the author's inscription and signature.

Keeping the pitchfork level with one hand, the man took the book with the other. He squinted to focus on the writing, blinked, extended his arm its full length, and squinted again. Apparently the words came into focus, because he read aloud the inscription. *To Jesse. May you find the strength that comes from goodness. Your aunt, Sarah Morgan Cooper.* Eyebrows raised when the man noticed that the signature matched the name of the author.

"You know the writer of this book?" the man asked.

"My aunt. See…her middle name is my last name."

"You could have stolen this book," the man said lamely.

"Yes, sir. I could have, but I didn't."

The pitchfork lowered as the man tossed the book back to Jesse. "No, you don't look the type." His tone was one of concession.

The book landed on Jesse's belly. He rolled over halfway and replaced it in his waistband, making no attempt to get up because the man still hovered over him.

"But you're no traveler either," the man said. "No extra clothes. No provisions. No weapon. My guess is that you're a man on the run."

It was difficult to argue with him since he was right. Quite disturbing though that his state of affairs was so easily recognizable. Jesse hadn't counted on that.

"When was the last time you ate?" the man asked.

Looking at the ground, Jesse tried to remember his last meal. Dinner? No, it must have been…

"That long? Come!"

Turning his back on Jesse, the man walked away. Jesse was tempted to run now that he was no longer pinned against the tree. It was the prospect of food that kept him there. Besides, the man had not been unkind to him. He was merely protecting his property.

Jesse struggled to his feet. The dampness of the earth had

crept into his joints and muscles. He stretched and moaned, then hobbled after the man with the pitchfork. After just a few steps a slow, rolling wave of white passed before his eyes, disorienting him and making him dizzy. He reached out an arm to steady himself even though nothing was nearby. Then the wave passed and the dizziness subsided.

What was that?

His stomach growled in answer to the question. It confirmed that Jesse was doing the right thing by staying. He needed to eat. Jesse followed the large man around the side of the massive building which proved to be a stable. As he did, the odor of eggs and bacon and freshly baked bread hit him. His stomach growled again, urging him on.

"You work; you eat."

The pitchfork was thrust at Jesse, this time handle first.

"Use the shovel over there to clean the stalls. Replace the soiled straw with fresh. Oats in one trough, water in the other. When you're done, come to the house. Use the back door."

With that brief introduction to the task, the man left Jesse standing in the midst of odors that were far less appetizing than the ones he'd smelled only a moment before. However, the odors did nothing to hinder his growing appetite. He got right to work. His stomach growled repeatedly while he shoveled and scooped. By the time he was finished cleaning the stable and feeding the horses, he was ravenous.

Stepping from the stable into the sunlight, Jesse stretched. He felt robust. His muscles were warm from the work and his hunger seemed to heighten his senses. Everything was bright, sharp, clear. It was his first full day out on his own and he was feeling adventurous. It felt good to feel good after having walked with depression all night long.

For some reason unpleasant memories seem worse at night. And the memory of little Jake's death worked on Jesse like leather against a blister. As he grew weary, the guilt weighed so heavily upon him that he stumbled under its load. Tears blurred rocks and holes that tripped him. At one point his invisible load became so unbearable that he collapsed in the dirt and wondered how he could live the rest of his life under such conditions. That was when he saw the dark silhouettes of the stable and the tree. He no sooner reached them when blessed sleep granted him a momentary escape from his guilt.

How different things looked this morning. The memory and guilt were still there. Jesse didn't expect it to be otherwise. However, they were dimmed by the fresh air and spring colors. And Jesse was grateful for that.

Approaching the back of the house, he followed the breakfast smells that escaped through the open top half of a Dutch door. He knocked on the door's bottom panel.

Inside, the large man sat at a wooden table behind a pewter plate filled to the edges with mounds of food. "Door's open!" the man said.

The kitchen into which Jesse stepped was spacious. A woman, almost as large as the man at the table, worked over a stove. Her back was to Jesse. She didn't turn around or greet him.

"Sit." The man motioned to the chair opposite him. To the woman: "Hedda, we need another plate of food over here."

The woman at the stove gave no indication she heard him. Behind the seated man, a door swung open. A stocky young woman appeared, looking much like a female version of the man at the table. Short blond pigtails swung as she walked. She was carrying two large empty bowls.

"More biscuits and potatoes," she said to the woman at the stove. Catching a glimpse of Jesse out of the corner of her eye, she slowed to get a better look at him, then glanced quickly away. She smiled at no one in particular. Her cheeks, already rosy, deepened in color. While the woman at the stove refilled the empty bowls with fried potatoes from a skillet and biscuits from the oven, the pigtailed lady sneaked several glances at Jesse.

"Hedda! I said we needed another plate of food!"

"Ya, ya! I only got two hands!"

With one last glance, the younger woman disappeared again through the doorway. At the stove there was the clang of metal utensils against a pewter plate. The woman at the stove swung around. Her face glistened with sweat. She plopped a plate of food in front of Jesse without even looking at him.

"My wife Hedda," the man said between bites.

A moment later the woman returned to drop a fork and knife on the table close to Jesse. Still without a word or a glance, she returned to her steaming pots.

The door behind the man swung open again. This time only a pigtailed head appeared. "Poppa, Mr. Elroy insists on speaking to you." When her father made no acknowledgment or move to get up, she remained in the doorway and waited, her head ticking back and forth like a metronome.

Across the table the man finished shoveling a forkful of scrambled eggs into his mouth. He began to scoop another load, then stopped. The man's lower lip worked back and forth. From the sour expression on his face it looked like foul words were attempting to escape from his mouth and he was fighting them back with his lip.

From the doorway: "I tried to tell him…"

The table shuddered as the man slammed down his fork. "I'll tell him myself!" the man boomed. He shoved himself away from the table, but because the table weighed less than him it moved more than he did. Jesse's plate of food and the edge of the table pressed against his stomach. Following his daughter, the man stormed out the door.

The only sound in the kitchen was the clatter lids make

when lifted from a pot and the scraping sound of a spoon against the side of a kettle when something is stirred. Jesse put his hands to the table's edge and attempted to discreetly push it back into place. His effort was rewarded with a long, high-pitched screech. He stopped. The table was only half the distance to its previous position. The noise didn't seem to bother the woman at all. She gave no indication that she'd even heard it. But it bothered Jesse. So, instead of pushing the table the remaining distance, he simply scooted his chair forward and concentrated on the food that was set before him.

The plate held more than generous portions of scrambled eggs, fried potatoes, and slices of ham. A huge biscuit perched victoriously atop the mountain of potatoes. Risking a breach of etiquette, he decided not to wait for his host to return. He attacked the eggs first. The first bite exploded with flavor. Those that followed in quick succession were no less wonderful.

Not until the plate was half empty did Jesse slow his eating pace. He sat back and chewed appreciatively. Then, remembering his manners, he swallowed and said to the woman's back, "Thank you, this is really quite good."

"Ya." The woman nodded. She didn't turn around.

The door swung open and the man reappeared. His facial expression had calmed since his departure, looking like the aftermath of a storm.

Eyeing Jesse's half-empty plate, he said without grinning, "You like my wife's cooking?"

With his mouth full of potatoes, Jesse nodded until he could swallow. "I was telling her how much I liked it just before you came in."

The man sat in his chair and instead of scooting up to the table pulled the table to him. Jesse stared haplessly at the canyon that formed between him and his plate. The man didn't seem to notice. He was busily shoveling cold eggs. As discreetly as he could and without standing up, Jesse grabbed the sides of his chair and scooted back up to the table.

After several minutes, the man looked up and eyed Jesse through his thick lids. He chewed and talked at the same time. Bits of scrambled egg and biscuits speckled his tongue and chin. "This is the Red Horse Inn," he said. "My name is Hans. I'm the owner." He paused, then added sardonically, "...and the butler, and the repairman, and the stable boy, and the bookkeeper, and the...." He chuckled at his own joke. It took two bites of food before his smile faded. "So tell me, Mr. Morgan, what are you running from? Are you a criminal?"

"No, sir!" Jesse said emphatically. Maybe too emphatically, for his enthusiasm to refute the question raised the innkeeper's hairy eyebrows. "I've done nothing illegal. Something happened—an incident of sorts—I'd like to forget. I just needed to get out of the city. I'm going West to start a new life."

The seasoned eyes of a man who had seen people of all sorts stared at Jesse as though weighing him in a balance. His next words would reveal whether or not he believed Jesse was telling the truth. "West?" the innkeeper said. "Where in the West? Texas? Oklahoma? San Francisco?"

The question took Jesse aback. He didn't know. He was just heading West. "Probably Oklahoma," he said, then after a moment's thought, "maybe San Francisco, since I'll almost be to the Pacific Ocean anyway."

"And what will you do once you get there?"

Another question for which he didn't have an answer! "I don't know," he stammered. "Farm. Join a cattle drive. Be a cowboy. I'll see what's available once I get out there."

"I see." An amused smirk grew on the man's face. "You gonna walk the whole way?"

Jesse felt like he was taking a test, one for which he was unprepared. Previously when he'd thought of the West, he'd always envisioned himself riding a horse, though he had no idea where or how he would obtain one. And although he'd driven a carriage on occasion, most of his travel had occurred on foot, sometimes on the city's horse-drawn carriages or the el. He didn't even know for sure if he could ride a horse. He'd just always assumed he would take to a saddle naturally.

Tired of providing inadequate answers, Jesse decided to avoid the question by asking one of his own. "If you were traveling West and had a choice of transportation," Jesse asked, "what mode would you choose?"

Without hesitation, the innkeeper said, "I'd go by water. Wagons are too slow and dusty. Trains too expensive. I'd glide my way West on the blue highway."

"Blue highway?"

"Steamboat, my boy!" The innkeeper's eyes lit up as he said the word. "If I were you, I'd head across Pennsylvania to the Ohio River where I'd board one of those two-deck stern-wheelers. I'd float leisurely down the Ohio to the Mississippi. Then I'd travel upstream to the Missouri and into Dakota Territory, smooth and easy."

"But I don't want to go to the Dakota Territory."

"Then take a steamboat as far as St. Louis. From there you can join a wagon train, or hop aboard the railroad." From the way the innkeeper talked—his eyes fixed on a vision seen only by him—it was evident this wasn't the first time he had thought about traveling West. "Boy, if I was your age again…"

Before the sentence was completed it spurred an immediate response from the innkeeper's wife. The woman spun around from the stove. She didn't say anything, but her eyes burrowed into her husband with sharp intensity. Her fiery anger showed evidence of a longstanding, unresolved battle between husband and wife. Until now Jesse had thought the woman was ignoring them. However, it was now evident she had been listening to them all along.

The innkeeper capitulated to his wife's stare. He changed

the subject and the woman returned to her work. To Jesse he said, "Do you have money?"

Jesse had a couple of coins in his pocket, but he thought it unwise to tell the innkeeper. His eyes darted from side-to-side as he searched his mind for an appropriate response.

The innkeeper blustered, "What? I look like a thief to you?" The hostility the man was feeling for his wife spilled over into his conversation with Jesse. The man seemed to recognize he had overreacted. He looked away and held up a hand in apology.

"I have some money," Jesse said quietly.

"Enough to get you to Oklahoma?"

"I don't know."

The innkeeper brushed aside Jesse's comment. In doing so he also brushed aside any trace of testiness. His voice was friendly again, even eager. "Doesn't matter," he said. "You're young, strong. If you're willing to work, you can always find a job for food or passage."

For a moment the innkeeper's gaze drifted again to that faraway vision in his mind. The look on his face was that of an old man pining after his youth. This time, however, he said nothing aloud.

With her back to him, his wife rattled pans and banged lids as she perspired heavily over the stove.

Out of his wife's hearing, Hans the innkeeper pulled Jesse aside. "I wish I were going," he whispered. "When I was young, I had my chance. Now I regret it."

Jesse didn't understand why the man was whispering. They stood a good distance beyond the stable in the middle of a field.

"Head due west to Brownsville, Pennsylvania," the innkeeper whispered. "It's on the Monongahela River. They build steamboats there, outfitted with engines built in Pittsburgh. Then, the steamboats are delivered to various cities along the

Mississippi and Missouri Rivers. Skeleton crews deliver them. That's where you come in! Imagine, having an entire steamboat to yourself! And getting paid for it!"

Jesse had to admit the idea sounded attractive.

"Here, take this." He shoved a canvas bag into Jesse's arms.

"What's this?" Jesse asked.

The innkeeper shrugged sheepishly with a touch of sadness as though his youthful dream was in the bag that he was giving to Jesse. "Some britches and shirts—I tried to pick out your size—and some food."

Reaching into the bag and following closely with his head, Jesse rummaged around to see what was in it. It was as the innkeeper said: a couple of flannel shirts, pants, and some bundles he assumed were food. There was also a coin purse. It jingled when Jesse touched it.

"Just a couple of dollars," Hans said.

Jesse grinned. "I don't know what to say. Thank you."

"You strike me as a good young man. Though I don't know what you're running from—and, mind you, I don't want to know—I wish you all the best. I couldn't go West. But by helping you today, I feel like I'm sending a part of me anyway."

Jesse thanked him again and began walking. After a few steps he turned to wave, but all he saw was the innkeeper's back. The man had already turned his back on what might have been and was returning to what was—his inn, his wife and daughter, and Mr. Elroy.

Chapter 14

JESSE crossed the Delaware River into Pennsylvania. After two days of hobbling on blistered feet and rubbing cramped legs, the innkeeper's blue highway sounded more and more inviting. Yet despite the pain, he was enjoying himself. He felt more like a traveler than a runaway. Before he could only imagine what Truly Noble felt when he initially journeyed West in *Noble Cowboy;* now he could identify with the experience. The only difference between him and his hero was that Truly traveled with Charity Increase and Jesse traveled alone.

Thoughts of Charity reminded him of Emily Barnes and his last night in New York. He remembered the dark loneliness which surrounded him as he stared at the river and how Emily emerged from the light and rescued him from the darkness. He remembered her face aglow in the lamplight. Her smiling eyes. The warmth of her nearness.

Jesse was surprised at how strongly the emotions of that night had attached themselves to his memory. The very thought of Emily on the bridge with the lights of the city as a backdrop caused his pulse to race again.

For the first time in his life, Jesse understood the attraction Truly Noble felt for Charity. He understood the passages where Tru rescued her from danger—something which Charity attracted to herself like ants to honey. Endangering his own life to save helpless females was the work of a hero.

The parts he didn't understand were the paragraphs his aunt wrote about how their eyes locked in silent communication, or the giddiness Tru felt whenever Charity was around. These were not hero qualities. And Jesse ignored them as the unrealistic imagination of a woman writer.

Now, he wasn't so sure. With Emily, he found himself feeling these very feelings. And they were far from imaginary.

Odd how things work out, he mused. *How after all these years of not caring for girls, I should be attracted to one just when I leave. But maybe it's not so odd. Emily is different from all the other girls. She isn't panting for a husband. She's an investigative reporter which means she likes mystery and she's not afraid of danger. Like me.*

Jesse chuckled aloud.

And, of course, now that I've met someone who might very well have been my Charity Increase, I'm forced to leave the lower east side. Now I'll never know for sure.

Another chuckle, this one louder.

Wouldn't Mother be surprised if she knew what I was feeling for Emily? What was it she used to call me? Oh, yeah...late bloomer. Like I was a flower or something. Then she'd tell me about Frank and Christopher and Gregory—all of them my age and how they had wives and jobs. And how Christopher was already a father. Then she'd tell me not to let it bother me, that my time would come, that I was a late bloomer. If she didn't want those things to bother me, why did she bother telling me about them?

The sun lowered itself gloriously in front of him. The orange orb stretched from one side of the road to the other, making it look like a tunnel through which Jesse would have to pass to reach the West. As he walked toward the sun Jesse had two thoughts on his mind: finding a place to bed down, and whether or not he would ever see Emily Barnes again.

Jesse's trek across Pennsylvania confirmed what Hans the innkeeper told him. As long as he was willing to work he would have something to eat and a place to lay his head at night. For these things he baled hay, cleaned horse stalls, hammered nails, chopped wood, hauled water, swept porches, plowed fields, sawed logs, milked cows, cleared land, and repaired fences all the way across the state.

He discovered he liked working outdoors. It felt good to sweat, to feel his chest heaving from exertion, and to quit at the end of the day, his muscles warm from work. There was something satisfying about fixing things or having the satisfaction of completing a difficult task. He'd never felt this way about his work in the city.

At night he would relax. He liked to lie on his back with his hands behind his head and look at the country sky. He loved the expansiveness of it, and the fact that there were more stars here than there were in the city. Before drifting off to sleep he would take stock of the day and of himself. Each day he grew stronger and more confident. And by the time he reached Brownsville, he was convinced that he would not only survive, but that he would succeed at whatever he set out to do. He thought of how pleased his mother would be when he sent for her. And then he would sleep the sleep of an exhausted, satisfied man.

"The economy's depressed. So's the steamboat buildin' business. Time was we could sell 'em faster'n we could build 'em. No more. Railroads changed all that. Steamboats can't compete with the blasted railroads."

Jesse sat in a squeaky chair in a small shack beside the Monongahela River. The man talking to him was propped up behind a heavily scarred wooden desk strewn with invoices and letters and plans and financial logs. His chair was tilted backward against the wall and the heels of his boots set atop the papers as he talked. Every time he repositioned himself in his chair, his boots crinkled or ripped the papers beneath them. The man didn't seem to mind.

His name was Edwards. Jesse wasn't told his first name and he didn't ask. Upon reaching Brownsville he went down to the river. From there it wasn't hard to find the steamboats. Three of them were under construction, two sternwheelers and one side-wheeler. They lay on the riverbank like beached whales. The wooden carcasses were covered with workers clinging to their exposed ribs, pounding and sawing and shaving them. Jesse had to approach four men before he could get one of them to answer him. And even then the man stopped hammering only long enough to point to the shack and say, "Talk to Edwards."

The man seated casually in front of Jesse was shorter than him. He wore a coarse black beard made up of thousands of tiny ringlets. His eyes were equally dark and, when he talked, they focused on Jesse in a judgmental way as though the man doubted Jesse was listening to him. From the man's tattered and dusty overalls, it was clear he was a working foreman. His pants had bits of sawdust all over them as did the hair on his forearms that protruded from rolled-up sleeves.

"Are you saying you can't hire me?" Jesse asked.

Edwards looked him over. "Ever held a hammer before?"

"I helped build a barn in Harrisburg."

"Barn's not a steamboat."

Jesse acknowledged the truth of his statement and added, "You asked if I'd used a hammer. You show me what you want hammered and I'll hammer it."

The man shook his head. "Got too many hammerers."

Jesse bit his tongue. He wanted to say, *Then why did you ask if I could hammer?* Instead, he asked, "What else is there?"

"Can you handle a saw?"

"Like I already told you, I helped build a barn in Harrisburg.

I used both a hammer and a saw."

"Don't need hammerers," Edwards said, using a fingernail to pick a piece of meat that had lodged in his teeth.

"Yes, I know. But do you need sawyers?"

"Nope."

Jesse bit his lower lip. He wondered if he could get a job before he chewed himself to death. He leaned forward, his elbows on his knees, his hands spread wide in a pleading manner, "Look, Mr. Edwards..."

"Edwards. No mister," the man said matter-of-factly. He was making progress with the meat between his teeth. His tongue slid over to help the fingernail.

"All right... listen, Edwards, tell me this: What kind of work do you need done around here?"

"Can you handle a ax?"

Jesse was wise to this approach. "Do you need someone who can handle an ax?"

"Maybe." The piece of meat was extracted. It lay on Edwards' fingertip while he examined it. Once the examination was over, he flicked it away.

"Mr. Edwards, let me tell you what I'm after. My goal is to get aboard one of those steamboats. I'm heading West and I don't mind working for my passage. I was told that once the steamboats were built, a skeleton crew sailed them down the Ohio River to their point of delivery."

"Who told ya that?"

"Hans. An innkeeper."

"An innkeeper told you that?"

Jesse's hopes began to fade. Maybe Hans had his facts wrong. "Is it true?" he asked.

"Yup."

Relief swept over him, followed by frustration. Why was Edwards making this so difficult for him? Jesse tried to pin him down. "Then, what can I do to become part of that crew?"

"Can ya handle a ax?"

Jesse wanted to bite something. He resisted. "Yes, I can handle an ax."

A scowling Edwards leaned forward. His chair banged onto all fours. "Then why didn't ya just say so? Steamboats burn wood. Plenty of it. Wood doesn't cut itself."

"Then you'll give me a job?"

A quizzical look came over Edwards' hairy face. "You gave your teachers a tough time in school, didn't you?"

"Mr. Edwards, just tell me plainly. Do I have a job chopping wood?"

Edwards leaned forward. With wide eyes he nodded his head in a very deliberate way and said, "Yeeeeessssss!"

Jesse ignored the sarcasm. "And when one of those steamboats is finished, I can be part of the crew that will deliver it?"

Again, Edwards nodded. "Yeeeeessssss!"

"Which boat?"

Edwards sat back in his chair, dropping the sarcasm. "The *Little Hawk* will be finished first. It already has a full crew. After that, the *Anabelle*. You can go on her. But you'll have to do whatever work the captain wants you to do, understand?"

"I'm willing to do anything," Jesse said eagerly. "Where is the *Anabelle* headed?"

"St. Louis."

"That's perfect!" Jesse cried.

"You start choppin' now," Edwards said. "Supper's in two hours. There's a tent with a cot near some spruce trees. You can sleep there. The wood's laid out nearby. So's the ax."

Jesse jumped to his feet, eager to get to work. He extended his hand. "Thank you, Mr., um, thank you, Edwards. You won't regret this."

Edwards replied with a smacking sound of his lips. He turned his attention to another piece of meat he found wedged between two teeth.

That night after the sun had set and it was too dark to chop wood, Jesse wandered to the shoreline and walked among the giant steamboats. The *Little Hawk* and the *Anabelle* were the two sternwheelers. As Edwards had indicated, the *Little Hawk* was further along in its development. It was missing its railing and several walls, but the deck was complete and portions of it were already painted white. The *Anabelle* still displayed portions of its skeletal frame and much of the deck had yet to be laid. But that didn't keep Jesse from seeing himself walking the decks on a moonlit night as the proud craft made its maiden voyage down the Ohio River.

So this is the craft that's going to deliver me to the doorstep of the West, he mused. Later that night Jesse fell asleep propped up against a tree outside his tent looking at the steamboat *Anabelle.*

For the most part, Jesse was left alone to chop wood. He was the sole occupant of the tent; he never learned who the previous occupant had been or why it had been erected in the first place. It sheltered him from the late spring rains and the occasional cold snap as the year grudgingly gave up its final hold on winter. At night he virtually had the riverbank to himself. Most of the other workers lived in the town and those who didn't either reveled the night away in a tavern or found lodging elsewhere. Neither did Jesse have much contact with them during the day. They did their jobs and he did his.

Twenty-three days after Jesse arrived in Brownsville a cheer rose along the bank as the *Little Hawk* was rolled on timbers into the river. The boat nestled itself into the Monongahela current. Shorelines held it in place while a final inspection was made by the captain.

Early the next morning after minor leaks were sealed, it was declared fit to sail. The boat was officially christened. To shouts and songs and gaiety, the lines anchoring it to shore were cut. Jesse watched with mounting anxiety as the steamboat was turned loose to sail downriver to the Ohio.

The next steamboat launched from this shore will be carrying me, he said to himself. By that evening he had increased his daily stack of wood by nearly half.

"Hey, boy! What did you do so awful that they set you to choppin' wood?"

Jesse kept his head down and swung his ax. *Crack! Thump!* The ax head split the wood cleanly. Two pieces of equal size fell to the side of the tree stump Jesse used as a block. Bending over, he retrieved the pieces, tossed them in his growing pile, and placed another log on the stump.

"He probably robbed a bank!"

"Or killed someone!"

The two men who were amusing themselves at Jesse's expense were seated on the ground about fifty feet distant. They had propped themselves against a fallen tree and were eating oranges. At first they entertained themselves by spitting the seeds and trying to hit Jesse with them. When their puckers failed to provide adequate power to make the game worthwhile, they turned to verbal jibes.

"He don't look the sort that could kill someone!"

"You're right. But he could bore them to death!"

The two men fell all over each other with laughter. The larger of the men was the rougher of the two. There were times in his jesting when he slapped or kicked or punched his partner. The partner never retaliated. Every time, he took the blow and laughed it off. The rough one was covered with black hair. Not only was his beard and mustache full, but his hair was shoulder length, and black hair sprouted from under his shirt at the base of his neck. Even the backs of his hands and his knuckles were fuzzy with hair.

The other man was of a slighter build and, because his hair

was thin and light, compared to his partner he looked like he had no body hair at all. His ears were wide, as was his grin. There were no teeth in his mouth that Jesse could see. While his voice was squeaky high, the hairy man's laughter boomed like a bass drum. By listening to them exchange names, Jesse had learned that the large man was called Bulfinch and the smaller man was Fritz. The britches of both men extended no further than the middle of their calves, and neither of them wore shoes.

Jesse saw them for the first time two days previous. There was a third man with them. They never worked, at least from what Jesse observed. He overheard one of the workers call them flatboaters. The man had said the name like it stuck to his tongue and left a bad taste.

"I know! I know!" Fritz cried. "He sassed his mommy and now he's being punished!" The slight man raised his eyebrows and waited for a response. When Bulfinch laughed, then he laughed too.

"Don't the two of you have anything better to do?" Jesse asked.

Bulfinch looked at Fritz with surprise. "He talks!"

Fritz giggled at the remark.

Jesse shook his head and split another log.

"Speak again, fair prince!" Bulfinch cried, placing folded hairy hands against his heart. He batted his eyelashes.

Ignoring them, Jesse bent over to pick up the split halves. As he did, a smooth rock bounced off the tree stump and hit him on the side of the nose.

"Got 'im!" Fritz yelled.

The blow stung, knocking the sight from Jesse's left eye momentarily. His anger rising within him, he rubbed the spot where the rock hit and blinked his eye until he could see again. Then he turned on his attackers.

It was Finn and his ruffians all over again. But this time Jesse had added some muscle to his arms and legs and chest from all the wood cutting and hauling. And this was a more confident Jesse. He didn't want to fight, but neither was he going to let two idlers abuse him while he was working.

Jesse stood tall beside the tree stump. His eyes narrowed. His hands balled into fists.

"Oooooo! Look like he wants to fight!" Fritz said in a childish tone.

Bulfinch said nothing. He stood and mirrored Jesse's posture.

"I don't want to fight you," Jesse said firmly. "But I'm not going to let you pelt me with rocks."

"And how are you gonna stop me?" Fritz cried.

"Just go on your way and let me get back to work," Jesse said.

Bulfinch began rolling up his sleeves. "We'll be on our way," he said, "as soon as I finish my work here—pounding you into pulp!"

Standing face-to-face with the burly man, Jesse caught his first clear glimpse of the man's eyes. They were blue—light blue, the color of the sky. And one was angled off to the side. Add to that the fact that the end of his nose looked like someone or something had chewed it. The combination of the man's eyes, his chewed nose, and his hairy covering made him look more like an animal than a man. He moved toward Jesse.

Jesse considered grabbing the ax, then decided against it. He doubted he could ever swing an ax at human flesh. So he looked for vulnerabilities. The man was taller, beefier, and from the looks of him, more experienced in fighting.

What would Truly Noble do?

Give peace a chance. Jesse raised his hands in front of him, palms out. "I said I didn't want to fight you. All I want is to do my work."

"FINCH! Leave the boy alone!"

The command sounded like a man ordering his dog to heel. It came from behind Bulfinch. Jesse glanced beyond his attacker and saw the third member of the trio walking toward him. He was a man of average height, sandy-colored hair, and had several flesh-colored moles on both sides of his face. He walked with an air of authority.

"FINCH! BACK AWAY!"

Bulfinch stopped, but he didn't back away.

"The boy's not worth it," the sandy-haired man said. "You start a fight with him and you'll have all them boatbuilders down on top of us. He's probably their mascot or something." The man stepped between them, his back to Jesse. Bulfinch glared over his head at Jesse. "We've got work to do," the man said, placing his hands on Bulfinch's arms and physically turning him away.

It took a second effort, but the sandy-haired man managed to turn Bulfinch around. To Fritz he said, "Meet me at the general store."

Fritz nodded. "Whatever you say, Phyfe."

Once they were gone, the man Fritz had called Phyfe turned toward Jesse. He was almost amused by Jesse's predicament. "What did you do to rile him?" he asked.

Jesse shrugged. "I'm just doing my job," he said. "They got bored and, well, I guess they just decided to have fun with me. When I tried to put a stop to it, the big one got mad."

Phyfe looked over his shoulder at the departing Bulfinch. "If I were you, son, I wouldn't make him mad again." Without another word he turned and followed after his partners.

For the next half hour Jesse's strokes hit the block with stronger than normal blows. It took him that long to work the anger out of his system. He knew the incident didn't warrant the amount of anger he felt. But he couldn't help it. The Finns and Bulfinches of the world affected him that way.

To calm himself, he diverted his attention to more pleasant thoughts. Seven more days. Only seven days and he would be sailing aboard the *Anabelle* to St. Louis.

WHEN the *Anabelle* sailed from Brownsville, Jesse was not aboard.

"You said I would be part of the *Anabelle's* crew!"

"I lied," Edwards said. The man was straddling a beam shoulder high on the yet-unnamed side-wheeler. He hammered on the beam above him. Sweat trickled down his temple and disappeared into the mass of hair rings that was his beard.

Jesse stood below him on a board stretched across the boat's ribs. "Why? Why would you lie to me?"

"Bad habit," Edwards sniggered. "I do it all the time."

Exasperated, Jesse placed his hands on his hips. He looked around as though searching for the right words that would command a direct response. All around him—above, below, and on all sides—workers hammered and sawed and planed the boat's ribbing and frame. Without exception they cocked an ear Jesse's direction while they worked, occasionally looking up to view the spectacle. Some looked sympathetic to his plight. Most, however, wore the same smirk as Edwards as if it had been replicated and distributed to them.

Jesse formulated his question. "What purpose did you have in telling me that I would be part of the *Anabelle's* crew when you knew that it wasn't your decision to make?"

That was how Jesse learned that Edwards lied. When the *Anabelle* was finished, the captain arrived for a preliminary inspection. Jesse expected Edwards would introduce him to the captain. He did not. At first Jesse reasoned that the captain had more important things to attend to. He told himself to be patient, that introductions would come in time. Then, after several days had passed, Jesse went to Edwards and inquired about his position on the boat. Edwards assured him his position was secure and that all the unskilled crewmen boarded the ship at one time just before the boat sailed. The answer made sense to him, so Jesse waited. And waited.

When the day of *Anabelle's* departure arrived, Jesse couldn't find Edwards anywhere. Spying the captain, he decided to take matters into his own hands. He introduced himself to the captain and received a blank-stare response. It was then that Jesse learned Edwards had lied to him. The crew was picked and trained by the captain months before the date of departure. Edwards had no say in it at all. And despite Jesse's fervent pleas, the captain refused to take him on.

Edwards looked down at Jesse. "You wanna know why I lied to you, is that it?"

"Exactly."

"Would you have stayed as long if you knew you would not be sailing on board the *Anabelle?*"

"Of course not!" Jesse cried.

"There you have it."

Jesse was so angry he wanted to spit, or hit something. "Of all the lowdown…"

"You opened the door yourself!" Edwards laughed.

"What do you mean?"

"With that story you told me. The one about workin' for passage…the one that tavern owner told you."

"Innkeeper."

"Huh?"

"He was an innkeeper, not a tavern owner."

"Doesn't matter. That's what gave me the idea. Before you

came along I couldn't get boys to stay and chop wood for longer than a week!"

Anger clouded Jesse's mind. He wanted to do something. Say something. But fury's fog was so thick he couldn't think of anything other than how angry he was.

"What are you bellyachin' for anyway?" Edwards cried. "You chopped wood for food and shelter. As for the rest, well, consider it a lesson! No extra charge!"

Laughter and catcalls and derogatory comments burst out all around Jesse. Edwards let it go on for a bit, then yelled, "Show's over! Get back to work!" The response was an immediate resumption of pounding and ripping of saws. To Jesse he said, "I take it you don't want to chop any more wood for me?"

"I wouldn't chop wood for you if..."

"Then get off my boat!" Edwards turned his back on Jesse and resumed hammering.

The road out of Brownsville crossed the river before turning north to Pittsburgh. It paralleled the river's route. With his canvas bag slung across his back, Jesse walked a good mile before he stopped muttering to himself.

Lesson. I learned a lesson all right. Never trust a hairy boat-builder.

"Hey! Woodsman!"

The voice came from the river valley. Just over the ridge Jesse could see a head with sandy-colored hair. It belonged to the man who had prevented the fight with the idler named Bulfinch.

"Where you headed?" the man shouted.

Jesse slowed his pace but didn't stop. "Pittsburgh," he shouted back.

"You live there or something?"

"Just hope to catch a ride there."

"A ride to where?"

Jesse looked away. The man was asking a lot of questions. It made Jesse realize that he did learn something from Edwards. *Don't be too free with the information you hand out. It can be used against you.*

It was as though the man sensed what Jesse was thinking. He said, "I'm just asking because we're going as far as Cincinnati. And we could use another hand. How about joining us?"

Us? From the road Jesse could see only the one man. And what was the mode of transportation? He could see no masts or sails or boat of any kind.

Jesse stepped to the edge of the road. His questions were answered. The "us" included Bulfinch and Fritz who reclined lazily on a flatboat. The craft was nothing more than a large floating platform with a tiller. That's why Jesse had not been able to see anything.

Taking one look at Bulfinch, Jesse said, "Thanks, but I think I'll walk."

"I hope it's not because of what happened between you and Finch earlier," the man said. "He doesn't normally act like that, only after he's been drinking."

Jesse hadn't seen any liquor bottles the day of the preempted fight. But Bulfinch could have been drinking earlier.

"You'd be helpin' us out a lot," the man said. "We really need at least four men to pilot this craft. And it would help you too. You can catch a steamboat in Cincinnati a lot easier than in Pittsburgh. More passenger traffic from there."

The man had a point. Still, Jesse felt uneasy. He didn't know if he wanted to share a flatboat with the likes of Bulfinch and Fritz. However, the sandy-haired fellow—what was his name? That's right, Phyfe—he seemed a likable sort. And he was able to control Bulfinch. He demonstrated that back in Brownsville.

Jesse stepped over the ridge and slid down to the flatboat. Bulfinch and Fritz eyed him all the way down. The flatboat bobbed as he stepped aboard. The less-than-stable flooring prompted him to hurriedly bring his other foot aboard and plant it flatly on the planks. It took Jesse a moment to gain his balance.

"Just stow your bag in the front with that pile of stuff," Phyfe said.

Jesse walked between the other two men. The path took him down the middle of the flatboat. It was fairly solid footing.

"Ever travel by flatboat before?" Phyfe asked.

"This is my first time," Jesse said.

"Nothing to it. We'll teach you everything you need to know." To Bulfinch and Fritz he said, "Looks like the river gods are smiling upon us, gentlemen. Now that we have a full complement, let's get underway."

Jesse couldn't help but cringe at Phyfe's use of the term *gentlemen* for Bulfinch and Fritz. He had to be using it sarcastically, didn't he? Nevertheless, the two "gentlemen" hopped to their feet and grabbed poles that must have been at least twelve feet long. Phyfe manned the tiller.

"Just sit there in the middle for the time being," he said to Jesse. "Watch for a bit. You'll get your hand on them poles soon enough."

The flatboat moved into the stream in a way that Jesse could only describe as a liquid lurch. It was a sudden movement, but the water kept it from being jerky. The platform beneath his feet likewise mimicked the liquid surface upon which it rode. Jesse was glad to sit down; it kept him from falling over. He'd heard about men getting their sea legs, but this was his first real experience, and the small size of the craft seemed to accentuate everything.

The craft merged with the flow of the stream. Overhead, the sun beat down on them brightly, enhanced by the reflection of the water. Jesse squinted to adjust the light to his eyes. The bill of his ever-present cap had been sufficient for the street, but out on the river he understood why so many men sported wide-brimmed hats.

For a time no one said a word. After pushing off from the shore Fritz and Bulfinch worked in unison, one on each side of the platform. They plunged their poles into the stream until they hit bottom. Then, holding tightly to the poles, they walked them to the back of the boat where they extracted them, carried them to the front, and started again. Phyfe pulled the tiller hard into his stomach until they were midstream, whereupon he moved it back to center. His eyes keenly searched the river ahead for obstructions, such as rocks, fallen trees, or driftwood of significant size.

Though Jesse had doubts about the company he was keeping, there was something about finally being on the river that excited him. It amazed him how different things looked from the middle of the river. It was an entirely new perspective, not anything like the road he had just been walking even though the road was only a couple of hundred yards to his left. Maybe the different perspective would extend to the people who shared the flatboat with him. He hoped so anyway.

The flatboat drifted lazily down the Ohio River. Jesse's introduction to river sailing had stretched into its fifth day. He had poled with both Fritz and Bulfinch. And Phyfe had even let him man the tiller for a while, until they approached Pittsburgh.

They stopped only long enough to get some supplies. Then the craft was nudged back into the Monongahela River and the foursome drifted into the confluence where the Monongahela joined the Allegheny River to create the Ohio River.

For Jesse it was something of a rite of passage as the craft slipped into the Ohio River. This was a river of history. Along with the Mississippi and the Missouri, it defined the West. Early explorers sailed down this river before the colonies ever conceived of declaring their independence. The river was a dividing line between North and South in the great Civil War. Fortunes were gained or lost aboard the steamboats that plied these waters, transporting cotton and sugar to the West. And now Jesse Morgan was sailing down the great Ohio River. It was as though this was his first step west and everything to this point was merely a prelude.

The river flowed northwest out of Pennsylvania. It would gradually wind its way around to a southwesterly course and seek the mighty Mississippi. Jesse was enjoying his first night on the Ohio. It was wider, almost a half mile across. Phyfe told him that by the time they reached Cincinnati it would be a mile across. They drifted peacefully under the stars as the water lapped the boat's shallow sides. The trees along the shore had grown black while the sky retained a hint of dark blue.

Bulfinch and Fritz sat near the front on wooden boxes. A third box between them served as a table. They were playing cards just like they did every night. A lantern sat on one side of the table. Its glow painted the front half of the two card players with color while their backs remained pitch-black.

To Jesse's surprise, they had left him alone during the trip. The two men rarely even spoke to him, which suited Jesse just fine. The only discord that occurred aboard the boat came when the two men argued over cards. This inevitably happened whenever Bulfinch drank. However, Phyfe was always quick to step between the two and settle them down. He ordered them around like children, and the two men obeyed him like he was their father.

Jesse didn't understand the relationship the three men had together, but he figured as long as they left him alone he could live with them until they reached Cincinnati. Phyfe leaned on the tiller and contentedly smoked a pipe. Wisps of gray smoke curled around his head, then disappeared into the night.

"What's in Cincinnati for you?" Jesse asked. It occurred to

him that they knew his reason for traveling downriver, but he had never asked theirs.

Phyfe didn't answer immediately. He drew long on his pipe, held it, then blew a steady stream of smoke that tumbled and swirled before it dissipated. Then he cleared his throat, turned his head, and spat in the wake of the boat. Jesse waited. He'd learned to wait. It wasn't a matter of hearing. Phyfe had heard him all right. In fact, in the stillness of the night river, any number of people standing along shore could have heard him even though he spoke in a soft voice. This was just Phyfe's way. Like the meandering river, he didn't hurry.

"You read the Bible, boy?" he asked at last.

"Some," Jesse replied tentatively. He'd never thought of Phyfe as a religious man.

"Do you know the story of the Good Samaritan?"

Jesse nodded hesitantly. It had been a long time since he'd heard any Bible stories. "A man was traveling and some thieves jumped him and took all his money. Then a good man—the Good Samaritan—came by and helped him."

Phyfe nodded approvingly. "Bulfinch, Fritz, and me... we're Good Samaritans."

Jesse had a hard time placing Bulfinch and Fritz in that role. Apparently he wasn't alone. Even the two card players paused their game and looked questioningly at the man holding the tiller.

"It's not what's in Cincinnati," Phyfe explained. "It's what's between here and Cincinnati."

Apparently the two card players understood where Phyfe was going with this, for they returned to their game. Jesse, however, remained puzzled.

"Occasionally a steamboat will get caught on a sandbar or get snagged by something in the river. In order to get unstuck, they have to unload their cargo and passengers. This makes the boat lighter and easier to free. That's where we come in.

Flatboats like this one are ideal for loading and unloading cargo from boat to shore and back again. We help ships in trouble. We're Good Samaritans."

Jesse nodded. He understood now.

"Captains and steamboat lines pay us for our services. And mighty handsomely too."

Bulfinch chuckled. Jesse couldn't tell if the man simply had a good hand or if it was something Phyfe said.

"So now that you're with us, that makes you a Good Samaritan too," Phyfe said.

"I'll be glad to do my part."

"Of that I have no doubt," Phyfe said. "Of that I have no doubt."

It was days before they encountered their first steamboat. Jesse watched in awe as it plowed effortlessly through the water in the opposite direction toward Pittsburgh. The stateliness of its pillared decks and the well-dressed passengers lining the rails and the powerful twin black towers belching smoke made the flatboat seem like a floating matchbox in comparison. It was hard to imagine such a magnificent river craft floundering on a sandbar while a little nothing of a flatboat came to its rescue.

Most days they encountered only smaller craft moving dutifully back and forth across the river or for short hops upstream or downstream in the course of an average day's work. Long hours afloat passed more quickly when stories were told. Phyfe and his crew learned of Jesse's upbringing in New York, about his father's death in the factory fire, and his mother's work for the sweater. Jesse learned that Phyfe's father was a riverboat captain and that Phyfe had been raised on the Mississippi as a cabin boy. His father too had died a violent death—shot by a drunken gambler.

The only thing Bulfinch mentioned was that his father, a

Pennsylvania farmer, beat him when he was young. Claimed his father hit him in the side of the head with a wooden plank; that's why his one eye was knocked crazy. He swore that if he ever saw his old man again, he'd kill him.

Fritz turned out to be the son of an overbearing storekeeper. He was raised to take over his father's retail business which was given to him and his new bride as a present on their wedding day. Three days later his new bride somehow managed to sell the store without his knowing it. She ran off with the cash. Fritz's father threw such a fit, he died of apoplexy the same day. Fritz's mother blamed her husband's death on him.

Jesse learned from Phyfe that the three men met at a tavern in Brownsville. On that particular night a steamboat captain was singing the praises of flatboaters. Claimed they were worth their weight in gold. That's when they decided to band together to get a little of that gold for themselves.

Of the three of them, Bulfinch especially had taken to life on the river, which was surprising considering he grew up on a farm. He not only loved the river, he loved everything associated with it, including river lore. He collected river stories.

At first Jesse was impressed at the big man's literary interests. He never would have guessed Bulfinch could collect anything other than enemies. Then, when he heard some of Bulfinch's stories, it all made sense.

"The Snapping Turtle, that's what they called him," Bulfinch mumbled.

Jesse found he had to listen hard to understand the man. Every word had two seemingly insurmountable obstacles they had to overcome in order to be heard: an uneducated tongue and mumbling lips which happened to be buried in a deep forest of facial hair.

"But most people know him as Mike Fink," Bulfinch said. "It was said that he could drink a gallon of whisky and still shoot the tail off a pig at ninety paces!" Bulfinch's wild eyes grew wide in admiration.

"He used to boast that he could out-run, out-hop, out-jump, throw-down, drag out, and lick any man in the country. And he could do it too!"

Phyfe added, "When I was just a tyke, I met a man who claimed to know Mike Fink himself. Said he watched him fight once. Fink gouged out the other man's eye and bit off his ear."

Jesse winced at the image of an eyeless, earless man. Bulfinch reached up and touched the chewed end of his nose.

Phyfe laughed as he remembered another Mike Fink anecdote. "The old man told me he also saw Fink's woman be stupid enough to wink at another man. Do you know what Fink did?"

"What?" Bulfinch cried with the enthusiasm of a little boy.

"He set her clothes on fire!"

Bulfinch howled.

"She saved herself by jumping into the river!"

Phyfe and Bulfinch laughed uproariously. Fritz joined them, but not as heartily.

"What's the matter with you, boy?" Phyfe asked Jesse. "You don't think that's funny?"

Jesse shook his head. "No...I just don't think someone on fire is a funny thing."

Bulfinch and Phyfe looked at him like he was demented.

"Do you know how Fink died?" Bulfinch asked.

"I've heard a couple different stories," Phyfe replied.

"The way I heard it, Fink and his partner...his partner..."

"Carpenter," Phyfe said.

"Yeah, Carpenter. He and his partner Carpenter were sharin' this Indian woman. And one day they got into an argument about her."

"It's always a woman, isn't it?" Fritz chimed in.

Phyfe found Fritz's unexpected commentary amusing. His laughter interrupted Bulfinch's story. Phyfe apologized and urged the big man to continue.

"Anyway...the two of them was drunk and Fink suggested they settle the matter by taking turns shooting a glass of whiskey off each other's head—this was somethin' they did all the time, Fink and Carpenter."

Of course, who doesn't? Jesse thought disgustedly.

"Carpenter agrees and they toss a coin to see who would go first. Fink wins. So Carpenter puts a glass of whiskey on top of his head. And Fink blows his brains out." Bulfinch started to chuckle. The chuckle turned into a laugh that made it difficult for him to continue. "And Fink, standing over his dead partner, says, 'Carpenter! You spilled the whiskey!' "

Bulfinch and Phyfe grabbed their bellies and roared. Fritz laughed a nasal laugh while his shoulders bounced up and down. Jesse couldn't believe that they thought the story was funny.

"What happened to Fink?" he asked. "You said he died."

"He did," Bulfinch said, sobering a little. "A man named Talbot didn't like what Fink did to Carpenter, so he pulled out his pistol and shot Fink through the heart."

"The man had no sense of humor at all!" Phyfe cried.

This started them up again. He and Bulfinch laughed until tears came to their eyes. The oversized storyteller took exception to Jesse's sober face.

"I suppose you have a better story," he said. The man's pale blue eyes challenged Jesse.

Shrugging aside the challenge, he said, "I don't mean to offend you, it's just that...." He stopped. This was the old Jesse, the one who ran from bullies.

Give peace a chance.

This was a solid maxim, one that he wanted to live by. But giving peace a chance didn't mean that he was not entitled to an opinion. It didn't mean that he should bow and scrape to everyone who challenged him.

"As a matter of fact, I do have a better story," he said, staring into Bulfinch's straight eye. Reaching behind him, he pulled out his Truly Noble book. He sat next to the lantern and began reading:

Deadwood was a mean town. As mean as they come. Normally Truly Noble would have taken the long way around the town to avoid trouble. But he couldn't do that today. His beloved Charity had volunteered to play the piano for her brother, the minister, at the town's only church.

The church was only two months old. But that was twice as old as any of the previous churches. The only reason it had survived this long was because Virgil Increase, Charity's brother, was stubborn and refused to give in to the bullying and threats of the corrupt sheriff and his deputies. Tru knew all about the Increase stubbornness. It must have been a family trait.

So when Charity insisted on staying the summer, Tru wasn't surprised. But he wasn't about to leave her to the mercy of a godless town. He rode to Deadwood to protect Charity, her brother, and the fledgling church.

As soon as he entered the town, he smelled trouble...

To Jesse's delight, the flatboaters' initial sniggers gave way to interest as Sarah Morgan Cooper's tale unfolded. For three nights Jesse read to them. The fourth night was so quiet, Bulfinch asked him to read the story again.

Chapter 16

THE *Liberty Belle* stood motionless in the river. Thick black smoke erupted from her twin stacks. The giant wooden paddle wheel slapped helplessly at the water, first forward, then in reverse. Anxious passengers lined the rails, staring into the water, talking to one another, and shaking their heads. The wheelhouse bristled with activity. The captain—his face noticeably red even from a distance—shouted, first at one crewman then at another. But they were as helpless as he to get the boat unstuck.

The boat did not list to one side or the other; nor were there any roots or limbs or visible obstructions of any kind. It had wedged itself on a sandbar, and had done a pretty good job of it too.

Phyfe and his crew sat aboard the flatboat which was tied up at river's edge. They watched and waited. "She's stuck good," Phyfe said. "They'll have to unload. Fritz, run up to the road and tell Mills we got ourselves a job."

Frank Mills was another one of the Good Samaritans. The first time Jesse met him, three days earlier, he thought they were about to be attacked by Indians. They were sailing peacefully downriver when Jesse caught a glimpse of something flashing in the forest. He saw it first and started to point it out to Phyfe when it disappeared. For a while, Jesse kept a cautious eye on the forest. Then, just when he relaxed, the light flashed again. It was a reflection. Jesse whispered to Phyfe that he thought they were being watched by Indians. Phyfe burst out laughing. This time Phyfe saw the reflection too. He steered the craft directly toward it. That's when Jesse met the mirror-signaling Mr. Mills.

Phyfe explained that Mills was their land contact. He shadowed their movement on shore and whenever they came across a ship, Mills would ride to the nearest town and round up extra men or horses or wagons—whatever was needed to complete the task.

So while the other three watched the *Liberty Belle* struggle in vain to break free of the sand's grip, Fritz scurried up the slope to the road to relay Phyfe's message to their land contact.

"Shouldn't we offer our services to the captain?" Jesse asked.

"He knows we're here. Can't appear too anxious, it'll only make him angry. When he's ready, he'll find a way of signaling us."

The signal came in the form of a shout from one of the crew. The man stood on the bow of the ship, cupped his hands around his mouth, and shouted, "You on the flatboat! Give us a hand!"

"That's what we're waiting for," Phyfe said. "All right, you two, push off."

"What about Fritz?"

"Never mind about him. He'll join us down there."

On the deck of the *Liberty Belle* Phyfe was a congenial smooth-talker. "Once heard Captain Joseph LaBarge say that he never lost any sleep over sandbars. 'The way the river constantly changes, every captain is bound to hit one sooner or later.'"

His words had no apparent effect on the angry captain. So Phyfe switched immediately to business.

"I can see you're in a hurry, so let me tell you what I can do for you. There's a little town just a few miles from here. Even as I speak, my associates are arranging transportation for your passengers. We'll unload the passengers first and take them to a tavern where they can refresh themselves with something to drink." As an aside, he whispered, "Besides, it will get them out of our hair."

The captain didn't comment, but the change in his expression and the way he looked at Phyfe showed he was impressed.

"Next," Phyfe said, "we'll unload the boat. What are you carrying?"

"Sugar," the captain said.

"Sugar! We're experts at handling sugar!" Phyfe said. "By the time we get that sugar off this boat, you'll glide over that bar like it wasn't even there."

The captain and Phyfe negotiated a price. The captain even offered to pay Phyfe half of the money upfront to cover his expenses. Phyfe good-naturedly refused the offer, saying he had everything under control; and they set to work unloading the boat.

Caught up by Phyfe's congenial spirit, Jesse smiled and extended his hand to the ladies as they stepped from the steamboat to the flatboat and were ferried the short distance to shore. He assured them they would be on their way shortly and waved as wagon-load after wagon-load took them to the nearby tavern.

Once the passengers were cared for, they began unloading the sugar. Once again Jesse was straining his muscles and working up a sweat. It felt good. And as he scurried back and forth from the hold to the flatboat, he realized how much stronger he'd become since he'd left New York. In fact, he felt good all around. He was assisting a steamboat in crisis, working as part of a team, and making his way West. The unfortunate delay in Brownsville may have been a blessing in disguise.

"We're getting close," Phyfe said to Jesse, pulling him aside. They had just completed loading the flatboat with another load. "Tell you what I need you to do," he said. "While we take this next load over and unload it, get all the crewmen you can find down into that hold. You see, the bulk of the load that's left on board is directly on top of the sandbar. If we can shift it to the empty side of the hold and off of the sandbar, we may be able to save ourselves a lot of back-and-forth time on the flatboat. Understand?"

Jesse nodded his head.

Leaning closer to him, Phyfe whispered, "See, we're getting paid a flat deal for this. So the faster we get it done, the better. Right?"

Jesse nodded again.

"As many crewmen as you can find," Phyfe emphasized.

"You can count on me," Jesse said.

"I knew I could."

With all the urgency of a man on a federal mission, Jesse rounded up crew members. For the most part they came willingly. More than anything they wanted to get the steamboat off the sandbar and back on course so that their schedule and duties could return to normal.

Like an army commander, Jesse set about to fulfill his superior officer's orders. He informed the workers of their task and organized them into fire lines; only instead of passing buckets of water, they passed sacks of sugar from one to the other. This made the task more efficient, eliminating the wasted time it would have taken each worker walking back empty-handed to get another sack. Jesse himself commanded the head of one of the lines, giving encouragement and verbal praise to his workers.

After nearly a half hour, the bulk of the sacks were moved from the center of the boat to the stern. All of a sudden, the boat shifted. It slipped on the bar. A cheer arose within the hold.

But no sooner had the echo of the cheer faded when a crewman from on deck bounded into the hold. He was rubbing his wrists and shouting, "We've been robbed! We've been robbed!"

The crew of the *Liberty Belle* jammed the steps leading to the deck. By the time Jesse got on deck, all the crew members were leaning on the railing looking toward shore. Phyfe, Bulfinch, Fritz, Mills, and other men were loading the last of the sugar sacks onto a wagon. Phyfe hopped on back of the wagon just as it was pulling away. The deserted flatboat bobbed happily beside the shore.

Jesse caught Phyfe's eye. The captain of the flatboat punched Bulfinch in the arm and pointed to Jesse. They both laughed and waved. Phyfe cupped his hands around his mouth. "I knew I could count on you!" he shouted. Then as an afterthought, he added, "Edwards said you worked good for him, so he passed you along to me. Next time I see him, I'll give him your regards!"

The wagon loaded with sugar disappeared behind a tuft of trees.

"Seize him! He's one of them!" the captain of the steamboat shouted.

More hands than Jesse could count came down upon him. They held him in place while the captain flew into a rage. "Where have you men been?" he bellowed.

One of the crew members told him about the work below deck.

"Well, while all of you were playing games in the hold, those vultures robbed us blind. They jumped the wheelhouse crew and put a gun to my head. Then they stole everything that wasn't tied down."

"They get into the safe, Captain?"

"They held a gun to my head!" the captain bellowed.

No wonder Phyfe didn't want the money upfront, Jesse

thought. *He knew he was going to take it all anyway!*

"The boat's ready to go, Captain," one crewman said. "We felt it slip. Why don't we just go after them? The road hugs the shoreline between here and…"

"They shut down the boiler," the captain said.

"Shut it down completely?"

"Completely."

A pall fell over the crewmen. Their hold on the sandbar, once a hindrance, was now an anchor. That is, if it continued to hold. They'd already felt the boat slip. And without power, they would be at the mercy of the river.

Several of the men scrambled toward the boiler at the captain's unspoken command. *Get that boiler going. We need steam if we're going to survive.* To the rest of the crew he shouted, "Get to your duty stations!" Looking at Jesse, he said, "Bring this boy to my cabin!"

All of the man's rage was concentrated into one hateful glare at Jesse—his fury over landing on the sandbar in the first place, of being taken in by a con man, and the humiliation of facing his crew as well as the abuse he knew would inevitably come when he retrieved his passengers from the tavern. And Jesse was the only outlet for his anger.

"But, Captain," Jesse cried. "I'm as much of a victim as you!"

"Take him to my cabin!"

The captain looked like a boiler about to explode. Jesse knew there would be no reasoning with the man. He was going to suffer the full punishment for Phyfe's carefully planned and executed robbery.

He was jerked so hard he felt something snap in his neck. Like spilled coffee sopped up by a cloth, so the pain spread up and down his neck. There was a man on each arm with a third man trailing behind as he was led down the passageway on the river side of the boat.

Jesse's head was swimming from the abrupt change of circumstances. The Good Samaritans were vultures all along. And he was a fool for believing anything the smooth-talking Phyfe said. Twice now he'd been played for a fool.

And I play the part so well!

But this was not the time to feel sorry for himself. If he remained onboard he was doomed for sure. No one would believe that he had no knowledge of the robbery. His only chance was to escape. But how? It was three against one.

His only chance was surprise. Sudden. Unexpected. But how do you do the unexpected when that's exactly what they're expecting? And what could he use? There were doors to cabins on his left. Railing and posts on the river side. They're expecting him to try to pull away. But what about...? It was his only chance. A sudden reversal.

He counted the steps from post to post. One. Two. Three. Four. Five. Post. He counted again. One. Two. Three. Four. Five. Post.

It was now or never.

One. Two. Three. Four...

Jesse leaned back into his captors. They gripped him tighter, just like he wanted. Lifting his left leg, he coiled it against the post and pushed off with all his might. Like a bowling ball striking pins, the four of them crashed to the deck. The crewman who was trailing took the weight of all three men in front of him. He groaned as the weight of three grown men forced the air from his lungs.

Unexpected. It had worked. But the unexpected doesn't last long. Jesse scrambled to get up. One of the crewmen recovered quickly enough to grab him by the ankle. Jesse tried to shake him off. The other crewman shook his head, his senses returning. In a moment, he too would be grabbing at Jesse.

Gripping the post, Jesse slammed his free foot down on the crewman's wrist. The man screamed. The fingers that were gripping Jesse's ankle opened like a sprung lock. The other crewman lunged for the same ankle. Jesse was able to pull it out of reach.

He pulled himself onto the railing and looked down at the river.

He hesitated.

From behind, a hand grabbed his waistband. Jesse turned and tried to swat it away, but the hand wouldn't let go. The second crewman grabbed his arm. They were too much for him, pulling him back to the deck side of the railing.

Holding onto the post with one hand, being pulled back with the other with his waistband cutting into his stomach, Jesse aligned his feet on the railing. With all the strength his legs could muster, he shoved off.

The hands couldn't hold him. He was free!

Free from the crewmen. Free from the railing. Free from the boat. Free from everything, except gravity. It was a strange sensation for him. He twisted around as he fell and saw the two crewmen reaching over the railing empty-handed. They grew smaller as he fell away. Beside him, falling at the same rate, was *Danger at Deadwood,* the novel his aunt had autographed.

Splash!

His head and neck took the brunt of the impact. There was a flash of light, then everything went dark. Dark and liquid. He remembered the floating sensation. And he remembered trying to breathe, to breathe the dark air. It filled his lungs. Now it was dark inside of him as well as without.

Voices penetrated his darkness. He no longer was floating. But his arms raised without him making any effort to raise them. First one, then the other.

"He looks dead."

"I don't think so, dear. I saw his eye twitch."

"You can't lift him by yourself. Let me help you."

The sensation of weight was coming back to him. And

there was another sensation with it—a gritty feeling in his mouth, covering his tongue. He tried to move it, to say something. But he didn't know what to say. His head lolled to one side. There was nothing he could do but let it loll. He was being moved, rather clumsily.

"Careful, dear. Grab the cap as well. It might be his."

Now he knew how a sack of sugar felt. Lifted. Carried. Plopped down on a wooden surface. Then the surface jolted and moved and bumped.

Then the voices came again.

"Oh, J.D., he looks so young."

Chapter 17

THE blackness thinned. No longer was it thick, liquid, and suffocating. He could inhale it now and it didn't burn his lungs. But only sips at a time. Too much at once set him to coughing, convulsive coughs that folded him over until his knees touched his nose. When that happened the hands came again. On his back and shoulders. They pulled on him. Held him down.

Got to fight them. Push them away. Can't be caught. They'll never believe you. Never believe.

Sometimes the voices returned in the interlude between coughing fits. Not the hands though, just the voices. But they made no sense.

"Second time for that stretch of sand. Almost lost a brother there."

"I remember. I've never seen you run so fast. You took off down that ridge like your pants were on fire."

"All I could think about was how angry Father would be if he drowned."

"He looks a little like your brother, don't you think?"

"Hair's too light."

"Look at his mouth. The structure of his chin."

"Slight resemblance."

"He seems to be calming down now."

"Let's let him get some rest."

"Are the ladies praying?"

"At church. I'm headed there now."

"Like some tea before you go?"

"Who would have thought you'd make such a thoughtful wife?"

"Not me, that's for sure."

Icy black fingers touched his spine. Like icicles they jabbed his arms and legs and feet, chilling his flesh deep to the bone. He shivered so hard it hurt. Curling up into a ball didn't help. Legs running didn't help. His head ached horribly, like a spike was wedged in the base of his skull splitting it in two. The shivering didn't help. It rattled his teeth and jaw, making the pain in his head worse. Then, when he thought it couldn't get worse, every time he moved his head the spike acted like a lightning rod for pain, grabbing bolts from the sky, redirecting them into his brain.

"Poor dear! He needs more blankets."

"I'll see if I can find some more."

The voices had returned; they brought the hands with them. Grabbing his shoulders. Turning him. Holding him down.

"These are all we had in the chest."

"Help me cover him."

Jesse fought to open his eyes. To see his captors.

Can't let them capture you. They'll never believe you. Get away! Get away!

"I think he's coming around!"

"Son? Son? Can you hear me?"

Each attempt Jesse made to open his eyes summoned additional bolts of pain. Still, he kept trying. Had to know who was holding him down.

"He's not shivering as much."

"Thank God for that."

Needles of light jabbed his eyes. Mingled among them

were two shadowy figures. Heads. Close together. Bending over him. They were dark. Blurry. Hard to make out their features. It was too painful. He had to close his eyes.

He rested, then tried again. This time features were added to the faces. Two people. A man and a woman. Both smiling. He had a mustache and thinning hair. She was blond. Happy eyes.

"Can you hear me, son?" he asked.

Son. The word confused Jesse. Son. Was he dead? He'd heard of a shadowy afterlife. Hades. The realm of shades. Was this it? He tried to speak. His mouth was a solid mass with no moving parts.

"Son, can you hear me?"

Jesse broke his tongue free. He pulled his lips apart. From deep within he summoned a gasp of breath, enough to utter a single word: "Father?"

"No...no, I'm not your father. We found you at the edge of the river. You've swallowed a lot of water. But the doct...you will...take time to...rush...as you want... home is..."

The blackness fought to reclaim him. It lapped the edges of his consciousness like waves on the shore. Each wave created a gap in what he heard. Jesse fought to hold it back. To hear.

"...your name, son? What's ...na...?"

Hold on just a moment longer, Jesse thought. *Fight...it...back.* He tried to form his name with his tongue and lips. The J sound was proving to be most difficult. "...ess..., ...esse."

"Your name begins with the letter S?"

"...ess...esseeee."

"I think he's trying to spell something!"

"You may be right. It sounded like S...E..."

Jesse tried to shake his head. A bolt of pain stopped him before he managed even half a shake. He worked his lips and tongue to loosen them. He tried again. "Zhh...Zhh..."

"Are you getting that?"

"No, are you?"

"Zhh...zhh...Je...Jess...Jess...eeee."

"I think he's saying Jesse!"

"You're right! Son, is your name Jesse?"

Jesse managed a half smile. Then the darkness carried him away.

Birdsong woke him. Outside the window a trio of cardinals chirped and chattered and squabbled. Jesse stirred. His insides felt like they were coated with sandpaper. Eyelids scraped open. A parched tongue rubbed roughly against moisture-barren cheeks and lips. His headache was nearly gone, although the numbing aftereffect was just as debilitating. He lifted his head. The room swayed and rocked. Was he back aboard the steamboat?

He sat up. Striped wallpaper surrounded him. A bureau with a mirror lay just beyond the foot of the bed. To his right there was a window. A large one with a wooden frame. That's where the sound of birds was coming from—tree limbs, and beyond the tree limbs a grassy field and a dirt road.

I'm not on the steamboat.

Peeling back the covers, he swung his feet over the edge of the bed. They touched down on a cold wooden floor. He inched forward slowly—because that's the only speed he could manage at the moment—and shifted his weight to his feet. He tried to stand. A flash of nausea swept through his head and he collapsed backward onto the bed.

His pulse raced. He was breathing like he'd just run a good mile. It was amazing to him how such a little thing like standing required such a great effort. He tried again. This time he kept one hand on the side of the bed as an anchor. Nausea flashed again. He steadied himself, leaning heavily on the bed. The wave passed and he was still standing.

Stand—that's all he did for a full minute. That's all he could do. Once his breathing and pulse slowed, he shuffled one foot forward, then the other, until he managed to make his way to the window. Propping himself up with his forearm against the frame, he tried to determine where he was.

He was on the ground floor of a house. Everything outside was dusted with the first light of dawn. He could see the Ohio River just beyond a ridge on the far side of the dirt road. What was it Phyfe had said to the captain of the steamboat? There was a town nearby. The passengers were carted there to get them out of the way.

Out of Phyfe's way so he could rob the boat.

By now the townspeople knew all about the robbery. They undoubtedly had also heard about the one robber who was caught and managed to escape. A description would have been circulated. The whole town would be looking for him.

I have to get out of here.

Jesse found his clothes draped across a chair next to the bed. His cap lay nearby. He was weak; his hands shook from the exertion. The sudden physical activity also caused the pounding in his head to resume. But at least all of his body parts seemed to be working. As badly as he felt right now, he was going to need all of them just to get away.

To his relief, the window slid open noiselessly. The morning chill slapped his sensitive skin. Sitting on the sill, he swung his legs outside. A moment later he was weaving an uncertain path across the field toward the dirt road.

Sarah yawned and stretched. This was her favorite time of morning. The freshness of a new day. The rosy glow in the sky. As much as she loved her life on a Virginia plantation with Daniel, a part of her was still here in Ohio. In this room. At this desk.

She stood over the small writing table placed beside the window. It was here as a young girl she sat and looked out the window and dreamed of being a famous writer. It was at this desk that she wrote the initial draft of her first manuscript. More than a few love letters to Daniel were penned at this desk too.

A grin formed on her lips, one that warmed her heart. Funny how she could smile about that day now. At the time the events occurred, she thought her life was ending.

The day she remembered was unforgettable for several reasons. The Coopers were visiting them. That meant she got to see Daniel again following a long absence. Pre-Civil War tensions had interrupted what had previously been an annual gathering of the two families. But for one week the Southern Coopers and Northern Morgans agreed to forget their sectional differences.

Everything was going well until Seth Cooper, Daniel's father, learned that the Morgan boys were running slaves during their stay. One of the skiffs Marshall and Willy used to transport the slaves across the Ohio River had fallen apart. Marshall nearly drowned. J.D. saw the accident from the ridge near the house and he, Daniel, and Willy managed to rescue Marshall.

When Daniel's father learned that his son had been pulled into a slave-running effort—even though it meant saving Marshall's life—he was livid. The Coopers departed for home within the hour. It was at this desk by the window that Sarah watched her beloved Daniel go. She thought her heart would break as she penned a letter to him, not knowing if she would ever see him again.

Sarah's grin broadened into a full smile. Who could have foreseen how wonderfully things worked out for her? Now, years later, she had the twin desires of her heart—her beloved Daniel and the opportunity to write. There was no other way to explain it than a testimony of God's grace.

As she stood by her old writing table, an odd thought occurred to her. Now that her parents were gone and J.D. and Jenny lived in the house, did they keep the table by the window all the time, or did they place it here just for her visit?

An outside movement caught her eye. Beyond the window in the field below she saw a lanky boy with a cap cross the field on uncertain legs. It was more than a walk, but slower than a run. At first she thought he might have been up to some mischief. But he carried nothing in his hands. And other than the fact that he was hurrying, there was nothing suspicious about him—he didn't glance over his shoulder repeatedly. Probably just a young boy taking a shortcut.

But there was something about him that disturbed her. The way he moved. His long legs, gangly arms. His clothes. That cap.

Jesse.

That's who the lad reminded her of. She watched him as he crossed the dirt road, stumbled over the ridge, and then— after hesitating a bit to negotiate the slope—disappeared over the side.

She shook her head and thought it strange how a person can mistake the back of a stranger for someone they know. Had she seen the boy's face, she probably would have laughed at the absurdity of mistaking him for Jesse.

Drawing the curtain, Sarah dressed for breakfast.

"Good morning, dear! Welcome home."

Jenny turned from the hot stove from which emanated odors of fresh coffee, frying sausage, and eggs. She wiped her hands on her apron and opened her arms wide. Sarah smiled and stepped into them. In her estimation, the wisest thing her brother J.D. ever did in his life was to marry Jenny Parsons.

"You came in so late last night," Jenny said, "I didn't get a chance to greet you adequately."

"It feels good to be home," Sarah said, closing her eyes to savor the embrace.

After the two women took a good look at each other, Jenny

turned her attention back to the stove. She rolled the sausages over and turned the eggs.

"How did you sleep, back in your old room again?" she asked. "Have you missed your bed?"

Sarah laughed. "It's amazing how much smaller the bed is now. It must have shrunk."

Jenny laughed with her. Then, noticing the book Sarah had placed on the table, she said, "I haven't seen that since our wedding day."

Sarah lay her hand on the book—the Morgan family Bible. "It gave me the excuse I needed to come back to Point Providence."

"Sarah Cooper! You may be a famous writer and all, but you never need an excuse to come home."

Sarah grinned at Jenny's chiding. "Poor choice of words," the writer said.

An uneven thumping sounded down the stairs.

"Sounds like the master of the house is up," Jenny said.

As if on cue, J.D. Morgan entered the kitchen, walking with the aid of a cane. A wooden leg had replaced the one he lost at the Battle of Fredericksburg. It was an inadequate replacement. He required the use of a cane to get around.

"The boy's not in his room," J.D. said. "Is he down here?"

Jenny turned from the stove, concerned. "He's not down here," she said.

"Boy?" Sarah asked.

J.D. and Jenny had no children. His war wound made that impossible. It was this inability to sire a Morgan heir that had prompted his father to present the family Bible to Benjamin Morgan. One of the responsibilities of the keeper of the Bible was to pass it along to the next generation of Morgans.

"We found him nearly drowned along that flat section that's used as a landing," J.D. said. "You know, the place where Marshall almost drowned."

"I was just thinking about that this morning," Sarah reflected. "I was standing by the window…"

"Did you look outside for him?" Jenny asked. "Maybe he's using the…"

"I looked there," J.D. said.

"Is he a local boy?" Sarah asked. "I saw a boy crossing the field this morning. He went down to the river. Had I only known…"

Jenny walked over and placed a hand on Sarah's shoulder. "There's no way you could have known, dear," she said.

"If he's local, maybe he was just going home," Sarah offered.

"Could be," J.D. mused. "Still, it wouldn't hurt to look around for him."

While Jenny removed things from the stove, Sarah said to J.D., "I want to help you look for him."

"That really isn't necessary," J.D. replied. "If he's well enough to move about, he's not too bad off. Why don't you and Jenny stay here and have breakfast. I'll take a look around."

"Nonsense. I want to help," Sarah said.

"We'll all go," Jenny said, taking off her apron.

"What can I say?" J.D. laughed. "I'm outvoted!"

Delaying long enough to get light sweaters, the three of them stepped into the early morning chill. "You said he went down to the river?" J.D. asked.

Sarah pointed to the spot.

"Well, let's start there," J.D. said. "Then, if necessary, we can split up."

"What did you say the boy's name is?" Sarah asked, walking toward the ridge.

"Jesse," Jenny replied.

The name brought Sarah to an abrupt halt. She wouldn't have stopped any quicker had she run into a brick wall. And the wall probably would not have stunned her as much as the name.

"What's wrong, dear?" Jenny cried.

Instantly J.D. was at his sister's side, holding her arm lest she fall.

"No," Sarah said. "It's just coincidence."

"What? What's coincidence, dear?"

"When I saw the boy crossing the field..."

"Yes?"

"...for a moment I thought...well, it just struck me, the similarities and all, and I just thought..."

"Thought what? Sarah, you're frightening me!" Jenny cried.

"I'm sorry," Sarah said. "It's probably my writer's imagination going wild, but I thought the boy looked a lot like our Jesse."

"Ben's Jesse?" J.D. cried. "From New York?"

"Crazy, isn't it?" Sarah said sheepishly. She was regaining her composure. "After all, how many Jesses are there between here and there?"

"Some coincidence," J.D. admitted. He released Sarah's arm and turned toward the river.

"Maybe not," Jenny said. "Remember last night? When I thought he looked like Ben..."

"This is too much!" J.D. cried. "I know Clara has kept her distance from us since Ben's death, but surely she would have told us if Jesse was coming to Ohio."

"*If* she knew he was coming," Jenny said.

"What does that mean?" J.D. wondered aloud.

"I don't know," Jenny said. "It's just a feeling. Let's see if we can find him."

They searched the ridge and along the river all the way to the landing where they'd found him. Then they searched the house and its vicinity again. When they found no trace of him, J.D. rode into town to see if he was there and ask around. He returned shortly before lunch.

J.D., Jenny, and Sarah stood on the ridge overlooking the river.

"It probably wasn't him," Sarah said. "But just in case, I'm going to send a telegram to Clara."

"What are you going to say?" J.D. asked.

"I don't know. But I'm a writer, I'll think of something."

Jenny said, "I can't explain it, but for some reason I can't shake the feeling that it was our Jesse. The way he looked on the bed. He reminded me of Ben."

J.D. took Jenny and Sarah by the hands. "Whether it was our Jesse or not, I think it would be a good idea to pray for him."

As the Ohio River flowed past them on its ancient course, J.D. Morgan prayed to the God of the Ages to watch over and protect both Jesses, should they indeed be two people, and to fill their Jesse with wisdom and strength wherever he might be.

Chapter 18

FOR two days Cincinnati's hills provided cover and a place for Jesse to recuperate while he waited for the *Liberty Belle* to continue her journey. Not wanting to risk being seen on the docks by her captain or crew, Jesse did odd jobs on nearby farms for food during the day and slept out in the open at night. At the end of each day, under cover of darkness, he ventured to the docks and, from a discreet distance, checked to see if the *Liberty Belle* was still there. On the second evening, to his delight, she was gone.

Early on the third morning he was at the docks looking for a job aboard a steamboat headed for St. Louis. He asked around and learned that there were two steamboats with St. Louis as their destinations—the *Tippecanoe* and the *Eagle*. On this particular morning, the *Tippecanoe* was loading cargo.

Jesse didn't have to ask around to find the captain. Everybody on the docks knew exactly where he was. They also knew every single word he was saying. Even though his nose was inches away from the nose of the dock foreman, his voice was loud enough to carry halfway into town.

"Eight o'clock sharp!" the captain thundered.

"Impossible!" the dock foreman yelled back. "I don't have the men to get you underway by then."

"Why don't you?"

"Because yesterday you told me you would depart at ten

o'clock. I can have you loaded by then."

"Well, now I'm telling you eight o'clock!"

"And I'm telling you that's impossible!" the dock foreman thundered back.

"Then hire some more men!" the captain boomed.

"I could never round them up in time!"

Jesse saw his opening. He took it. "I can help load. I'm looking for work."

"See! Here's one more worker already! You're just not trying, Jonathan!" the captain cried. Leaning closer and speaking more discreetly, the captain added, "If I didn't know you better, I might suspect that you took money from Marsh to do this to me."

The dock foreman was stunned to the point of stammering. "Captain Lakanal, I resent that remark!"

"Then get my boat loaded by eight o'clock!" Considering the matter settled, the captain turned toward the gangplank of the *Tippecanoe*. Jesse followed after him.

"Captain!" he cried.

The captain turned around. He was a handsome man in his mid-fifties with a neatly trimmed, full white beard and mustache. Deep-set eyes and bronze, leathery skin gave testimony to a lifetime of standing in the sun and reading rivers in much the same way palm readers study the lines on one's hand.

The captain turned back. "What?"

"I want to go to St. Louis."

"Buy a ticket."

"No, you don't understand. I don't have any money. I want to work my way to St. Louis. I want to be a part of your crew."

The captain turned seasoned eyes on him. The same eyes that scrutinized rivers for potential danger examined Jesse for the same reason. "What can you do?" the captain asked.

"Anything you want me to do. I'm a hard worker."

"I mean, what skills do you have that are useful on a steamboat?"

Steamboat skills. He didn't want to mention Brownsville, or anything about the flatboat. "I've chopped a lot of wood," he stammered.

"Bah! You're wasting my time!"

"Wait, Captain, please. I admit I don't have any riverboat experience. In New York I was an office boy, and since then I've..."

"Office boy?"

Jesse's eyes brightened. "Yessir. At Ruger's Glassworks Factory."

"I lost my cabin boy," the captain said.

"I could be your cabin boy!" Jesse cried.

The captain looked at him like he was crazy. "You're too old to be a cabin boy!"

"Then, call me your assistant or personal servant or slave. And I don't expect any pay. All I need is food and a place to sleep."

Deep eyes narrowed as the captain focused on Jesse. He held up an index finger for emphasis. "I only say things once," he said. "And I expect every order to be carried out without question."

"Yessir," Jesse said.

"I need someone who can get things done. I can't be following you around making sure you've done your job right."

"No, sir. There will be no need for that."

"I'll tell you what," the captain said. "You help load that cargo. If we can depart by eight o'clock, you've got yourself passage to St. Louis."

"Yessir!" Jesse beamed. Without wasting a second, he turned and ran toward where they were loading sacks and wooden crates aboard the *Tippecanoe*.

Jesse's eagerness to get aboard the *Tippecanoe* nearly killed him. With his passage aboard ship riding on the quickness with which the steamboat was loaded, he launched into hauling cargo with complete disregard for his recent bout with drowning. It didn't take long before he was dripping with sweat and he could barely lift his arms. Still, he pressed forward—while urging on everyone else around him. He was determined to beat the eight o'clock deadline.

When the last load was being lifted by the forward derrick, Jesse called out for the time. Five minutes after nine o'clock. Jesse's heart sank. He had feared it was after eight o'clock, but he was hoping that they were only ten or fifteen minutes late. But more than an hour?

Jesse stood on the dock and stared at the steamboat. He'd tried his best. It just wasn't enough. There just were not enough dockhands. The captain was expecting the impossible. Standing on the dock Jesse felt like one of the limp sacks of grain he'd been toting all morning. He was surprised he didn't feel more disappointed. But there wasn't enough energy left in him to feel anything.

Get some rest and try the Eagle, he told himself. *After all, it's barely mid-morning. Maybe you can have better luck with her captain.* He hoped the captain of the *Eagle* didn't have a dockfull of goods to load.

Still, he just stood there. His body refused to listen to any commands to move. It had worked hard to get on board the *Tippecanoe;* and it wasn't going to leave the dock without one more effort. Somehow his legs found enough strength to carry him to the gangplank.

Jesse told the smug crewman at the head of the gangplank that he had been ordered to report to the captain. The crewman looked at the sweat rings under Jesse's arms.

"I suppose the captain has invited you to share tea with him in the stateroom before we depart," the thin-lipped crewman drawled sarcastically.

It took him several minutes of verbal thrust and parry with the drawling crewman, but Jesse wouldn't go away and the crewman had little choice but to look into the matter. With strained civility he escorted Jesse personally to the wheelhouse. Jesse didn't even want to think what the return trip with this crewman would be like should the captain turn him away.

As they approached the wheelhouse, through the glass Jesse could see the captain and his pilot. They were bending over a map. The captain was speaking. With the opening of the wheelhouse door, Captain Lakanal's bass voice said something about the Falls of the Ohio near Louisville. Cut off midsentence, he glared at the interrupters.

The crewman escort began, "Captain, this man said that you..."

Jesse interjected, "Captain, I know you told me..."

"Where have you been?" the captain interrupted Jesse. "Here! Take this message to the engineer. Wait for a reply." He lifted the corner of the map, shuffled a few papers until he found the one he was looking for, and handed it to Jesse. "What are you dawdling for? You should be halfway there by now!"

"Yessir!" Jesse said, grinning at the captain who was no longer looking at him. His grin widened as he looked at his escort, a small but significant vindication.

"Just a minute!" the captain shouted.

The crewman, sensing a reversal, grabbed Jesse's arm to keep him from running away.

"What's your name?" the captain asked.

"Jesse Morgan, sir."

"Well, get to it, Morgan!"

At precisely ten o'clock the *Tippecanoe* whistled its departure and cast off. Right on schedule, as always. This was Captain "Punctual" Lakanal's riverboat legacy. His nickname, pronounced "Punk-choo-AL" to rhyme with his French surname, reflected his reputation of prompt arrivals and departures. The son of French-Canadian parents, Lakanal was a throwback to the glory days of the steamboat when captains were treated like kings and the river was their kingdom.

Jesse soon learned the secret to the captain's punctuality. When it came to time, the captain always demanded the impossible. As in the case of the dock loading, he knew it was impossible to have the boat loaded by eight o'clock; but by demanding that it be completed by eight, he was assured that it would be done in plenty of time for him to keep his schedule of a ten o'clock departure. And it was. He had nearly an hour following the loading before he sailed. On the other hand, had he told the dock foreman that he needed the boat loaded for a ten o'clock departure, the foreman would have aimed at a ten o'clock deadline, and probably missed it, causing a delay in his departure.

And on those rare occasions when the impossible was somehow made possible, Lakanal would leisurely wait until time caught up with them. Never early. Never late. He was Captain "Punctual" Lakanal.

There was an element of nostalgia for Jesse about the captain's time expectations. Especially when he yelled, "What took you so long?" Memories of the thin bespectacled office manager with his white shirt and red suspenders flashed in his mind. That made him think of his position at Ruger's Glassworks, home, his mother, and Emily. The strength of the tug these memories had on his heart surprised him. It was amazing how at the time those things were commonplace and boring. Now, miles and months distant, Hester Street and his life on the lower east side brought a lump of emotion to his throat.

Jesse logged several weary miles his first day aboard the *Tippecanoe*. By the end of the day he had almost covered every inch of the boat running messages and errands for the captain. His accommodations—pointed out by a steward in passing—proved to be little more than a closet with a hammock. Somehow, it didn't matter. He doubted he'd be spending much time there anyway.

When the captain learned he had no clothing other than what he was wearing, he was instructed to sort through the unclaimed belongings that had been left on board by previous passengers. He found several quality shirts and pairs of pants that fit him, as well as a good pair of shoes.

Jesse had once heard a Bible story about a day when the sun stood still. This felt like one of those days. It was exceedingly long, which shouldn't have come as a surprise to him considering he was exhausted before he came on board. By evening, Jesse could barely function. And just when he thought he'd completed his last task for the day and was heading mindlessly toward his hammock, a crewman shouted out to him. The captain wanted to see him in his quarters immediately.

Shuffling down the passageway, Jesse was so tired he didn't notice the way the silver moonlight sparkled on the river and trimmed the silhouetted trees that graced the shoreline. He was too exhausted to feel the thrill of his first night aboard a floating palace as it glided downstream to the Mississippi and St. Louis. All these things were lost on him. He could think only of his hammock and how luxurious it would feel to be allowed to close his eyes.

He rapped on the captain's door and waited for a response. "Enter!"

Jesse stretched his eyes open with his fingers, hoping that he didn't look as tired as he felt. He swung open the door. In the next instant, his fatigue vanished. His eyelids no longer needed props. His arms and legs filled with new life. Gone were any thoughts of sleep. He felt like a new man.

"Morgan," the captain rose from his chair. "I'd like you to meet someone." Then, speaking to his guest who remained seated, he said, "This is the young man I was telling you about. He will assist you in whatever you need." Turning to Jesse again, he motioned to his guest with a gracious sweep of his hand. "Morgan," he said, "this is Miss Emily Barnes. She's a reporter for the New York *Evening Post.*"

Emily sat demurely with her hands folded in her lap. She wore an emerald green walking dress with long sleeves. From the sleeves, to the high neck, to the waist, to her ankles, it clung tightly to her body revealing a slender form. A matching hat decorated with small, colorful dried flowers sat elegantly atop her head, and was fastened there with a large black and white striped bow tied under her chin.

"Mr. Morgan," she greeted him. Her eyes sparkled for an instant. Then, she modestly glanced away.

"Miss Barnes," Jesse returned the greeting.

"You treat her with respect, Morgan," the captain growled. "She's interviewing me for a newspaper article and I don't want you to louse it up! Understand?"

"Yessir. Whatever you say."

Chapter 19

L IKE a lover's sigh the evening breeze whisked airily through the stray hairs that framed her pale temples. Her brown eyes, so discreet in the captain's cabin, now boldly embraced his gaze. The highlight on her nose and cheeks and lips and chin reminded Jesse of the last time he had seen her. There was a river that night too; the East River. Now, they met on the Ohio. Then, the soft light of the promenade's gas lamps caressed her face; tonight, it was the brilliant western moon.

While other things were similar, there was one constant. The way he felt inside when he looked at her. It was as though a devil moon had cast a spell over him. Everything about her enchanted him. The way the corners of her mouth curled up mischievously the instant before she broke into a full smile. The way the gentle softness of her skin resembled undisturbed drifts of new-fallen snow. The way her tongue and teeth moved in easy rhythm as one word, then another, and another waltzed effortlessly on her lips. He could watch her forever and never grow tired.

Jesse sat on the forward steps. Emily leaned on the banister that separated them. With the bulk of the ship behind them and only the gentle upward slope of the bow in front of them, it was easy to imagine they were sailing alone aboard a private yacht.

"I can't believe this!" Jesse said. He had smiled so much since leaving the captain's cabin with Emily that his grin ached.

"What can't you believe?" Emily asked. Her arms rested on the banister and her chin rested on her arms. From the way her eyes smiled, she was as happy to see him as he was to see her.

"This coincidence!" Jesse said. "You and me ending up on the same boat hundreds of miles from New York. You don't find that amazing?"

The corners of her mouth curled up mischievously. Then, like curtains parting, her lips pulled back to reveal perfect white teeth.

"What are you smiling about?" Jesse asked.

"Nothing." She was toying with him.

"Tell me!" Jesse pleaded.

She tilted her head so that her mouth rested on her forearm and looked at him through the tops of her eyes as though she was debating whether or not to tell him. She smiled again, a smile that pressed against her forearm.

Jesse leaned back against the next highest step, his arms folded. He was content to wait her out. It gave him a chance to look at her longer.

She lifted her lips from her arm. "What if..." she began, "...I were to tell you that it's not that big of a coincidence?"

"You don't think it's a coincidence that we should happen to bump into each other in Cincinnati?"

"Well, no...not when you know all the facts."

Jesse straightened up on the step, placed his palms on either side of him, and leaned toward her. "And just what are the facts?"

Emily smiled and pressed her lips to her arm again. She obviously knew something but was hesitant to tell him.

"If it makes you feel uncomfortable..."

She shook her head. "I have to tell you sometime."

"Well? What better time than now?"

Emily stared into his eyes. He loved it when she did that. "All right," she said, "here goes. I followed you out here."

That wasn't what he was expecting to hear. Jesse didn't know what he was expecting to hear, but he knew that wasn't it. "Followed me...no, you couldn't have! You expect me to believe that ever since I left New York you have been with me?"

"No, that's not how I did it. I used my investigative skills. I tracked you."

There was something about being tracked—even if it was by a beautiful woman—that disturbed him. Not wanting to admit that she had tracked him, he said, "Prove it."

"Prove it?"

"Yes, prove it. Tell me how you did it."

His challenging tone took some of the sparkle out of her eyes. Jesse was genuinely sorry for that. Nor did he like the uneasy feeling inside of him that was rapidly replacing the warm glow of romance. However, it wasn't his fault. His was a natural response. No matter how attractive, the prey rarely harbors warm feelings for the hunter.

"Well, when I hadn't seen you for a couple of days and another boy delivered the envelope from Ruger's Glassworks, I got concerned. So I started asking around and learned that you were missing."

"Who did you talk to?"

Emily frowned at his prosecutorial tone. "Mr. Sagean, for one."

"Did you talk to my mother?"

"No, I went to your tenement. She wasn't there. But I left her a note."

"What did the note say?"

Another frown. "There wasn't much I could say at the time and the paper I was writing on wasn't very big."

"What did the note say?"

"Jesse Morgan! You stop that this instant!"

So concerned was he about the content of the note, her outburst caught him by surprise. He was so focused on the note's possible impact on his mother, he became oblivious to everything else, including the fact that Emily was trying to help him. Her outburst snapped his narrow obsession and rudely pulled him back to present surroundings.

"Stop what?" he cried.

"This badgering! You're making me feel like I did something wrong!" Her eyes, that had just a few minutes earlier sparkled with the happiness of seeing him again, now glistened in the moonlight. She was on the verge of tears.

Jesse reached out tentatively and touched her arm. "I'm sorry," he said softly. "I'm...it's just that you don't know all the circumstances that led to my departure from New York. And...well...I'm rather sensitive about it."

Emily blinked back her tears. She sniffed once. "Do you want me to continue?"

"Please."

Another sniff, then, "In the note, I told your mother that I knew you had left and that I thought I knew where you were going."

"How did you know that?"

She shot him a warning glance. His hands went up in surrender.

"The night you left. I saw you walking toward the Hudson River. Heading west."

Jesse started to ask how she could have seen him heading west when he didn't actually begin his journey west for some time after they parted. At this point, he figured it didn't matter. So he said nothing.

"You had a couple of days headstart on me," Emily continued, "so I knew if I was going to find you I would need a lucky break. I took the same road you took and began asking people if they had seen you. I began to suspect that you had left the road completely when person after person said they had not seen you. And just when I was ready to reconsider the direction I was heading, I hit pay dirt."

"Pay dirt?"

Emily grinned. "In all those Western stories you read you've never heard the words 'pay dirt' before? It's a mining term that means you struck the mother lode. In this case, my mother lode was a talkative innkeeper by the name of..."

"Hans!" Jesse cried.

Emily smiled and nodded. "He recognized you by my description. He told me he sent you to Brownsville. So I hired a carriage and traveled there."

"Then you talked to Edwards..."

"Briefly. When I mentioned your name, he suddenly became uncooperative, even hostile. What did you do to him?"

"Ha! What did I do to him? It's what he did to me!" Jesse told her how Edwards tricked him into chopping wood.

"Luckily for me," Emily continued, "some of the other workers were more cooperative. They told me the last they saw you, you were headed for Pittsburgh by foot. Some of them remembered you saying something about Cincinnati and St. Louis. One man added that he thought he'd seen you aboard a flatboat with three other men. Although your mode of transportation was questionable, in general everyone agreed that you were following the river's course. So I did too."

Jesse wanted to tell her about Bulfinch and Phyfe and Fritz, but he didn't want to suspend her story for one of his own. He would tell her later.

"Well," Emily sighed, "Pittsburgh proved to be disappointing. No one along the waterfront remembered you. So I continued to Cincinnati, fully intending to go to St. Louis if necessary. But, as you know, that wasn't necessary. I spotted you this morning on the docks hauling wooden boxes onto the *Tippecanoe*."

Jesse gave an appreciative nod. "Your investigative skills are quite impressive, Miss Barnes."

"Why thank you, Mr. Morgan."

"So you're not here to do a story on Captain Lakanal for the New York *Evening Post* after all?"

"I'm here to do a story," Emily insisted. "Where do you think the money comes from for my travel? We working girls don't have rich fathers, you know."

Jesse smiled; he loved looking at her. Emily smiled too, but her smile faded after a moment.

"There's more," she said.

"I thought there would be. You told me how you managed to find me, but you didn't tell me why you did it. We've not known each other long, and I can't help but wonder why would a successful writer like yourself chase after me all this way."

"Chase after you?" Emily chuckled. "Why, Mr. Morgan, what a high opinion you have of yourself."

Jesse's face reddened. "That came out wrong," he said. "What I meant was, why did you do it? Why did you follow me?"

Emily's face sobered. "I know why you left home."

A rogue shiver skittered up Jesse's spine. *Impossible! She just thinks she knows. She couldn't know, could she? Yet she looks so confident. No, she couldn't know. She'll give a reason that's totally unrelated.* "So you think you know why I left?" Jesse said calmly, trying to mask his uneasiness. "All right, tell me. Why did I leave home?"

"Think? No. I *know* why you left."

Her confidence was unnerving. Jesse gestured openly. "Then tell me."

She stared at him with all seriousness, then lowered her eyes. Almost in a whisper, she said, "Little Jake."

Two words. Like bullets, they pierced Jesse's chest and penetrated his heart. The grief that he thought he'd left behind swept over him like a wave crashing over the bow. She knew! But how could she know? What did it matter? It hurt just the same.

"You think you killed him," Emily said softly.

Familiar pictures caught up with his grief, flooding his mind. Jake on the ledge. Jesse's own arm reaching out to him. Jake pleading for help. Something catching Jesse's foot. Stumbling. Falling into Jake. The boy's arms waving like windmills, waving...waving... but they couldn't pull him back to the ledge. The look on little Jake's face. Frightened. Afraid...afraid to die. A scream. Jake's scream. So young...so young. Then nothing. No sound. No Jake. Nothing but an empty night sky.

"It was my fault," Jesse said softly, his head bowed.

"Jesse, you just think you killed him," Emily said.

"I *did* kill him!"

"No you didn't!"

Jesse turned away from her. He shook his head. She didn't understand. He didn't want platitudes. He knew what happened. He went there to save Jake, but pushed him over the ledge instead. It was an accident. But it didn't change the fact that because of his clumsiness, a little boy was dead.

"Jake is alive!"

Jesse looked up at her. Confused. No, she's wrong. He didn't hear her right. Maybe she said, "I wish Jake was alive."

"Jesse, listen to me! Jake is alive!"

Why is she saying something that he knows is not true? She wasn't there. He saw Jake fall. He heard Jake scream!

"They played a practical joke on you!" Emily said. "They made you believe you killed Jake, but you didn't! Jake is alive!"

It was hard for Jesse to let go of his guilt. He had grown comfortable with it. He'd worn it so long and had convinced himself that he would wear it to his grave. To strip it off now seemed wrong. "You've seen him? Actually seen him?"

Emily nodded. "In the alley where we met. Finn was picking on him like he always does."

Her sincerity tugged on his guilt, trying to strip it from

him. Jesse wanted to believe her; he really did! But it was hard for him. If he could just see Jake for himself...then, he might be able to believe.

"How...how did you find out all of this?" Jesse asked.

Emily shrugged. "Let's just say I'm a good investigator and leave it at that."

Like a snake shedding skin, he felt the guilt being peeled away. The more he shed, the better it felt. "A practical joke, huh?"

Emily nodded. "A practical joke."

Jesse stood and walked slowly up the incline to the bow of the boat. He leaned against the derrick and watched the water go by. "A practical joke," he muttered.

Emily followed him. Standing a discreet distance from him, she clasped her hands and gave him the time he needed to acclimate himself to the truth.

"So I ran away from nothing," he said. "All of this...everything I've done from that day until now...all of it because of a practical joke. Boy, if Finn only knew. He and those two oafs of his would be howling."

Emily touched his arm. Her fingers were warm. Tender. "Forget them," she said. "You can go home now."

"Yes," he chuckled. "I guess I can."

The latch clicked softly behind her. Emily leaned against the door, her eyes closed, her heart pounding. While she waited, she began remembering everything that had happened today—the way her pulse quickened when she first caught sight of Jesse on the docks. It was the cap that grabbed her attention. His back was to her. He lifted a sack and tossed it over his shoulder, carried it to a pallet, flung it onto the stack of sacks to be lifted by the derrick, and then turned back for another one.

That was the moment she knew she'd found him! Even

though his feet shuffled when he didn't have a load on his back, there was no mistaking his gait. He looked tired, but it was Jesse. It was definitely Jesse! She had found him!

In her cabin aboard the steamboat, Emily's pulse raced with the memory the same way it did that moment on the docks. Getting on board the *Tippecanoe* was easy once she met the captain. She knew she had passage when she saw the way Lakanal strode toward her with his air of self-importance; the attention to detail he obviously paid to the trimming of his beard gave testimony to a man who thought himself handsome; the fact that shortly before departure he readily found time for a newspaper reporter—all these things attested to the man's vanity. Men like him embraced every opportunity to say something that might be quoted in a newspaper. While they usually disdained all human life but their own, they were always friendly to someone who had it within her power to see that the story of their success would appear in a major newspaper.

Emily grinned to herself when she remembered how once inside the captain's cabin she heard him send for Morgan. She shivered with excitement at the remembrance. It was too good. Too easy. The captain was actually summoning him into her presence!

Then the waiting. Oh, the horrible, agonizing eternity of waiting! All the while pretending to listen to the captain as he droned on and on about his boring life. Casting anxious glances at the doorway, knowing that at any moment Jesse would appear. The captain saying something that drew her attention back to him again. And again she acted like she was interested, yet in reality she was dying for the door to open and Jesse to step into the cabin.

What would his reaction be when he saw her? Would he be pleased? Surely, he would recognize her, wouldn't he? What if he didn't?

Then the knock came. He was so close! Just on the other

side of the door! Then the moment she'd dreamed about happened. The door opened. He saw her.

Emily sighed as she remembered their reunion. A giggle escaped her throat. The look on his face! Surprised. Then...pleased, more than pleased, happy to see her. She wanted to run to him. Instead, she folded her hands. She wanted to stare at him, but she knew if she did she would melt in her chair. All professionalism would be gone. The captain would suspect something. So she forced herself to glance away. She tried to act demure.

But the best...oh, the best was this last hour with Jesse on the stairs at the boat's bow. They were so close to each other. She could smell him...a scent she remembered from the bridge. Even now, when she closed her eyes, she could smell him! And the way he kept looking at her! He couldn't take his eyes off of her! Then...he reached out and touched her!

In the cabin, Emily's hand tenderly stroked the place on her arm where he'd touched her. Just a light touch, but it was warm. Tender. A deposit of more to come? Yes, she was sure of it! Someday he would hold her. Touch her. Kiss her.

Leaning against the cabin door, she listened for Jesse's footsteps outside on the passageway. They had faded away. All was silent. He was gone.

"Waaaaaaahoooooooo!" Emily squealed. She bounded across the room and jumped onto her bed. Grabbing her pillow, she hugged it tightly. Then, she began again remembering the first moment she realized it was Jesse on the docks.

"Tykas! What are you doing in Louisville?"

Richard Tykas ran a hand through his oily hair in the manner of a man who was self-conscious about his appearance. He extended his hand to the man who had hailed him and, with a straight face, relished the man's expression when he realized he was gripping a greasy palm and tried not to act disgusted.

Tykas was anything but self-conscious. His hand-in-the-hair handshake was a little game he liked to play.

"Warren! What a surprise!" he said. "You on official business?"

The man who had hailed him was young and impeccably dressed. Though his black hair was receding near his temples, he seemed to make up for the thinning line with bushy sideburns that extended all the way down his jaw then, at the chin, turned abruptly upward at the corners of his mouth, curving up and over his lips and meeting beneath his nose. In response to Tykas' question, Warren nodded in the affirmative. He was here on official business.

"The Austin girl?" Tykas asked.

"You know about that?" Warren looked surprised.

Tykas shrugged nonchalantly. "When you've been in the security business for as long as I have, word gets around." Then, grinning wryly, he said, "She's a long way from home this time."

"Not for long." Warren smiled confidently.

"Oh? So you've located her?"

"Hatch did. Spotted her in Cincinnati, but couldn't apprehend her." Warren chuckled. "He saw her aboard a steamboat just as it was pulling away from the docks. What could he do, start swimming? So, he telegraphed me."

Tykas imitated Warren's chuckle and shook his head in a similar manner. The veteran agent didn't do it to mimic the man, but to establish rapport. From years of observation he had learned that people feel more at ease with someone similar to them. And Tykas wanted Warren to feel at ease with him.

"I'd be willing to bet her father could be heard halfway to California when he learned she'd run away," he said.

"That's not what I heard," Warren replied. "The way it came down to me, after reading the girl's note, Austin calmly issued orders to find her and bring her back. Very businesslike. Just like he was managing one of his properties."

Tykas chuckled another Warren-like chuckle. "I worked for the man all these years and still don't understand the relationship he has with his family. Far be it from me ever to understand wealthy people." He studied the young agent a moment, then asked, "Do you think the young lady will go back willingly?"

"I don't know what to expect from her," Warren confessed. Then his eyes lit up as a thought came to him. "You've known the Austins longer than me," he said. "I've only seen her once. What kind of a person is she?"

Tykas folded his arms and grinned as one who was about to share a piece of knowledge that had been forged in the fires of experience. "She's a handful, that's for sure. Be prepared for anything."

Warren grimaced. "That's what I was afraid you'd say." He reflected on this information a moment, then changed the subject. "What about you? What are you doing these days? You know, most of us feel Austin was wrong in dismissing you."

Tykas shrugged. "The hazards of being in security these days," he said. "Austin really had no choice. It was either dismiss me or face a possible scandal."

"But there was no evidence! The charges were never proved! You would think he'd take your years of service into consideration."

"You would think..." Tykas echoed. He smiled, enjoying the young man's defense on his behalf.

Warren added, "It just makes it difficult for the rest of us to be loyal to a man who so readily dismisses a person with your record on the unproved accusations of one man."

"Another security officer," Tykas reminded him. He argued Austin's side of the issue knowing that Warren would come to his defense. Which he did.

"But Logan couldn't prove the charges! It was his word against yours!"

Tykas sighed a martyr's sigh. "The worst part of the whole thing is that Logan was my friend."

"Some friend!" Warren exclaimed sarcastically. "So what are you doing now?"

Tykas glanced around him, indicating that what he was about to say was not for public hearing. "Too many people," he said. "Step over here." Tykas stepped toward a double row of crates. The space between them would provide some privacy. Warren didn't follow immediately. He peered upriver. Tykas dug into his pocket and produced a watch. "You still have twenty minutes!" he cried. "It'll take just a moment. I don't want just anybody to hear this."

Warren pulled out his own watch and checked the time. He glanced about at the growing crowd of people. "All right," he conceded.

Tykas smiled and led him behind the crates. He knew Warren had interpreted his smile as that of a friend thanking him for his indulgence. He couldn't have been more wrong. Tykas' smile was the grin of a veteran who had just bested a beginner. When Warren agreed that he had twenty minutes to spare, he had confirmed to Tykas that Emily Austin was aboard the *Tippecanoe*—the only steamboat scheduled to arrive in twenty minutes.

With a hand gesture, Tykas invited the junior security agent to step into a closed-end hallway formed by the two parallel rows of crates stacked ten feet high. Even in the privacy the space afforded, Tykas leaned forward and spoke softly.

"I'm going to Illinois," he said.

"That's your secret?"

Tykas laughed. "No, the secret is one word—Christianopolis."

"Christianopolis?"

"The city of Christ," Tykas explained. "I'm going to build it." A sick look crossed Warren's face. Tykas had trapped him.

The elder agent's reputation was well-known among the other Austin agents. When it came to security, there was none better. When it came to religion, the consensus was that the man was crazy. Tykas had just crossed the line from business talk to crazy religion and Warren could do nothing about it. He was trapped.

Over the years the veteran agent had made no secret of the fact that he was a Putney Perfectionist, a follower of John Humphrey Noyes who founded the now defunct Oneida Community, a utopian society that believed all sin was cleansed at conversion, thus rendering Christians perfect. After nearly four decades, the utopian community was forced to dissolve following Noyes' failed endeavor to produce a superior spiritual generation through selective breeding.

"I know where Noyes went wrong!" Tykas said excitedly.

Warren's response was a deadpan expression of patronizing indifference.

"His millennial timetable was corrupt and his philosophical foundation too simplistic. These things will be corrected in New Oneida. I will build a community founded upon the principles commended by Plato, Lord Bacon, and Sir Thomas More, as well as the Bible! And, as you undoubtedly guessed, it will be erected in Illinois, not New York."

Warren looked at his watch.

"Think of it! A utopia—on earth as it is in heaven! Thousands of people will flock to this ideal community," he said. "And when the number reaches five thousand, the world will no longer be able to ignore us. All world leaders will finally be convinced by the example of our New Moral World. And then…oh, then we will invite Christ to return to earth to take His rightful place on earth's throne."

His eyes glazed, Warren stifled a yawn.

Tykas was not blind to the disinterested agent's symptoms. He concluded that the man's spiritual depth could be measured by the width of a hair. But Warren and his kind would someday be convinced. Their eyes would be opened. They would see the things Tykas could already see; they would understand what Tykas already understood. But that day was not now. And for his present purposes Tykas used a popular teaching technique to corral Warren's wandering interest.

"So when do you think all this will take place?" Tykas asked.

"Huh? Sorry...could you repeat what you just said?"

Smiling indulgently, Tykas asked again, "When do you think Christ will assume His rightful place and sit on the world's throne?"

"God alone knows!" Warren chuckled at his own cleverness.

Tykas plunged both hands in his pockets in a relaxed, if not condescending way. "Partially true. He knows, but He's also told me. Nineteen hundred. The turn of the century. It's less than a decade away."

Clearing his throat, Warren said, "Tykas, thanks for telling me what to expect with Emily. And best of luck on your new venture..."

Removing his left hand from the pocket, Tykas held it up in the manner of a police officer. "And who do you think will be funding this new community?" he asked.

Pursing his lips, Warren shook his head impatiently. "I really don't know. But I do know I have to be on my way."

"Austin."

The word pulled Warren up short, leaving his mouth partially open.

"Franklin Grant Austin." Tykas gave the man's full name for emphasis.

"You're joking!" Warren cried.

"Deadly serious."

A steam whistle could be heard in the distance. Both men cocked an ear to the sound.

"I wish I had time to explain it to you," Tykas said. "But

time is short. So I'll do something even better."

All Warren saw was the blur of a hand. The knife plunged into him before he could react. His knees buckled. His eyes turned heavenward.

Tykas caught him before he fell. A clamped hand over Warren's mouth kept him from crying out while he was dying. Laying Warren gently onto the wooden dock, Tykas whispered in his ear. "Like I said, time is short. I wish I had time to convince you to join us. For now, it's enough that you know Emily is the key to funding the community, and you're in my way. So I'm doing you this favor: I'm sending you straight to God. He will answer all your questions to your satisfaction."

Agent Warren took his last breaths as the *Tippecanoe* drew near the docks.

Tykas leaned closer and spoke intimately into the ear of the dying man. "I envy you, Warren. In just a few moments you will see God's glory—unparalleled glory the rest of us can only dream about."

After Warren breathed his last, Tykas lowered the dead agent onto the dock's wooden planks. He emptied the agent's pockets, including his credentials, money, and the telegram from Hatch informing him that Emily had been spotted boarding the *Tippecanoe*.

Stepping smartly from between the rows of crates, Richard Tykas joined the others who awaited the docking of the steamboat. He scanned the faces of the passengers that lined the railing, looking for Franklin Austin's daughter.

Chapter 20

PEACOCK proud, Captain Louis Lakanal escorted Emily from bow to stern regaling her with river stories about himself.

"Once, many years ago on the Missouri River, I was transporting a contingent of loud-talking mountain men who were headed toward the Rockies. While we were loading wood, and just as the gangplank was jammed with mountain men coming on board, a band of Sioux Indians attacked us. The Sioux charged the boat with rawhide whips, flailing at the helpless mountain men who were loaded down with all their baggage and gear. In the confusion, bundles of clothing and equipment flew every direction and mountain men tumbled all over themselves trying to get on deck."

Emily took notes while the captain talked. They strolled side-by-side along the upper deck; he with his hands clasped behind him, she with her head bent over a pad as she outlined his comments and captured what she considered to be key quotes. The *Tippecanoe* was docked. Deckhands loaded and unloaded crates. Some passengers departed while others came on board.

There was an occasional pause in the storytelling. While the captain's mind was back on the Missouri River with the Sioux Indians, his eyes oversaw the progress of his crew on the docks. Occasionally something would catch his attention and he would stop his story. Sometimes he would bark an order to a nearby deckhand who would scurry away to fulfill it; sometimes he would lean over the railing and shout at a worker on the dock directly; and sometimes he would pause, start to shout something, swallow his words, mutter something in French that, to Emily, sounded obscene, and then say to her, "Where was I?"

During these occasional pauses in the story, Emily would steal a glance herself at the deckhands below. Among them was Jesse. After telling him about the hoax that had been played on him by Finn, she had thought they would be getting off the boat at Louisville and returning to New York together. But Jesse said he wasn't sure he wanted to return. This was a setback she hadn't anticipated, so she improvised.

She said that to get the captain's story she would stay on board until they reached Cairo, the confluence of the Ohio and Mississippi Rivers. Then she would return to New York. She intimated that the return trip would be long and possibly dangerous for a young woman traveling alone and that she would appreciate his company if at all possible. Jesse agreed to make up his mind by the time the boat reached Cairo.

"Where was I?" Captain Lakanal asked.

"The Sioux were attacking the boat with whips while the mountain men were boarding," Emily replied.

"Ah, yes. Well, the commander of the mountain men ran to the plank and began shouting at his men and the Indians. He rallied enough of his men that the Indians saw they were outnumbered and retreated."

Lakanal stepped to the railing and shouted below, "No! NO! Watkins! WATKINS! Over there! OVER THERE!"

He stepped back and muttered, "Idiot! Now, where was I?"

But Emily didn't hear him. As usual she was taking advantage of the interruption to snatch a glimpse of Jesse. She couldn't spot him immediately and thought he might have moved below them on deck or into the hold. When she looked again, a passenger caught her attention. A man. Middle-aged. Dark, thin, slick hair. Plump cheeks. A stylish mustache and a patch of beard that looked like it was pasted to his chin. She had seen this man before! But where? The office? No, that didn't seem right. She couldn't remember and it disturbed her.

As the man boarded, he glanced at the upper deck. Emily stepped back from the railing so he couldn't see her. It was best to be safe until she could remember where she had seen him before.

"Miss Barnes?" the captain said.

"Oh...the Indians backed away," she replied.

"But they weren't finished yet!" he added with a twinkle in his eye. "We'd had similar incidents before and that was usually the end of the matter. So after watching them depart, I went down to the passenger's deck and sat and read while the rest of the mountain men boarded and the crew finished loading the wood. When, all of a sudden a volley of gunshot slammed into the side of the boat!"

He waited for her reaction and smiled when she expressed surprised shock.

"Yes, indeed! The Indians had come back! They were insulted that the commander had run them off. They killed one deckhand and managed to board the boat virtually unopposed; after all, they took us by surprise. Well, apparently they'd learned a few things by observing steamboats, because they seized buckets, opened the boat's fire doors, and flooded the banks of embers under our boilers!"

Another look of shock prompted another grin. Lakanal was enjoying himself, even more so knowing that his story was being recorded for print.

"Needless to say, my reading was rudely interrupted by the howls of the invaders, and I was showered with glass from the volley of shot."

"Were you hurt?"

"Minor cuts. It was nothing," the captain said with bravado.

Emily wrote down his quote which pleased the captain.

"I ran to the river side of the boat," he continued, "and while trying to make my way up to the wheelhouse, I came face-to-face with the savages. They had captured the commander of the mountain men. He interpreted their demands. 'They want the boat,' he said. 'They say they'll let the crew go if they get it. If not, they're going to kill everybody.'"

Emily was writing furiously. Lakanal waited for her to catch up with him. When she did, she looked up. "What did you do?" she asked.

"I noticed something odd about the behavior of the Indians. Apparently there were parts of the boat that were unfamiliar to them, because only a few of them—the ones that doused the boiler fire and who now held the commander—had pressed forward on the boat. The others huddled near the plank at the boat's middle. So I tried to think of how I might use that to my advantage.

"Then, I considered what weapons were available to me. Unfortunately, our brass cannon had been damaged and the weapon was in the engine room awaiting repair."

"Oh no!"

"Oh yes! But I took that apparent problem and turned it to my advantage. Under the pretense of ordering my crew from the boat, I leaped down to the engine space and quietly ordered my engineer to begin stuffing the cannon with powder. He had no shot, so we had to use a double handful of boiler rivets for our ammunition!"

Emily wrote that down.

"Then, we rigged a pulley and lifted the cannon up to the deck and maneuvered it so that it was pointing at the huddled Indians. I lit a cigar, puffed confidently on it, and lowered it toward the cannon. Then I told the commander to tell the Indians that if they did not get off my boat, I'd blow them all to pieces!"

The captain struck a chest-high pose as he related his heroics.

"Did it work?" Emily asked, then caught herself. "Well, of course it worked. You're here, aren't you?"

Lakanal laughed the laugh of the victorious. "Those savages fought one another to get off my boat. We swung the cannon around and kept it trained on the shore until we completed loading our wood."

"Good story!" Emily said as she recorded his last comments.

"That's not the end of it!" Lakanal said.

"Oh?"

He shook his head and grinned. "While I set about looking for my crew who had strangely enough vanished, I also looked for those brave mountaineers. Where had they hidden themselves during this attack, leaving my boat defenseless?"

He paused for effect.

"Guess where I found them?" he asked.

Emily shrugged and shook her head.

"On the paddles of the sternwheel! They were hanging all over the paddles. Thick as sardines! I was so disgusted with them that I threatened to set the wheel in motion and give them all a good dunking! And I would have too! Only, the Indians had put out the fire and I had no steam!"

Her pencil scratching feverishly, Emily said, "Great story, Captain! Great story!"

Lakanal nodded. He thought so too.

With the ship loaded and the passenger transfer complete, the captain busied himself with getting underway. So Emily busied herself by looking for Jesse.

She wandered by his cabin, but he wasn't there. So she strolled casually to the lower deck and circled the perimeter of the boat. She tried not to look like she was searching for someone. Her pace was aimless. She paused to examine a detail or two about the boat, or to gaze at the dock as they slowly slipped further away from it. But her mind and her eyes were sharply attuned to anything that might resemble Jesse.

Reaching the bow of the boat again, she was ascending the stairs to the upper deck when she saw him—not Jesse, the man with the black patch of beard on his chin. He was standing next to the railing and looking straight at her.

His was a steady gaze. Not the kind of glance where two strangers lock eyes for a moment, then look away. This was a bold stare. He didn't smile. He didn't nod or make any indication that he knew her, or even that he knew he was blatantly staring at her. He just stared.

His boldness stopped Emily mid-step. She had seen this man before. But where? The way he was looking at her made her shiver. She broke eye contact with him and hurried up the stairs. Even though she had stepped from his sight, the man's face haunted her. Where had she seen him before?

Father's study!

He was one of her father's agents! She remembered that he and another man had stepped from her father's study on the night she was caught sneaking back into the house! They were the ones arguing about the factory fire, the one that Emily had been investigating before she was dismissed at the office. Two people had died in that fire. A girl named Molly and Benjamin Morgan. Emily had not yet had the chance to ask Jesse if Benjamin Morgan was his father. Which raised a question. Was the man on the boat after her, or Jesse?

Or maybe he's not after anybody and you're just being paranoid, Emily said to herself.

But no matter what she said to herself, she could not escape the cold feeling that came over her when she thought of the man with the oily black hair. For the time being, she decided not to say anything to Jesse. How could she tell him about the man without admitting that she had run away from home and that her father was looking for her? She decided it was best just to wait and let the man make the first move. Once she knew what he was after, then she could plan a response.

Working her way toward Jesse's cabin again, an idea came to her. She began to formulate some way she could ask the captain about the man. Maybe he had some information that would be useful to her.

The captain proved to be unhelpful in the matter of the Austin agent's identity. Emily was careful to inquire about the agent without raising any suspicions. The last thing she wanted was for the captain to intervene on her behalf and confront the man. If that were to happen, the captain would quickly learn the truth about her—that she had run away and she was not an investigative reporter for the *Evening Post*.

On this latter point she was hopeful that her ruse would pay dividends. Although the *Post* had not sent her to interview the captain, she thought his story had the makings of an interesting article, one that she could sell to the newspaper.

Her working title was: "Louis Lakanal: The Last of a Dying Breed." Her angle for the article was to contrast the romance and nobility of steamboats over against their increasingly popular railroad competition. She would do this by portraying Captain Lakanal as something of a white knight on the rivers. She thought she would lead the article using a quote from one of Lakanal's favorite authors, a man who himself spent a good deal of his life on riverboats:

> *In order to be a pilot a man had to learn more than any man ought to be allowed to know. He must learn it all over again in a different way every twenty-four hours. —Mark Twain*

Following this opening quote she added, "The captains of these noble steamboats learned the fundamentals of their craft as lowly deckhands or cabin boys. They had to learn how to cope with Indians, unreliable machinery, and raucous crews as they guided their boats, according to one log entry, 'just a little beyond no place.'"

When she told the captain the angle she would use, he insisted he be allowed to read her opening. Emily knew she had scored a hit with him by the self-satisfied grin that creased his face as he read.

The mystery of the Austin agent remained a mystery for several days out of Louisville. This in itself was curious to Emily. She saw the man on several occasions, and each time he stared at her with purpose. Yet never once did he approach her.

One night, when the captain was preoccupied with things other than his life's story, and Jesse was detained by boat's business, she caught the agent staring at her across the large public passenger cabin. The cabin was the social gathering place for the passengers, furnished with a bar and private tables. It was lighted by an elegant crystal chandelier. Royal purple carpeting stretched from wall to wall. And large ferns added a touch of green against the mahogany paneled walls. One side of the room was lined with windows so the passengers could view the passing scenery as they drank, or conversed, or—as many of them did—gambled.

Emily had just entered the room when she spotted the Austin agent. He was leaning against the bar. He took note of her entrance and, like he always did, stared at her brazenly. Deciding it was better to know than not to know the man's purpose, and feeling safe with so many other passengers around, Emily concluded it was time to approach the man herself.

This time, instead of walking away from him, she stood at the entrance and returned his stare, hoping it would make him uncomfortable. It did not. He lifted his glass and drank without taking his eyes off her.

All right, Emily said to herself, *let's get it out in the open.*

She strode purposefully toward him without lowering her gaze. He watched her with unchanged expression. He neither grinned, nor frowned, nor sneered. Nothing. Undaunted, Emily continued walking toward him. He lifted his glass and finished his drink.

When she was within five feet of him, she raised her hand. With her index finger pointing at him, she was just about to say, "I want to know who you are and why you have been staring at me ever since you've come aboard!"

But the words never had a chance to leave her mouth.

The man set down his glass on the bar and walked out, leaving Emily standing there looking ridiculous with her index finger pointing at a person who was no longer in the room.

Self-consciously lowering her hand, she thought, *You can't get away from me that easily. I'm going to find out who you are!*

She didn't have to wait long.

A knock on her door awakened her.

Emily had just drifted off to sleep. It was late. Still dressed, she was lying on top of her bed waiting for Jesse. It was nearly midnight by the time the captain released him. Being the only non-gambler left in the passenger cabin, Emily had just given up on him for the night and was leaving. She saw him on the passageway, and even though he looked like he could barely keep his eyes open, she persuaded him to stroll with her around the deck once before retiring.

Holding up grimy hands, he told her he wanted at least to wash up, and that he would come by her cabin to get her. That was nearly a quarter of an hour ago and Emily had fallen asleep waiting for him. Then came the expected knock on the door.

"Coming!" she yelled, trying not to sound sleepy. She

jumped off the bed and opened her eyes wide in an attempt to wake up. Straightening her hair, she reached for the latch. "It's about time!" she said, opening the door. "What took you so…"

The black-haired Austin agent stood on the threshold. "It's a little late to be expecting someone, isn't it, Emily?" His eyes had a wicked glint in them.

"I don't see that it's any of your business," Emily said.

"You're wrong in that," he said. "As a security agent for your father, it *is* my business. You see, he sent me to find you. My name is Richard Tykas. You may call me Mr. Tykas."

"Well, Mr. Tykas. As you said, it's late. You can find me again in the morning. Good-night."

Emily attempted to close the door. Tykas stopped her.

"It is my duty to inform you, Miss Austin…it is Miss Austin, isn't it? For some reason everyone on board seems to think your name is Barnes, and that you're some kind of newspaper reporter for the *Evening Post* and that you're writing an article on the captain. I wonder where they could have gotten that idea?"

The chill that Emily felt whenever he looked at her returned, but this time it was much stronger. While she had been trying to find out about him, he had been investigating her. And from what he had just said, he had had more success than she did.

He waved aside his last comment. "It really doesn't matter where they got that idea, does it? It is my duty to inform you, Miss *Austin* (he emphasized her last name) that your father has sent me to find *and* to bring you back to New York."

He paused for a response. Emily did not give him one.

"So. This is what we'll do," he said. "We reach Cairo tomorrow at 4 P.M., at which time I will escort you off this ship and we will begin our journey home. I assume you will still be on board since we don't dock any place between here and Cairo. Please don't make this difficult for yourself, Miss Austin. If necessary, I will inform the captain of your true identity, at which time I will request additional security measures both on board the ship and at the docks."

He paused again. Emily simply glared at him.

"You will notice," Tykas continued, "that I did not ask if these accommodations are suitable to you. The way I see it, you have no choice. So I suggest you prepare yourself for the journey home." He smiled a syrupy smile and added, "Goodnight, Miss Austin. Sleep well."

Tykas attempted to close the door behind him, but Emily clung to the latch and wouldn't let him. When he saw she was determined not to let him have the door, he shrugged and left. He was no more than three steps down the passageway when she slammed the door with all her might.

Emily lay on her bed, fully clothed, all night long. She hardly slept, and what little sleep she did get was fitful and restless. Now that the guessing was over, she had plenty to think about and be angry about.

Why had Tykas waited so long to approach her? The ship had docked at several towns since Louisville. Why wait until they were in Illinois?

The fact that he told her just hours before they docked at Cairo was obvious. He didn't want to give her time to get away.

And where was Jesse? It should have been him at the door, not Tykas. If Jesse had come on time, she would have been strolling with him on the passageway when Tykas came to her room!

Even though she was furious at Jesse, she still waited for him. Her wait lasted all night long, because Jesse never arrived.

Chapter 21

HOW many times can I say it? I'm sorry, I fell asleep!"
Standing on the passageway, Jesse pleaded with Emily who was clearly upset, more so than he thought she should have been given the circumstances. He had fallen asleep; he admitted that. They didn't get to stroll around the deck together; he regretted that. What more could he say?

Jesse had chastised himself vigorously when he awoke in his cabin. He was disappointed in himself. There was nothing he would rather do than be with Emily. But he made a mistake. He was only going to lie down for a moment—a moment that happened to stretch into the daylight hours. Why was Emily treating this like it was a life or death issue?

"I don't have time to argue with you now," Emily said huffily. "The captain sent for me."

"I don't see that there's anything *to* argue about!" Jesse cried.

"I don't have time to get into it!" She pushed past Jesse on her way to the wheelhouse. Suddenly swinging around, she asked, "Do you know why the captain wants to see me?"

"Listen," was all Jesse said.

Her brow wrinkled. She wasn't following him. "Listen to...?"

Jesse held his finger to his lips in a shushing gesture. He mouthed the word, *Listen.* In the distance three distinct whistle blasts sounded. "It's the steamboat *Eagle*. Her captain is Lakanal's rival. From what I hear, they're cut from the same cloth, both proud old steamboat captains. I was in the wheelhouse when the captain sent a steward for you. When the engineer heard that, he turned to me and said, 'If he's sending for the reporter, we're gonna have a race for sure.'"

"A race?"

Jesse nodded. "From what I hear, it won't be the first time. There's a standing grudge between the two captains. The *Eagle's* coming up fast from astern, and according to the engineer there's only one reason it would do that—to challenge Lakanal and attempt to beat him to Cairo."

"So what do I have to do with this?"

"Everything! How can Lakanal let the *Eagle* beat him to Cairo with you on board? You're writing his story. If you were to put in his article that Marsh overtook him and got to Cairo first, he'd be humiliated! But if Marsh were to challenge him—which he's apparently doing—and Lakanal were to beat him to Cairo, then he'd come off as a hero in the old steamboat tradition!"

"What possible difference could it make which boat reaches Cairo first?" Emily said. "It sounds like two little boys fighting to me!"

Jesse laughed. "Maybe so, but there's a lot of interest in the outcome. The crew of the *Tippecanoe* is excited. And from what I've heard already this morning, word is spreading quickly among the passengers. No one on board wants to lose to the *Eagle*."

Emily shook her head in disgust. "Well, here's one passenger who doesn't care if another ship docks before us, as long as we make it there safely! This is silly."

"Emily! It's part of riverboat history! Competition between steamboat captains is legendary! Joiner—he's the engineer—was telling me that he saw the start of the race between the

Natchez and the *Robert E. Lee* twenty years ago. They raced from New Orleans to St. Louis. According to Joiner, ten thousand people watched the start of the race and bets were placed from as far away as London and Paris!"

"I still think it's silly," Emily said.

"Well, if I were you, I wouldn't say that to the captain."

Emily's response was the clicking of her heels on the wooden passageway on her way to the wheelhouse. Jesse watched her for about a dozen steps, then turned the opposite direction toward the boiler room.

Jesse hadn't told Emily everything the captain said in the wheelhouse. When the *Eagle* was sighted and it became clear the other ship was overtaking them, the captain pulled Jesse aside and whispered special instructions to him. He would be used to shuttle private communication between the wheelhouse and the boiler room. Jesse would need to be swift and discreet. However, Lakanal emphasized, the private communication was secondary. What he wanted most from Jesse was observation. The captain wanted Jesse to observe and report on Joiner, the engineer—everything he said and did, not only his response to the captain's communication, but his overall disposition during the race.

It sounded a lot like spying to Jesse. From what the captain said next, apparently Jesse's eyes had communicated his thoughts; for the captain added, "Normally, I wouldn't ask you to do this. But today I have my reasons. Let's just say that in times past Joiner's courage has been tested and found wanting. Let's leave it at that, shall we?"

Jesse was on his way to the boiler room with the captain's first scripted message when he bumped into Emily on the passageway. He hadn't seen her since he missed their stroll. Now, as he approached the boiler room, Jesse mentally kicked himself again for falling asleep. He would have to make it up to Emily. However, he didn't have much time. They'd be docking in

Cairo later today and he'd promised her an answer about New York. She wasn't going to be happy about that either.

"Oops! Sorry!" The man with whom Jesse collided bounced backward, even though he was the bigger of the two. The man's face wrinkled up like a bulldog itching for a scrap.

"Why don't you watch where you're going!" the man cried.

Jesse found himself chest-to-chest with a man who smelled heavily of stale perspiration. Slick, oily black hair was plastered against his forehead.

"Sorry, sir. It was my fault," Jesse apologized.

"Is it policy for members of the crew to bowl over paying passengers? This is inexcusable! What's your name, boy?"

"Jesse, sir. Jesse Morgan."

The man's head snapped back in exaggerated fashion. "Morgan?" It was as though the name left a familiar taste in the man's mouth but he couldn't place it. The longer it lingered on his lips, the more sour his face grew. He said it again, "Morgan."

"Yes, sir. And I truly am sorry, sir."

The man grabbed Jesse by the front of his shirt, completely taking Jesse by surprise. One moment, the man was backing away tasting his name, the next instant he had pulled Jesse within an inch of his own face. The smell of sweat mingled with coffee breath.

Whispering through clenched teeth, the man said, "Listen, Morgan. I'm only going to tell you this once. Stay away from Emily. If you value your life, stay away from her."

He shoved Jesse aside and continued down the passage-way—casually, as though he were out taking a morning stroll. The man's threat knocked Jesse off-balance much more than the physical collision. What had just happened here? Who was this man? And what did he have to do with Emily?

It began to dawn on Jesse that the collision had been no accident after all. He started to follow after the man.

Three blasts of a steam whistle from the wheelhouse stopped him. Another three followed, these from the *Eagle*. She was much closer now.

"MORGAN!"

The captain's voice bellowed across the water. Jesse hesitated. He wanted to catch up with the man who had just threatened him and find out what this was all about. But he hadn't gone to the boiler room yet and the captain was yelling for him to come to the wheelhouse. The man would have to wait. Now his choice was narrowed to two. The boiler room or the wheelhouse?

Jesse took a last look at the back of the man who had threatened him. Then, slapping the handrail in frustration, he sprinted toward the boiler room.

"Where have you been?"

Jesse was out of breath by the time he got back to the wheelhouse. Barging through the door, he handed a scrap of paper to the captain—the engineer's response to Lakanal's previous message. While the captain unfolded and read the message, Jesse looked for Emily. In the cramped wheelhouse it wasn't hard to find her. She was backed into a corner out of the way, writing on her pad of paper. She hadn't looked up when he came in, and she didn't look up now.

Gripping the wheel, the pilot looked over at him. The man's mouth was a grim line of determination. He glanced nervously over his shoulder. Jesse followed his gaze. The *Eagle*—her twin smokestacks belching flame and smoke—was clearly gaining on them.

Lakanal crumpled the message and looked up. "Give me a report!"

Jesse relayed what he had observed: "Everyone in the boiler room is confident and ready to take on the *Eagle.*"

Emily rolled her eyes when she heard the report.

The captain leaned closer to Jesse. "Everyone?" he questioned.

"Everyone," Jesse replied.

"Good!" Turning to the pilot he said, "Mr. Barker, it's time to show Marsh what the *Tippecanoe* can do!"

The grim line which marked the pilot's mouth went unchanged. He nodded a single nod in response to the captain.

Lakanal consulted his map, pointed a weathered finger to a place where the river curved radically, and said, "Here."

Without releasing the wheel, the pilot leaned over and looked at the spot to which the captain was pointing. There was no change of expression when he looked up. His eyes met the captain's.

"The element of surprise, Mr. Barker," the captain said. "Marsh will never expect it!"

"The sandbar?" Barker asked.

"There's room. We can clear it!" the captain said.

The grim line on Barker's face grew even grimmer. Still, his response was an affirmative nod.

Lakanal snatched a scrap of paper and wrote furiously. He folded it and handed it to Jesse. "Don't forget my instructions, Mr. Morgan," he said. "After you deliver this to Joiner, stay down there. At the first sign of any change in status, you report to me. Understood?" The way the captain caught Jesse's eye and held it communicated an underlying message which came through loud and clear.

Before he raced out the door, Jesse shot one more glance at Emily. This time she looked at him. The edges of her mouth pulled back with a look of chagrin, as if to say, "This is so silly!"

This time Jesse didn't run into any passengers. In fact, the passageway was clear of all activity. Most of the passengers, having heard of the race by now, were lined up along the railing on the other side of the boat. The *Eagle* had pulled up beside them and the river was charged with excitement.

Money exchanged hands as bets were made. Verbal bets were shouted across the water between the passengers of both boats. Young women bounced up and down excitedly as though the *Tippecanoe* were a horse and they were urging her to run faster.

Captain Marsh and the pilot stood proudly behind the glass of the *Eagle's* wheelhouse. Marsh had gray hair like Lakanal's, but thinner and shorter. He sported only a mustache. A satisfied grin beneath the mustache indicated he was pleased that the *Eagle* had closed the gap between him and his rival. He looked over at the *Tippecanoe's* wheelhouse. The transformation in his face the moment his eyes locked onto Lakanal's was striking, like an electrical storm that blew in without warning.

Jesse reached the boiler. Gasping for breath, he handed the captain's note to the engineer. Joiner received it, read it, and nodded. Jesse watched for reaction. There was none. Joiner had simply acknowledged the order. So Jesse stood off to the side and waited for any change as he was ordered to do.

Bare-chested deckhands, sweaty and splotched with soot, lined up to cast wood under the boiler at the engineer's command. Jesse recognized the size and shape of the logs in their hands; he'd chopped enough of them at Brownsville.

He had angled himself in such a way that he could not see the flames under the boiler directly. It was something he did without thinking about it. For as long as he could remember, the sight of flames made him feel uncomfortable. Whenever he saw exposed flames, a nervous knot formed in his stomach making him feel sick. His hands would perspire, and he would start to shake. If he stopped to think about it, he knew why he reacted to fire this way. But since he instinctively avoided the sight of flames, he didn't often have to think about it.

The glow of the boiler's fire painted everyone around it

with yellow and orange highlight—yellow for those who were closest to the flames, orange for those who were farther away. Joiner stood with his hands on his hips and inspected the boiler. He cocked his head this way and that, bent down and looked at the fiery underbelly, and down the length of each side. He wrung his hands.

Jesse took note of the engineer's reaction, but did not move. A disturbing question came to him. The captain said to report any change in status. Certainly he didn't mean this, did he? Joiner had gone from a man with his hands on his hips to a man wringing his hands. A change in status. But was it a significant enough change to report? Jesse decided to wait and observe a little longer.

The order came down from the captain to proceed to full speed. With the order came an admonition! "Give it everything she's got, Joiner!"

The engineer paused long enough to wipe sweat from his chin and brow. Then he ordered his men to stoke the fire. Within seconds, the fire responded to the added fuel. The boiler fizzled and creaked. The slapping of the paddlewheel on the water was faster. They were picking up speed.

Joiner studied the boiler again. To Jesse, the engineer looked like a mother examining her child for chickenpox or some other symptom of disease. He didn't like what he saw. Shaking his head from side to side, he cursed.

Jesse took note. Now? Hand-wringing and cursing? Was that enough? Should he report it to the captain? He decided to wait a little longer.

Another order came down from the wheelhouse. "We need more speed! Pile it on, Mr. Joiner!"

The engineer stood there. His men looked at him in anticipation of his order. None was immediately forthcoming.

Jesse began to worry that he had waited too long. Joiner's eyes were closed. His chest heaved. Then, just as Jesse had decided to go back to the wheelhouse, the engineer ordered his men to stoke the fire faster.

The resulting blaze was so hot, the yellow glow of the fire turned to white. The men throwing on the logs had to pitch them from farther away. They backed up, shielding their faces with their forearms. The boiler shuddered from the increased temperature. Outside on the water the paddlewheel slapped faster and faster until the slaps blended into a single sound.

Turning away from his men, engineer Joiner cursed the captain under his breath. Jesse saw it because he was looking for it. He didn't know for sure if he would have caught the words had he been depending on his ears alone. But he saw the words on Joiner's lips. Saw them and recognized them.

Stepping from the boiler room, Jesse was greeted by a variety of sensory sensations. The first thing he noticed was the breeze. The temperature difference outside was remarkably refreshing. The sound of cheers and hoots could be heard from the passengers urging their boat even faster. The shoreline whisked by at a pace that seemed unnaturally swift compared to the leisurely rate to which he was accustomed.

He raced down the passageway and up the steps, bursting into the wheelhouse. His sudden appearance startled Emily, whose attention had been focused on the *Eagle*. The two ships were bow to bow, both of them plowing through the waters at breakneck speed.

The captain cursed when he saw Jesse; not because it was Jesse, but because Jesse's presence meant the engineer was beginning to falter. "Report!" he shouted.

Speaking while bending over to catch his breath, Jesse whispered, "There is an increasing delay in obeying your orders," he said. "He's wringing his hands, muttering, and cursing."

"Come outside!" The captain led Jesse outside the wheelhouse, closing the door behind him. The river air cooled

Jesse's glistening skin. The captain spoke directly into Jesse's ear. He had to speak loud enough to be heard over the rush of the wind and the water and the slapping of the paddles; yet he didn't want anyone else to hear what he was saying. "Has Joiner disheartened his men in any way?"

Jesse wasn't sure exactly what the captain was implying. "No...I don't think so."

The captain was more direct. "Has Joiner said or implied that if we go any faster, the boiler is going to explode?"

Jesse was glad the captain's face was next to his; that way the captain couldn't see the surprised look in his eyes. "No," Jesse said. "He's said nothing like that."

The captain nodded enthusiastically. "Go back down there," he ordered. "If Joiner expresses doubts to his men of any kind, I want to know about it!"

Jesse nodded.

The captain reached for the wheelhouse latch just as Emily was coming out. "Miss Barnes?" he said.

"Captain," she almost had to shout to be heard, "allow me to accompany Mr. Morgan to the boiler. I want to see the men in action for my story."

The captain was about to refuse. Jesse could see it in his eyes. Apparently so could Emily.

"I'll just be a moment," she assured him. "I want to be here in the wheelhouse when we pull ahead."

It took the captain a silent moment to work through his reservations. But in the end he agreed she could accompany Jesse.

No sooner had the wheelhouse door closed and they were on the passageway when Emily turned to Jesse. "What did he say to you?" she asked.

For a moment Jesse was confused. Who was she talking about? Did she know about the man who had threatened him? Or was she talking about the captain?

"What do you mean?" he asked.

"Back there, a moment ago. The captain said something to you. You should have seen your face!"

Jesse told her about his assignment in the boiler room.

"Explode! Is that possible?"

"It's happened before during steamboat races."

"Oh my," Emily said, walking a short distance away. She bit her fingernails as she thought. "Oh my," she said again.

"What? Have you heard something?"

She nodded her head and continued biting her fingernails. "Up ahead there's a divided turn in the river. On the short side are two sandbars with barely enough room for a steamboat to get through. Normally, the steamboats take the long way around. To beat the *Eagle*, Lakanal is going to shoot between the sandbars. According to the pilot, it's risky enough trying to navigate the bars at a snail's pace, but Lakanal…"

Jesse finished her sentence, "…is attempting to do it full speed."

"Faster than the *Tippecanoe* has ever gone before," Emily added.

"Is that what the captain said?" Jesse asked.

Emily nodded.

"Come with me," Jesse said.

"Where are we going?"

"To the boiler. We can use Joiner as a gauge. If there's any sign of trouble he'll be the first one to know. And he's not a man who easily hides his feelings. If anything should go wrong…"

This time Emily finished Jesse's sentence, "…we're over the side."

Jesse nodded.

"Let me go to my room first," Emily said. "I want to get some things."

"We don't have time!"

"They're important!" Emily cried. "I'll meet you at the boiler room."

Jesse looked at her. Now was not the time for them to separate. "No," he said. "I'll go with you." He grabbed her by the hand and they ran to her room.

She took only a few moments to throw some things into a bag, talking as she did. "My credentials and money mostly," she explained. "I already have my story notes. That is, if they survive a drenching in the river should it come to that."

Slinging the strap of her bag over her shoulder, she turned to go. She came straight at Jesse who was standing in the doorway. He didn't move. "Strange it should come to this," he said.

Emily cocked her head to one side. "So tell me. Are we going back to New York together?"

Jesse smiled. "We haven't reached Cairo yet. I told you I'd give you my answer when we reached Cairo."

Emily moved closer to him. In a low husky voice she said, "It seems to me you're just trying to be evasive. Come on. You can tell me."

For a long moment, the two of them stood closer together than they'd ever stood before.

"Sorry," Jesse said abruptly, "I'll tell you when we get to Cairo." He grabbed her by the hand and pulled her into the passageway.

Jesse and Emily never reached the boiler room. No sooner had they put foot on the main deck when a stream of sweaty, sooty bodies flew past them and over the side of the boat.

Sploosh! Sploosh! Sploosh!

One man dove over the railing screaming, "She's gonna blow!"

As fast as the steamboat was traveling, most of the men cleared the stern before they even surfaced. Some, however, didn't jump far enough away from the boat and the force of the paddlewheel pulled them under.

The screams from the boiler room alarmed the passengers who were still at the railing urging their boat to victory. Within moments the main deck erupted with panic.

Jesse grabbed Emily by the hand. "Hold tight!" he yelled. "Let's not get separated!"

Emily nodded nervously. The two of them prepared to slip over the railing.

"Morgan! You! Morgan!"

The cry came from behind them. It was the man who had threatened Jesse earlier.

"Stay right where you are!" he cried.

Emily looked at Jesse angrily. "You know him? You know Tykas?"

The man Emily called Tykas was running toward them. Jesse started to say something, to defend himself; then he stopped. This wasn't the time for explanations. He looked at Emily and pushed her over the railing.

"Jesseee!" she screamed.

Sploosh!

He watched long enough to see Emily surface. She was clear of the paddlewheel.

Tykas lunged at Jesse, but came up empty. Jesse ducked under the man's grasp and managed to slip away. He ran up the passageway, weaving in and out of screaming, distraught passengers. Tykas was right behind him.

The *Tippecanoe's* whistle blasted. Short blasts in rapid succession. Next to the passageway the river and shoreline rushed by madly. As Jesse reached the bow, he could see two tan sandbars laying parallel to the boat's path. Between them the water was darker, deeper. But was it wide enough? Sandbars were notorious for the way they shifted from day to day.

The whistle blasted over and over. From inside the wheelhouse Jesse could hear the captain yelling, "Speed, Mr. Joiner!

I need more speed!"

With all the congestion on the passageway, Jesse couldn't get to the railing and over the side. Tykas would be on him before he could jump. Jesse looked toward the bow. No good. If he jumped there, the boat would plow right over him. He looked all around him. How to get off the boat?

What would Truly Noble do?

The upper deck. Yes, it was probably less crowded.

Jesse reversed his direction and bounded up the main stairway, the same one that he had sat on while he stared at Emily their first night on board. Tykas tried to cut him off by reaching over the railing. The man got a piece of Jesse's shirt.

Jesse tried to pull away. His legs churned on the stairs, but Tykas' grip held him back. Jesse changed tactics. Instead of trying to pull way, he placed both hands on Tykas' forearm. Then he leaned all his weight on it, using the railing as a fulcrum. Tykas screamed in pain. The next instant, Jesse was free.

He raced up the stairs. His hunch had been right. So many people had been down below on the main deck watching the race that the passageways were not nearly as crowded as below. Running full speed past the rows of cabins, Jesse knew exactly what Truly Noble would do; he just wasn't sure he had the courage to do it himself.

He glanced behind him. Tykas was charging up the stairs.

The boat's whistle shrieked incessantly as the steamboat hurtled toward the gap in the sandbars. The *Eagle* had pulled away. She was taking the longer route.

Suddenly, the deck beneath Jesse's feet shuddered. People screamed. The boat shuddered again, this time convulsively.

Jesse was halfway down the passageway. Tykas was right behind him. For an older man, he was fast—faster than Jesse now that there were no hindrances between them. Jesse could hear the man's labored breathing. The man sounded like a bull charging. Jesse put his head down and urged his legs to move faster down the passageway. He looked up. It was a dead end.

What would Truly Noble do?

Exactly what Jesse was about to do.

With a leap, Jesse sailed over the railing between two posts. For an instant, he hovered there, almost as if time was frozen. He hung between heaven and earth. Above him was only sky. Beneath him, he could see the shoreline and the steamboat and the river that ran between them.

Then he plunged. Like a rock. The river plummeted toward him.

Sploosh!

Everything was suddenly and strangely quiet. Other than a gurgling sound, little else could be heard until the churning of the paddlewheel passed by. Beneath him Jesse could see the slippery surface of the river's bottom, interspersed with rocks and flowing reeds. Above him, he could see the sky and clouds distorted by the water's surface. He swam toward the blue.

As soon as he broke the surface of the water, he looked back at the steamboat. The paddlewheel churned mightily, propelling the steamboat toward the gap. Fire and smoke and ash erupted from her twin stacks. But there was another source of smoke and fire. The third column of smoke rose from the boiler room.

Jesse saw Tykas standing on the outside of the railing, clinging onto it with both hands and looking down at the water. It looked like he was trying to work up enough courage to jump. Just as it seemed he was going to climb back over the railing, his foot slipped. He plunged into the water below. Jesse didn't see him surface.

The *Tippecanoe* plunged toward the gap, its whistle blasting repeatedly. Lakanal was determined to go through with it. He was going to shoot the gap between the sandbars. If he succeeded, he would most assuredly win the race against his rival as well as a place in riverboat history for his courage and daring.

The closer the steamboat came to the gap, the faster its whistle blew.

It hit the gap. The boat jerked and shuddered. It slipped between the sandbars, and for a moment it looked like it was going to make it. Then it jerked again, violently. The stern of the boat swung to the left so that the name *Tippecanoe* on its side could be seen by those downriver, as though the boat itself wanted everyone to know the correct spelling of its name when they recorded the day's events.

The boat's two magnificent stacks skewed awkwardly, one forward, the other back. An instant later, there was a monstrous explosion. An enormous fireball rose from the belly of the vessel. Wood and glass littered the air and splashed onto the water's surface. Another explosion soon followed and the boat listed to one side, giving up its ghost.

Captain Lakanal had lost his race—and his place in history.

Jesse swam toward the shoreline.

Chapter 22

AT the southernmost tip of Illinois, Jesse and Emily sat side-by-side as the Ohio River on their left and the Mississippi River on their right joined forces in front of them. This location was Emily's request. Although she said nothing to Jesse, she thought it was a suitably symbolic locale for the occasion, anticipating as she was that her path and Jesse's path would be joining together for a return trip to New York. In fact, given time, the location might even prove to be prophetic as a symbol of the joining together of their two lives in marriage.

Following the explosion on board the *Tippecanoe,* Captain Marsh and the *Eagle* circled back to assist the survivors. Jesse and Emily found each other on shore soon after the blast. Having swum to shore, Emily had made her way downriver and witnessed the explosion. She spotted Jesse swimming ashore a few moments later. Among the confirmed dead were Captain Lakanal, the pilot, and engineer Joiner who stayed with the boiler until it blew. Among the missing was Richard Tykas.

The *Eagle* transported the survivors the rest of the way to Cairo. It was a solemn journey. Gossip aboard the boat was that following the rescue efforts, Captain Marsh had locked himself in his cabin. No one had heard from him since and he wouldn't answer knocks on his door.

The steamboat company provided lodging and meals for the survivors. Emily and Jesse spent much of the next morning answering questions regarding the incident. They told their stories so many times—to company officials, newspaper reporters, hotel employees, and anyone else who learned they had been on board the *Tippecanoe*—that their comments began to sound like memorized speeches.

By late afternoon, the excitement had died down. Jesse and Emily took a couple of hours to rest and refresh themselves. They agreed to meet for dinner and an evening stroll. Emily arranged for a carriage which took them past many imposing residences that had been built by wealth generated from the steamboat industry before the railroads branched out and dominated shipping and transportation.

It was twilight. Cool wind rose up from the rivers on both sides of them.

"I was worried about you," Emily said.

She didn't look at him when she spoke. They sat on a blanket inches from each other. Emily's legs were stretched out and crossed at the ankles; leaning back, she propped herself up with her hands. Jesse sat with his knees up; resting his arms on his knees, he sifted through a cupped hand of tiny pebbles looking for suitable ones to flick with his thumb and forefinger.

"Worried? When?" he asked.

"During the explosion. I didn't know if you'd gotten off or not. Then I saw a head bobbing in the river wearing that cap and I knew you were all right."

Jesse grinned and touched the cap. "After all I've been through, it's amazing this cap is still around."

Their thoughts drifted back to the events on board the *Tippecanoe.*

"Who is that Tykas fellow?" Jesse said suddenly. His attention diverted from flicking pebbles to the man who was chasing him when he jumped overboard.

Emily sat up defensively. "How is it that you know him?" she asked.

"I don't know him!" Jesse protested. "I bumped into him on the passageway and the next thing I know, he's threatening me and warning me to stay away from you!"

His response seemed to ease Emily's mind. She relaxed and leaned back, this time lower, supporting herself on her elbows. "He works for a rival newspaper," she explained. "He's attracted to me and can be a real nuisance. He was fired from the *Evening Post* for threatening other men who showed an interest in me. Which reminds me...you pushed me overboard!"

"You make it sound like a bad thing!" Jesse cried.

"Well, isn't it?"

"No! That Tykas fellow was charging toward us, and the boiler was about to explode, and we were going to jump anyway! I was saving your life!"

"I know," Emily said, smiling. "And I've not had the chance to thank you for it."

She rose up and pecked him on the cheek, then reclined back on her elbows as if nothing had happened. But something had happened. Jesse tossed the pebbles aside and brushed the dirt from his hands. He turned and sat cross-legged so that he was facing Emily. For a moment, she gazed up at him and he stared down at her under a canopy of emerging stars while the two great rivers merged at Emily's feet.

Jesse broke the silence. "Was that difficult for you today?"

"What?"

"Talking to reporters. I mean, since you are one and you're usually the one asking the questions instead of answering them."

"Oh, that," Emily said. "No, it wasn't difficult. Our jobs are different. They cover daily news and events while I'm an investigative reporter. My research takes more time because the issues are more complicated. While they're just reporting events, I'm scratching below the surface for a story. There's really no comparison at all."

Jesse nodded. He lowered his head. "I'm sure you're very good at what you do."

"Thank you, Jesse. That's sweet."

"So you probably already know what I'm going to say next."

Emily smiled confidently. She said nothing, allowing him time to find his own words. While she waited, she listened to the rush of the two rivers joining.

Leaning to one side, Jesse pulled an envelope from his back pocket. It was folded over in half. He held it out to her.

Emily had to lean on one side to free a hand to take it. She leaned closer to Jesse. "What's this?" she asked, smiling.

"A letter to my mother. I will be in your debt if you will deliver it to her when you reach New York."

When you *reach New York. When* you *reach New York.*

The words hung in the air and stared her in the face. Emily wanted to swat them away, to smash them out of existence and pretend they had never been spoken. But there was nothing she could do. The words were out there—invincible syllables that could never be destroyed.

"You're not going back?"

Hers was a feeble question masquerading as casual inquiry, the cry of a wounded dreamer. Maybe she had misunderstood him. Maybe an explanation would provide some unseen breath of information that would somehow resuscitate her dying fantasy.

"I'm continuing west," Jesse said.

Like a stake to the heart, his response laid to rest forever Emily's dream of the two of them going home together. With the envelope in her hand she fell back onto her elbows and stared at nothing.

"I feel like I belong out here," Jesse explained. "I love the openness of the sky and the land. When I think about going back to the city, I get a closed-in feeling, like someone is trying to lock me up in a closet. Out here I've learned to depend upon myself. I've learned that I can survive...more than that, I've learned that with hard work I can make a life for myself. I've changed since the night I left New York. I'm stronger. I'm more confident. For the first time in my life, I feel good about myself."

Emily had to admit that Jesse had changed. His arms were thicker, his skin darker, and he was more confident about himself. He was less of a boy and more of a man. All of which only served to hurt her more at the thought that they were parting ways.

"Besides, nothing is back there for me. I mean, as far as a job or a future. After all I've been through, can you see me going back to Ruger's Glassworks as an office boy? And I still can't see myself going to college. That's my mother's dream, not mine. This is where I want to be. I want to work with my hands. I want to build something for myself that will last."

Still shaken by his announcement, Emily did her best to steady her voice. "What about your mother?" she asked.

"That's all in the letter," Jesse said. "I explained why I left as I did, and apologized for the pain I know I've caused her. And I told her that as soon as I get settled, I'm going to build us a house and send for her. She can use the money she's saved for my college education for a train ticket."

Emily nodded. He had it all figured out. And none of it included her. "So then, where do you think you'll settle down?"

"I don't rightly know for sure," he replied. "I'll probably head up the Missouri River on another steamboat."

"The Missouri? I thought you were going to St. Louis."

Jesse chuckled.

"What?"

"Oh, I was just thinking about old Hans back at the Red Horse Inn. He was the one who told me about Brownsville and how I could work my way West. Only his information was about fifty years old. Brownsville was no longer the booming town he'd described, and St. Louis is no longer the Western gateway it once was. Then, on the *Tippecanoe* someone told me I needed to go to Independence, Missouri. He said wagon trains leave there for the West two hundred at a time. And now, I come to find out, that's no longer true. A flood destroyed the wharves at Independence and now wagons are outfitted at Westport Landing. So I guess that's where I'm going."

"Kansas City," Emily said.

"What?"

"You're going to Kansas City. Westport Landing's name was changed to Town of Kansas, and then to Kansas City."

Jesse stared at her, not sure whether to believe her or not.

"I'm a journalist! I know these things!" she cried. In truth, she'd learned of the name change while tracing some documents at the office when she was investigating her father's business.

"Well, tell me this, Miss Journalist," Jesse said, "is the West still out there? And is it still called the West?"

"Last I heard, the West is still the West," Emily said, going along with Jesse's dry bit of humor. "But I can't guarantee that the West will still be there by the time you get there."

The lighthearted give-and-take between them eased Emily's pain momentarily. Then, as silence set in between them, the pain returned.

"Earlier? When I said there was nothing for me in New York?"

Emily nodded.

"I wasn't being truthful."

Emily nodded again. "Your mother. I think I know how you feel about her."

"And there's you."

Emily looked at him with a grin, prepared for another round of give-and-take. But Jesse was looking down at his hands as he spoke. He glanced up at her. There was no humor in his eyes. They were soft and warm, and serious.

"Emily, I wish you could go with me. I know you can't—you're a successful reporter and have your career and all. It's just that...well, I wish things were different. I wish you were free to go West with me."

Stunned, Emily could do nothing more than stare at him. With just a handful of words from Jesse, all of her dreams had come true. Yet she couldn't claim it. Her own made-up story was getting in the way!

What was she to say? "Jesse, I've been lying to you all this time. The truth is, I'm not a reporter and my real name isn't Barnes. I ran away from home and followed you out West because I love you. My father's rich and he's sent one of his agents to take me back home, but please don't hold all of this against me because I love you and I'd love to go West with you."

Jesse interpreted her pondering as embarrassed silence. "I'm sorry," Jesse said. "I've obviously embarrassed you. A successful woman like yourself must have a line of suitors a mile long back in New York. Please, forgive me. It's just that when I saw you on the steamboat...well, I felt...." He shook his head. "That doesn't matter now."

He jumped up before she could say anything.

"We need to be heading back," he said.

"Jesse, wait!"

But he didn't wait. He walked toward the carriage.

Emily caught up with him. "Jesse." She touched his arm. He stopped. Gently, she turned him around until they were facing each other. "I would love to go West with you," she said.

Assuming her statement was an incomplete sentence, he added, "...if it weren't for your story about Captain Lakanal and the *Tippecanoe.*" He smiled. "It's a good one, Emily. And you were there. You can write an eyewitness account for the *Evening Post* the last days of a legendary steamboat captain I hope I can read it someday."

Emily moved into him and put her head against his chest and her arms around his waist. He responded with his arms around her neck and shoulders.

At the confluence of the Ohio and Mississippi Rivers Emily and Jesse came together for a brief moment in time.

The next morning when Emily came to the hotel lobby, Jesse was already gone.

"Clara! How good it is to see you again!"

"Yes, dear! Welcome back to Point Providence."

Sarah and Jenny greeted Clara at the doorway while J.D. unloaded her baggage from the buggy.

"My, you do look weary from your trip," Jenny said. "Please, come in. May I get you some refreshments? Lemonade? Tea?"

"Tea, please," Clara said.

She was indeed weary. In fact, weary didn't begin to describe how tired she felt. The train ride from New York was but a small part of her exhaustion. Fatigue had been Clara's daily companion months before Jesse left home. The unrelenting schedule she kept to maintain a high volume of piecework did not come without a price. Add to that her constant worry over Jesse since the day he disappeared, the stress of leaving New York knowing that she would lose her piecework to other workers, and the weariness from a several-state train ride.

"Let's all sit around the kitchen table," Jenny said. "I have some molasses cookies that will go well with the tea."

For several minutes Clara sat at the kitchen table alone. While the others busied themselves with small tasks—J.D. taking her baggage upstairs, Jenny preparing the tea, and Sarah placing cookies on a plate—an uneasy silence hung in the air. It had always been this way between Clara and the Morgans, and she didn't expect anything would be different even considering the unusual circumstances that brought them together.

When Ben first took Clara to meet his family, he did so with great enthusiasm. Having been raised by an eccentric and vengeful grandfather, Ben's true heritage had been concealed from him until he was an adult. It was during the war that he discovered he had brothers and a sister. And once he was finally reunited with them, Ben did all he could to make up for the many lost years when he thought he was an only child.

At times, Clara thought her husband went beyond normal expectations in his attempts to be a good brother. The Morgans were a proud family with a rich heritage, and she felt her husband worried too much about living up to the Morgan name.

And now she shared their name; but only the name, not the heritage behind it. The Morgan family heritage had been Ben's heritage, not hers. It had been that way from the beginning. At that first Morgan family gathering when Ben excitedly introduced her to one Morgan after another, she felt like an intruder into a secret organization. She'd never felt comfortable around the Morgans. Not then. Not now.

At the table they all descended upon her at once. *Strength in numbers,* she supposed. J.D. came down the stairs, Jenny arrived with a teapot and cups, and Sarah carried the cookies. Clara studied Jenny in particular.

She was a delicate woman who had aged beautifully. Her shiny black hair was parted down the middle and drawn back across her forehead like theater curtains opening. Her eyes were bright and lively, and she had a ready smile. While J.D. and Sarah were true Morgans, Jenny had married into the family. Yet she might as well have had Morgan blood flowing through her. She was just as much a part of the family as any of them. But then Jenny grew up with the Morgan children. They'd known her all their lives. And in a small town like Point Providence, that's almost as close as family. She and J.D. had probably been sweethearts from the time the two of them could walk.

Jenny poured the tea. Clara first, then J.D., then Sarah, finally her own cup.

At the sight of the tea and cookies, J.D. rubbed his hands together like a little boy. Looking at Clara, he said, "I've been waiting for you to get here all day! Since early this morning the smell of these cookies has been torturing me! And these two Pharisees"—he nodded at his wife and Sarah—"insisted they were for our guest and wouldn't let me have a single one until you arrived! As if you would miss one! You wouldn't, would you?"

Jenny spoke to Clara: "Don't mind him. Some men never grow up!"

Clara managed a polite smile. She sipped her tea.

They ate in silence.

After a while, Sarah said, "Have you heard from Jesse yet?"

Clara shook her head no. "But Jesse's boss told me that a young lady inquired after him at the glassworks factory. He said he recognized her as Franklin Austin's daughter."

J.D. frowned. "Austin...wasn't it an Austin factory that burned down when Ben was killed?"

Clara nodded.

"Does Jesse know the Austin girl?" Jenny asked.

"I've never heard him mention her," Clara replied.

"Have you talked to the Austin girl?" Sarah asked.

"I've tried," Clara replied. "So has Mr. Sagean. But we can't get past the front door of the Austin mansion."

"They don't even have the decency to talk to you?" J.D. thundered.

Clara thought his question rhetorical, so she didn't answer.

"Well, there's been a development here," Sarah said.

Clara put down her cookie mid-bite.

Sarah, Jenny, and J.D. exchanged glances.

"Well?" Clara asked. It infuriated her the way the three of them looked at each other. Secret society. They knew something about Jesse and were deciding whether or not to let her in on it.

Sarah's chair scraped back. She left the table.

J.D. said, "We've determined it was Jesse who was in our house."

Jenny reached across the table and touched Clara's hand. "We wish we had known it was him at the time. I'm not saying we could have done anything differently, but maybe somehow just knowing it was him would have made a difference!"

"How do you know for sure?" Clara asked.

"Because of this."

Sarah returned carrying a swollen book. She handed it to Clara. "Recognize it?"

Clara examined the book. The pages were crisp and dry now, but it was evident the book had been doused with water. That's what had made its pages swell. The corners were turned up; some stuck together, others were a series of curls lying atop one another. The title and the cover pictures were washed and faded, but still readable: *Danger at Deadwood: Another Exciting Truly Noble Adventure.* By Sarah Morgan Cooper.

Glancing at the author, Clara lifted the cover. It cracked and threatened to tear as she lifted it. Inside, on the title page, there was this inscription: *To Jesse. May you find the strength that comes from goodness. Your aunt, Sarah Morgan Cooper.*

"It was found floating in the river near Cincinnati," J.D. explained. "The boy who found it showed it to his father. His father recognized Sarah's name. He used to have a farm near Point Providence. Because it had Sarah's signature in it, he thought it might have some value to us, so he had it delivered to me."

Clara gently turned one page after another of the book.

Jenny said, "Clara, dear, you have such a handsome son. Ben would be so proud of him!"

Tears came to Clara's eyes. She continued flipping pages.

"We've asked around between here and Cincinnati," J.D. said. "No one we've talked to has seen him."

"And we have folk at the church praying for him regularly," Jenny offered.

Clara sniffed. "Where is Deadwood?" she asked.

"The town in my book?" Sarah asked.

Clara nodded, still not looking up from the pages.

"It's a fictitious town," Sarah said.

"Is it near something that's real?"

"The setting for the book is the New Mexico Territory. In the story Deadwood is a few miles west of Santa Fe."

"Are there trains to Santa Fe?"

"In the book?" Sarah asked.

"You're not thinking of going there, are you?" J.D. asked.

"It's the only lead I have," Clara said. "For some reason my son is headed West. This Truly Noble character has been his hero for years. If Truly Noble went to Santa Fe, chances are my son has gone to Santa Fe."

"Mmmm," J.D. shook his head questionably, "that seems unlikely, Clara."

"It's my last hope."

"You wouldn't go alone, would you?" Jenny asked.

"Why not?"

"A woman traveling West alone," Sarah said. "It's just not wise."

"Seems like I've been doing a lot of things alone lately," Clara said. "The labor riots of '77, the New York blizzard of '88, living in squalor and misery, yet somehow we've managed to survive. I suppose I'll survive this too."

"It sounds like God has been watching over you," Jenny said.

Clara shook her head. "I don't think God knows where Hester Street is." Her comment prompted downcast eyes all around the table. And silence.

"Listen," Clara said, "I don't want to be a bother to you. I'll leave tomorrow."

"Nonsense!" Jenny cried. "You're welcome to stay as long as you like."

Clara pushed back her chair and stood. The other three followed her example.

"I still think it would be wise for someone to accompany you," Sarah said.

"Let me send a telegram to Marshall," J.D. offered. "I'm sure we could get him to meet you in St. Louis, and from there you could..."

"I don't want your help!" Clara cried. It came out a little more strongly than she had intended, but now that it had, a flood of emotion followed it. "This isn't a Morgan rescue mission!" she said. "He's my son, and if he's gone West, I'll find him."

"Clara, dear," Jenny said, "it's just that we think the world of Jesse and..."

"Then just leave him be!" Clara yelled. She figured that since she had gone this far, she might as well get it out once and for all. "It's this ridiculous Morgan notion that you have to be the saviors of the world that got my Ben killed! I don't want it to kill my Jesse too!" She broke down in tears and ran from the room saying, "If it hasn't already!"

Chapter 23

THE first day Jesse set foot on the prairie he thought his dreams had finally come true. By the fourteenth day on the prairie, he wasn't so sure.

A pair of oxen and an army of flies were his daily travel companions. His job was to walk beside the beasts as they pulled a Conestoga-style wagon just like they had done the day before, and the day before that, and the day before that for two weeks. The oxen were black and sweaty and smelly. The sun beat down upon them mercilessly. Flies buzzed annoyingly around his face, trying to find a bit of shade under the bill of his cap, or in his ears or nose. Along with them came a host of other smaller insects which inflicted him with what was popularly termed "prairie itch."

There was no need for a scout to guide them. They didn't even have to steer the wagons. The Santa Fe Trail upon which they traveled was so deeply rutted it looked like an inverse railroad track. The wagon wheels slipped neatly into the dirt grooves. All that was needed now for them to reach their destination was locomotion, which the oxen supplied.

Day after day as he kept the oxen company, Jesse couldn't help but stare at the ruts in the trail and become more and more moody. The deep parallel track was a reminder of the thousands of men, women, and children who had preceded him across the prairie. And all those who had gone before had managed to take all of the "wild" out of the West.

There was no longer any danger of being attacked by Indians on the trail. Treaties had been signed, reservations appointed, and the Indians had been moved. With a string of forts and regular patrols along the trail it was safer than it had ever been to travel. Even the size of Jesse's wagon train bore testimony to the trail's safety. Time was when as many as two hundred wagons traveled together for protection. Jesse's group was smaller. Much smaller. It was comprised of two wagons.

Jesse groused to himself: *So this will be the legacy I leave my children: He was the last man to travel West on the Santa Fe Trail.*

There were actually ten people traveling with the two wagons. Allen Waterman owned both wagons. He needed two wagons because he was moving his business to Pueblo, Colorado. Waterman was a Chicago druggist. The first wagon contained bottle upon bottle of potions and pills and elixirs, along with his beakers and scales and measuring spoons—all the things he needed to ply his craft. The second wagon carried the usual fare for pioneers—clothing, food, utensils, weapons, tools, and repair parts should either of the wagons break down.

The two wagons were typical prairie schooners, aptly named because with their white canvas covering they looked like ships plying an ocean of grass as they moved across the flatlands. They were basically four-feet-by-ten feet oak boxes on wheels. The cover was made of canvas which was stretched across ribs of hickory. The wagons lacked the comfort of springs, which seemed to encourage those who could walk to do so.

Allen Waterman, a small obsessive man with thinning dark hair, drove the lead wagon filled with his medicines. He was usually accompanied by his wife, Daisy, a stern-faced woman who was slightly taller than he, and one of their two daughters: Cora Belle, age seven; and Lillie, age five. Because there was such limited space in the wagon, only one daughter could ride at a time, which left one to ride in the second wagon.

The trailing wagon was driven by Waterman's brother-in-law, George McFarland, who was married to Waterman's older sister, Matilda. He was a slow, round man who was horseshoe bald, while she was more like her brother—small, precise, and neat. Their two daughters, Cordelia, age thirteen, and Clarina, age ten, kept the spare Waterman girl company in the back of the wagon with both family's personal belongings and food-stuffs. A lone mule trailed behind the second wagon. Waterman planned to use the mule for plowing once they reached Pueblo.

It didn't take long for Jesse to learn that McFarland was something of a leach. He drank much and did little work. Unlike the Watermans, McFarland had no discernible plans for when they reached Pueblo. The entire excursion was Waterman's doing. All McFarland did was drive a wagon. The best thing he contributed to the party was his family. His girls and the Waterman girls entertained each other famously, and Matilda provided companionship for Daisy.

The remaining two in the party were given meals and passage for work. While Jesse had been hired to assist the Watermans, a bashful young boy named Slate Pickens assisted the McFarlands and the second wagon.

Without exception, each day was identical. They broke camp at six o'clock in the morning, stowed the gear, and got underway. Twice a day they would stop to water the teams. On an average day they would travel fifteen miles; twenty on a good day. At four in the afternoon they would make camp for the night. Campfires were started, the oxen were set out to graze, and dinner was made. After dinner—which Jesse had always heard was a social time of talking and singing—was always a disappointment. Waterman would examine and dust his bottles of medicine, and growl at anyone who came near. The two women sat off by themselves and chattered while the girls played around them. McFarland would slap Slate around for being slow and lazy after which he'd prop himself against a tree and get drunk. Slate would suffer the unwarranted discipline in silence and keep to himself. As soon as he finished his chores he would stretch out under the wagon and go to sleep. And every night Jesse was left to find something with which to amuse himself.

After two weeks, the vastness of the night sky and the flatness of the plains failed to be a source of wonder. He learned that there were only so many days a man could marvel at the number of stars there were on the prairie compared to what could be seen in the city. He had nothing to read, no one to talk to, and nothing to do. Even dreaming about the future or remembering Emily proved to be less than satisfying. That's what he did all day long while walking beside the wagons. Until now, he never realized that memories, like fabric, can fade and wear out from daily use.

Jesse yearned for some excitement. He longed for a swarm of locusts, or a flash flood, or a cyclone just to break up the monotony.

His arms hung heavily from the weight of two full water buckets. Jesse trudged up the rocky incline from the river and the two prairie schooners came back into view. They were engulfed in a thick sea of sunflowers waving in the breeze, and he could readily see how they got their name. Hidden from sight were the road and the wagon wheels so that all Jesse could make out were the top edges of the wagons and white canvas. The ties on the canvas were loosed and the corners, pulled back to reveal one of the wagon's hickory bows, flapped in the wind like unloosed sails.

On the far side of the wagons stood a small unnatural clearing, another reminder of the hundreds of pioneers that had gone before them. There was no reason to doubt that sunflowers had once occupied the site. But with the proximity of the river to the road and the regularity of a wagon's daily schedule, the place had become a common campground.

Waterman was standing in the wagon bed with the canvas peeled back inspecting his cargo. The lid on a wooden box was up and he was pulling one glass vial after another out of it, holding them up to the waning sun, examining them with squinting eyes, shaking some, then wiping them off with a rag before returning them to the box.

He did this methodically, just as he did everything. Jesse had observed that in Waterman's mind everything and everyone had their place in life. If people and things were in their place and on schedule, he was contentedly, if not sullenly, silent. But let things get out of place or let the schedule slip and he became surly, sarcastic, and unbearable. To keep him in good spirits, everyone in the party performed their tasks to his liking.

When Jesse first hired on with him in Kansas City, he felt himself fortunate. Jesse had first tried securing passage aboard a train, but found little opportunity to work himself West on a train like he had done on the steamships. Not as many hands were needed to run a train as were needed to sail a boat. And he found he was not qualified to be a conductor, engineer, or porter. Although loading and unloading cargo was always needed, the task was performed by men and boys who lived in the towns. When the train pulled out, they were not on board.

However, Jesse learned that he might find passage West as an extra hand with a wagon train, though they were dwindling in number. After a few more inquiries he learned that the Watermans were planning to pull out soon and that they were looking for a man to accompany them since they had only young daughters.

Upon finding them, Jesse was readily hired and he counted

himself fortunate to have the chance to travel West with a learned man. What he didn't know at the time was that the learned man was also very private. He talked little and that was just to speak orders. When he drove the wagon, if he had anything to say to his wife, which was seldom, he leaned toward her and spoke in low tones. Jesse never knew what he said to her, but doubted it was anything worth hearing, for rarely did Daisy Waterman react to her husband's words. She jostled in silence next to him with a fixed look in her eyes.

As Jesse neared the wagons, through the gap between them he could see the clearing. The women were bent over the open fire. Matilda scooped coffee into the pot and awaited Jesse's arrival with the water. Thin wisps of smoke rose from an iron skillet attended by Daisy. Jesse could hear the crackle and smell the bacon even from a distance.

Beyond them, McFarland supervised Slate as the young boy chopped wood. The boy was having a rough time of it, missing every other stroke. Each time he did, McFarland cursed at him or cuffed him behind the ear.

Because of his shyness, Slate was something of a mystery. He had joined them just an hour before they pulled out of Kansas City. When the boy approached Waterman and said he'd heard they were looking for help, Waterman dismissed him with word that the position had already been filled. McFarland whined like a small child. Waterman had help, why couldn't he? The grown man threw such a tantrum that Waterman gave in and hired the boy just to shut up his brother-in-law.

Slate Pickens was a frail boy who had not yet developed a man's body. His arms, always hidden beneath long sleeves or a coat, must have been rail thin. He was not very strong, and though he did everything that was asked of him, he struggled with some of the simplest chores. He wore a broad-brimmed hat, always kept his head down, and rarely spoke. Jesse's guess was that the boy had probably been beaten much of his life and was running away from home. Unfortunately for him, Slate had not improved his lot in life. McFarland, whiskey bottle in hand, shouted, cursed, and mocked the boy's awkward wood-chopping skills.

A squeal of little girl laughter jumped from behind the sunflowers. Jesse jumped.

"We scared him, we scared him!"

Four girls sprang from their hiding places and ran in front of Jesse, each one pointing a teasing finger at him.

"We scared you, we scared you!"

Cordelia, the eldest, had eyes for Jesse. Seeing that his hands were safely occupied with water-filled buckets, she boldly reached out and touched a button on his shirt. "We scared you!" she said in a flirtatious tone. Lillie, the smallest and youngest, was the last to tease him. She planted herself in front of him, grinning from ear to ear, slapped his knee, and shouted, "We scare you!" Squealing in a pitch that caused Jesse to wince, she ran after the older girls.

Not wanting to rob them of the satisfaction of their game, Jesse nodded and smiled. "You scared me good," he admitted.

Jesse passed between the wagons. Waterman paid him no attention as he lifted one more vial to the sun, which was now more orange than yellow.

"What took you so long?" Matilda said when he set the buckets down next to the fire.

The question seemed to follow Jesse wherever he went. Knowing she wanted the water and not an answer, Jesse lifted one bucket to pour. Matilda placed the coffee pot near the rim and Jesse filled it. He poured the remainder of the water in a water barrel.

"Didn't your pappy teach you nothin'?" McFarland screamed.

Jesse looked up to see Slate try to balance a half log on its end to split it in two. Before he could get the ax raised, it would fall over again.

"We're gonna need two more buckets of water," Matilda said to Jesse.

"Yes, ma'am," Jesse said. But instead of carrying the buckets to the river, he took them to the place where Slate was chopping wood.

"Here," Jesse said. Dropping the buckets, he took the ax from Slate. "I'll do that. You go get some more water."

"What do you think you're doing, Morgan? That's his job!" McFarland bellowed.

The man's whining complaint attracted the attention of the other adults. Waterman stood up in the wagon and glared their direction. The two women looked up from their cooking at the disturbance.

Jesse pleaded his case to Waterman. "It's more efficient this way." He demonstrated by setting up the log and splitting it with a single blow. "I've chopped enough wood in my life to fuel a steamboat for a year," he exaggerated for emphasis. "I can have this job done in no time."

All eyes turned to Waterman for a verdict. The druggist said nothing. He simply returned to his bottles. Jesse took his response as a verdict in his favor. So did the women; they returned to their cooking. With a nod of appreciation, Slate picked up the buckets and headed for the river. McFarland glared at Jesse with yellow eyes, then followed after Slate.

"I'll bet you don't know how to fetch water from a river either!" he whined.

Jesse split the remaining logs, which were becoming an increasingly rare commodity the further west they traveled.

I hope we survive all this excitement, he said to himself.

After supper Jesse stood on the edge of the sunflower field and looked at the stars that stretched from horizon to horizon at all four compass points. The only thing to interrupt his view was the profile of the wagons. He settled in for another long evening.

The women, having finished their after-supper chores, were seated next to each other on campstools. Cordelia sat on the ground in front of her mother as her mother brushed her hair. The women chattered back and forth actively while Cordelia listened. Occasionally, one of the women would bend over and whisper something in the young woman's ear. Cordelia's eyes would grow wide, her mouth would drop open, and she'd blush. Following each blush, the young girl leaned back for more, clearly enjoying being included in women's talk. Her mother playfully shoved the girl forward whenever her eagerness to hear impeded the brushing of her hair.

Bottles clinked as Waterman cleaned them. McFarland had found a rock to lean against, bottle still in hand, his head fallen to one side in an unnatural manner. He was snoring. Not far from the wagons came an occasional bray from the mule and grunt from the oxen as they foraged for bits of grass. The three younger girls ran around the wagons chasing each other. And Slate was stretching a ground cloth under the second wagon, preparing for bed.

Oh, to be in Dodge City, Jesse thought, *the town of Bat Masterson, buffalo hunter, Indian scout, and lawman.* Then, with a chagrined look on his face, he thought, *They've probably tamed Dodge City by now too. Nothing exciting ever happens out here anymore.*

"Do you mind, young man?" Matilda cried. All three women had turned to scowl at Slate who was on his knees unrolling his bedroll under the wagon. "We're trying to have a private conversation here!"

Slate said nothing. He got up and walked to the far side of the road where he stood with his back turned and his hands plunged into his pockets. For one of the few times since they had left Kansas City, it was still early and Slate was not asleep under the wagon. Jesse decided to take advantage of the situation and talk to him. Since they were both runaways—though Jesse still didn't like to think of himself in those terms—maybe they could find something in common.

Stepping between the wagons, Jesse approached the boy. His path was cut off by three little girls running in front of him.

"Jesse is soooo charming!" Clarina said, imitating her older sister's voice.

"Shut up, Clarina!" Cordelia yelled, still sitting in front of her mother getting her hair brushed.

"Jesse is soooo charming!" Cora Belle echoed.

"Mother, please! Will you make them shut up!" Cordelia screamed.

Little Lillie trailed behind. Carrying her bonnet in her hand, she slapped Jesse playfully on the leg with it. "Jesse's soooo charming!" she giggled, then ran away.

"Mother!" Cordelia objected.

"Girls! Leave Mr. Jesse alone!" Matilda said, sharing a smirk with Daisy.

Jesse smiled at the girls. He looked up just as Slate turned his head away, but not before Jesse thought he caught a glimpse of a smile on the boy's face. Approaching the boy from behind, he said, "We haven't had much chance to get to know each other."

The boy didn't respond.

Undaunted, Jesse said, "Seems to me this is going to be a long trip. Might as well get to know one another."

No response.

Jesse placed a hand on the boy's shoulder. The shoulders beneath the boy's coat were scrawnier than Jesse had originally thought. Slate jumped at Jesse's touch, but made no attempt to shrug off Jesse's hand. Moving slightly to one side in an attempt to look the boy in the eyes, Jesse said, "I think I know how you feel."

Silence.

"You're a runaway, aren't you?"

A slight nod.

"So am I!" Jesse said, feeling he was making progress.

For some reason, Jesse looked up for a moment. Clarina was chasing Cora Belle past the oxen and mule. Little Lillie was trailing behind, waving her bonnet and squealing happily. As she passed behind the mule, she swatted one leg with her bonnet.

The mule reacted instinctively. Its leg lashed out, catching Lillie in the head. Her happy squealing ended abruptly. She dropped to the ground. Stone still.

"MOMMA!"

Clarina's scream cut the air. Laced with panic, it penetrated Waterman's concentration on his bottles, halted the women's gossip, even roused the drunken slumber of George McFarland. The girl had turned to check on her playful pursuer just as the donkey kicked.

"Oh, my little girl!" Daisy's campstool flew backward as she jumped to run to her youngest daughter.

"O God, no!" Waterman cried as he left his bottles for Lillie.

Jesse was the first to reach her; but once he did, he wasn't sure what to do. He placed his hand on her tiny back. It was warm, but he could feel no breathing.

Daisy pushed him aside and scooped up her daughter. "My baby! My baby!" She crushed the child against her breast.

"Let me see her!" Waterman yelled.

Daisy rocked the child and wept.

"Let me see her!" Waterman yelled again. He managed to get his wife to loosen her hold on Lillie long enough that he could examine the little girl's head. There was a deep gash, but little blood.

The other girls stood silently watching with tear-filled eyes, their hands held to their mouths. Even in his drunken state McFarland managed a look of concern.

Ordering his wife to quit her bawling, Waterman placed his ear to Lillie's lips. He felt her chest. Everyone else held their breath.

He looked up at his wife. "She's dead."

"No!" Daisy whispered. "She's just asleep!"

"Are you sure, Allen?" Matilda asked. "Are you sure?"

Waterman nodded solemnly. His eyes were dry, but there was no mistaking that Lillie had taken some of the life from her father's eyes when she left.

"You have a whole wagon load of medicines!" Daisy yelled at him. "Concoct something that will wake her up!"

"Daisy, she's gone. Nothing will wake her up!" Waterman said.

Matilda gathered the girls—all of them reduced to tears now—and took them back to the wagon. McFarland returned to his rock and drank in silence. Slate crawled under the wagon and into his bedroll. Waterman stood by his wife as she wailed. He offered her no comfort.

In the tamed West, in the midst of boredom, death came suddenly.

Chapter 24

THERE was little rest in the camp on the night of Lillie's death. Early the next morning a grave was made among the sunflowers where the girl was tenderly laid. Daisy insisted that Waterman shoot the donkey. He refused. They would need it when they reached Pueblo. After privately warning everyone not to let Daisy near firearms, Waterman did his best to restore their daily routine.

But Daisy was not the same after Lillie's death. She spoke little and sat alone at nights while her husband cleaned his bottles and McFarland drank and Matilda cared for the girls.

Routine returned within a week. Up at six, walk, two stops to water the animals, make camp at four, finish chores, and go to bed, only to do the exact same thing the next day. The only change was in those who lived the routine. Cora Belle lost not only her little sister, she lost her mother to a silent world of grief. And for some reason McFarland changed in the way he treated Slate. He dogged the boy more than ever.

From sunup to well past sundown, the bulging McFarland watched Slate's every step. He was still physical with the boy, but in a different way, and the change in tactic seemed to annoy Slate even more. Jesse figured that's why McFarland did it.

The inebriated McFarland, who drank half the day now as well as at night, acted as Slate's shadow, always staying within touching distance and never leaving the boy alone. Instead of shouting at the boy, he whispered things in his ear—off-color remarks was Jesse's guess, based on the way Slate pushed the drunk away. And instead of criticizing, McFarland teased him. He laughed and sniggered and made fun of almost everything Slate did.

After a couple of days of this, Jesse had seen enough. He told McFarland to leave the boy alone. McFarland's reaction was to take a swing at Jesse and tell him to mind his own business. Afterward, the bully was all the more aggressive in his actions with Slate, only now he leered at Jesse while he pestered the boy.

Jesse couldn't believe Waterman had failed to notice the abuse. He could only conclude Waterman chose not to confront his brother-in-law for whatever reason. So Jesse brought the abuse to the druggist's attention, hoping that it would force Waterman to deal with it. It didn't. He shrugged it off. He said the reason he hired the boy was to keep McFarland out of his hair and so far it was working. In addition, he instructed Jesse to leave McFarland and the boy alone, saying he didn't want Jesse to stir up a hornet's nest needlessly.

Late that same night Jesse was awakened by the sounds of a struggle. Beneath the second wagon McFarland was wrestling with Slate. Although McFarland's speech was heavily slurred and his actions clumsy, he had a distinct advantage in that he outweighed the boy two to one. He had managed to pin the boy's arms to the ground.

"Get off of me!" Slate hissed.

The boy's words had no effect on the drunk. He squirmed and struggled, but was making no headway.

Jesse looked around. Everyone else was still asleep. While Jesse slept by the fire, the Watermans and their daughter slept under the drugstore wagon. Matilda and her girls had found sleeping room inside the second wagon.

Slate managed to unpin a leg. He tried to kick the bottom

of the wagon, undoubtedly hoping to waken Mrs. McFarland so she would come and take care of her husband. However, McFarland managed to pin the freed leg and foil the boy's attempt.

Mindful of Waterman's admonition to leave well enough alone, Jesse yelled at McFarland in a half-whisper so as not to wake the others. "Come on, McFarland!" he yelled. "You badger the boy all day long. Let him get some sleep!"

McFarland gave no indication he heard Jesse. With all the scuffling, chances are he didn't. Slate didn't seem to hear either; he grunted as he tried to push the heavier man off of him.

"McFarland!"

The struggle continued.

"McFarland!"

It was no use. If Jesse yelled louder, he would wake up everyone. But if he got up and confronted McFarland, the abusive drunk would probably come after him. He wasn't so concerned about that as much as he was concerned about "stirring up the hornet's nest." He didn't want to make things even worse for Slate. Nor did he want Waterman to leave him high and dry in the middle of Kansas for interfering when he was told not to.

What would Truly Noble do?

That settled it. This time the answer came easily. There were occasions when stirring up hornets could not be avoided. This was one of those times.

Jesse threw back his blanket and walked to the edge of the wagon. Bending down, he shoved McFarland in the back and said, "Leave the boy alone!"

McFarland swung around like a bear disturbed in his cave. He glared at the intruder with yellow, bloodshot eyes. He showed his teeth. And, unless Jesse was imagining things, he even growled.

"Mind your own business!" McFarland roared.

"Jesse...help...me..."

The boy's voice was barely audible; his chest bore the full weight of the drunk. But it was enough to stir Jesse to action. He reached under the wagon and grabbed McFarland by the collar and the back of the shirt, and he pulled with all his might.

Because McFarland outweighed him too, Jesse had put everything he had into the initial tug. Either he had gained more muscle than he realized, or drinking made a man lighter, Jesse didn't know which, but McFarland came off the boy with surprising ease. In fact, the drunk almost flew off, banging his head against the top of the wagon.

McFarland let out a howl of pain.

The moment the drunk was off him, Slate scrambled from underneath the wagon and escaped out the other side. Circling the end of the wagon, the boy ran across a field toward the stream.

The bump and howl were loud enough to wake one of the girls inside the wagon. "Momma, I heard something outside. I think it's a bear. Or maybe Indians!"

Her alarm set off her sister who started screaming. Matilda, not knowing it was her husband doing the howling, called for him to protect them. Waterman was on his feet reaching for a rifle. Under the first wagon Cora Belle was in her mother's arms screaming. Daisy held her tight saying, "We're comin' to be with you, Lillie! We're comin' to be with you!"

Jesse looked at the chaos all around him. There was no other way to describe it—it was a hornet's nest.

"Waterman! Don't shoot! It's just us!"

The druggist peered his direction without lowering the rifle barrel.

Jesse looked around for Slate. The boy had taken off across a field and was still running. He looked back at the wagons and stumbled, falling to the ground.

The druggist swung the weapon toward the field.

"Don't shoot! It's Slate!" Jesse cried. Turning to the boy he cupped his hands around his mouth and shouted, "It's all right! Stay there!"

The boy scrambled to get up.

"I'll go get him!" Jesse said. He started after the boy.

McFarland grabbed Jesse's shirt from behind. Warm, sour whiskey breath hit him in the face as the drunk cursed him and said, "You keep your stinkin' hands off her!"

Jesse broke away from him. "What are you talking about?" he cried. "You're out of your mind!" When he turned to go after Slate, he saw the boy picking up his hat which had fallen to the ground. It was the first time Jesse had seen the boy without his hat. There was something familiar about him.

Jesse ran after him. Slate turned and continued running. Behind them McFarland kept shouting that he had seen her first.

On the far side of the field where the ground had been cut away by a creek, Jesse caught up with the boy. Jesse grabbed the back of his coat just as Slate slipped over the ridge. Together they tumbled down the pebble-strewn side. When they finally came to a stop, Jesse's back was in the creek. The cool water soaked through his shirt quickly and chilled him. Slate ended up on top of him.

For the first time since they set out, Jesse got a clear glimpse of Slate's face. As he did, his mind flashed back to a New York alley and the sound of a police whistle. A wooden gate crashed open and a dark form flew toward him, knocking him to the ground and landing on top of him. Just like now. In fact, exactly like now.

"Emily!"

"I can explain, Jesse, if you'll just give me a chance!"

Chapter 25

CLARA Morgan found herself sandwiched among hundreds of emigrants as she stood on the Kansas City platform of the Santa Fe Railroad. Clouds of white vapor escaped from various connections as station hands readied the train for departure. She caught an occasional glimpse of the engineer checking gauges in the locomotive's cab. He had personalized his cab with a stag's antlers mounted overhead. He stepped aside while a fireman shoveled coal into the furnace to keep the pressure up.

A railroad conductor mounted a step so he could be seen above the throng. Holding a list in front of him, he began calling out names. All around, people strained to hear. The conductor called each name only once and ignored all pleas for clarification. In fact, he refused to answer questions of any kind. He simply stood on his step and woodenly continued his task.

Those who heard their name called hastily gathered up packages, luggage, and children and hurried to board the train. The conductor droned on calling name after name. Clara Morgan was not among them. She wondered what she would do if she did not get on board. Ticket lines were long and station officials refused to bother themselves with questions asked by those with emigrant tickets, even when it came to simple questions like train schedules. It was the least expensive fare and it was all Clara could afford.

She had enough money to get to Santa Fe. After that, she didn't know what she was going to do. Everything depended upon finding Jesse. If she found him in Santa Fe, then they would figure a way to get back home. If she didn't find him there...well, she would worry about that when the time came.

The crowd of emigrants around her thinned considerably. She scanned the windows of the passenger cars. There were fifteen of them per car, and every one of them had a face in it. She inched closer to the conductor. By doing so she knew it wouldn't change anything, still it was a few feet closer to getting on board. The conductor barked:

Mr. and Mrs. John G. Shreves...

Phoebe Ann Park...

Nathaniel Hardman...

Mr. and Mrs. Thomas Galbraith.

He paused and lowered his list. Pivoting on the step he craned his neck to look behind him. Waiting for a signal.

Would that be all? Clara worried about what she would do now. When would the next train come along? Where could she find out? Did she have to exchange tickets to get back on the list or did they just continue with the names on the current list?

The conductor nodded to some unseen signal. He lifted his board and began reading again:

Mr. and Mrs. Amos Matthews Harris...

Charlotte O'Dell Gilmore...

Henry Dutton...

Clara Cassidy Morgan...

Spencer Philips...

The conductor had called her name! Clara snatched up her bag and stepped smartly toward the first passenger car. Just as she reached the steps, another conductor blocked her way.

"Not this one...down the line." He shooed her away like she was a little child caught in the wrong place.

Conductors blocked her entrance to the third and fourth passenger cars. The steps to the fifth car were clear. Clara climbed on board.

The car in which Clara found herself was crammed with adults and children of every size and description on both sides of the aisle. The scene reminded Clara of Noah's ark. The seats were straight-backed and small, with thinly padded cushions and little leg room. There were gas lamps at either end of the compartment. To get to the aisle, she had to step around a wood-burning stove that sat on a platform. An enclosed space at the far end of the car held the toilet.

Leading herself with her bag, Clara worked her way down the aisle looking for an open seat. On both sides of the aisle adults spilled over the edges of the short benches, narrowing the passage and making it difficult for her to pass. If she said "excuse me" once, she said it a hundred times.

Three quarters of the way down the aisle she spotted two empty seats. The one on the left was next to a woman dressed in black who held a drooling child on her lap. The empty seat on the right was next to a man with a full brown beard and thinning hair. He occupied himself staring out the window.

Given the choice, Clara preferred the company of a woman over that of a strange man. But when she made her way toward the empty seat, the woman with the child looked up, saw what Clara was thinking, and with a scowl, snatched the child from her lap and plopped him in the seat next to her. The child took exception to his mother's action and began to howl as he tried to climb back onto his mother's lap. But the mother would have none of it. She scolded him and held him in place.

Clara turned toward the other empty seat.

"Is this seat taken?" she asked.

The man next to the window turned and looked at her. His eyes were kind though he didn't smile. Looking quickly away, he pulled himself closer to the window and tugged at the ends of his long-sleeved shirt. "No," he said softly.

Clara looked around for a place to put her bag. Every available space seemed to be taken already.

"Do you need help with that?"

He had spoken so softly, at first Clara didn't hear him. Then, when she realized he'd said something, she saw he was staring at her bag. "Oh, I just can't seem to find a place to put this," she said.

The man got up from his seat. She handed him her bag and he managed to wedge it beneath their seat, though it cut into his already cramped foot space.

"Are you sure that will be all right?" Clara asked.

The man smiled and nodded. He took his place and Clara sat next to him.

Shortly afterward, the train crawled out of the station. Clara expected the train to pick up speed once it cleared the station. However, after a full hour it chugged along at a pace that seemed no faster than a brisk walk. No one came to offer an explanation. But that didn't stop some of the passengers around her from offering guesses.

"Probably a train wreck ahead," a man across the aisle and three seats up said. He was a large man with a full white beard and a red nose. Although he spoke to the person across the aisle from him, by the way he kept glancing around it was evident he wanted everyone to hear what he was saying.

"Took an East Coast train once," he said, "from New York to Philadelphia. Same thing happened. Someone forgot to turn a switch and two trains goin' sixty miles an hour hit head-on! BOOM!" He made a crashing sound to illustrate his story. "Took them two full days to clear the tracks afore we could get through. Even then, when we passed there was bodies everywhere. 'Course they were covered with blankets and tarps. But you could see their feet stickin' out just the same."

Clara didn't want to hear this, not while she was riding the train. She didn't seem to be alone. Heads turned this way and that away from the man. So Clara thought that would be the end of it. It wasn't.

"Train wrecks are common things, happen every day," the man started up again. "Read someplace that in the mid-seventies there were a hundred-an'-four head-on collisions!" He waited for a response and was satisfied to get a few raised eyebrows. "'Course, the railroad companies have made some improvements since then. But that doesn't mean it still doesn't happen regularly."

He sat back and seemed to bask in the small response he managed to get. Again, Clara hoped that would be the end of it.

"'Course, train wrecks can happen for all kinds of reasons," the man continued. "Boilers blow up, bridges decay and collapse when the trains pass over them, tracks get old and crack, brakes overheat or fail, and sometimes they're set on fire by these kerosene lamps or that wood stove! Once read about the Camp Hill Disaster and the Angola Horror. Forty-two passengers were burned to a crisp when their car fell off a bridge!"

The man next to Clara shifted in his seat uncomfortably. He pulled on the cuffs of his sleeves and stared at the flatlands creeping by.

"'Course, the best wrecks are head-on collisions," the morbid storyteller went on. "I have a photographic print of a head-on collision that took place in Pawtucket, Rhode Island in '56. It's rolled up in my bag. First chance we get, I'll show it to anyone who's interested."

The man across the aisle from him said, "I heard that some railroad companies are staging wrecks for entertainment."

Clara moaned. *Please don't encourage him!*

The self-appointed train wreck expert brightened. "I seen one of those!" he cried. "Thirty thousand people came out to watch it!" Glancing around at some of the other passengers he defended himself against their unspoken thoughts. "So I guess

I'm not as strange as some of you might think when thirty thousand come out to see a wreck!"

For the next twenty minutes he described the event in lurid detail of how two locomotives destroyed each other as they steamed toward a sixty-mile-an-hour crash.

To distract herself, Clara closed her eyes and leaned her head back. Her thoughts turned to the immediate past—a head-on collision of her own. *Why do I act that way around the Morgans? Every time I'm around them, the worst comes out in me. You'd think that after all these years I would be able to control my feelings when I'm around them. Yet I always come away feeling like a dog! They mean well, I know that. It's just that they don't realize that you can't change the world. There are some things you just have to live...*

"Are you going to Topeka?"

Clara opened her eyes. The man next to her looked at her with kind eyes. "Topeka? No, actually, Santa Fe."

He nodded and looked away.

"And you?" Clara asked.

"Denver," the man said. "By way of La Junta."

Clara nodded.

"Joining your family in Santa Fe?"

"No...well, yes...I think...at least I hope," Clara stammered.

This brought a smile from the man. He had a naturally warm smile that hinted at an equally warm and friendly disposition.

"And you? Do you have family in Denver?"

The man shook his head. He pulled at the cuffs on his sleeves. "No family..." he lost himself in thought for a moment, then said, "...an employment opportunity. Security firm, like the Pinkertons, only much smaller. I've been corresponding with the man who owns the company. He said if I could make it out to La Junta, he would give me a job. He has a ranch there. The job would be in Denver."

"I see," said Clara.

An uneasy moment of transition passed between them. Would there be a transition to a different topic, or a transition to silence and their separate private thoughts? Clara stared at the back of the seat as she waited to see which would develop.

"By the way, my name is Logan," the man said. He didn't offer a hand.

"Logan," Clara repeated.

"Actually, it's Woodhull Logan." He grinned and shrugged. "But people just call me Logan...you can call me...just Logan...I thought since we were traveling so far together, we might as well..."

"Clara."

"Clara?" Logan repeated.

"Clara Morgan."

Logan cocked his head and gave her an unusual look.

"What is it?" Clara asked.

"Are you from Kansas City?"

"No," she said tentatively. "I'm from New York."

"Lower east side?"

"Yes."

Logan sat back and smiled. "This is amazing," he mused, "no...it would be..."

"What?"

Logan turned toward her. "He's been dead for some years now, but by any chance would you be a relation to Benjamin Morgan? He used to be..."

"...the preacher at the Heritage Church mission."

"That's the one!" Logan said excitedly.

"I knew him," Clara said. "He was my husband."

Woodhull Logan closed his eyes and whispered, "Thank You, Lord!" To Clara he said, "Mrs. Morgan, this is an answer to prayer. I just want to tell you how much your husband meant to me. He..." Logan paused to blink back tears. "...your husband saved my life. Twice."

As he spoke he pulled down on the cuffs of his shirtsleeves. It was then that Clara noticed that both of the man's hands bore heavy burn scars.

Chapter 26

WATERMAN had warned Jesse not to stir up a hornet's nest. Lying on the water side of the river's edge, Jesse couldn't imagine things being stirred up any more than they were right now.

Cold river water soaked his clothing and chilled his back. Slate lay on top of him; only it wasn't Slate, it was Emily with short hair. Not far from them was a drunkard who wanted to smash Jesse's face and a druggist with a rifle who would somehow find a way to blame Jesse for this unforeseen turn of events. Meanwhile, the closeness of Emily's smooth, pale skin set against a black canvas of glistening stars tantalized him more than he cared to admit to himself. At the same time, the prairie itch was attacking his bottom with a vengeance, undoubtedly aggravated by his wet trousers. But somehow everything came back to Emily. He couldn't take his eyes off her. One moment she looked like Slate, and the next moment she looked like Emily—alluring and attractive. What was she doing dressed as a boy? And why had he not recognized her before now?

The hornet's nest was Jesse's head and all these thoughts buzzed inside.

Emily rolled off him, allowing Jesse to climb out of the river.

As he did, he moaned and said, "All right, you said you could explain. Well, go ahead. Explain!"

"Not here!" Emily whispered. She crawled up the ridge until she could see the clearing. "Waterman and McFarland are coming!" she cried.

Jesse peeked over the ridge for himself. The druggist Waterman led the way, his rifle at the ready. McFarland staggered behind him, weaving from side to side. Daisy and Matilda huddled with the children beside the wagons, the mothers' arms encircling their offspring like hens protecting chicks.

"Don't let him touch me again!" Emily cried. Her eyes—fastened on McFarland—were filled with horror and loathing; her lips curled with disgust.

Jesse looked around them for someplace to go. "Come on!" he said.

Taking Emily by the hand, he led her upstream about a quarter of a mile. There, they found an abandoned campsite sheltered by boulders. They waited in silence and listened. After a few minutes of hearing nothing but an occasional rustle of wind, Jesse concluded the druggist and the drunk hadn't followed them. He figured it was a safe assumption. McFarland was so drunk he couldn't sneak up on a circus.

"Now," Jesse said, turning to Emily who was seated on a boulder. "You said you could explain."

Emily stared at the ground. "It's hard to know where to begin," she said.

Maybe it was the cold, wet clothes; or maybe the prairie itch was finally getting to him; or maybe things had been stirred up beyond his ability to cope, but for whatever reason, Jesse was feeling waspish.

"All right, then, let me guess," he said. "You're doing a feature story on Chicago druggists who are moving to Pueblo, Colorado. No, no...I got it...you're writing an investigative article about the danger of drunks on the Santa Fe Trail! Or maybe this...you're following a man across the continent seeing how many ways you can ruin his life before he goes insane!"

"Jesse Morgan!" Emily cried, jumping down from the boulder. "You have no right to talk to me that way!"

"I have every right to talk to you this way!" Jesse yelled. "Who are you, anyway? I don't even know for sure who I'm talking to—Slate or Emily Barnes? What's worse, I'm not even sure I know your gender! Are you male or female? You're driving me crazy!"

"Jesse Morgan! You're an unfeeling brute!" Emily cried. "Just a little while ago a drunken man tried to force himself on me! It took you long enough to come to my aid!"

"It took me so long," Jesse cried, "because I thought you were a boy!"

"McFarland knew I wasn't a boy!" Emily cried. Fresh tear tracks glimmered on her cheeks lit by the moon.

"How long has he known?"

Emily sniffed and dried her cheeks with the palms of her hands. "Since the day we buried Lillie," she said. "He stumbled upon me while I was…" she hesitated, "…while I was…"

Jesse held up a hand and nodded. He understood. *So that explains the change in the way McFarland was treating Slate…er, Emily.* "If McFarland knew, why didn't he tell anybody?" Jesse asked.

"He threatened to tell Waterman every day," Emily cried. "I guess he thought he could pressure me into granting him favors for his silence."

"Did you?"

"Of course not!" Emily cried. "Is that what it looked like I was doing under that wagon? Granting him favors? I was fighting for my life!"

"I'm sorry," Jesse said softly. He stared at her. "It's just that I'm still having a hard time believing that you're not Slate. For some reason I keep thinking that you've put on Slate's clothes and poor Slate is running around somewhere in his long johns."

Emily sniffed and laughed. "You're the one who gave me the idea."

"Me?"

"That night on the bridge. You told me about Julia, your other aunt, the Confederate belle who dressed up like a soldier."

Jesse shook his head and grinned. Before, whenever he had heard the story of Julia and Marshall, he'd always wondered how his Uncle Marshall could be so blind that he wouldn't be able to recognize a woman in man's clothing. Now that it happened to him, he wouldn't be so hard on his uncle.

"You still haven't explained what you're doing here!" Jesse said. "I mean...who are you? The first time I saw you, you were a typist in an office. Then you're some kind of crusader who comes barging through a gate blowing a police whistle. Then, you're this glamorous woman I happen to meet on the Brooklyn Bridge. And the next thing I know, we bump into each other on a steamboat in Cincinnati and you're an investigative reporter doing a story on the captain while this hulking man threatens to hurt me for being near you. Now you show up disguised as a boy on the Santa Fe Trail in the middle of Kansas!" He paused for effect. "Have I missed anything?"

Emily could think of a couple of things she could have added to his list that he didn't know about, but she held her tongue.

"Who is Emily Barnes?" Jesse cried.

"Austin," Emily said.

"Austin? What do you mean, Austin?"

"My last name is not Barnes. It's Austin."

Jesse was dumbfounded. His eyebrows were raised high while his jaw hung low. "Austin," he repeated. "As in..."

Emily nodded. "The Austin Factory. Austin Enterprises. Franklin Austin. I'm his daughter."

Jesse threw his hands high and twirled around. "I can't believe this! I'm standing in the middle of Kansas with a millionaire's daughter who's dressed like a boy!"

Emily slipped off the wide-brimmed hat and held it in her hands. That helped considerably. Even though her hair was cut short, without the hat her features looked more feminine.

"Any more surprises?" Jesse asked.

"I'm not a reporter with the *Evening Post.*"

Again his mouth dropped like a lead weight. "You're not a reporter? All that time...Captain Lakanal leading you around the boat...the race against the *Eagle* to impress you..."

Emily flapped her hands. "Well, I want to be a reporter!" she cried. "It's just that I've never had anything published yet."

"This is unbelievable!" Jesse cried. "Completely and totally unbelievable! I've got to sit down." He made his way to a rock and plunked down on it, slope-shouldered and bewildered.

"There's more," Emily said.

"Of course there is! Why wouldn't there be?" Jesse cried sarcastically.

"That man on the steamboat? Mr. Tykas?"

"Yeah?"

"He works for my father. He was sent to find me and take me home."

Jesse winced. "Don't tell me you ran away from home."

"My father wouldn't let me go. So I went anyway."

Jesse rolled his eyes.

"You ran away!" Emily cried.

"I thought I'd killed a boy! Besides, I'm old enough to be out on my own."

"So am I!"

"How old are you?" Jesse asked.

Emily sniffed. "A lady doesn't reveal her age."

"Ohhhhh," Jesse moaned. "You're sixteen years old, aren't you? Or, better yet, fifteen!"

Emily straightened. "I am not! I'm eighteen!"

"Still young enough that your father sends someone to

fetch you home!"

Emily hopped off her rock. "I think I've had enough of this conversation, thank you," she said.

"What? I've hurt your feelings? What are you going to do? Run home? Oh! That's right, you can't! 'Cause home is more than a thousand miles away!"

Emily just stood there, stunned by Jesse's sarcastic volley. The way she looked—frightened, defeated, hurt—made Jesse wish he hadn't said the things he did. But his anger drove him. He still needed to know one thing.

Jesse stood. "You haven't told me why you did it."

"Did what?"

"All of this!" Jesse said with grandiose arm gestures. "This whole charade! Pretending to be a reporter. Running away. Becoming a boy! Everything!"

Emily started to walk away. "I don't care to discuss this anymore."

"Well, you're going to discuss it!" Jesse said.

"Jesse Morgan, if you think for one moment I'm going to stand here and let you..."

Jesse grabbed her by the shoulders. "Tell me!" he shouted.

"Jesse Morgan, you let me go!"

"Not until you tell me."

Emily struggled to break free. Jesse's hold on her was too strong.

"Look at me!" Jesse said.

Emily looked away.

"Look at me!" Jesse said again. This time he grabbed the sides of her head and forced her to look at him. "Tell me why you did this!"

"Let me go!"

"Not until you tell me why you did this!"

"Jesse, I'm warning you..."

"We can stand here all night," Jesse said. "Tell me why you

did this!"

Emily began to weep.

"Tell me!"

"No...I..." Tears escalated to sobs.

"Tell me!"

"Jesse..."

"Tell me!"

"I love you..." Emily sobbed. "I love you...I did it because I love you!"

Jesse loosed his grip on her shoulders and Emily's head fell against his chest.

"I love you," she wept softly. "You silly fool!"

The eastern sky was robin's egg blue when Emily and Jesse made their way back downstream. When they crested the ridge that separated the river from the field, Emily gasped.

"They're gone!" she said.

"I don't believe it!" Jesse cried. "They left us!"

On the far side of the road the campsite was deserted. Not a wagon or druggist or drunk was in sight. Jesse raced across the field and a short distance up the rutted road. There was no sign of the Waterman party, not even rising dust from the wagons.

Emily caught up with him. "What do we do now?" she asked.

Biting his lower lip, Jesse stared at the trail, then slowly turned around in a circle, stopping at each compass point and straining his eyes into the distance. There wasn't much to see. Flat land, mild rises and depressions, but no signs of any other roads or structures.

"Do you know where we are?" Emily asked.

"Waterman kept the maps. He looked at them while we were traveling. I never got to see them."

"Then we're lost?" Emily asked.

"I just don't know how far we have to travel before we find a town or something," Jesse said, staring up the road again. He started walking; his clothes were damp and heavy, and the prairie itch flaired from his backside down to his ankles.

Emily waited a moment; then, realizing he wasn't scouting the territory but had decided to move on, ran to catch him. "We're just going to walk?" she asked.

"Do you have any better ideas?"

She fell in beside him.

"Put your hat on and keep it on," Jesse said. "If anybody sees us, it's best they think you're a boy for now."

That was all he said to her the entire day.

Chapter 27

JESSE and Emily staggered into the safety of Fort Larned, weary and exhausted after two days of walking. Earlier that morning they had happened upon a small hill with a rock face. In any other part of the country this minor geographical structure would have gone unnoticed. But this was Kansas and the rock was the constellation of the prairie; it not only served as a constant point of reference, it attracted plains travelers to it.

Inscriptions covered the rock, scratched in the surface by those who had traveled the trail before Jesse and Emily. Later, Jesse learned that the outcropping was called Pawnee Rock. It had been a major campground for caravans for years. It was also the site of more than one Indian ambush. According to the colonel at Fort Larned, practically every square yard of sod below the rock contained the grave of a Santa Fe Trail traveler.

However, Jesse saw no Pawnees at the rock. He sensed no danger there. The rock only served to remind him that he had arrived in the West long after the real excitement had passed on. There was no longer any real adventure on the trail, only obsessed druggists with their drunken brothers-in-law, and runaway girls who dressed up to look like boys.

The colonel in charge at Fort Larned was sympathetic to Jesse and Emily's plight, at least as much of it as they told him. Basically, their story was that Waterman abandoned them while they were down by the river. They didn't hide the fact that Emily was a girl, nor did they tell the colonel what they were doing at the river, and he didn't ask.

The colonel confirmed that two wagons had indeed passed by the fort without stopping, which he thought doubly odd—first, because wagon travelers were growing increasingly scarce; and second, because they didn't stop. Usually this far into the journey across Kansas nearly everyone needed some kind of supplies; and even if they didn't, they would stop to inquire about the road ahead or just to chat for a while.

"I had a strange feeling about them two wagons," the colonel said. He was a small man with red hair and an easygoing manner about him. But from what Jesse observed, the man's genial personality in no way lessened his authority at the post. From the way the soldiers came and went, it was evident that they greatly respected their superior.

"I can send a detachment to bring those wagons back here," the colonel offered.

Jesse pondered the offer; he looked at Emily. Her eyes reflected a horror at the prospect of having to confront McFarland. "No sir," Jesse replied. "We're safe now. No real harm was done."

"Think it over carefully, boy. Abandoning two people on the plains with no food or water or weapons is not something we take lightly around here," the colonel said.

"Waterman checked his maps frequently," Jesse said. "He probably knew that Fort Larned was within walking distance. I see no point in going after him." Jesse felt uneasy about defending the druggist, but it was necessary to protect Emily.

The colonel shook his head. "You're a more forgiving man than I would be if our situations were reversed," he said. "So then, what now for you?"

"Do you have a telegraph?" Jesse asked.

"Of course."

"Then, if possible, we would like to telegraph New York. Miss Barnes...I mean, Miss Austin needs to contact her father to make arrangements for her return."

The disappointment and hurt in Emily's eyes were unmistakable. She and Jesse had pointedly argued about this very issue. Jesse insisted that Emily return to her father; Emily insisted she would not. Furthermore, Emily predicted that when the time came for a decision to be made, Jesse would relent and the two of them would stay together. Jesse had just proven her wrong. He was sending her away.

Jesse looked straight at her when he made arrangements for the telegram, expecting some kind of argument from Emily. There was none. In silent resignation, Emily lowered her head.

The telegraph message was sent.

"I'm still amazed at modern-day communications," Jesse said, holding a telegraph dispatch in his hand. "We sent a message to your father only two hours ago, and already we have a response! In the old days, it would have taken months for correspondence to be answered between Kansas and New York."

Jesse stood in the doorway of Emily's room. In the compound behind him, the last of the sun's shadows had disappeared for the evening. Soldiers lowered the fort's flag. Others marched dutifully around the compound to secure the outpost for the night.

The interior of Emily's cabin was dark enough to warrant a lamp. However, none were lit. Emily slumped in a wooden chair beside a quilted bed. From the look of indifference upon her face, she did not share Jesse's enthusiasm for modern communication devices.

She sighed. With a flat, lifeless voice, she asked, "What does the telegram say?"

"Emily, don't be like this," Jesse said.

"That's what my father said? 'Emily, don't be like this?'"

Jesse leaned heavily against the door jamb. The woman before him was nothing like the cannonball that had burst through the gate in the alley and landed on top of him. Nor did she resemble the cocky investigative reporter aboard the *Tippecanoe*. And there was nothing similar between the woman in this cabin and the alluring beauty who had walked with Jesse on the Brooklyn Bridge. Slouched in the chair, she was nothing more than a pouting little girl who wasn't getting her way.

"I'm not being like anything," Emily said. "Just read the telegram."

Without looking at the paper in his hand, Jesse told her what the message said. "Your father is glad you're safe. He's sending one of his agents to escort you back to New York. The agent should arrive in two to three days."

A suspicious glint appeared in her eyes. "My father said he was glad I was safe?"

Jesse shrugged. "He implied it."

"Specifically, how did he imply it?"

Jesse sighed in exasperation, "He didn't imply it, all right? I assumed it. After all, he's your father."

Emily slumped further down in her chair. "You don't know my father," she said.

For a time, nothing further was said by either one of them. Jesse felt like some things needed to be said, he just couldn't get the words out. His unspoken words clotted in his throat in a painful lump.

"Unless you have some more good news you want to pass along to me..." Emily said.

With a shuffle of his feet, Jesse turned to leave. He turned back. "Emily..."

Quickly, Emily was out of her chair. "Good-night, Mr. Morgan," she said.

"Wait!" Jesse pleaded.

Emily folded her arms angrily.

"This may be our last night together," Jesse said softly. "There's a supply wagon leaving for Dodge City tomorrow afternoon. The colonel said I could hitch a ride on it."

"Dodge City...how nice for you."

Ignoring the sarcasm, Jesse continued, "And since we may not see each other again...couldn't we just talk? The moon is on the rise. I thought we might stroll around the compound together."

"Thank you, but no," Emily said firmly. "You have already made known your feelings for me. It's time I stopped making a spectacle of myself."

"But since that night by the river, I haven't spoken a word to you about how I feel!" Jesse protested.

"My point exactly!"

Emily shut the door on him.

Jesse spotted Tykas first. The agent was driving a buckboard wagon into the fort. Upon seeing Tykas again, Jesse's reactions were mixed. The last time he had seen the agent was when the *Tippecanoe* exploded. And although Jesse was glad that the agent hadn't perished in the river, he was chagrined that Tykas would be the one to escort Emily home. It only made sense though. If Tykas was tracking them, naturally he would be the closest Austin agent to them—apparently even closer than Austin knew when he sent the dispatch, for the agent arrived at the fort the day after the dispatch arrived.

"Mr. Tykas!" Jesse yelled.

The agent pulled his horse to a halt and turned suddenly in Jesse's direction. When the agent saw who had hailed him, he reached for something inside his coat.

"I want to apologize for my actions," Jesse said quickly. "On board the *Tippecanoe* I didn't know you worked for Mr. Austin."

Tykas looked at him suspiciously and said nothing.

"I understand now that you were just doing your job," Jesse explained.

"You understand now," Tykas repeated.

Jesse grinned and nodded sheepishly. "Until just a few days ago, I didn't know that Emily had run away from home. I didn't even know that she was Franklin Austin's daughter. I thought her name was Barnes."

"I see. So you will take me to her?"

"Of course!" Jesse cried. "She's right over there." He pointed to Emily's room on the far side of the compound. "But I'm sure you'll want to talk to the colonel first. Besides, it may take Emily a little while to get ready, though I don't know why it would—she doesn't have any clothes other than the ones she's wearing. It's just that your arrival is something of a surprise. Mr. Austin's dispatch said you wouldn't be here for another day or two."

"Let's get on with this," Tykas said.

In the colonel's office, Jesse introduced Tykas to the commander of the fort as the Austin agent who had been sent to escort Emily home. The colonel sent for Emily and while they waited for her to arrive, Tykas spoke knowledgeably about Emily and Austin family affairs. He also sketched their return journey.

"I'm to take the young lady to Great Bend. There, we will catch a train east. Naturally, we'll get her some suitable clothing."

Emily was led into the office. Her appearance illustrated her need for suitable clothing. She still wore the boots and britches and shirt and vest she wore as Slate. Upon seeing Tykas, she reacted visibly. However, her initial resistance melted quickly. While the colonel and Tykas talked, Emily stood silently like a prisoner resigned to her fate.

The buckboard left the fort two hours before Jesse was

scheduled to leave for Dodge City. Tykas insisted Mr. Austin would want them to leave immediately. He said that with luck they could catch the late-afternoon train out of Great Bend.

In all the haste, Jesse did not have an opportunity to tell Emily good-bye privately. He watched as Tykas shepherded her into the buckboard. Then, just as the buckboard pulled away, Emily's eyes met his.

Jesse smiled. "Good-bye, Emily."

Emily returned neither the smile nor the good-bye. Sitting sullenly beside Tykas, she turned her head and stared forward. Jesse could only watch as the buckboard disappeared through the fort gates in a cloud of dust.

Following Emily's departure, a gray mood settled inside Jesse. It was like one of those gloomy neither/nor weather days when it was neither sunny nor rainy; the kind of day when the sky is flat gray and the air hangs heavy, when time drags because it is impossible to distinguish one hour from the next because morning and afternoon look exactly the same.

Jesse fought the mood with activity. He volunteered for odd jobs around the compound to pass the time until the supply wagon was due to depart for Dodge City. Although he didn't want to admit it to himself, it bothered him that Emily was gone and that she didn't say good-bye to him when she left. And it bothered him that it was Tykas who was escorting her back to New York, though he didn't know why. Somehow, it just would have been easier for him if the agent was someone he'd never met before.

The supply wagon pulled out of the fort on schedule. Two soldiers sat on the wagon seat. One drove while the other stood guard. Two additional soldiers flanked the wagon on horseback. Jesse sat alone in the empty wagon bed.

They had been gone from the fort for less than fifteen minutes when Jesse noticed someone riding up on them from behind. He alerted the flanking guards. In a precautionary move, the wagon was pulled to a stop and all rifles were trained on the approaching rider.

As soon as the rider came clearly into view, the rifles were lowered. It was another soldier from the fort, a private.

"Colonel sent me to return Morgan to the fort," the private said.

All eyes turned suspiciously toward Jesse. "All of us, or just Morgan?" the driver asked.

"You're to continue on to Dodge City. Morgan will ride back with me."

"What's this all about?" Jesse asked.

"I can't answer that," the private said. "All I know is that the colonel sent me to get you and return you to the fort."

Jesse glanced at the suspicious eyes that surrounded him. He wasn't being given a choice. Climbing out of the wagon, he accepted the private's outstretched hand and was pulled onto the horse. With the supply wagon soldiers watching, the private and his passenger turned back to Fort Larned.

"Morgan!" A scowling colonel rose from his chair and crossed to the front of his desk when Jesse was ushered into the room. While the colonel sat on the edge of his desk, he motioned Jesse toward a chair. As Jesse sat, the colonel handed him a piece of paper.

"We received this dispatch minutes after you left," the colonel said. "Would you care to explain it to me?"

Jesse read the telegram:

COLONEL,

I AM IN YOUR DEBT FOR THE SAFE RETURN OF MY DAUGHTER. MR. NELSON MERIWEATHER, ONE OF MY AGENTS, WILL ARRIVE AT FORT LARNED DAY AFTER NEXT. HE WILL ESCORT

MY DAUGHTER BACK TO NEW YORK. MR. MERIWEATHER HAS
MY FULL AUTHORITY TO REIMBURSE YOU FOR ANY AND ALL
EXPENDITURES YOU MIGHT HAVE SUSTAINED DURING MY
DAUGHTER'S STAY.

FRANKLIN AUSTIN

As Jesse read the dispatch, a feeling of dread crept over
him.

With arms folded and in a voice heavy with authority, the
colonel said, "So tell me, Mr. Morgan, who is this Tykas fellow you brought into my office? And what are his plans for
Emily Austin?"

From the tone of the man's voice and the way he was scruti-
nizing Jesse, it was clear the colonel suspected Jesse of conspir-
acy. To offset the colonel's suspicions, Jesse related everything
he knew about Tykas—his encounter with the man on board
the *Tippecanoe,* and everything Emily had told him. "It was
Emily who told me Tykas works for Mr. Austin," Jesse said,
"and that he had been sent to take her back to New York!"

The colonel rubbed his eyes while he weighed Jesse's words.
"There's only one way to clear this up," he said. The colonel
called in his assistant and dictated a dispatch to Franklin
Austin in which he inquired about both Tykas and Jesse
Morgan. "Meanwhile," the colonel said to Jesse, "you're not
going anywhere!"

A couple hours later Jesse was called again to the colonel's
office.

"Franklin Austin never heard of you," the colonel told him.
The red-haired commander held a fresh telegram in his hand.
"As for Tykas...the man is a *former* agent for Austin."

"Former?"

The colonel nodded. "Austin fired him."

Jesse sat forward in his seat and worried his cap with his

hands. "Then what does Richard Tykas want with Emily?"

"That's exactly what I intend to ask him!" The colonel called for his horse and a detachment of soldiers to accompany him to Great Bend. Then he ordered a dispatch sent to the train station instructing them to detain passengers Tykas and Austin until he arrived.

"Let me go with you, Colonel!" Jesse pleaded.

The colonel looked at him askance.

"I feel responsible!" Jesse said. "I handed Emily over to the wrong man!"

"Private!" the colonel yelled to his assistant. "Saddle an extra horse for Mr. Morgan!"

Chapter 28

THE station master at Great Bend had no passengers by the name of Tykas or Austin. At the colonel's insistence, the man checked his passenger list twice. No Tykas. No Austin. Nor had he seen a man and young woman fitting their description. The colonel questioned everyone at the station—baggage handlers, ticket sellers, even passengers who were waiting for the next train. No one had seen Emily or Tykas.

After a visit to the sheriff, the colonel concluded there was little else he could do. "My guess is Tykas had no intention of bringing her to Great Bend. For all we know, he doubled back and went to Dodge City. Or he could have headed south to Texas, or north to catch the Kansas Pacific Railroad."

"You're not giving up, are you?" Jesse asked.

"As much as I hate telling Mr. Austin that I handed his daughter over to the wrong man, I don't see that I have much choice."

"Can't you form a posse to go after them?"

"Which direction do you suggest I send them?" the colonel asked.

Jesse didn't have a ready answer.

"Look, son, I'll alert all my patrols to keep a ready eye open. In addition, I'll send dispatches to the neighboring cities and the stations along the railroad line. But after that, I don't know what else I can do."

Jesse nodded sadly. "I think I'll stay here," he said. "I'm going to ask around some more. Maybe somebody has seen them."

"Let me know if you learn anything," the colonel said.

The red-haired colonel and the detachment from Fort Larned left Great Bend and Jesse behind them.

For the second time in as many days, Jesse saw Tykas first.

It was night. The former Austin agent walked out of a hotel and crossed the street to a saloon. Jesse was slumped against the side of a closed barber shop on the boardwalk. He was low and in the shadows; that's why Tykas didn't see him. For the rest of the afternoon he had gone from street to street, business to business, and house to house asking if anyone had seen Tykas and Emily. He had come up dry. Until now.

Jesse waited a few minutes after Tykas entered the saloon before he got up. He wanted to make sure the man wasn't just going in and coming right back out. Hugging the shadows, Jesse made his way to the hotel.

The lobby was nothing more than a long room with a counter. Two heavily scarred chairs rested against the wall opposite the counter. Had there been people sitting in them, they would have had to move their legs to one side to let someone pass, so narrow was the distance between them and the counter. There were no fancy trappings. The walls were bare, as was the floor. At the far end of the lobby, a stairway led upstairs to the guest rooms. A silver-haired woman stood behind the counter. She sorted through some kind of paper slips while she puffed on a cigar.

"Can you tell me what room Emily Austin is in?" Jesse asked her.

The woman puffed, but didn't look up. "Don't give out room numbers," she said.

"I'm a friend of hers," Jesse said. "I've been looking for her all day."

"What makes you think she's here?" the woman asked, still not looking up.

"I just saw the man she was traveling with," Jesse said. "So I know she's here."

The cigar-smoking woman looked up. She stared at Jesse, then blew smoke in his face. "So, why don't you ask *him* what room she's in?" the woman asked with a yellow-toothed grin.

Jesse didn't have an answer for her.

"You're crowding my lobby," the woman said.

Jesse looked at the stairs.

"Get out!" the woman shouted. "Get out or I call the sheriff!"

Jesse left the hotel lobby and stood on the boardwalk. With an eye on the saloon, Jesse considered his options. He thought about simply calling out to Emily, hoping that she could hear him. But if she could hear him, chances were that Tykas would hear him too. He had to find Emily quietly, and he couldn't get to the rooms through the lobby. What else was there?

Walking out into the middle of the street, Jesse turned and looked back at the hotel. Above the porch covering, there were windows. He would have to climb onto the porch, though. Very conspicuous. So he made his way around to the back.

The first thing he saw surprised him. Tykas' buckboard. The horses were harnessed and tied to a railing. They were still hitched to the wagon. Either Tykas and Emily had just arrived at this location, or they were soon leaving. Jesse had to work fast. Someone would be tending the horses soon, quite possibly Tykas himself.

There was another stairway that led to a small landing and a back door. All along the back was a row of windows, but no way to peer into them. Unless…

Jesse made his way upstairs. He tried the back door. Locked. He didn't expect it to be that easy, but he had to try. Using the stair railing as a ladder, he pulled himself onto the roof of the building. He walked along the edge until he was near the first window, at least as close as he could get to it by guessing. Getting down on his belly, Jesse inched his way down the slanted roof until his head and shoulders hung over the edge. His head began to throb as blood rushed to it.

Holding onto the ledge with his hands, he peeked into the first room. It was completely dark. He couldn't see anything. Pulling himself back up, Jesse went to the next window. It was a tedious process, but one window at a time, Jesse worked his way down the back of the hotel. By the time he had looked in half the windows, he was growing discouraged. Some of the rooms were dark and he could see very little, but that didn't mean that Emily was not in one of them. Others had the shades drawn and Jesse could see nothing at all. Emily could have been behind any one of them. In one window, Jesse saw a woman brushing her hair in front of a vanity. In another, he saw a man meticulously laying out his bedclothes on the edge of the bed. In still another, he saw a bare-chested man standing sideways in front of a mirror as he scrutinized the bulge around his middle. In none of them did he see Emily.

Jesse's hands and stomach were getting raw from all the scraping on the rooftop. Still, he had to continue. He had to at least try to find Emily. Finally, he saw something.

There were a pair of men's boots at the end of a bed. Jesse could see no further than the top of the boots, so he could not see who was filling the boots. But the thing that grabbed his attention was that the boots were tied together by rope.

"Emily! Is that you?"

The boots didn't move.

Jesse leaned over the ledge dangerously far. Stretching as far forward as he could, he barely managed to tap the glass. "Emily! Emily! Can you hear me?"

The boots shook, then rocked side to side.

"Emily. If that's you, raise your boots and lower them three consecutive times." Jesse stared at the boots. They raised up and fell to the bed. Once. Twice. Three times!

"I'm coming in!" Jesse said.

Pulling himself onto the roof, Jesse reversed his position and lowered himself over the edge feet first. When he was balancing halfway on and halfway off, he began to doubt whether this was such a good idea. His feet dangled in air, searching for something but finding nothing.

Allowing himself to slip even more, he slid until at last his momentum gave way and the rest of his body slid off the roof. The only thing that kept him from falling were his fingers which were clinging desperately to the edge of the roof. There he dangled over the back alley.

Now what?

His legs ran in mid-air as though he were riding an invisible bicycle. He was trying to get a toe-hold on something, anything! He managed to hit the window a couple of times which rocked him back and forth, giving him an idea.

He got himself to rocking. With one kick, he broke the window. He rocked some more. As he did, he knocked out the remaining glass. Now, if he could just get enough momentum to swing into the open window.

Jesse's fingers were scraped, bleeding, and aching. But if he let go now, he would plunge to the alley and fail Emily in the process. His arms, likewise, complained about the weight pulling on them.

On the count of three, Jesse told himself.

One.

Jesse pushed off the side of the hotel.

Two.

It felt like his fingers were going to snap.

Three.

He swung toward the window and let loose. His foot hit the window sill, instantly stopping his forward swing. He began to fall.

Reaching, grabbing at anything, somehow Jesse managed to get an arm in the window. Grabbing the sill with his arm, he managed to swing another arm over the sill. Now, instead of hanging off the roof, he was hanging out a window. But at least his feet had something to work with.

Jesse's shoes scraped against the side of the hotel as he managed to scramble through the window into the hotel room. He fell onto some glass, cutting his arms in the process. He wasn't even aware of the cuts or the blood that soon followed. Jumping to his feet, he looked at the person on the bed.

It was Emily.

Jesse untied her legs and arms. Emily removed the gag from her mouth on her own. She began to weep.

"O Jesse!" she cried. "He was going to kidnap me!"

"Let's get out of here!" Jesse helped her off the bed.

"For ransom!" Emily cried. "He was going to hold me for ransom!"

"We'll talk about it later," Jesse whispered. "Right now, let's get out of here!"

Emily whimpered as he helped her toward the door. She moved stiffly.

From the other side of the door, Jesse heard footsteps. They hit the floorboards heavily and were widely spaced. A man. Tykas?

Jesse shoved Emily to one side of the door. He stood on the other. If it was Tykas, he planned on jumping the man as soon as the door opened. He looked around for a weapon. Nothing convenient was in sight.

The footsteps grew louder. Then they slowed.

Jesse held his breath. Tykas was larger than him. Heavier. More experienced in this kind of confrontation. What chance did Jesse have against him?

The footsteps picked up again. Then they passed the door and continued down the hallway. A moment later Jesse heard a door open and close.

Jesse bowed his head and sighed in relief. "Let's go!" he said to Emily.

There was a hint of disappointment on Emily's face, as though she wanted it to be Tykas so that she could get some measure of revenge against him.

Jesse poked his head out the door and looked up and down the hallway before stepping into it. It was clear. Grabbing Emily's hand, he pulled her along behind him. They stepped quickly the length of the hallway.

At the far end two stairways met at the top of the same platform. The one set went down to the lobby; the other set, which lay just beyond a closed door, went down the back stairs to alley. Jesse tried the alley stairs door first, hoping it was locked only from the outside. He winced upon discovering it was locked from the inside too.

Then, just as they turned around toward the other set of stairs, he saw Tykas. Again, Jesse saw him before he saw Jesse. The man was climbing the stairs with one hand digging in his pocket for the room key. He looked up and saw Jesse. But by then, it was too late.

Jesse rammed his shoulder into the man, sending him tumbling down the stairs. Turning toward the locked door, Jesse applied the same tactic. He rammed his shoulder against the door. There was a sound of splitting wood, but the door held.

"What's going on up there?"

Jesse recognized the voice of the cigar-smoking woman at the front desk. On the steps, Tykas had come to a halt. He was struggling to get up.

Another blow to the door, and another crack. But the door held.

"Together," Emily said.

Jesse nodded. "One, two, three!"

Both of them hit the door. It flew open.

As Tykas ran up the one set of stairs, Jesse and Emily ran down the other.

A groomsman stood next to the buckboard, holding the reins is his hand, about to remove the horse's bridle.

Jesse grabbed the reins from the groomsman and jumped into the buckboard. Emily jumped in the other side.

"Stop them!" Tykas yelled from the stairs.

The frightened groomsman didn't know what to do. He stood there helplessly.

Jesse urged the horses onward, just as Tykas reached the back of the buckboard. The agent got a hold on the baggage railing.

"Hyah!" Jesse cried.

Tykas was dragged behind, yet he refused to let go. Finally, his fingers gave out. And as Tykas skid and rolled in the dirt alley, Jesse and Emily fled town.

Chapter 29

WHAT the emigrant trains lacked in accommodations, they more than made up for in rudeness. The conductors came through the train only to issue orders. They did not answer questions, nor did they converse with the passengers. Even the newsboys were rude. At each stop, which occurred every forty to fifty miles, the train was swarmed by young boys selling newspapers, books, fruits, lollipops, cigars, soap, towels, tin washing dishes, coffee, tea, sugar, and tinned edibles—mostly hash or beans. They hawked their goods with a generous dash of insolence not used with first- or second-class passengers.

Meal stops were nothing less than chaos. Passengers were granted twenty minutes to eat while the train took on fuel and water. Consequently, there was a mad rush to the closest restaurant. The secret to successful dining was to enter the restaurant on the run while simultaneously shouting out a food order and grabbing a table. Diners then shoveled their food and tried to get a second cup of coffee from the frantic waiters who pushed through the crowds with overloaded trays. For this, they paid a dollar—seventy-five cents if payment was made in silver instead of paper money.

In general, aboard emigrant trains, the train conductors never bothered to announce their departure with the familiar warning cry, *All aboard!* When the allotted twenty-minute dining time was up, the engineer simply opened the throttle and the train stole away from the station. This meant that diners had to keep one eye on the train while they ate, and reboarding was as frantic as the initial departure.

After only one day of this routine, Clara realized how much a person could miss the comfort of civility. It was night and the windows were coal black. They were not covered with anything, it was just that there was no moon, and the absence of light and any scenery for it to shine upon combined to give the appearance that they were traveling through a hundred-mile-long tunnel. Several oil wall lamps gave off feeble illumination and reflected the inside activity against the glass.

"Chumming boards! Two dollars!" The conductor made his way down the aisle shouting the announcement.

Clara leaned toward Woodhull Logan. "What are chumming boards?" she asked.

"These benches can be made to face each other," Logan explained. "A chumming board is a wide piece of lumber that is laid from bench to bench, making a bed."

The idea of laying down and stretching out for the night was an appealing vision. Clara was cramped, dirty, and exhausted. She reached out and stopped the conductor by grabbing his arm. "Is there a women's car where I could go to lie down?" she asked.

The conductor, a wide man with round, chapped cheeks and a mustache that hung over his lip so far it concealed his mouth, said, "Do you want a chumming board?"

"I think I want one," Clara said. "It's just that I would need to go to a women's car if I were to share a board..."

"If you wanted the women's car, you should have gone there when you initially boarded," the man said. He spoke to her with a tone a disappointed and angry parent would use on a child.

"At the time, I didn't know..."

"Do you want a chumming board or not?" the conductor said.

Logan spoke up. "I would like one," he said, handing the conductor the money.

The conductor pocketed the money and continued on his way. A crewman followed behind him, delivering the board. In short order, the front bench was reversed and the board was in place. Clara stood in the aisle looking helpless. Up and down the car, passengers were settling in for the night by either settling onto chumming boards or wedging themselves between the seats and windows. Nearly every inch of floor space was taken. There were only enough islands of space for a person to make his way down the aisle, or to stand.

Clara looked at the chumming board, the only remaining available space in the car. She was tired, her emotions were on edge, and the one pushing itself to the forefront was anger. "And where am I supposed to sleep?" she asked.

"Right here," Logan said.

"I'm not sleeping next to you!"

Logan chuckled. "I don't expect you to. You are obviously exhausted. You need to lie down. This is for you," he said.

"Then, where…"

"All my professional life I've been a security agent. I can sleep anywhere. Standing up, if need be. I'll be fine. You get a good night's rest."

Clara looked at the chumming board. How she longed to lie down. Still, she hesitated. "Mr. Logan, this is very kind, but I can't…"

"Mrs. Morgan," he cut her off, "please, let me do this for you. It's the least I can do after all your husband did for me." He turned and made his way toward the wood-burning stove. The way he tiptoed through the scattered bodies, it looked like he was crossing a stream by stepping from rock to rock.

Again, Clara hesitated. She was not accustomed to accepting things from people. She was perfectly capable of taking care of herself. Yet the promise of sleep was a powerful lure. It won out over her pride.

Once situated on the board, she thought of something. Lifting herself up, she motioned to Logan. With a puzzled look on his face, he made his way back to the benches.

"Mr. Logan," Clara said, "I didn't thank you for your kindness."

"There was no need to," he replied.

"Also," she said, "if you would like...well, this board is large enough for two. And if you get tired, I wouldn't mind you sitting on that side of the board."

Logan grinned. "How very kind," he said sincerely.

"Good-night, Mr. Logan."

"Good-night, Mrs. Morgan."

Clara turned over facing the windows. She felt the chumming board sag with Logan's weight at he sat down. She glanced over her shoulder at him. His back was straight and his arms were folded across his chest. Turning back, she adjusted herself until she was comfortable. She fell asleep with a smile on her face.

After two full days of travel, Clara was well acquainted with the man who shared her bench. She discovered that he was a generous man. Not only did he provide her with a chumming board at night, but he also purchased and shared other supplies—a tin washing dish and a brick of soap. He bought two towels, one for himself and one for her. No amount of objections on her part seemed to dissuade him.

During their long conversations, Clara learned that when Logan first arrived in New York, he was indigent and drank heavily. One night he stumbled into the Heritage Church Mission looking for food. He not only found a hot meal, but he found a friend in Benjamin Morgan, who helped dry him out and find employment with the Austin Factory.

She also learned that Logan went out of his way to believe the best in people, and that he longed to live in a town where people treated each other like family, the way Ben made everyone feel at the mission, only on a grander scale. She learned that Logan was in the same factory fire that killed her husband; that after a beam fell on him, knocking him unconscious, it was Ben who carried him to safety.

"How did you know it was Ben who rescued you?" Clara asked.

"When I came around, one of the firefighters told me." As he spoke, he pulled nervously on the cuffs of his sleeves. "That's why I say Ben saved me twice. He saved me from destroying myself, and he saved me from the fire."

Logan struck Clara as a forthright, honest man. For two days he had spoken openly about his difficult life. However, when he described the events of the fire that led to Ben's death, she couldn't help but get the feeling that there was something he was hiding.

"Is that when you burned your hands, in the factory fire?" Clara asked.

Self-consciously, Logan glanced at his scarred hands. One tried to cover the other. Clearly, the scars made him uneasy about his appearance. "No," he said. "That happened a long time before the factory fire."

"You were in another fire?"

Logan pulled on his cuffs and nodded.

"How awful!"

He blinked self-consciously, and winced as visions of a past horror came to mind. "I was a child," he said.

Clara placed a reassuring hand on Logan's forearm. "This is painful for you," she said. "You don't have to tell me this. We can change the subject."

Kind, brown eyes turned to her. "I haven't told many people about this," he said. "But there's something about you...I felt it about your husband too...it just feels perfectly natural for me to share these things with you."

Now it was Clara's turn to feel self-conscious. It had been a long time since anyone had compared her to Ben and accused her of showing compassion. It used to be that people did it all the time. But since her husband's death, Clara had withdrawn from people. She didn't want to talk to anyone. Didn't want to listen. It was as though she had scraped the bottom of her compassion barrel and there was only enough left for herself and her son. But somehow, like the Zarephath widow's oil jug in the Old Testament, Clara felt certain that she could share some compassion with the man sitting next to her and it would not deplete her supply.

"I lost my family in a fire when I was seven years old," Logan said softly. His head bowed at the memory that Clara guessed was at least four decades old.

"And that's when you burned your hands?"

For the first time since she had known him, Logan stretched out his hands so that the scars could be seen plainly. They stretched up his wrists. "My arms are like this too," he said. "And my legs and feet and torso. Even my face and cheeks. That's why I have this full beard." He chuckled self-consciously. "I hate the thing. It itches all the time. But it hides the scars." He pulled his arms up so that they were in front of his eyes and nose, like he was shielding himself. "To get out of the house I ran through a wall of flame like this. That's why everything is burned except the upper portion of my face."

"I'm so sorry," Clara said. "I didn't know. I couldn't tell."

Logan took her comment as a compliment. "Over the years, I've learned to cover up well. Besides, I learned to live with this a long time ago. That fire hurt me much deeper."

"The loss of your parents," Emily said.

Logan nodded. "And an older brother and a baby sister.

But that still wasn't the worst of it."

A dark shadow of emotion swept over him, a foreboding force that twisted his features with pain.

"I was blamed for setting the fire."

"O dear God," Clara said. "But you didn't set it, did you?"

Tears that had accumulated for decades deep beneath his scarred skin welled to the surface and formed pools in his eyes.

"Do you know who started the fire?" Clara asked.

Logan nodded. "My older brother, Brett. He sneaked Poppa's pipe into the barn. Said he wanted to see what it felt like to smoke one. That's how the fire started. We tried to put it out, but it spread too fast. Pretty soon, Poppa saw it and he helped us fight the fire. Then, all of a sudden, the wind shifted and the house went up. Mother and little Christie were in there. First Poppa went in to save them. When he didn't come out, Brett went in. And when Brett didn't come out, I went in. But it was too late. They were all dead. As you might expect, when the neighbors saw the smoke they came running to help. They found me sitting on the ground holding the pipe."

"Why didn't you tell them it was your brother who started the fire?"

Logan shook his head. "I couldn't. I worshiped my brother. Everybody in town liked Brett. He was smart. Handsome. Strong. Smoking that pipe...he wasn't like that at all. He made one stupid mistake! And I knew that if I told everyone Brett started the fire, that's all they would ever remember of him. I wanted them to remember the good things about him."

"And you've lived with that secret all these years?"

"I set the course," Logan said. "I'm not about to change it now."

"Thank you for sharing that with me."

"I've only told two people. First Ben, now you."

"You've never had a wife to tell?" Clara asked.

Logan scoffed. "Married? Who would ever marry a monster

like me? The first time I took off my shirt, my wife would faint."

Clara reached out and touched the back of Logan's hand. Instinctively, he tensed and almost pulled it away. But the incomparable sensation of human touch from which he had been deprived since a child stilled his hand. Lightly, Clara rested her hand on his.

"Mr. Logan," she said, "you should know by now that a person's worth is not determined by the comeliness of his skin."

The train beat a monotonous rhythm as it crossed the Kansas plains. Frequent stops gave opportunity for cramped legs to stretch and aching backs to arch. But at all times an eye had to be kept on the train, for without warning it would chug into motion again.

"You said you had relatives in Santa Fe?" Logan asked as they boarded the train at a stop so small it had no name. Some stops, like Topeka, had large two-story train stations. People from all over town would come to meet departing and arriving relatives and friends, or just come to see the train. Some stops had small towns attached to them. Then there were stops like this one. Water and coal and nothing else but wide open space.

Clara did her best to hide a grimace at Logan's question. It was one thing to be friendly enough to listen to someone's story; it was quite another thing to tell your own. And Clara wasn't sure she wanted to tell Logan her troubles.

"Hopefully, my son will be there," she said. Then she looked out the window as the train picked up speed. She hoped that would be the end of the conversation.

"Does he live there?"

There was an awkward pause. Logan noticed it.

"I don't mean to pry," he said, turning his head to look at nothing along with Clara.

A few moments later, Clara said, "Jesse ran away from

home. I don't know why. But I have reason to believe he may be in Santa Fe. I'm going there hoping to find him."

Logan turned sympathetic eyes her direction. "This trip must be very difficult for you," he said. "Is there anything I can do to help?"

This time it was Logan who reached out and placed his hand on hers. It was a simple gesture. But the warmth of his touch breached a dam that had held back personal thoughts and emotions for fifteen years. And for the first time since the death of her husband, Clara Morgan talked to someone about personal matters.

She told Logan about Jesse's mysterious disappearance, Sagean's information about the Austin girl, Jesse's book that washed up near Cincinnati, her reasons for suspecting Jesse was in Santa Fe.

"I've seen the Austin girl once at her home," Logan said. "It was my last night as an employee of Franklin Austin."

"What did she have to do with…"

Logan waved off the question before it was fully formed. "She had nothing to do with my dismissal. I just happened to see her in the house that night." He hesitated, then added, "I might as well tell you."

"Tell me what?" Clara asked.

Logan took a deep breath before beginning. "I was forced to leave Austin's security agency," he said. "It was either leave, or be brought up on charges for starting the factory fire that killed Ben."

Clara shook her head sadly. "I'm sorry," she said.

"Aren't you going to ask me if I started the fire?"

Clara stared at him as if to say, *That is the dumbest question I've ever heard in my life.* She said, "I know you didn't start it."

"How do you know?" Logan asked.

"For the last two days I've done nothing else but get to know you. It's not in you to hurt others. You couldn't have started that fire."

"Thank you," Logan said. "I didn't. The report said it was an accident, sparks from a piece of electrical machinery. But just a couple of months ago, I heard a rumor from inside security that Austin ordered the blaze set and then covered it up with a false report."

"Do you really think Austin did it?"

"No. At first I did, but not now. But I am convinced it was deliberately set. I was dismissed before I could prove it."

"Do you know who set the fire?"

Logan nodded. "I think I do, but I can't prove it. But let's get back to Jesse. You say you have no idea what the connection is between him and the Austin girl?"

"I didn't even know Jesse was acquainted with her."

"Have you ever met her?"

"No. I've never seen the girl."

Logan squinted his eyes in thought. "Odd," he said. "And you said Jesse was seen by relatives in Ohio."

"He was at their house. Then he slipped away before they knew who he was."

"Did he know who *they* were?"

"No," Clara said. "I don't think so. Jesse was so young the last time he saw them, too young to remember them."

Still working on the puzzle, Logan shook his head side-to-side. "I'm surprised the Morgans didn't offer to help you look for him."

Clara looked at him suspiciously. "Why do you say that?"

"Ben spoke of his family constantly. He told me that bizarre story about how he discovered he was a Morgan after all those years of hating them. I have never heard a man speak of his family with such love and admiration. It made a strong impact on me. In fact, I must confess, I was rather envious. The Morgans, as Ben described them, were everything I ever wanted in a family. So naturally, it surprises me that they didn't offer to help you find Jesse." Logan's eyes brightened as he remembered something. "Yes...especially since he would be the next recipient of the Morgan family Bible! Isn't he?"

Clara didn't want to talk about this. She had her reasons for not liking the Morgans and for refusing their help. They were good reasons too. At least they had always sounded good in her mind. Only now as she sought to justify her anger to Logan, all of her ironclad arguments suddenly seemed like straw.

"I can see the bitterness in your eyes, Clara." Logan spoke in a soothing tone. "I recognize it. For years bitterness was my daily companion. I was bitter that everybody had a family but me. I was bitter that I had been robbed of a good name and a handsome body. Do you know what I learned, Clara? I learned that bitterness is a parasite. Every day it eats away at you until finally nothing is left, and you become a walking shell with no feelings, no friends, no life. And do you want to know the strangest thing about bitterness? All the time it was devouring me, I defended it! Because I believed I had a right to be bitter."

Clara rallied her defenses. She wasn't bitter; she was realistic. Life is cruel. You can't depend on anything or anyone. When it came to the Morgans, she had a right to... *All the time it was devouring me, I defended it!* Her husband had been taken from her and she had to raise her son without help from anyone, she had a right to... *All the time it was devouring me, I defended it!*

"Let me ask you this, Clara," Logan said. "Do you feel toward God the same way you feel toward the Morgans?"

"Let's not bring God into this," Clara said.

Logan started laughing, which didn't sit well with Clara.

"Are you laughing at me?"

"No...no, not at all," Logan said, still laughing. "It's just that those were my exact words to Ben."

Clara looked at him skeptically.

"Do you know how he answered me? He told me a story."

Logan adjusted into what Clara assumed was a storytelling position. He squared his shoulders toward her and freed his hands. "There once was a woman," he began, "who was driving a wagon home from town. She had been to town to pick up a few supplies and had talked with a friend longer than she expected. The sun was going down and it would be dark before she arrived home, something she had wanted to avoid.

"With the town behind her, she set out for home. After a couple of minutes, she happened to glance behind her. There was a rider following her. No one else was on the road, just her and the rider, and it frightened her. So she urged the horses to go faster. She waited a few minutes before she dared to turn around and look again. When she did, the rider was still behind her. He had matched her speed. To make matters worse, it was dark now.

"The woman's mind raced. What should she do? She was still far from home and no one else was in sight. Just ahead of her, there was a fork in the road. To the left, the road split off to the next town; to the right, there was a bridge which led to her home. She reached the fork and went over the bridge. Looking behind her, she waited and hoped that the rider would veer to the left. He didn't. He rode over the bridge after her.

"By now, the woman was nearly beside herself. Her mind raced frantically. She turned down the first farm road she saw, off the main road. The rider followed her. Until now, it could have been coincidence, but now she knew for sure the rider was after her. Urging the horses to a full gallop, she raced toward the lights of a distant farmhouse. The rider's horse likewise broke into a full gallop. He began to close the distance between them.

"Nearly out of her mind, the woman reached the farmhouse just as the rider was catching up to her. She reined the horses to a stop and jumped out of the wagon. The rider jumped from his horse and ran toward her. The woman screamed for help as she ran toward the house. But the rider didn't follow her. He stopped at the wagon and threw back the canvas covering. Beneath the canvas was a man with a knife. The rider had seen the man crawl under the canvas just as the woman was leaving town. All this time, the woman was running from the very person who was trying to save her."

Logan leaned back to signal that the story had concluded. Then he said, "Clara, you're the woman in that story. And you're running from God, the very one who is trying to save you."

Chapter 30

FLEEING from Tykas in the man's own buckboard, Jesse steered a large circuitous route. His plan was simple: head north, double back, sneak behind their pursuer to a train station, and get Emily on a train heading east. Details—such as where the money would come from for Emily's train ticket—would have to be worked out as they went along. Jesse figured he could always exchange work for the ticket.

He made one other decision. He decided to put off telling Emily his plan for as long as possible.

"Tykas had no intention of returning me to New York," Emily said. Her voice was shaking and it wasn't because of the bouncing buckboard.

"He's no longer an Austin agent," Jesse said. "Your father dismissed him. We found that out after you left."

"The man's a lunatic!" Emily cried. "He was going to hold me for ransom... somewhere in Illinois. He said I was going to provide the seed money he needed for some kind of utopian community."

Jesse glanced over his shoulder. The road was clear.

"Illinois!" Emily cried. "It makes sense now."

"What makes sense?"

"Aboard the *Tippecanoe*. Tykas boarded in Louisville and told me right away he'd been sent to take me home. But then he did nothing. Apparently he was waiting until we got to

Cairo. Only the boat never got that far."

The buckboard clattered along at a quick pace. Any faster and it would bounce out of control. Jesse checked the road behind them again. Still clear. As he turned his eyes forward, he caught sight of Emily. She was staring at him.

An eerie tingle flashed up and down his spine, the kind of feeling he would get whenever he recognized something that he had previously dreamed. Only this time it wasn't something he'd dreamed, but something he'd imagined—a million times. A smile crossed his face as he thought about it. *I'm out West, speeding along in a buckboard, being chased by an evil man after just having rescued a young woman from danger. Just like Truly Noble!*

"Thank you for coming after me," Emily said. She looked at him the same way Charity Increase looked at Truly Noble following a rescue, all warm and affectionate.

"I'm just doing what is right," Jesse said, echoing the printed words of his hero.

As the buckboard bounded north, Jesse made it a point to talk to everyone they came across—a few travelers on the road and a couple of sod house homesteaders, not more than a handful of people. To each one, he asked the same thing. "How far north would they have to travel to reach the closest Kansas Pacific Railroad train station?" Jesse was hoping to use the agent's training against him. If Tykas was indeed following them, he would probably ask people along the way if they saw a man and a woman heading north in a buckboard. Any of these people would, of course, tell Tykas exactly what Jesse wanted him to hear.

Just as Jesse was thinking it might be time to reverse direction, they came upon a large lake. He concluded fortune was smiling upon them. He used the lake as the hub for their turn. This way, the body of water shielded them as they swung around and headed southward.

"Where are we going?" Emily cried.

The change in direction prompted the question. He could not put off telling her any longer, and so divulged his plan.

"So all this talk of a train wasn't just a ruse?" she said angrily. "You really are taking me to a train station?"

Jesse nodded. "Just not the Kansas Pacific."

"Very clever, Mr. Morgan. So tell me, why did you wait until now to inform me of my plans?"

"The plans haven't changed since Fort Larned," Jesse said, defensively. "Tykas only interrupted them."

"I see."

Emily folded her arms. There was no lingering trace of the warmth that was there a few moments ago. From then on, Emily rode in silence.

When it became too dark for them to travel, Jesse pulled off the road. There were no lights in sight, so he suggested they use the buckboard as cover and sleep under it. Emily made no response. She sat stone still with her arms folded. Jesse could not get her to climb down from her seat, nor could he get her to say a word, or even acknowledge his presence. So he climbed under the buckboard and curled up to sleep.

It was nearly two hours before slumber came, while overhead the buckboard bounced and squeaked and groaned.

In the morning they continued south until they came upon the Santa Fe Railroad tracks. Turning east, they followed the tracks until a small town came into sight, a sign announcing its name:

REDEMPTION
Where Everybody Gets A Second Chance

Redemption was nothing more than a small cluster of buildings jutting up in the midst of a sea of prairie grass. Plain frame buildings lined the town's main—and only—street.

One end of the street butted up against the train depot. It was a small building painted red with a long platform that paralleled the tracks. There was a ticket window, but it was closed, and no one else was to be seen.

"Where is everybody?" Jesse wondered aloud, for the place looked deserted.

Emily didn't respond; Jesse didn't expect her to.

They stood on the platform and looked toward the town. The far end of the street opened up to the prairie and outlying farms and ranches.

"Let's see if anyone's home," Jesse said.

The sound of the horse's hooves echoed between the buildings as they traveled the length of the street. Hand-painted signs identified the businesses—Curtis Rickhart's Outfitting Store; Dalton's Restaurant; G.S. Nichols' Saloon and Faro House; Hosea Milburn, Justice of the Peace; Charles Woolcott's General Store and Post Office; Humphrey's Clothing Store; and Kate Coffee's Hotel.

There was not a soul in sight. The street was deserted. The boardwalk that lined the businesses bore no traffic. None of the doors were open and there were no faces in any of the windows.

Stopping at the hotel, Jesse said, "Wait here." He hopped down and tried the door. It was unlocked, but when he stepped inside there was no one to greet him. There was a bell on the counter. Jesse rang it. No one answered it. He shouted, "Hey! Is anyone here?" If there was, they didn't respond.

Back outside he shrugged his shoulders at Emily. "It's like they all disappeared," he said. "I'll try the next door."

The next door was the general store. The door was unlocked, just like the hotel. And, also like the hotel, there was no one inside. Everything else looked normal. Canned fruit and vegetables lined the shelves. Sacks of potatoes, turnips, cabbage, pumpkins, and long-neck squashes formed aisles. Barrels of nails were set in front of the counter. Barrels of flour—white and middling—were stacked against a wall. The only things missing were an owner and customers.

Walking across the street, Jesse tried a barber shop and the sheriff's office. The results were the same. Empty barber chairs. Even the jail cell was empty.

"This is spooky," Jesse said.

"Real spooky," Emily agreed.

What was also spooky was the fact that those were the first two words Emily had spoken to him since the previous afternoon.

Slowly, the two of them made their way down the street toward the open prairie. They were almost to the end when Emily heard something.

"Listen!" she said.

Jesse pulled the horse to a halt and listened hard.

"Do you hear it?"

"Just barely."

In front of them the prairie grass fluttered in the wind. The sound was faint, almost imperceptible. And odd. Very odd. It sounded to Jesse like the prairie grass was singing to them.

"I hear music," he said. "But where is it coming from?"

"I can't tell. Go forward a bit."

Jesse flicked the reins. As the buckboard cleared the end of the street, the music grew louder and the direction became clear. As they passed the last building on the street they could see it. About a quarter of a mile beyond the town, in a small clearing next to a solitary tree, stood a white frame church. It was surrounded by horses and wagons and buggies.

"So that's where everyone is!" Jesse exclaimed. "This must be Sunday!"

They smiled at each other, relieved that the mystery was solved. Jesse steered the buckboard toward the church.

"I'm not going in there!" Emily said as Jesse started to hop out of the buckboard.

"Why not?"

"Why not?" Emily echoed his question in disbelief. "Look at the way I'm dressed."

She was still wearing the clothes of Slate Pickens.

"We're not here to impress them," Jesse said. "We're here to get help."

"I don't care," Emily insisted. "I'm not going into church dressed like this!"

"Fine. Then I'll go in alone, and you can…"

"Wait in the buckboard like a pet dog?"

Her analogy was fitting. There were a variety of dogs waiting in the wagons that encircled the church. Without exception they were pointed at the church door waiting for their masters to appear.

"You win! I'll stay here with you until the service is over!" Jesse conceded. "Will that make you happy?"

It didn't, of course. But Emily was less angry with him than she would have been had he gone inside without her.

As it turned out, they didn't have to wait long. The double doors of the church swung open and the residents of Redemption, Kansas poured out into the sunshine. The first person to come their way was an elderly man. Beside him, holding his hand, was a happy little girl with hair curled in ringlets and wearing a red dress.

"Excuse me, sir," Jesse said. "Can you tell me when the next train is scheduled to arrive?"

"Headin' east or west?" the man asked as he slowed to a stop.

The little girl, not happy that her escort had stopped to talk, pulled on his hand. "Come on, Grandpa!" Gripping the man's forefinger with one hand and his little finger with her other hand, she pulled with all her might. Grandfather didn't budge.

"East," Jesse said. "We need the eastbound train."

The old man's face grimaced, bunching his wrinkles into more wrinkles. "Eastbound train doesn't arrive until Thursday. From the looks of ya, I thought ya might be headin' west. That train comes on Tuesday."

"Grandpa!" The girl had released her grandfather's hand. She stood impatiently with her hands on her hips. She tapped an angry toe.

"Thursday, huh?" Jesse said.

"If ya need a place to stay 'til then, there's Kate Coffee's Hotel. Kate's a mighty fine hostess."

"Grandpa!"

Jesse rubbed his chin. "We don't exactly have any money for a hotel," he said.

The old man studied Jesse, then Emily. He looked at the buckboard and noticed it was empty. "I think it best you talk to our preacher," he said.

Before Jesse could respond, the old man turned and whistled. It was a sharp whistle that quieted every conversation. Heads turned their direction.

"We need a preacher over here!" the man yelled.

The crowd parted to let a tall man through. A large brown mustache draped over the man's upper lip; matching sun-streaked brown hair fell to his collar. The man strode confidently toward them. Several interested bystanders indiscreetly followed in his wake, always maintaining a safe distance.

"This here's the preacher," the old man said. "He's also the sheriff." Following the introduction, the man stepped back, dragging his granddaughter with him. But he stayed close enough to hear what was being said.

An easy grin formed beneath the preacher's mustache. He held out his hand to Jesse. The man's grip was rock-hard, but the squeeze was controlled. It didn't feel like a preacher's grip.

"Name's Sheriff Clark," the preacher said warmly. "How

can I be of help to you folks?"

"Well, we were asking about the train...the eastbound train," Jesse said, correcting himself before the elderly man did. "And we learned that it wouldn't arrive until Thursday..."

"And they don't got no money or place to stay," the elderly man finished Jesse's sentence for him.

"Do you live in these parts?" the sheriff asked Jesse.

"No, sir. We're both from New York."

"New York?" the sheriff exclaimed. "What are you doing all the way out here without money or food?"

Jesse didn't quite know where to begin, especially since he had thought he was going to be speaking to a preacher, but found himself being questioned by a sheriff. "I...we..." Jesse stammered. He glanced back at Emily. "...were left behind by two families traveling West in wagons. We'd been hired on to help them in return for food."

"You steal from them?" Clark's voice hardened. The sheriff in him began to overshadow the preacher.

"No, sir," Jesse replied.

"Threaten them?"

"No, sir."

"Then why did they abandon you?"

Jesse glanced back at Emily who looked nervously about at the people. It was clear to him that she didn't want McFarland's indiscretions with her to become public knowledge. He said, "It was a personal matter. But we did nothing wrong."

The sheriff's blue eyes focused on him with intensity. Looking at the man's finely focused eyes, Jesse was reminded of how a looking-glass lens could concentrate the sun's light to a point capable of starting a fire. Had the man's eyes been a looking-glass, Jesse's forehead would have been smoldering.

"Is this their buckboard and horse?"

"Um...," Jesse cleared his throat, "...no..."

"Did you steal it?"

"That one's a little harder to explain," Jesse said.

Sheriff Clark nodded his head. "I think I'd better take you two boys to my office. This sounds like it's going to be a long story."

Jesse laughed. He tried to stop himself, but he couldn't. Emily wasn't amused—at the sheriff's failure to recognize her gender, or at Jesse for laughing at his mistake.

"What are you laughing at?" Clark asked.

"I mean no disrespect, Sheriff. But this is Emily. She's a girl."

A bright feminine voice came from behind the sheriff. "Of course she is!" A plump woman in a pale yellow dress appeared. From her sparkling eyes to her toothy smile, it was clear the woman's personality was as bright as her dress. "Any fool can see that she's a lady," she berated the sheriff.

Crimson colored the sheriff's face. "Pardon me, Miss," he said to Emily. "I was so busy…"

The plump woman brushed by him. "He was so busy jawing and acting like a sheriff that he didn't have manners enough to take a good look at you," she said. The woman crossed over to Emily's side of the wagon, took Emily by the hand, and said, "Please forgive my brother, he's a good man. It's just that he doesn't always come across that way." Turning to the sheriff, she said, "Oliver, let's get these two young people out of the sun. They don't want to be a spectacle for the whole town. And from the look of them, they're probably famished."

The sheriff led Jesse and Emily back to the town and to his office. The woman in the yellow dress accompanied them.

Chapter 31

IN the sheriff's office the whole story came out. The Watermans. McFarland. Even Fort Larned and Tykas.

"You poor dear!" the woman in yellow cried, comforting Emily.

"Well," Sheriff Clark concluded, "there's little we can do until tomorrow. In the morning I'll notify your father by telegram."

"There's plenty we can do today," the woman in yellow said to her brother. "These two poor young things have been through a horrible experience. We can at least show them some prairie hospitality."

Jesse wondered how old the woman was. She called them young things, yet she didn't seem to be but a few years older than them.

"Molly," the sheriff said with a note of exasperation, "give me credit for having at least an ounce of good sense. I wasn't exactly planning to lock them up for the night."

His sister wasn't listening to him. She assisted Emily to her feet and said, "The first thing we're going to do is interrupt Charles Woolcott's Sunday afternoon dinner. He owns the general store. Charles may growl a little over the interruption, but just ignore him. He's a kind man. It's just that sometimes he forgets that he is."

Molly led Emily out into the street. Jesse followed.

"Then we'll get Ann Humphrey to open her clothing store," Molly continued. "We must get you something a little more fitting to wear."

Sheriff Clark closed the door to his office behind him. He called after his sister: "Molly, I'm starved. Do I have your permission to go home now?"

Molly turned around. She recognized her brother's playful taunting. Responding in kind, she said, "Oliver, we could have done all this without your help in the first place." Then, staring at his middle, she added, "By all means, go stuff yourself. But from where I'm standing, Oliver dear, you could miss a few meals and it wouldn't hurt you one bit!"

If the sheriff was offended, he didn't show it. The boardwalk clacked under his heels as he ambled down the street.

Arm-in-arm, Molly led Emily across the street to the general store. "Our stores aren't open for business on the Sabbath," she explained. "But this is something special. This is a mission of mercy."

Charles Woolcott, the owner of the general goods store, did indeed grumble, but he also dutifully gathered up everything Molly instructed him to get. She saw to it that Emily and Jesse had everything they needed to clean and refresh themselves. As they left the store, Molly thanked Woolcott for his generosity, telling him that God would reward him generously in heaven for his kindness to these two strangers on earth. Woolcott grunted and returned to his Sunday meal.

"He gave us these things?" Emily asked.

Molly smiled and nodded. "This is the Sabbath day," she said. "It would be wrong of him to sell them. However, I know of no Bible verse that forbids a person from giving things away on the Sabbath."

At the clothing shop, Molly assisted Emily as she tried on dresses. The shop's owner, Ann Humphrey, a tall, stocky redhead, offered assistance when it was needed, and stood beside

Jesse and talked when she wasn't shuffling through dresses.

"What do you think of our Molly?" Ann asked him.

"She's been very kind to us," Jesse replied.

"She's that way with everyone."

Jesse nodded in response as Emily twirled around in a flowing summer afternoon dress.

"We call Molly our Prairie Saint," Ann continued. "You saw the name of the town when you rode in, didn't you?"

"Redemption."

"That's right. It was Molly's idea to change the name of the town. Do you know what the town was called before she came?"

Jesse shook his head.

"Acrimony."

Jesse smiled a half-smile. He didn't know whether Ann Humphrey was joking with him or not.

"It's true. Acrimony, Kansas. And the name fit too. It was a bitter place. Until then, the only thing this town was known for was its wars between ranchers over water rights. It was an ugly time. Entire families would sometimes be killed during a shootout."

Emily whispered something into Molly's ear. The two girls looked at Jesse and giggled.

"Oliver Clark came to the town to be our preacher. Then, when we heard he'd been a sheriff before his call to the ministry, we asked him to be our sheriff too. Worked out well for us as a town," Ann commented. "By combining two paltry paychecks, we almost give him enough to live on."

Molly called across the room: "Ann, I think we have it narrowed down to four dresses."

"Take as much time as you need," Ann said. "Cyrus is taking his Sunday afternoon nap. He doesn't even know I'm gone."

Molly and Emily returned to the dresses. Emily held up the summer dress for one last look and Jesse silently hoped she would choose it.

"Then one day Sheriff Clark sent for his little sister," Ann continued her story. She chuckled. "This town hasn't been the same since. 'Course, back then she was no bigger than a bar of soap after a hard day's wash."

Jesse looked at Molly. It was hard to imagine her little and skinny. He had known her for little more than an hour, but he liked her just the way she was.

"It all started with our church," Ann said. "The cornerstone had been laid, but times were rough and building came to a halt. A workman's lien was about to be placed on the four walls that were standing. And our church was going to be sold at an auction. That's when Molly stepped in. She went around town carrying a little basket asking people to make donations to the church. Not in money. In materials. She would say, 'Surely you have a dozen nails you can donate,' or 'Surely you have a few pieces of lumber you can give to the Lord.' Well, she made the whole town realize that although we might not have the money to complete the building, together we had the materials we needed in our barns and sheds. If it wasn't for little Molly, our church might never have been built. We met in it for the first time on a Christmas Eve. The town has never been the same since."

Jesse looked at Molly. No longer a little girl. For some reason, it wasn't difficult for him to imagine her carrying a basket around town and getting people to do something nice in spite of themselves.

"I never thought I'd live in a town where you didn't have to lock your doors at night," Ann said. "Especially this town. There's just something special about Molly. She loves the Lord so much, it's contagious; and the whole town has been infected."

"How about these two, Ann?" Molly held two dresses up to Emily's shoulders. The first one was a simple blue calico dress; the other was the breezy summer dress.

Ann smiled. "Smart choice. You know, Emily, that summer dress was stitched by Molly."

"It's so beautiful," Emily said.

Ann replied: "Take them both with my blessings." To Molly she said, "Are you taking them home with you?" She was referring to Jesse and Emily.

Molly beamed. She said, "The Lord has given me two new friends, and now instead of spending the afternoon alone, I intend to spend it getting to know all about them."

After a lengthy departure at the clothing store—Emily couldn't stop thanking Ann for the dresses—the three of them rode to Molly's house. Molly insisted on driving since she knew the way; Emily sat next to her; and Jesse sat in the back holding the boxes from the clothing shop and general store. The two girls got to talking and almost completely forgot that Jesse was behind them. It was good to see Emily talking and smiling again, even if it wasn't at him. But by the time they reached the house, Jesse found himself glad the trip was over. It seemed to him that Emily was having too good of a time without involving him.

Molly's house was situated a little less than a mile from town. It was a whitewashed two-story house with a spacious front porch and a swing. After showing Emily and Jesse to their rooms, Molly prepared lunch while the two travelers cleaned up.

The bedroom in which Jesse found himself was small but comfortable. The way everything was laid out, it looked like Molly had known they were coming. The bed had fresh linens; towels were laid out; the vanity had brushes and combs and powders neatly arranged on top. When he first saw the room Jesse thought it was someone's bedroom and he insisted he didn't want to inconvenience anyone. Molly laughed. It was a guest room and all the things in it were there for his use.

After Jesse had washed up, he joined Molly downstairs. As

he passed through the sitting room, he was amazed by the number of pillows that were laying about. Round pillows. Square pillows. Triangular pillows. Pillows of different sizes and colors. It struck him as odd, but who could fault a woman as friendly and generous as Molly for liking pillows?

It was easy for him to find his hostess. She was singing hymns as she worked in the kitchen fixing the afternoon meal. In honor of the Sabbath, the cooking had all been done on Saturday. Molly was simply setting the table and placing the food on serving dishes.

A few moments later, Emily appeared. She descended the stairs accompanied by the light swishing of the summer dress. She had never looked more beautiful to Jesse. The dress was a blending of soft white and gray shades, making it look like she was enveloped by a cloud. For nearly five minutes Molly made a fuss over her.

The afternoon meal consisted of fresh ham and chicken, both served cold; bread; freshly churned butter; green beans; corn; potatoes; milk; and a cream cake in three layers. Jesse couldn't remember ever having a meal like it in his life.

For the rest of the afternoon and into the evening, they sat on the porch and talked. Molly and Emily shared the porch swing. Jesse sat in a rocker. The Kansas prairie stretched endlessly before them as they watched the sun slowly dip itself behind the western horizon. As soon as the daylight orb disappeared, a cool breeze swept across the porch and refreshed them.

"You're from New York? Really?" Molly said. "I spent my childhood in New York, until Oliver brought me out here." Her mind wandered back to the city. "The thing I remember most is all those tall buildings," she mused, "and the huge churches with their steeples pointing toward heaven. And the horse cars! And the steam train that ran on tracks that looked a mile high to me at the time. Do either of you miss the city?"

Jesse shrugged. "Not me. For as long as I can remember I

wanted to leave the city and come West."

"There are some things I miss," Emily said. "Some of the conveniences. Indoor plumbing. Electricity. The newspapers. I haven't seen a good newspaper in weeks."

"I'm afraid you'll be disappointed in our little newspaper," Molly said. "The little man and woman who print it mean well, but it's more gossip than news. And even then the gossip isn't news. Their presses can't compete with the speed of wagging tongues."

"Come to think of it," Jesse said, "I do miss the books. I used to read a lot before I came West."

"Oh? Do you like to read stories?" Molly asked.

"He *loves* stories!" Emily said.

"Have you read *Ben Hur?*" Molly asked. "It's a wonderful story of perseverance and love set in Bible times."

"Mostly I read dime novels," Jesse replied. "Stories by Sarah Morgan Cooper in particular. She's my aunt."

"Sarah Morgan Cooper is your aunt? How interesting! I've read some of her stories. Truly Noble, right? And the girl's name is Faith...no, Hope..."

"Charity!" A laughing Jesse corrected her. "Did you like her stories?"

Molly smiled. "They're a bit simplistic, but Mrs. Cooper always manages to include moral teachings in her stories. I like that a lot."

"I prefer Nellie Bly and a good investigative article myself," Emily sniffed. "She deals with actual events, even creates the event herself if need be. For me, made-up stories just don't have the same impact."

"In what parts of the city did you live?" Molly asked both of them.

Jesse responded first. "Lower east side."

"Really? That's where I was raised. Which street?"

"Hester."

Molly leaned her head back, trying to visualize the streets of New York. "I don't remember Hester," she said.

"Near Grand Street," Jesse offered.

"The horse cars were on Grand!" Molly said excitedly.

Jesse smiled. The lady in the clothing store had been right about Molly. Her enthusiasm and happiness were contagious. Until now, he had never thought he could be attracted to a plump woman. But Molly was proving to be an exception. He couldn't imagine ever tiring of the sparkle in her eyes, her laugh, the way she brought out the best in other people. He felt good around her. He found himself wanting—no, needing to make her laugh. He wanted to do something for her that would make her happy, that would somehow pay her back for all the happiness she brought to others.

Just then Jesse caught Emily looking at him. Her eyes were glassy with tears.

"So, you're a relation to Sarah Morgan Cooper," Molly said. "Does that mean your last name is Cooper too?"

Jesse shook his head. "She was my father's sister. Her middle name is her maiden name. I'm a Morgan."

"Morgan?" Molly said rather eerily. Turning to Emily she said, "And your last name..."

"Is Austin," Emily said. "My father owns..."

"...factories," Molly said.

The hostess looked like she had been stunned twice. Once by each name.

"Is something wrong?" Emily asked.

"Both of those names bring back memories," Molly said, looking like she was in a trance. "Unpleasant ones."

The porch fell silent. Jesse and Emily glanced at each other, neither knowing whether to say something or to wait for Molly to speak first. For the first time since they had met her, the sparkle had fled from Molly's eyes. They were fixed in a dull, flat stare as she looked at nothing.

Then she rallied. "Please forgive me," she said. "Those things are past and gone. I haven't thought of them in years."

Emily leaned toward her and placed a comforting hand on her arm. "Let's talk of more pleasant things," she offered. But Molly had momentarily slipped back into the privacy of her thoughts. Emily's words had no power to penetrate the thick swarm of memories that clouded Molly's eyes.

It took a moment for their hostess to find the words to explain what she was seeing in her mind. "The Lord does indeed work in mysterious ways," she said. "Who would have thought that after all these years?"

"Molly...are you all right?" Jesse asked.

"I'm so embarrassed," she said, placing a hand against her chest.

"Would it help to get it out?" Jesse asked.

Molly took a deep breath. Then another. Her complexion was pale. She was perspiring despite the prairie breeze. "When I was a little girl," she began, "I worked in an Austin factory. It was a difficult time for us. Both of my parents were sickly and couldn't work. I earned our only income. Fourteen to sixteen hours a day I worked. Still, I didn't make enough money to buy the food and medicine we needed. First Momma died. Then Poppa. When Poppa died, I was evicted from the tenement." She brightened for a moment. "Of course, Oliver was out West already. He sent us money and when he heard Momma and Poppa were sick, he wanted to bring us all out West to be with him."

Molly began to weep. Tears and anguish were a double tragedy on a face that was normally so happy.

"I lived on the street for a while. Then I learned of a Christian mission. They took me in, fed me, and gave me a place to sleep." Looking at Jesse, she said, "The mission was run by a Mr. Morgan."

"My father," Jesse said.

Molly raised a hand to her chest. She wept freely now. "After all these years," she said. "He was such a good man. So kind...so..." Molly was interrupted by her own sobs.

"What is it?" Emily asked. "Molly, what's wrong?"

"Jesse...do you know how your father died?"

"He died in a factory fire."

Molly nodded. "That's true. He was in the factory when he died and the building was on fire. But he didn't die from the fire."

"What?"

"Jesse...I'm so sorry I have to be the one to tell you this. Your father was murdered."

"Murdered!"

"I was there."

"The little girl!" Emily said. "The report said that there was one fatality. Benjamin Morgan. And that he died after saving another man and a little girl."

Molly nodded. "Mr. Morgan pulled me out of the flames. Then, when he was going back to see if there were any more workers inside..." her voice broke, "he was killed by the man who set the fire."

"You saw who set the fire?" Emily said.

Molly nodded. "And he saw me. He was chasing me until I became trapped behind a fallen beam. He couldn't reach me, so he left me there to die."

Jesse sat in silence, staring at the ground.

"Who did this?" Emily said. "Do you know who did this?"

"I don't know the man's name, but I'll never forget how he looked. He was big and bulky. His eyes were hard black. His hair was black too—slicked down and oily. He wore a mustache and..." she placed her index finger to her chin, "...he had a small patch right here for a beard."

"Tykas!" Jesse murmured.

"Tykas!" Emily agreed.

Chapter 32

TWO telegrams were sent to New York the next day. One to Franklin Austin informing him of Emily's safety and her scheduled departure on Thursday. The second was sent to Clara Morgan. The recent news of his father's death prompted Jesse at least to inform her of his location. He told her that he had met the girl his father had rescued in the factory fire and that he would write a letter with details soon. He told her nothing about his father's murder, thinking it best to explain it to her in his own way and in his own handwriting.

To Sheriff Clark, Jesse explained in detail how he led Tykas to believe they had fled north. The sheriff wrote down Jesse's description of the man and set about to notify the nearby towns of the killer's presence in the area.

By midafternoon, tensions had eased. Molly returned to her usual ebullient self as she escorted Jesse and Emily around town, introducing them to everyone.

Jesse loved everything about Redemption, Kansas. It was a Western town just like he'd always imagined, except much tamer of course. The people were genuinely warm and friendly. And for the first time since crossing the New York City boundaries, he thought seriously about settling down.

And Molly Clark figured into those thoughts.

He had known her such a short time, but with each passing hour she grew more attractive to him. And, unless he was mistaken, she felt the attraction too. When she looked at him, her gaze lingered. She seemed to welcome opportunities to touch him. She laughed readily at the things he said. Jesse couldn't help but think that somehow his father had rescued Molly from the fire just for him.

Some of the townspeople noticed the difference in her too.

When they visited Ann Humphrey again, the stocky red-head whispered in Jesse's ear, "You bring out a side of Molly I've never seen before. I always thought it would take a special man to make her happy." She stepped back and winked at him knowingly. "A word to the wise..." she said.

At Woolcott's General Store, Jesse got similar advice, only in a different way: "Watch your step, boy," the gruff store owner told him. "You hurt that young lady and we'll string you up faster than a horse thief."

Emily seemed to sense there was something between them too. When it was just she and Molly together, the two of them got along famously. However, whenever Jesse and Molly were together, Jesse would catch Emily casting pained glances at him from a distance. And whenever the three of them were together, Emily was strangely quiet.

The first Monday of every month was music night in Redemption, Kansas. The whole town congregated at Zimmerman's barn for an evening of song and laughter. The elderly Elijah Zimmerman had converted his barn into a stage just for the occasion. He had reconstructed one side of the barn into two large doors that swung open on tracks. Mounted on the inside of the doors were hats of every size, shape, color, and nationality: cowboy hats, firemen's hats, derbys, top hats, and a variety of tam-o'-shanters with pompoms, tassels, or feathers in the center.

Families from all over gathered in front of the barn—some in their wagons, others on picnic blankets—for a night of music and frivolity. Zimmerman hosted the event with his banjo, harmonica, and fiddle. A small band accompanied him. And everyone was welcome to sing or play an instrument of their choice. Part of the fun was Zimmerman's selection of an appropriate hat for each song.

Before each song, with mock seriousness the horseshoe bald Zimmerman would pace back and forth in front of the hats. He would select one and try it on. Then he would face the audience and elicit their response. Not until he had sufficient applause over his hat selection did the music continue.

"It's so much fun," Molly said as they rode in the buckboard. Jesse drove and Molly sat next to him. Emily sat alone in the back.

"What kind of music do you like, Emily?" Molly looked over her shoulder to ask.

"Popular tunes," Emily said halfheartedly. "'Frankie and Johnny,' 'Listen to the Mockingbird,' that sort of thing."

"How about you, Jesse?" Molly asked. "What kind of music do you like?"

Jesse shrugged. "Can't rightly say that I'm partial to any kind of music. Haven't heard much. Truly Noble likes Western songs," Jesse said. "So I guess if I had to choose, I'd say Western songs. How about you? What do you like?"

"Gospel songs," Molly said. "I can't get enough of them."

"There's a surprise," Emily quipped, a little more sharply than she had intended.

Something Jesse said caught Molly's attention. "Whenever you speak of Truly Noble, you do so almost with a reverence in your voice. Have you noticed that?"

Jesse shrugged. "I guess so. He's the kind of person I want to be."

"Oh?"

"Sure!" Jesse exclaimed. "He fights evil and lives for good. In fact..." he paused.

Both girls were looking at him intently. Molly was turned slightly toward him; Emily rested on one hand to see him. Jesse was reminded of when he was younger, how the girls made fun of him over his fascination with the fictional Truly.

"In fact, what?" Molly prompted.

"Nothing," Jesse said. "It was nothing."

"Tell me!" Molly said.

Jesse looked at the woman sitting next to him. There was no guile in her. And Jesse knew that he could tell her anything.

Still, it took a while before the words came out. "Whenever I face a difficult situation and I don't know what to do, I ask myself, 'What would Truly Noble do?'"

He braced himself for mocking laughter. It was a reflex action.

"Hmmm." Molly pondered what he said like it was a deep philosophical insight.

Emily looked at him with a knowing look, like she had just found the last piece of information to a puzzle.

"Where does Jesus fit into all of this?" Molly asked.

Both Jesse and Emily stared at her. It was the kind of question they would expect from her preacher/sheriff brother.

"Jesus fits into Sunday morning," Jesse said, "at church."

Another "hmmm" formed on Molly's face. "Do you attend church often, Jesse?"

Jesse shook his head. "Of course, we used to when my father preached at the mission. But I can barely remember it."

"And you and your mother stopped going after your father died?" Molly asked.

"Except on holidays. Why do you ask?"

"The question you ask yourself," Molly said. "It's similar to one I heard from a preacher in Topeka. A couple of us women went there to attend a National Women's Christian Temperance Union meeting. On Sunday we attended a Congregational church—Central Congregational, if memory serves. Following the sermon the pastor graciously chatted with us ladies for a while. He mentioned the same question, only with a different twist to it. He pondered what the world would be like if, whenever a person had a decision to make, he asked himself, 'What would Jesus do in this situation?' So, you see, you have the right idea. But you have the wrong man."

Jesse shook his head in disagreement. This was one time when Molly was wrong. "You can't compare the two," he said.

"I agree," Molly responded.

Jesse laughed. "No, I mean Truly Noble is a hero. Jesus wasn't."

"How can you say that?" Molly was offended. It was obvious.

"Don't get me wrong," Jesse said defensively. "Jesus healed people and gave us all those good Bible verses. But He wasn't a hero."

Molly visibly restrained herself. "How do you figure?" she asked.

"Simple. He lost. His enemies defeated Him. They killed Him on a cross. Truly Noble never loses. He always defeats the evil enemy." Jesse's voice quivered. "And he always rescues Charity."

Molly's ire eased; it was replaced with understanding compassion. "And if Jesus were really a hero," Molly concluded his line of thought, "He would have rescued your father from that fire and Tykas would have been killed instead."

With a hasty brush of his hand, Jesse wiped away a tear.

When Molly spoke next, she spoke softly. "I understand what you're saying," she said. "And I know what you're feeling. But you're wrong about Jesus. It's true, His enemies killed Him, but it wasn't because they were stronger. It was because by dying, Jesus gained a victory over two far greater enemies— sin and death. The cross wasn't Jesus' downfall, it was His path to victory. The Pharisees were no enduring threat to Him. Do you want to know the greatest threat Jesus faced on earth? It came in the wilderness when Satan tempted Him to live for Himself. Had Jesus failed there, He never would have been able to gain the victory later. You see, Jesse, dying isn't the worst thing that can happen to us. Living only for ourselves is far worse than death because it wastes the life God has given us. If Jesus had come down from the cross and defeated His enemies, He would have won a victory for Himself only and the rest of us would have lost. Your father knew this. He was just like Jesus. You see, Jesse, I am who I am today because two men gave their lives for me—Jesus on the cross, and your father in a factory fire. Both of them are heroes in my book."

"You sound like a preacher," Jesse joked.

Molly didn't laugh. "I won't apologize for the things I believe."

In the buckboard behind them, Emily listened and stared across the dark prairie.

Elijah Zimmerman was in rare form. Nearly two dozen families had already arrived by the time Jesse, Molly, and Emily got there. Without exception, the families waved, smiled, or shouted greetings to Molly. Seeing their response to her presence, one would have thought the queen of the province had just arrived.

"Do you mind?" Zimmerman cried out in mock indignation at the interruption Molly's arrival caused. "I'm trying to perform up here!"

"Sorry, Mr. Zimmerman," Molly shouted cheerfully.

A ripple of laughter echoed across the prairie.

Zimmerman stood on the stage. He wore overalls, a checkered long-sleeved shirt, and a silk top hat. Beside him stood a pudgy man, also wearing overalls. He had thinning hair and wore no covering.

"Goodness gracious!" the pudgy sidekick cried in a stage

voice. "What in thunder are you doing?"

Zimmerman twisted his arms and legs in several comical contortions. "Loosening up!" he said.

"But do you always do that?"

"Yes...*now!*"

"Why now?"

"Well, I'm a little older than I was when I began this business..."

A husky farmer in the audience stood and shouted, "You're much older now, Zim!"

Everyone laughed.

Zimmerman broke character. "Do you want to do this, Jim?" he shouted good-naturedly at the heckler.

The heckler laughed.

Zimmerman resumed his contortions. "As I was saying before I was so rudely interrupted..." More laughter. "...I'm a little older than I was when I began this business..." He broke character again and stared at Jim for a response. None was forthcoming, so he continued. "...and my legs get stiff, you know?"

"I can imagine!" the pudgy man chuckled. He was having a difficult time staying in character as he watched Zimmerman entwine his arms in a pretzel-shape behind his head.

"Why, I can remember when I could tie a knot in either leg without crackin' a joint!" Zimmerman exclaimed. "But no longer!"

While the pudgy straight man found his way offstage, the elderly Zimmerman twisted himself in a variety of contortions while members of the band, seated farther upstage, accompanied him with a series of pops, ratchet noises, and sliding strings.

The audience howled.

After a few songs of his own, Zimmerman called for volunteers to come onstage and entertain. A middle-aged rancher came up and played the hymn, "Amazing Grace" on a saw. An adolescent girl played a portion of Beethoven. It was painful to listen to, but that seemed to make the audience cheer all the louder.

"Molly! Get up there!"

It was Jim, the man who heckled the opening act. His call prompted a chorus of cries for Molly to sing. She waved them off for as long as she could. Finally, bowing to their insistence, she blushed and walked onstage.

"Hat! Hat! Hat! Hat! Hat!" the audience cheered.

While Molly stood self-consciously onstage, Zimmerman scurried behind her, trying on different hats.

A fireman's hat.

"Noooooo!" the audience cried.

The derby.

"Noooooo!"

Zimmerman donned a colonial woman's mobcap. He tied the white straps under his chin in a bow and batted his eyes in an overly flirtatious manner.

A cheer from the audience signaled he had found the right cap for Molly.

She turned to Zimmerman and the band and told them the song she wanted to sing.

Holding his violin, he turned to the band and asked, "Anybody know that one?" They all shook their heads no.

At first, Molly thought they were toying with her. But Zimmerman, looking ridiculous holding a violin and wearing a mobcap and overalls, confessed he didn't know the song. "Makes no difference," he assured her. "You begin singing, we'll catch on."

"Maybe it would be best if I just sit down." Molly tried to walk offstage. Zimmerman pulled her back. It was just as well. From the reaction of the audience, they wouldn't have let her get away without singing.

Standing center stage, Molly bowed her head to compose herself. Then, when she was ready, she raised her head. With her gaze lifted heavenward, she sang. Her voice was an alto instrument that rang with a melancholy sweetness.

> How sad by state our nature is
> Our sin how deep it stains,
> And Satan binds our captive souls
> Fast in his slavish chains.

Her voice, her demeanor, and the passion with which she articulated the words stilled the prairie audience. On the second verse, Zimmerman and the band picked up the tune and accompanied her. As she reached the climax of the song, her face beamed like the sun as she sang:

> Let every mortal ear attend
> And every heart rejoice
> The trumpet of the Gospel sounds
> With an inviting voice.

Her voice and the instruments faded to a silence which held for a poignant time. A resounding cheer, hand-clapping, and a smattering of "Amens" broke the silence.

As Molly descended the side steps leading to the stage, Zimmerman called out for more volunteers. There were no ready hands.

"We all know Molly is the only person in twenty counties who can carry a tune!" he cried. "That makes no nevermind! It's not like there's a New York drama director lurking in our midst. It's just us folks. Come on up and sing!"

"How about Molly's guests?" It was Jim the heckler again.

Jesse looked at Emily. He hadn't counted on this, and by the look on Emily's face, neither had she. "You first," Jesse said.

"Oh, no!" Emily cried. "I don't sing. You go!"

"You couldn't drag me up there!"

Zimmerman called from the stage. "Young lady! Young lady!"

Emily pointed to herself. "Me?" She looked at Jesse. "Is he talking to me?"

"Yes, you!" Zimmerman answered for Jesse. "Come up here!" He motioned for her to join him onstage.

Emily tried to wave him off. "Thank you, but no!" she said.

"Come on! I won't force you to do anything you don't want to do."

Jesse grinned. "Go on, Emily. Go up there!"

Zimmerman placed his hands on his hips. He was still wearing the mobcap and was hardly the picture of authority. "Do I have to send two good-looking gentlemen to escort you up here?"

A couple of male cheers sounded at the suggestion.

By this time Molly had rejoined them. "Go on, Emily," she whispered. "It's all in fun."

Reluctantly, very reluctantly, Emily stood and made her way to the stage. Her progress was accompanied by cheers.

Standing beside Zimmerman, the host placed his arm around her. "Now tell me, young lady. Be honest now. Do you sing?"

"No," Emily said.

"Do you play an instrument?"

"No."

"Then what exactly do you do?"

Emily looked down at Jesse. "I'm a writer," she said.

"Ah, a writer! That's good." Turning to the audience Zimmerman said, "Isn't that good?"

They responded with clapping and cheers.

"One more question, dear," Zimmerman said. "With what do you write? Pencil? Pen? Typewriter?"

"Mostly I write with a pencil, but I prefer the typewriter."

"The typewriter!" Zimmerman exclaimed in loud triumph. While the audience applauded, Zimmerman whispered in Emily's ear, "I was hoping you'd say that." To the audience: "I just happen to know a song about a typewriter!"

"Hat! Hat! Hat! Hat! Hat! Hat!"

After several rejected hat choices, the audience and Zimmerman settled on a French beret. Emily tried to sneak offstage, but Zimmerman pulled her back to stand next to him while he sang.

Accompanying himself with the banjo, the elderly host sang a woeful tune in a bad French accent. The song's title was: "Since My Daughter Plays on the Typewriter." Sung from a father's point of view, the lyrics bemoaned the fact that since his daughter learned to play the typewriter she began putting on airs, and coming home late from the office, and walking with a swagger like a fighter, and telling her mother to drop on herself—all because his daughter learned to play the typewriter.

The audience loved it. Even Emily had to laugh.

Later that night, after Jesse had excused himself and went upstairs to bed, Molly and Emily sat alone on the porch swing. Molly had fixed them some tea. Other than the sound of their own voices, the only noise was the creak of the swing and the chirp of crickets.

"Emily?"

"Hmmm?"

"I hope you don't think this too personal," Molly said, "but what are your feelings for Jesse?"

"What do you mean?" Emily asked coyly.

"I'm sorry," Molly said, genuinely flustered. "I shouldn't have asked."

Now it was Emily's turn to be flustered. Molly had broached

a subject that needed to be discussed. "You have every right to ask," Emily said. She sighed, took a sip of tea, and said, "I followed him out here. In fact, *chased* would be a better word."

"I see," Molly said.

"I'm not sure you do," Emily replied. "Jesse has no feelings for me. It's at his insistence that I'm going back to New York."

"I'm sorry," Molly said.

"Me too," Emily replied.

They sipped a while.

"What about you?" Emily said. "It's obvious Jesse has feelings for you. And, unless I miss my guess, you have feelings for him."

Molly blushed and tittered nervously. "Does it show that much?"

"It's something that's hard to hide," Emily chuckled with her. "Believe me, I know."

Molly spoke softly. "At first, I told myself that you and he belonged together. But that didn't stop the feelings I was feeling. And it bothered me. That is, until tonight."

"Oh? What happened tonight?"

Molly took a sip of tea. Her voice was firm and resolute. "The way things are right now, there could never be a future for Jesse and me."

Emily thought back on the night's events. The connection was eluding her.

"He's not a Christian," Molly said. "Jesus means nothing to him. He means everything to me."

"You mean, you would refuse to marry Jesse just because he doesn't believe like you do?"

"Without question," Molly said. "My faith means everything to me. I could never be yoked with a man who did not share it."

Emily wanted to shout for joy. Molly had effectively relinquished all interest in Jesse. Yet at the same time, she couldn't help but wonder why. It was evident that Molly felt very deeply about this. But she couldn't understand how a woman could turn from a man she loved for a prophet who lived so long ago.

"Molly?"

"Yes?"

"Tell me about Jesus. I've heard about Jesus during Christmas sermons and at Easter and all. Tell me about *your* Jesus."

As the hour grew late, Molly Clark told Emily about the source of her faith. It was a simple declaration. Without fanfare. Without theological jargon. To Emily it sounded like a love story. And before the night was over, Emily fell in love with Molly's Jesus too.

Chapter 33

WITH the rattle of the train against its track providing
percussion background, Logan read to Clara from a
book of verse. Slumped down in her seat, with eyes closed,
Clara listened to the tender, soft voice of the man who had
been her traveling companion.

> I fled Him, down the nights and down the days;
> I fled Him, down the arches of the years;
> I fled Him, down the labyrinthine ways
>   Of my own mind; and in the mist of tears
> I hid from Him, and under running laughter.
>   Up vistaed hopes I sped;
>   And shot, precipitated,
> Adown Titanic glooms of chasmed fears,
> From those strong Feet that followed, followed after.
>   But with unhurrying chase,
>   And unperturbed pace,
> Deliberate speed, majestic instancy,
>   They beat—and a Voice beat
>   More instant than the Feet—
> "All things betray thee, who betrayest Me."
>
> How little worthy of any love thou art!
> Whom wilt thou find to love ignoble thee

> Save Me, save only Me?
> All which I took from thee I did but take,
> Not for thy harms,
> But just that thou might'st seek it in My arms,
> All which thy child's mistake
> Fancies as lost, I have stored for thee at home:
> Rise, clasp My hand, and come!

A single tear escaped from under Clara's eyelid and trickled down her cheek. Without opening her eyes, she smiled. "How beautifully appropriate," she said. "Who wrote it?"

"An Englishman by the name of Francis Thompson," Logan replied. "Listen to this…" Logan read from a biographical paragraph printed under the poem. "It says here that three times Thompson tried to obtain a medical degree, and three times he failed. After that he drifted in abject poverty and was so poor, he couldn't even afford stationery to write. It seems he was supplied account books by a bootmaker. It was on those ledger sheets that he wrote his early poems." Logan chuckled softly. "Abject poverty…almost sounds like me…except for the writing part. I guess there's still hope that someday I'll make something of myself."

"If you ask me," Clara said in a sleepy voice, "you've done well for yourself. You may not have a financial empire, but you're at peace with yourself. Not many people can say that."

Logan looked lovingly at the woman beside him.

The train slowed.

"We're coming into a town," Logan said. "Now, look at that! The name of the town is Redemption."

Emily and Molly rode the buckboard into town. From casual observance, anyone who saw them might have mistaken them for lifelong friends who hadn't seen each other in years by the way they giggled and carried on with each other.

Truth was, they were feeling the effects of a sleepless night.

At one point during the late-night session, as the sky glowed by dawn's early light, Molly exclaimed to Emily, "Child, you're so filled with God's Spirit, you're going to have to backslide to get to sleep!"

For Emily it was the dawn of a new life. As the two women rode into town, Emily could barely stop smiling. She never would have guessed she could feel as close to another woman as she felt to Molly. And as wonderful as that felt, it only explained part of her exuberance. Suddenly, the whole world had taken on a new perspective. She couldn't believe how invigorating a ride to town could be. Never before had she smelled the air so fresh, or seen the sky so blue, or felt so alive.

The buckboard pulled up in front of the clothing store. "I have to deliver these dresses to Ann," Molly said. She climbed down and retrieved a large box from the wagon bed. "Why don't you go to Woolcott's and look for the things you need. I'll meet you there."

Emily agreed. As she crossed the street to the general store, she breathed deeply the prairie air. She smiled at the irony of traveling so far for romance only to find something even greater and more enduring—faith.

Logan stepped from the train, then turned to assist Clara. The platform was busy, but not crowded. People stood in clusters, some to greet friends and relatives arriving on the train; others to say their farewells. And, as at all the other train stops, a good number of people had come simply to watch the train. There was an aura about the mechanical monsters that still mesmerized the American public.

Clara and Logan stood beside the small red station house and gazed down the town's only street. For Redemption, it was a normal business day.

"After living in New York for so long," Logan commented,

"when I see a little town like this, I can't help but feel like I've stepped back in time to a tiny English hamlet."

"It is quaint, isn't it?" Clara replied. "But you know, I never had an inclination to move to the West until now. Given the choice, I would much rather settle in a little town like this than return to the tenements."

Logan pointed down the street. "On the left-hand side," he said, "about halfway down the street." He read the hand-painted sign: "Charles Woolcott's General Store and Post Office."

"Oh, good," Clara said. "I need to pick up a few things."

She stepped from the platform onto the street. After several steps she realized Logan was no longer beside her. She turned back. He was distracted by something she could not see behind the station house.

"Go ahead," Logan said to her. "I'll catch up with you in a minute."

Still staring at whatever it was that had distracted him, he strode down the platform and disappeared behind the station house. Although Clara was curious, she thought nothing of it. The man's affairs were none of her business. Following a couple of other passengers from the train, she walked down the street toward the general store.

With his shirt draped over a tree limb, Jesse swung the ax. With a crack and a thud, two pieces of wood fell to the sides of the block. The sun felt good on his back. His breathing had quickened from the exertion, and his skin glistened with sweat. After chopping so much wood for Edwards at Brownsville, Jesse never thought he'd hear himself say this again, but it felt good to chop wood. It was a perfect day, the work required little thought, and it felt good to stretch his muscles again.

Earlier that morning, Molly and Emily had breakfast ready

for him when he came downstairs. It struck him as odd that both girls were dressed in the same clothes they'd worn the night before. And when he learned they had stayed up all night talking, he thought them crazy, even more so when he learned they'd been talking about religious things. After further thought though, he didn't consider it quite as odd.

Somehow, Molly always found a way to slip religion into things. She never forced it into conversation like some people. It was as natural for Molly to talk about Jesus as it was for a cobbler to talk about shoes, or a sailor to use nautical terminology when he spoke. Molly wouldn't be Molly without her faith.

This morning, for lack of sleep or some other reason, the girls had been full of themselves and Jesse was glad to see them go into town. It would allow him some quiet time. He planned to use it to work through his thoughts—about Molly...and Emily...and his future. He couldn't shake the urge he was feeling to stake his claim in Redemption. As for Molly, his attraction to her had dimmed somewhat following their discussion on the way to Zimmerman's barn. He liked Molly as a person; he just didn't know if he wanted to spend his life with a woman who was so religious. And then there was Emily. Seeing her in a dress again nearly made him forget all about Slate Pickens. For her own safety, it was best that she go back to New York. But the more he thought about her leaving, the less he wanted to let her go.

Jesse was nearly done chopping all the wood he could find and still he had not come to any conclusions. Not about the girls. Not about the town.

"Tykas! What are you doing here?"

The oily-haired man jumped at the sound of his name. When he swung around and saw who it was that addressed him, he grinned widely. Smiles traveled only one direction.

"Logan! What are you doing in this God-forsaken town?"

"I just asked you the same thing."

Tykas glanced around. At the end of the train platform he spotted a sheriff watching passengers deboard the train. "Not here," he said. "Come with me."

Without waiting for a reply, Tykas stepped from the sheriff's view around the far side of the station house and walked down the back side of Redemption's businesses to an alley.

Reluctantly, Logan followed. If he had a choice, he wouldn't have anything to do with Tykas. But the former agent's presence out West was unsettling. It would be best to find out what the man was planning. So Logan walked after him.

In the alley, Logan could see across the street to the front door of the general store. He maneuvered himself so that Tykas' back was to the store. Logan didn't know if Tykas had ever met Clara Morgan, but he took the precaution anyway.

"Tell me what this is all about, Tykas."

The former agent didn't speak right away. With a grin he looked Logan over, then said, "I know that lately we've had our differences, but then we had our good days too, didn't we? The early days? Remember how we used to sit and talk for hours?"

Logan remembered. It was soon after Austin had hired him. Richard Tykas was assigned to acquaint the new security agent with his duties. During the long, empty hours of a few of their security assignments, the two men would talk philosophically. They learned that they both dreamed of an ordered society, free from strife and turmoil. And their shared dream initially formed a bond between the two men. However, after a while, it became evident to Logan that Tykas' idea of utopia was a world in which he was supreme and everybody did exactly what he wanted them to do. That was when Logan started to distance himself from the man.

"I'm on the verge of funding our longtime dream!" Tykas exclaimed. His eyes grew wide with excitement, showing a grotesque proportion of white.

"You've found someone out here to fund a community?"

Tykas laughed. "There's no money out here. New York money will fund it."

"Then what are you doing in Redemption?" Tykas seemed to delight in the fact that Logan was asking questions. Logan figured he interpreted the questions as a sign of interest.

"The incentive is out here," Tykas said.

"Incentive?"

Tykas nodded. "The incentive that will free up the money." Reading the puzzled look on Logan's face, he continued, "It will make sense once you know the source of the funds. Guess who is going to fund our dream?"

"Just tell me," Logan said.

Tykas folded his arms. "You have to guess!"

"I wouldn't even know where to begin," Logan said.

"Franklin Austin!" Tykas exclaimed gleefully. When he saw the surprised look on Logan's face, he nodded enthusiastically. "That's right! The old man himself!"

"And the incentive is…?"

"The Austin girl!"

"Austin's daughter Emily? What's she doing out here?"

"Ran away from home." Tykas laughed. "Couldn't have gotten luckier than if I'd planned it myself, could I?" He sobered a bit, then said, "I had her, but she slipped through my fingers. Tried to make me believe she went north. But I happen to know she's in this general area. I'll find her. And then, I'll telegraph her poppa."

It was this kind of thinking that made Logan detest Tykas. "You plan to hold the girl for ransom," Logan said.

Tykas winked. "That's the idea. How about it? Do you want in?"

Clara sorted through a barrel of apples. The sign above the

barrel said they were from Missouri. She had picked out two that were large, red, and crisp. She searched for two more. Another hand joined hers among the apples. Clara looked up. The hand belonged to a young woman with short, brown hair and innocent, wide eyes. She said, "Have you ever seen apples so red?"

"They do look delicious," Clara said.

The two women examined one apple after another.

"You have such a wonderful town!" the young woman exclaimed. "I think I'm falling in love with it."

Confused by the statement, Clara didn't know how to respond. Then she realized the young lady had confused her for a resident. "Oh, I don't live here," Clara smiled. "I just stepped off the train."

The young woman blushed. "I'm sorry," she giggled. "I just arrived myself on Sunday, and well, obviously, I don't know many of the people yet."

Clara laughed. "I thought *you* were a resident. But I do have to agree with you. It seems to be a lovely town."

"Where are you from?" the young lady asked.

"New York."

"New York, really? What a coincidence! I'm from New York too! My name's Emily. And you are?"

"Emily…" Clara repeated the name. "I'm glad to meet you. My name's…"

"TRAIN'S PULLIN' OUT!"

The bearded passenger who had delighted in telling train wreck stories had stuck his head in the doorway and shouted the announcement.

"Oh dear," Clara cried. "I've got to go, Emily."

"I didn't hear any whistle," Emily said.

Clara laughed again. "Seems like our engineer has an aversion to whistles," she said, racing to the counter. She hurriedly produced a few coins to pay Mr. Woolcott for the apples, then ran out the door.

"Have a nice journey!" Emily called after her.

Running up the street to the train, Clara looked around for Logan. A gnawing feeling of concern generated in her belly. Logan had failed to show up at the store like he said he would. Although she'd known him only a few days, she knew enough about him to deduce that this was unusual behavior. She remembered the look on his face when he told her to go on without him. What was it he had seen behind the station that would prompt such a look?

Ahead of her, the train shuddered, then shuddered again as it slowly moved forward. Clara glanced around her. There was no sign of Logan. She hoped he was already on board. Lifting her dress to keep from tripping, Clara stepped up onto the platform, and a few steps later onto the moving train step.

With her heart pounding from her hasty boarding, Clara navigated her way down the aisle to the bench she and Logan shared. Logan's book of poetry was its only occupant.

Clara bent over to look out the train's windows. She had to look around and past the people who had preceded her on board as they put packages away and began settling back into their places for the next leg of the journey.

Beyond the windows of the train, the buildings of Redemption slowly slipped by. Up and down the street people were milling about. Emily stood in the street, watching the train depart. On the station platform others waved good-bye and wiped away tears. Drivers of carriages that had lined the tracks clucked at their horses, turning them away from the train toward home.

Clara's heart began to pound again, but not from running. Logan was not on board and he was nowhere to be seen.

Chapter 34

FROM the alley Logan saw Clara burst out of the general store. He also heard the heavy chugs of the steam engine as it strained to set its emigrant load back into motion. Then, to his amazement, he saw her—the Austin girl.

Tykas didn't see her. His back was to the street. "Don't you see?" he cried. "This is the opportunity we've been waiting for! The community we dreamed about is within our grasp. After all, who knows Austin better than us? Right? We could ask for any amount and he'd pay it! So what do you think? Are you in or not?"

The Austin girl stood in the middle of the street. All Tykas had to do was glance over his shoulder and he'd see her. Logan couldn't let that happen.

The chugging of the train increased its rhythm. He thought of Clara. "So, once we nab the girl," he said, "where do we keep her?"

The patch of hair on the man's chin twitched excitedly. "I have a place in Illinois," he said. "We'll take her there."

"You wouldn't hurt her, would you?"

A hint of disappointment flashed in Tykas' eyes. In a less excited voice he said, "She's no good to us dead."

Logan looked past Tykas, hoping that the Austin girl had moved on.

She was staring straight at him! Her hand flew to her

mouth. She dropped the bag she was holding and ran in the direction of the train station.

Thoughts swirled in Logan's mind like a prairie twister. He had to distract Tykas, warn Emily, and catch up with Clara. It seemed impossible. But he had to try. The Austin girl was the key. She had run toward the train station. It just might work.

"Listen," Logan said. He spoke quickly. "I want to hear more about this, but the train is leaving and my things are on board. Let me catch it, get my things, and I'll meet you…" He spotted the church in the distance beyond the opposite end of town. "…under the tree by the church." He pointed to the church in case Tykas didn't know where it was. At the same time he began stepping toward the tracks.

The sound of the chugging train began to grow faint.

"You don't need nothing," Tykas said. "Soon, we'll have enough money to replace anything you have to leave behind."

"These are personal items," Logan insisted. "Family things. Irreplaceable. The church, by the tree, just give me a few minutes…" He turned toward the sound of the train.

Tykas squinted his eyes. "I'll wait for you under the tree," he said.

To Logan, his words signaled the start of a race. He was off as fast as he could run.

Clearing the end of the building closest to the station, the train came into view. Logan didn't know if he'd be able to catch it. Large puffs of black smoke erupted from the engine, which looked so far distant. It indicated the train was picking up speed.

Why this time? Logan said to himself.

Sometimes when the train pulled out of a station, for reasons unknown to the passengers, the train crept along at a turtle's pace for upwards of an hour. This time, however, the increasingly steady chugging sound from the engine indicated it was working up to full steam right away.

Logan pushed himself harder.

He had no intention of joining Tykas. His plan was to get the man away from Emily, then quickly warn her about him; catch up with Clara; stop the train; then come back to town. Hopefully, he would convince Clara to come back with him.

He knew all this was impossible, but he had to try. There was absolutely no way he could ride away on the train knowing that he was leaving a young lady at the mercy of a man like Tykas.

Just as he reached the platform, he spied Emily. She saw him too. Her hand was on the arm of a tall man wearing a mustache and a badge.

"There he is!" Emily cried, pointing at Logan. "He's one of them!"

When Emily stepped from the general store, she stood in the street and watched the departing train. She looked for the lady she'd met at the apple barrel. She saw Sheriff Clark; and there were several people waving good-bye to the train. But Emily didn't see the apple barrel lady, which meant she probably made it to the train on time.

Emily wondered what was keeping Molly. Apparently, her business with Ann was taking longer than she had expected. So Emily turned toward the clothing store.

Her heart stopped cold when she saw two men in an alley.

She didn't recognize Tykas immediately. He had his back to her. But there was something familiar about the other man that caught her attention. She had seen him before. But where? Full brown beard...thinning hair on top of his head...calm, almost sad eyes...that looked up at her.

Then she remembered; and the memory reached inside her chest with icy hands and stopped her heart. She had seen him in her house. At the foot of the steps in the entryway. It was the night her father caught her sneaking into the house. Two men emerged from her father's study. Tykas and his partner!

And the man with his back to her? Tykas! Now she recognized the back of his black, oily head.

There was but a single thought in Emily's mind. Run to Sheriff Clark!

The sheriff saw her coming. From the concerned look on her face, he knew she was frightened. Just as she reached him, out of the corner of her eye, she saw Tykas' partner emerge from the end of the building. He was running straight at her!

"There he is!" Emily cried. "He's one of them!"

Sheriff Clark stepped between her and the approaching man.

"He's Tykas' partner!" Emily screamed. She looked nervously around for Tykas, expecting him to appear from a different direction. She didn't see him.

"Hold it right there!" the sheriff cried.

The man kept running toward them. The sheriff drew his pistol.

The man shouted, "Sheriff, I don't have time to explain! Emily is in danger. Keep her with you until I get back. I must catch that train!"

The man showed no indication of slowing down.

"I said hold it right there!" the sheriff warned again.

The man had changed his course and was no longer running straight at them. Now, he was running toward the train. Sheriff Clark moved to keep himself between Emily and the man.

"I said hold it!" the sheriff shouted.

The man's hands were in full sight. He had no weapon.

"I'll explain in a few minutes!" he shouted. "I must catch that train!"

The man ran past the sheriff and Emily, closing the distance between himself and the train. It was clear that if his legs held out, he would catch up with it.

"Stop or I'll shoot!" the sheriff shouted.

The man kept running.

BLAM!

The sound of the sheriff's gun reverberated against the side of the red station. Smoke circled the barrel of his gun, which was pointed at the sky. The sound was enough to stop the man.

He stood at the edge of the platform. With slumped shoulders he watched the train as it continued down the track with increasing speed.

Concealed by the edge of Curtis Rickhart's Outfitting Store, Tykas observed Logan's arrest on the train platform with mixed feelings. On the one hand, he was fuming when he realized Logan had no intention of joining him; on the other hand, he now knew exactly where to find Emily.

"Fool!" he muttered under his breath as he watched the sheriff lead Logan away.

With no more wood to chop, Jesse had cleaned himself up and sat on the porch swing waiting for the girls to return. After a while, he grew tired of waiting and tired of thinking. Instead of coming to any conclusions about Molly, Emily, and the town of Redemption, he had only succeeded in muddying the issues.

With the town less than a mile away, he decided to walk that direction. If he met the girls on the road, he'd simply hitch a ride back with them. After all, it wasn't that he had any business in town; he was just lonely for some company.

Adjusting the cap that had traveled with him all the way from New York, he set out down the dirt road that led to Redemption.

"Sheriff, I know how this must look," Logan pleaded, "but I'm not in league with Richard Tykas. In fact, I was trying to warn Emily about him!"

Logan was led to the back of the sheriff's office and through a door to two jail cells. The sheriff gave no indication that he was even listening to Logan until after the door of the cell was closed and locked.

Then the sheriff said, "Looked to me like you were trying to escape on that train."

Logan nodded as he said, "Yes, I was trying to catch the train. I wanted to get my things which are still on board. But I was coming back. As God is my witness, I was coming back."

The sheriff turned to Emily who had followed them. "You say this is Tykas' partner?"

"I'm not his partner!" Logan insisted.

Emily nodded. "The two of them used to work together for my father. I saw them one night in my father's study."

"We *used* to work together," Logan explained. "We were partners for a while when we worked for Mr. Austin. But I am not Tykas' partner now."

"I saw the two of them together in the alley," Emily said.

The sheriff looked to Logan for an explanation.

"Yes, she saw us in the alley. But today is the first time I've seen the man in months! When I stepped off the train, I spotted him. He tried to enlist my help. That's what I've been trying to warn you about."

"Help with what?" the sheriff asked.

Logan sighed. He looked sadly at Emily. "Tykas plans to kidnap Emily and hold her for ransom. He wants to use the money to build a utopia."

"That's exactly what Tykas told me after abducting me from Fort Larned!" Emily said.

"That's *his* plan, not *mine!*" Logan insisted.

It was the sheriff's turn to sigh. "Mr. Logan, is there anything you can say, or show me, that will convince me of your story?"

Logan looked at the ceiling of the cell as he searched his mind for some tangible proof that he was telling the truth. "I have someone on board the train who can vouch for me," he offered.

"I'm afraid that doesn't do you much good right now. Is there anything else?" the sheriff replied.

Logan shrugged in resignation.

"Then I guess I'm just going to have to hold you until I can catch up with this Tykas fellow and get his story."

Clara stared absently out the train window. Her hands caressed Logan's book of poems on her lap. Tenderly she opened the book. Her gaze fell on the words of Francis Thompson's poem:

> I fled Him, down the nights and down the days;
> I fled Him, down the arches of the years;
> I fled Him, down the labyrinthine ways
>   Of my own mind; and in the mist of tears
> I hid from Him...

In the mist of tears... Clara's eyes grew moist as she thought of the book's owner; how, after all these years of living on a diet of bitter ire, he reacquainted her with the sweet things of life. He made her think of God.

It had been mere minutes since she had last seen Logan. Yet already she missed him. She wondered if she would ever have the chance to thank him for all he had done for her.

A single tear fell and marked the page of Thompson's poem; and for the first time since the death of her husband, Clara prayed.

When she opened her eyes, it took a moment for them to adjust to the midday sunlight. As they did, she stared out the window, content that God had heard her prayer. In the distance, a lone form strode across the prairie grass.

Tall. Lanky, with a familiar gait. And a cap, just like...

Jesse? Clara pressed close to the window, afraid to believe that it was her son.

The young man removed his cap to mop his forehead with his shirtsleeve. Brown hair with red highlights sparkled in the sunlight.

It was him!

"Jesse!" Clara yelled. Her voice bounced off the window back at her. Looking for a conductor, she yelled, "Stop the train! Stop the train!"

In the absence of a conductor, the bearded railroad storyteller said, "Ma'am, what is it? Are you ill?"

"That's my son out there!" Clara cried, tears rolling down her cheeks. "I've got to get off!"

The man peered across the aisle through the window. He spotted the boy.

"I've traveled all the way from New York to find him!" Clara wailed.

"Then this is an emergency?" the man asked.

"Yes! I've got to get off!"

The bearded man grinned. "I've always wanted to do this," he said. He reached for the emergency cord and pulled.

The squeal of train brakes sounded in the distance. Jesse returned his hat to his head and squinted his eyes against the brightness of the sun.

Odd, he thought. From what he could see, the train had no reason to be stopping so suddenly. Nothing seemed to be on the tracks.

Then a woman emerged from one of the middle cars. She ran as though someone were chasing her. A bearded man appeared on the train steps behind her, but didn't follow.

The woman was running and waving her arms. And yelling something.

Before he heard his name, he recognized her.

"Mother? Mother!" he shouted. He ran toward her.

Several hundred feet from the Santa Fe Railroad tracks Clara Morgan found her son. With passenger faces pressed against the windows of the train watching them, mother and son embraced, and wept, and embraced again.

"Jesse! Jesse! Thank God I found you! Thank God!"

Chapter 35

E MILY swept through the door of the dress shop and ran headlong into Molly, nearly bowling her over.

"Whoa!" Molly cried. "Miss me that much?"

"Tykas is here!" Emily shouted.

The name was enough to dissipate all traces of levity on Molly's face. "You saw him?" she asked.

"And his partner," Emily said. "Your brother has the partner locked up and is out looking for Tykas."

Ann approached the two women. "Molly, what's wrong, dear?" she asked. "You look like you've seen a ghost."

"Something like that," Molly said. "My past is haunting me."

"It's all my fault!" Emily said. "I led him here."

"Emily, don't do that. Don't blame yourself for another person's evil," Molly said. "Did my brother say what we are supposed to do?"

"We're supposed to go straight to his office and wait for him there," Emily replied.

"Then let's go," Molly said.

"Is there anything I can do?" Ann asked.

"Pray," Molly replied. "Pray without ceasing."

Arm-in-arm, the two women stepped outside. Nervously, they looked up and down the street. To Molly it looked like any other day in Redemption, Kansas. They could see Sheriff

Clark at the end of the street. He looked down an alley, then crossed over to the train station. He disappeared around the corner of the building.

Without saying a word, Emily and Molly slowly made their way toward the sheriff's office. They wouldn't have to cross the street, merely walk past three businesses on the boardwalk and they were there. Both of them kept vigilant eyes on the street. Emily wondered what they would do if they actually saw Tykas. She wished she had her police whistle with her.

Suddenly, a figure stepped from between the buildings. Emily felt a sharp point press against her back. Startled, she swiveled around to find she was inches from the black patch of hair on Tykas' chin.

"Make a sound and you're dead," he muttered.

Molly turned to see why Emily had stopped. It didn't take her but an instant to figure it out. "You!" she said disgustedly.

Tykas didn't know what to make of Molly or her remark. He wasted no time trying to figure it out. "Both of you, step this way." Gripping Emily's arm with iron fingers just below her shoulder, the man pulled her into the alley. "Unless you want this girl's blood on your hands," Tykas said to Molly, "you'll come along quietly. Make one chirp, and she's dead. Understand?"

From her past experience with the man, Molly had no doubt that he was capable of doing what he threatened. Fearing for Emily's life, Molly stepped into the alley with Emily and Tykas.

"He knew your father," Clara said.

Jesse's mother strolled beside him, her arm linked with his, a happy smile adorning her face. The train had continued on its journey without her. Clara didn't care. While others came West looking for a new start or sudden riches, Clara had found what she was looking for. Her journey at an end, she walked contentedly with her son toward the town of Redemption. She was describing to him her traveling companion.

As for Jesse, he was having a difficult time accepting the fact that it was indeed his mother on his arm. She came out of nowhere. She looked happier and healthier than Jesse could ever remember seeing her. And she was aglow about this man named Logan.

"A nicer man you'll never meet," she said. "And knowledgeable too. He must still be in town. I really want you to meet him, and him you."

While they were still several hundred yards away from the end of the town's only street, without warning, a wagon bolted from behind the buildings. With a plume of dust in its wake, it bounded away from the town in the general direction of the church. Jesse recognized the plump driver.

"Molly!" he cried. In the bed of the wagon were two other people sitting close together. *Emily. And Tykas!*

Tykas had a forearm around her neck. His other elbow was bent, suggesting that he had some kind of weapon pressed against her back.

"That girl in the wagon," Clara said, unsure what to make of her son's alarm. "That's the girl I met in the general store."

Jesse didn't hear her. Breaking their arm link, he ran after the wagon, shouting. His shouts caught the attention of Emily. Her lips mouthed his name. Tykas saw him too. He said something Jesse didn't quite make out, but showed no visible sign of concern. It was apparent to everyone that Jesse had no chance of catching the wagon.

When Jesse finally admitted that fact to himself, he turned to his mother. "They're being kidnapped!" he explained. "We need to alert the sheriff!"

He ran the rest of the way into town. Clara ran after him.

Jesse barged into the sheriff's office. "Sheriff Clark!" he yelled.

No one answered. The place looked deserted. The door leading to the jail cells was ajar.

"He must be patrolling the street," Jesse concluded out loud. "I've got to find him! Mother, you stay here. I'll be right back."

"Oh no!" Clara said. "I haven't come this far only to lose you again. I'm going wherever you go!"

"Clara?" The voice came through the door to the adjoining jail cells. "Clara? Clara, is that you?"

A puzzled expression crossed Clara's face. "Logan?" Tentatively Clara stepped through the door. "Logan! It is you! What are you doing in jail?"

"What are you doing here?" Logan cried. "Why aren't you on the train?"

"I found Jesse!" She grasped Logan's hands through the bars. "I found Jesse!"

Jesse poked his head around the door to see who his mother was talking to. The man behind the bars looked kindly at him, genuinely pleased by his mother's good fortune.

"Mother, are you all right?" Jesse asked, looking at the man in the cell, but wanting to run out the door.

Noting his concern, Clara nodded. "Go find the sheriff," she said. "But come right back here! Don't go anywhere else without me!" Her tone was heavy with motherly authority.

Jesse nodded. An instant later the slamming of a door indicated he was gone.

"What's happening?" Logan asked.

"Jesse saw a friend of his in a wagon with a man. He thinks the man is kidnapping her."

"Emily?" Logan shouted.

Clara stared at him with a look of bewilderment, as though everybody in the world was in on a secret except her. "Yes, Emily...I met her in the store..."

"I've got to get out of here!" Logan said.

Five minutes later, Jesse returned with the sheriff.

"Let me out of here, Sheriff," Logan cried. "I can help!"

"Can't do that," the sheriff said flatly. Staring at Clara, he said, "Who are you?"

Jesse quickly introduced his mother. The sheriff nodded and unlocked a gun rack. He grabbed a shotgun.

Clara spoke to him. "I know you suspect Logan of being in league with this other man," she said, "but he couldn't be. He's been beside me on the train for the last several days."

"Just like I've been telling you, Sheriff!" Logan pleaded. "I'm not that man's partner! But I know him. He's dangerous! And I can help you catch him!"

Sheriff Clark stepped in front of the jail cell. He stood nose-to-nose with Logan. In a low voice, he said, "That man has my sister!"

"Then let me help you catch him!" Logan said.

"Hurry, Sheriff!" Jesse cried.

Sheriff Clark unlocked the jail cell door. To Jesse he said, "Show me which way the wagon was heading."

After shouting to several men on the street that Molly had been kidnapped, the sheriff and Logan rode out on horses. Jesse drove his mother in the buckboard that had been left in front of the dress shop. The horses soon outdistanced the buckboard. If the terrain had greater geographical features, it would have been next to impossible for Jesse to follow them. As it was, even though he lost sight of the riders, he never lost sight of their trailing dust.

They caught up with the riders at an old house. The wagon which had been used to spirit the girls away was in front of the house. The sheriff and Logan were about a hundred yards away behind a small cluster of trees. The house looked deserted. And there was nothing between it and the trees that could provide cover for them.

Inside the house, Molly and Emily huddled in a corner. Tykas stood to one side of a window, occasionally poking his head just far enough around the frame to see what was going on outside.

From behind a cluster of trees came a voice. "This is Sheriff Clark," the voice identified itself.

This prompted an exchange of glances and smiles between the girls, which quickly withered under Tykas' murderous scowl.

"Let the women go, Tykas!" the sheriff shouted.

"This is no concern of yours, Sheriff!" Tykas yelled. "I'm a duly authorized agent of Franklin Austin. My assignment is to find his daughter and return her safely to him."

There was a moment of silence.

"All right, Mr. Tykas," the sheriff shouted. "I'll take you at your word."

"What?" Emily cried. A glare from Tykas brought her up short.

"Come out of the house and we'll all ride peacefully back to town. We'll send a telegram to Mr. Austin, and if he confirms your assignment, you and the girl are free to go."

From the lack of frustration on Tykas' face it was evident that he hadn't really expected the sheriff just to let him go. It was simply an opening gambit.

"What do we do now?" Jesse asked.

Without taking his eyes off the building, Sheriff Clark said, "We wait."

Jesse didn't want to hear that. "We've got to do something!" he cried. "Tykas will kill them!"

The sheriff looked at Logan. "Is he capable of it?"

"If provoked, yes," Logan said.

Calmly returning his attention to the building, Sheriff

Clark said, "Then we won't provoke him."

A commotion stirred behind them. Jesse turned and saw a great cloud of dust. It was the people of Redemption. Men and women. Swarming like a small army of locusts. In short order the entire house was surrounded. Tykas had nowhere to go.

The sun had slipped beneath the horizon. It was dark. Darker still because no one lit a fire. They didn't want to give the enemy any easy targets. The house was dark too. The moon had not yet risen. Behind the tree, Sheriff Clark huddled with a select group of men, Logan and Jesse among them. They were discussing a plan to use the cover of darkness to hide their approach to the house.

Emily could barely see Molly even though the girls were pressed shoulder-to-shoulder. At any given moment they didn't know where Tykas was, only that he appeared suddenly if they made the slightest sound, while he moved about on cat's paws. Emily guessed the man's training as an agent taught him how to come and go so quietly.

Once, when they had not seen him for several minutes, they tried to make a quiet break for the front door. He was upon them before they gained their footing. The memory of sharp-edged steel against their throats combined with the foul smell of Tykas' murderous threats kept them from trying again. Together, the girls determined their strongest effort was prayer, and faith in Oliver and Jesse.

Huddled in the dark corner, the two women took turns praying.

Tykas heard them. "Shut up!" he screamed. "I warned you about trying to escape!"

"We were just praying," Emily said.

"It'll do you no good," Tykas replied. "God's on my side."

Molly erupted. "How can you possibly think..."

Emily shushed her. Now was not the time for a theological debate.

Tykas had gathered a handful of loose papers. He stuffed these into a corner, then went in search for more. Back again, he stuffed papers in another corner.

"Here's the plan, ladies," he said. "In a minute, this place is going to be an inferno. Now, you have a choice. You can stick with me and escape when I escape, or you can stay here and be burned alive. It's your choice."

"You're crazy!" Molly said. "What makes you think you can escape with all those…"

"…people out there?" Tykas concluded her sentence for her. "Why, my dear lady, it is those people who will help me escape." He squatted in front of them so that their heads were on the same level. "Trust me!" he said. "It's not like this is the first time I've done this. Fire is a wonderful diversion. People running everywhere…frantic…with one thought on their mind, and one thought only…put the fire out! For calm, rational, sane people like myself, a good fire can become a wonderful cover for all sorts of—how shall I put it?—interesting developments. Afterward, the fire completes my job for me by cleansing the scene of all incriminating evidence."

"It doesn't do as good a job as you think," Molly said. "Sometimes it leaves behind witnesses. Like in New York fifteen years ago when you murdered Benjamin Morgan!"

Tykas was so stunned by her accusation, it was almost comical.

"That's right," Molly pressed. "I was there. I saw you kill him."

"The little girl…" Tykas muttered.

Fright visited the man's eyes. He wore a graveyard expression, the kind people wear in cemeteries late at night when they expect a ghost to appear from behind every tree or tombstone. Only for Tykas, the ghost was not imaginary. He was face-to-face with someone who, in his mind, had indeed risen from the dead.

He got up and moved away without a word.

Emily leaned closer to Molly and whispered, "I wish you hadn't told him that."

"I couldn't help myself," Molly confessed.

"Fire!"

The alarm disrupted the sheriff's planning. All eyes turned toward the house. Through the windows yellow and orange flames could be seen. In an instant, the old house was nearly engulfed.

Tykas' prediction was right on target. He had disrupted the anthill; people scurried everywhere, shouting, screaming, looking for a well, buckets, blankets, anything they could put their hands on to douse the flames. But there was nothing to find. The well was dry. There were no buckets. No blankets. No one thought to bring shovels. And no amount of agitation had any effect on the fire.

The sheriff's plans to use the cover of darkness went up in the smoke of the fire. The blaze illuminated the entire area surrounding the house. Anybody going near the house would be ablaze with light.

"What's he trying to do? Commit suicide?" the sheriff screamed.

"No," Logan replied. "He's done this before. He'll use the confusion of the fire to make his escape. Keep everyone away from the house."

"But they'll burn!" the sheriff cried.

"You can't give him a chance to get lost in a crowd of people fighting the fire!" Logan said. "Keep everyone away. I'll go in and get the girls. But I'll need help. Tykas will be lying in wait for us. If three of us go in, chances are that one of us will succeed in rescuing the girls."

"No!" Clara cried. "Let someone else go."

The sheriff barked orders to the men of Redemption to keep everyone away from the building. Then, to Logan, he said, "You take the north side. I'll take the east side. We need one more."

"I'll go," Jesse said.

Clara smothered her son in her arms. "Oh no, you don't. You're not going in there! I won't let you!"

Sheriff Clark placed a hand on Jesse's shoulder. "Son, you stay here with your mother."

Jesse shook his head. "Sheriff, you're going because your sister is in there, right?"

The sheriff conceded his point.

"Well, the woman I love is in there. How can you expect me to stand out here and do nothing?"

Sheriff Clark looked into his eyes and nodded. "You take the west side."

"Jesse, I lost your father this way, I won't…"

Firmly releasing himself from his mother's arms, Jesse said, "Father died doing what he thought was right. Maybe it's my father coming out in me, but I have to try. I can't let fear determine the course of my life."

Clara cradled her son's face in her hands. "You are so much like your father," she whispered. Embracing him, she said, "Go. And God be with you."

The west side of the house was a sheet of flame. It called to him.

As demonic spirits issue forth from the same hell, so flames come from a single source of all flames. At least, that's how it seemed to Jesse. How else could he explain that these flames, hundreds of miles from New York, knew his name?

These were the same flames that had killed his father. The flames that called to him from the barrel in the alley. The flames that would not be satisfied until they had consumed him too.

Jesse stepped tentatively toward them.

The flames jumped with glee at his approach. "Your luck has finally run out," they seemed to say. "It was inevitable. You were destined to be ours. Just like your father…just like your father."

The heat against his face was suffocating. Jesse stopped.

"Don't stop now!" the flames called to him. Fiery fingers beckoned him. "Come closer, come closer…"

A few more steps. Jesse could feel his face burning like it did after a long, hot day in the sun.

From behind him came a voice: "It's no use, son! Back away! Back away!"

Jesse turned to look behind him. An entire chorus of townspeople were waving him back, encouraging him to flee the flames.

The flames countered their call. "Come to us! It's your destiny. You can't run from us forever."

Jesse stood still, caught between the call of the townspeople and the call of the flames.

What would Truly Noble do?

Looking at the burning building, there was no question as to what Truly Noble would do. He would leap through the flames, fight off the evil men, scoop Charity Increase up in his arms, and emerge from the house unscathed. Always unscathed.

"But he isn't real…" Jesse muttered. "Truly Noble isn't a real person. He can do things like that and escape unscathed because he's just a story."

Jesse backed away from the fire.

"That's right, son!" the man behind him cried. "You did your best. Nobody could survive that fire!"

What would Jesus do?

The question came to him. Molly's question. A question not based on fiction, but based on the life of a real man.

What would Jesus do?

Jesse stared at the flaming house. *Jesus would put the well-being of others before His own well-being. Jesus would give His life to save Molly and Emily.*

With a burst of speed Jesse ran toward the house. Shielding his face with his arms, he threw himself at a window. The sound of shattering glass accompanied his crash to the floor. As he struggled to get up, he was stinging and sticky from cuts to his arms and legs.

He heard coughing. Getting to his feet, he saw Tykas standing in the center of the room. He was holding a board in one hand and a knife in the other. Sheriff Clark lay at his feet. Motionless. Apparently, Tykas had just turned to face Logan when Jesse crashed through the window. Now the man was caught between them.

Logan shouted to Jesse. "You get the girls out of here! I'll take care of Tykas!"

Tykas moved toward the girls. Logan countered his move. Jesse stepped toward Tykas. In order to keep both men at bay, Tykas was forced to back away.

The heat was incredible. Jesse felt like he was standing inside an iron stove. Smoke filled his lungs and he began to cough. Logan and Tykas were coughing too. They all staggered about like drunks fighting.

"Get the girls!" Logan cried.

Jesse stepped toward the girls huddled in the corner, coughing uncontrollably.

Tykas moved to cut him off.

That's when Logan launched himself toward the man, catching him from the side. The board in Tykas' hand went flying, but he managed to hold onto the knife. The two men rolled on the floor, wrestling for the weapon.

Jesse ran to the girls. "Molly! Emily! Let's get out of here!"

He helped them to their feet, and while Logan and Tykas wrestled, Jesse led the girls through the fire and out the door. Once they were outside, they were met by a wave of townspeople.

Molly and Emily doubled over with coughing spasms.

Between coughs, Molly managed to say, "Oliver!"

Jesse had no idea if her brother was dead or alive.

Clara ran to her son and grabbed his arm. "Logan! Did you see Logan?"

Coughing, Jesse nodded. "Needs help. I'm going...back in."

At first, Clara refused to release his arm. Jesse looked at his mother. Her grip eased. "Bring him out for me," she said.

Jesse ran back into the burning house.

The smoke was heavier now. Jesse pulled his shirt up and used it to cover his mouth. Stepping over the sheriff, Jesse scanned the floor for two men wrestling. He couldn't find them.

He almost saw Tykas too late.

The man had Logan backed against a flaming wall. The knife was leveled at Logan's belly.

"Tykas!" Jesse shouted.

The man spun around. Logan tried to grab Tykas' knife hand, but Tykas was too quick. The knife slashed, cutting open Logan's forearm.

But now Tykas was caught in the middle again. He backed away from them.

Like two hounds cornering a fox, Logan moved toward him on one side while Jesse approached from the other. Tykas brandished the knife, first at one man, then the other. He backed away.

All of a sudden, the flooring beneath Tykas gave way and one of his feet crashed through. He lost his balance. In his attempt to regain it, the knife flew from his hands. Jesse bent down and scooped it up.

"It's over, Tykas!" Logan said.

The man's foot was caught in the floorboards. No amount of struggling pulled it free.

Logan walked over to him and offered him his hand.

Tykas looked at his former partner, reached out, and took Logan's hand. Suddenly, he jerked with all his might. Logan was pulled down to the floor. Tykas put his arm around Logan's neck and began choking him.

"Let him go!" Jesse shouted. He pointed the knife at Tykas in a threatening manner. But he knew he could never use the knife on someone, and Tykas seemed to know it too.

"Get out," Logan wheezed as he struggled to free himself. "Get out!" Logan's eyes encouraged Jesse to look up. He did. The roof was creaking. It was beginning to collapse.

"I can't leave you!" Jesse cried.

"Get out!"

In the next instant, the discussion became moot. The ceiling crashed down upon all three of them. Jesse felt himself crushed beneath the weight of falling timbers and sensed the floor beneath him give way.

He was stunned, but the collapsing roof didn't knock him unconscious. Woozy, Jesse pushed the rubble off himself, using a cool board to push the hotter ones away. When he finally managed to free himself, he looked for Logan.

A pile of wood stirred, indicating life. As quickly as he could, despite the heat, his cuts and burns, and the smoke in his lungs, Jesse pulled the boards off Logan. He was alive and in much the same condition as Jesse. Unsteady, but functional.

There was a gaping hole in the roof over them. Other sections threatened to collapse at any moment.

Together, they uncovered Tykas. When they tried to lift him, the man offered them no help. Logan bent over him. The man wasn't breathing.

"Let's get the sheriff and get out of here!" Logan screamed.

"Is the sheriff alive?"

"He came in first," Logan said. "Tykas walloped him with a board. I think he's just unconscious."

Staggering across failing floorboard and shielding themselves from falling shingles, Logan and Jesse made their way to the door and Sheriff Clark. It took both of them to lift the man. But with one of them under each arm, they managed to get him out of the house just as another section of roof collapsed behind them.

As they emerged into the cool prairie air, a cheer went up from the citizens of Redemption.

Chapter 36

I THOUGHT I'd lost you," Emily said.

She sat beside Jesse's bed in the upstairs bedroom of Molly's house. Jesse felt his hand cradled in hers.

"How long have I been asleep?" Jesse asked.

"Most of the afternoon."

His eyelids were heavy. He gave into them and let them close.

"Would you like me to leave?" Emily asked.

"Please stay."

She squeezed his hand. The burns and cuts on it hurt, but he didn't let on. The pleasure of her touch was worth the pain.

"How is everyone else?" he asked.

"Sheriff Clark has a nasty bump on the back of his head. Mr. Logan is no worse off than you. Molly and I are still coughing." As if to illustrate her commentary, she turned her head and coughed. Turning toward him again, she made a sour face. "I can still taste the smoke," she said.

Jesse chuckled at the look on her face. It set him to coughing too.

"We make quite a pair, don't we?" Emily said.

"Speaking of that," Jesse said. He paused. "I've been thinking."

"Oh?"

"When I thought I was going to lose you in that fire…well, I couldn't bear the thought of you not being around."

Emily's eyes grew moist.

"And I realized how much a part of me you've become," he said. "And, well, what I want to say is, I don't want you to return to New York. I want you to stay with me…forever."

Emily smiled and wept openly. "Jesse Morgan, after all this time, is this a proposal of marriage?"

Jesse nodded. "Marry me?"

With closed eyes, Emily said, "You don't know how many times I've dreamed of this moment."

The warmth and happiness Jesse felt inside overpowered all the pain of his burns and cuts and bruises. "Emily, I'll make you very happy."

"I can't marry you, Jesse," she said.

In that moment, it was as though the entire world became silent and the earth halted on its axis. Apparently, the dumbfounded look on his face prompted Emily to repeat what she had said.

"As much as I want to, I can't marry you."

"Why not?" Jesse cried.

Emily released his hand. Her fingers played with a corner of the bed sheet as she spoke. "I've changed," she said. "And although I still love you, I love my Lord even more. And He says I can't marry a man who is not a Christian."

Approaching footsteps signaled the arrival of Clara and Logan.

"It's about time you woke up!" Logan jibbed.

Clara laughed. "Don't let him fool you, Jesse," she said. "He's been up barely five minutes."

"We have some news to share with you," Logan said. His arm was around Jesse's mother. "I've asked Clara to marry me."

"And I've consented," Clara blushed.

"Congratulations!" Emily squealed. She jumped up from

Jesse's bedside and hugged Clara.

"Yeah, congratulations," Jesse said.

A week later the eastbound train carried Emily Austin away to New York. The following week Jesse said good-bye to Molly and Sheriff Clark as he boarded a train for Denver. He was accompanied by Woodhull Logan and his mother.

Clara reached over and placed her hand on top of her son's. As the train rocked side-to-side, mountains loomed in the distance. Jesse and his mother sat alone; Logan was stretching his legs in the front of the car.

"I know it's hard to understand, Jesse," Clara said. "But Emily had to return to New York. She has to set things straight with her family."

"I'll never see her again," Jesse moped.

"If it's God's will, you'll see her again."

Jesse chuckled sarcastically. "That's a good one, considering that God is the one who is keeping us apart."

Clara closed her eyes and sighed. "Jesse, I've been a terrible mother."

"Don't say that! You've worked hard all your life to provide for me."

"Yes, I've provided for your physical needs. But not your spiritual needs. I was so angry at God for taking your father away from me, I hid you from God's influence. I was wrong. And I regret it."

"What is it about the West?" Jesse said. "Everybody I know who has come out here has suddenly come down with a case of religion."

If Clara was offended by his remark, she didn't show it. "When I first left New York," she said, "I was angry that you had run away. But, somehow, God has worked all of this for His good. He's brought us closer together. You've grown up and become a man. And I've found Logan. But most importantly, I've found God again."

"You sound just like Emily."

"There's something about the West...wait, I copied it down." Clara dug in her bag until she found the piece of paper she was looking for. "I read this in one of Molly's books," she said. "Listen: 'Pioneering is really a wilderness experience. We all need the wisdom of the wilderness—Moses did, Jesus did, and Paul did. The wilderness is the place to find God.'"

"I didn't come West to search for God," Jesse said.

"No, son, you came West because God was searching for you. And He still is."

As the train approached Denver, Colorado, Clara Morgan told her son the story about the woman who ran from the very man who was trying to rescue her.

Jesse listened.

EPILOGUE

"I don't know," Clara said. "He won't tell me."

Jesse looked in the mirror and finished shoving a brush through his hair. He stood in a room at the recently completed Brown Palace Hotel in Denver. Six tiers of balconies with cast iron railings encompassed the hotel's lobby. The railings were an intricate design featuring dancing ladies. According to the clerk who checked them into their rooms, two panels in the railings were deliberately installed upside down to create a diversion for visitors sitting in the lobby. A stained glass ceiling in the lobby provided a soft, natural lighting.

"Is Logan always full of surprises?" Jesse asked his mother.

"How should I know? I've only been married to him for five months."

"It must be some surprise. This is a pretty fancy place," Jesse said.

"I think it has to do with his work," Clara said. "He told you that they want to make him head of the Denver branch of the agency, didn't he?"

Jesse looked up, surprised. "No, he didn't!"

Clara smiled. "I think that's what this is all about."

Jesse set down the brush. "Well, let's find out," he said.

Pulling the door closed behind him, he followed his mother to the railing. They were on the third floor. Like a cathedral canopy, the stained glass covered them overhead. But when

Jesse looked down into the lobby, he didn't see the polished floor, or the Mexican onyx stone. He saw four people looking up at him.

"Oh my goodness!" Clara cried.

She took the words out of Jesse's mouth.

Standing next to Logan was Sarah Morgan Cooper. Next to her was another man and woman who looked vaguely familiar to Jesse.

"That's J.D. and Jenny Morgan," Clara said to Jesse. "Your uncle and aunt. The ones who pulled you from the Ohio River."

Descending to the lobby, Clara and Jesse joined the others.

"So this is what he looks like with his eyes open," J.D. joked.

Jesse recognized the book in his hands. It was the Morgan family Bible.

Jenny reached out and hugged her nephew. "We're so proud of you," she said. Likewise, Sarah hugged him. "Quite frankly, I'm not surprised at all you've done," she said. "I always knew you had it in you."

Clara stood awkwardly before J.D. and Jenny. With downcast eyes, she said, "I can't tell you how grateful I am for this opportunity." She glanced at Logan and smiled. "It gives me a chance to tell you how sorry I am for the dreadful…"

Jenny cut her off with an embrace. "No apologies are necessary," she said. "We're family."

"Save one of those hugs for me," Sarah said.

"You!" Clara said, pointing an accusing finger at Logan. "You arranged all this and I didn't know about it?"

Logan grinned and shrugged. "Why should you be surprised? My business is security."

J.D. said, "Logan has been keeping us informed ever since you arrived in Denver. He told us all that has happened. And I can't think of anyone else who has demonstrated with their lives how God is able to bring good out of adversity. I can't help but think how proud Benjamin would be."

Clara put an arm around Jesse and hugged him.

"During the trip out here," J.D. continued, "it suddenly struck me how Benjamin's sacrifice planted the seeds that would one day be his family's salvation. Two people were saved in the fire that claimed his life—Woodhull Logan and Molly Clark. Who would have believed that years later these same two people would be a blessing to his wife and only son?"

A murmur of agreement circled among them.

"But we're here for a reason," J.D. said. He lifted up the family Bible. He addressed Jesse. "According to Mr. Logan, you surrendered your life to Jesus Christ on the train trip to Denver. Is that true?"

"Yes, sir," Jesse said.

J.D. smiled. "Then it is my privilege to do today for you what my father once did for Benjamin, your father…"

"Wait!" Logan interrupted him. "We're not all here yet."

He glanced toward the lobby entrance. Others followed his glance.

Standing at the entrance in a black silk dress was Emily Austin. Standing behind her were her parents, Franklin and Eleanor Austin.

The ceremony concluded, the Morgans and Logans and Austins relaxed in the elegant hotel lobby. Jesse and Emily sat beside each other on a sofa. The Bible rested on Jesse's lap. They were looking at the names printed inside the front cover:

Drew Morgan, 1630, Zechariah 4:6
Christopher Morgan, 1654, Matthew 28:19
Philip Morgan, 1729, Philippians 2:3-4
Jared Morgan, 1741, John 15:13
Jacob Morgan, Esau's brother, 1786, 1 John 2:10

Seth Morgan, 1804, 2 Timothy 2:15
Jeremiah Morgan, 1833, Hebrews 4:1
Benjamin McKenna Morgan, 1865, Romans 8:28
Jesse Morgan, 1892, Genesis 50:20

"He was the pirate," Jesse said, pointing to Jared's name. "And he was the missionary to Indians," Jesse said, pointing to Christopher's name. "And these were twins," he said, pointing to Jacob and Esau's names.

"And he was the most handsome of all," Emily said, pointing to Jesse's name. She leaned over and kissed him on the cheek.

Jesse started to close the Bible.

"Wait!" Emily said. "Read your verse to me."

Jesse found Genesis 50:20. He read: "But as for you, ye thought evil against me; but God meant it unto good, to bring to pass, as it is this day, to save much people alive."

"Joseph said that to his brothers after they sold him into slavery in Egypt," Emily said.

Jesse was amazed. "You've been studying your Bible!" he said.

"If I can have your attention!" J.D. brought a halt to the rash of conversations around him. "There is one more duty that is my privilege to perform," he said. He motioned everyone to gather around him. "Get comfortable. Each time this is done, it takes a little bit longer."

"Probably because each man who does it embellishes the stories just a little bit more!" Sarah said.

Everyone laughed.

"Very funny," J.D. said. "Of course, this from the woman who earns money making up stories and telling them."

As everyone else settled, Emily snuggled into Jesse's arm.

"Don't distract him too much," J.D. said, noticing the snuggle. "He's going to have to do this himself someday."

Emily looked at Jesse and winked.

J.D. Morgan cleared his throat. "I can't tell you what a great privilege this is for me," he said. "All of my life I was raised for this moment. But then the war between the states interrupted things rather dramatically. And in God's wisdom, I was not able to have children of my own. But even in my loss, I gained an older brother. And now, in his untimely absence, I get to do what I always thought I'd do someday. Tell the Morgan story. This is our spiritual heritage. One that began with Drew Morgan and now continues on through Jesse."

J.D. paused. When he spoke next, his voice took on a tone of reverence.

"The story begins at Windsor Castle," he said, "the day Drew Morgan met Bishop Laud. For it was on that day his life began its downward direction..."

It was late. Everyone else had gone to bed. Jesse and Emily had the lobby to themselves.

"I can't believe this day," Jesse said. "When I awoke this morning, I had no idea any of this would be happening."

"Logan is a special man, isn't he?" Emily said. "He fits right into the family."

"And to think, you had him arrested in Redemption," Jesse said.

Emily freed an arm and punched him.

"I guess I deserved that," Jesse said, rubbing the spot. "Oh, by the way, there's a letter waiting for you in New York. I mailed it two days ago."

"Anything important in it?"

Jesse shook his head. "Just that nothing exciting ever happens around here."

Emily laughed.

Jesse looked at her. He remembered the first time he was this close to her. She had crashed through a gate and was sprawled out on top of him with a police whistle dangling from her lower lip. Then, as now, he couldn't believe how incredibly gorgeous her eyes were, how smooth her skin.

"What are you looking at?" Emily asked.

Jesse replied by leaning into her. Their lips met.

"Emily?" he said.

"Hmm?" Her eyes were still closed.

"Marry me?"

Now they were open. And they glassed over with tears. "I thought you'd never ask," she said.

For more than an hour they sat on the sofa in the Brown Palace Hotel lobby savoring their love and each other's nearness.

"Think we should tell somebody?" Emily whispered.

"Later," Jesse said, kissing her again.

AFTERWORD

One government official in the mid-1800s predicted it would take over five hundred years to settle the West. By the end of the century, however, it was effectively closed. It is this startling quickness with which the pioneers covered the continent that became the basis for Jesse Morgan's story.

I chose a late time setting for the pioneer story of the "American Family Portrait" series, because I wanted to demonstrate the rapid changes that were taking place by the end of the century. On the one hand, dramatic technological achievements were occurring almost on a daily basis. Wagons gave way to steamboats which gave way to railroads. Steam power was being replaced by electric power. Machines were revolutionizing how people worked. The typewriter itself introduced women into the workplace like never before.

But for all the technological advances, we paid a price, oftentimes with human lives. The early chapters of this novel do not begin to describe adequately the working and living conditions in the tenements. For those who wish further study about the tenements, I recommend the writing and photographs of Jacob Riis who documented them in all their gruesome detail. The conditions of the tenements prompted one observer to lament:

O God! That bread should be so dear,

And flesh and blood so cheap!

Labor reforms were being implemented during this time. However, the conditions described in the glass factory were still a part of everyday life for many children living on the lower east side.

By contrasting the crowded tenements with the wide open Kansas prairies, I hoped to show that the pioneers who were lured to the West were uprooted Easterners living in an alien environment. The people we call pioneers didn't just spring up on the prairie like sunflowers. They survived by learning to adapt in the face of hardship.

Within the New York area, there was a growing disparity of classes as seen in the differences of housing in which Jesse and Emily were raised; he in the tenements and she in the exclusive district.

Sarah Morgan Cooper and her dime novels featuring Truly Noble are fictional. However, her stories are representative of the dime novels that were popular in that day. Nellie Bly, however, is not fictional. Her investigative reporting and around-the-world trip mesmerized the nation.

Although the steamboat *Tippecanoe* and its colorful captain, Louis Lakanal, are fictional, his character, the steamboat race, and Lakanal's lament over the decline of this romantic mode of transportation is based on fact.

The flatboaters' stories of Mike Fink are based on his legend. And Richard Tykas' desire for a utopian settlement is based on the historical Oneida (N.Y.) Community of the Putney Perfectionists.

By the time of this story, the pioneering West that Jesse longed for—wagon trains a hundred wagons long, attacks by Indians, cavalry charges—had for the most part become lessons in history primers. The Santa Fe Trail and Oregon Trail had given way to the railroads. Some, like the fictional

Watermans, still chose to travel by wagon when the shipping costs of their goods was prohibitive; in this case, Waterman's stock of medicines. The tragic accident that took the life of the Waterman's daughter is based on a true incident.

Pawnee Rock and Fort Larned are real places and can still be visited today. For the sake of the story, I extended Fort Larned's use as a military post by a few years.

Francis Thompson's poem, "Hound of Heaven," did not actually appear in print until 1893. But since it was indicative of the times and fit the story so well, I anticipated its release by a couple of years.

Redemption is a fictional town, as are all of its residents and businesses. It is a composite of small prairie towns of this era. Travel aboard the emigrant train is based upon historical documents.

A special thanks to Ken and Jan Miles who described to me a barn gathering in the Paso Robles, California area which was the inspiration for Elijah Zimmerman and his musical sing-along in Redemption.

Finally, the Brown Palace Hotel is an actual location on the corner of Broadway and 17th Streets in Denver. Visitors can still admire its decorative iron railings and its stained glass ceiling, which is a replacement of the original. It is a relaxing setting to enjoy afternoon tea.

Jack Cavanaugh
San Diego, 1996

The Morgan Family

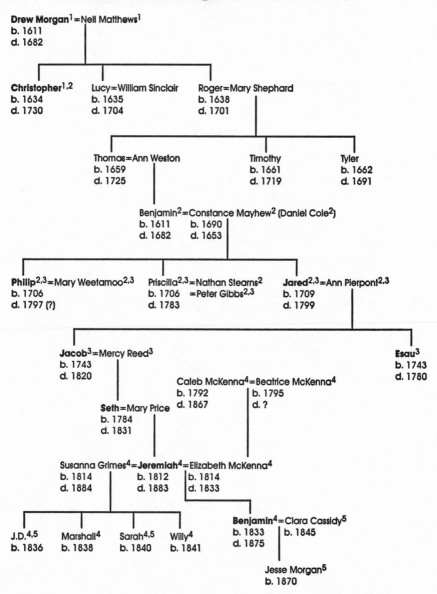

Drew Morgan[1]=Nell Matthews[1]
b. 1611
d. 1682

Christopher[1,2]   Lucy=William Sinclair   Roger=Mary Shephard
b. 1634   b. 1635   b. 1638
d. 1730   d. 1704   d. 1701

Thomas=Ann Weston   Timothy   Tyler
b. 1659   b. 1661   b. 1662
d. 1725   d. 1719   d. 1691

Benjamin[2]=Constance Mayhew[2] (Daniel Cole[2])
b. 1611   b. 1690
d. 1682   d. 1653

Philip[2,3]=Mary Weetamoo[2,3]   Priscilla[2,3]=Nathan Stearns[2]   **Jared**[2,3]=Ann Pierpont[2,3]
b. 1706   b. 1706   =Peter Gibbs[2,3]   b. 1709
d. 1797 (?)   d. 1783   d. 1799

Jacob[3]=Mercy Reed[3]   **Esau**[3]
b. 1743   b. 1743
d. 1820   d. 1780

Caleb McKenna[4]=Beatrice McKenna[4]
b. 1792   b. 1795
d. 1867   d. ?

Seth=Mary Price
b. 1784
d. 1831

Susanna Grimes[4]=**Jeremiah**[4]=Elizabeth McKenna[4]
b. 1814   b. 1812   b. 1814
d. 1884   d. 1883   d. 1833

J.D.[4,5]   Marshall[4]   Sarah[4,5]   Willy[4]   **Benjamin**[4]=Clara Cassidy[5]
b. 1836   b. 1838   b. 1840   b. 1841   b. 1833   b. 1845
                                                     d. 1875

Jesse Morgan[5]
b. 1870

* Names in **bold** appear in the Morgan family Bible.

* Superscript numbers indicate which characters appear in which books.

**An American
Family Portrait**
1. *The Puritans*
2. *The Colonists*
3. *The Patriots*
4. *The Adversaries*
5. *The Pioneers*